SHADOW REPUBLIC

JERRY AUTIERI

1

Varro sat at his cubiculum desk and shuffled the wax tablets before him. The wooden slates clapped together as each one vanished to the bottom of the pile. It kept his hands busy while his mind wandered over all he had experienced since returning to Rome. A bronze lamp, a luxury item, ensconced him in golden light. The door opened to the atrium. He allowed the reflected morning sunlight undulating across the wall to distract him from his work. That he did not want to address it was an understatement. He wanted to melt the tablets, flip the desk, and reenlist with the infantry.

But his villa demanded attention. In the time he had been away, he had gained new guards, repaired the outer walls, and lost a horse. That was what he garnered through a scan of the wax slates. His Macedonian steward and slave, Siculus, had more to tell him. But Varro had declined.

"Unless someone died or is at risk of death, speak of it later. I've been home for a single day, and I'm already exhausted."

He had been anticipating time away from the others. Both Falco and Curio were like brothers to him. Yet even tight-knit brothers needed a break from each other. But within a day of his independence, he was already longing to speak with them again.

He sat back in his chair, and it creaked under his weight. His chest was thick and his shoulders wide from hard exercise. He wondered how long he would remain in condition if he had to sit at this desk for months, maybe even years. Of course, he knew it was an exaggeration to think so. Flamininus had promised them action in short order. But even a week felt too long in the small cubiculum. The wax tablets spread on the desk crowded the room with their demand for attention.

At last, he surrendered to the tablet atop the pile. He lifted it and raised his brows as he scanned the neatly incised words. He reread the text twice, his mind willfully defying full attention. The wall repair had cost him twenty-five denarii. Siculus had made detailed notes of the transaction, but only the cost was of interest. Such a sum would have choked him in his early years. But now it was nothing. He had contracted for grain sales this year over ten times that amount. Indeed, Senator Flamininus had not been wrong to say his money was better placed in real estate and farms than in a bank. He still was unsure of what a bank did other than make it hard to access his wealth.

He rotated through two more slates until he came to the details of his horse. Siculus had explained the basic situation already, and the report only contained more details of the incident. The poor beast had caught a hoof in a crack created by the recent earthquakes. It must've been a deep crack, Varro thought, since the horse tripped and broke its leg. Its body was sold to a local merchant to recoup some of its cost. Siculus then noted the going rates of replacement horses. Varro knew too well how expensive they were. He was down to his main mount and a replacement, which would suffice.

A knock sounded from the half-opened door, and Varro nearly jumped out of his chair. He was glad for anything to relieve the tedium of reviewing reports. Siculus appeared in the narrow frame as a shadow against the light spilling in from the atrium. He ran his rough hands over a lush black beard. He waited for Varro's permission to enter, then stood before the desk like a soldier at attention. Varro appreciated this and suspected Siculus knew it as well. He was a capable slave and a shrewd judge of a man's inclinations. Varro counted himself lucky to have found him.

"Master, you wanted to see me. Is it about the horse?"

"Actually, it's about the guards. Five of them? It seems a large number considering the size of the estate."

Siculus dragged his knobby fingers through the tangle of his beard and considered.

"I calculated the costs, master. The guards need to sleep and have leave days. Five seemed a good number to keep on rotation."

Varro pursed his lips. He was already turning into a miser and he hadn't run his villa for a full year yet. When he bought the farm, he resolved to be more generous than he remembered his father being. However, the economic reality of running a farm was already apparent only after a few months. He leaned back and groaned.

"I suppose you're right. I haven't met all of them. Get them together for me. I'll give them a review to remind them of their legionary days." He gave Siculus a wry smile. The slave inclined his head.

"I'll do it immediately, sir. But remember, they are not legionaries any longer. One had only served a single campaign."

"Noble of you to beg for their comfort, but I expect only the best. I am paying them well. I won't damage my investment, but I won't tolerate anything less than legion standard."

Siculus bowed deeper, but Varro saw a thin smile. He was bold for a slave. But Varro trusted him. As long as he remembered his place, he expected good things from Siculus. He backed out the door and returned it to its half-closed position.

The distraction had not relieved the malaise he felt at the pile of wax slates stacked before him. Again, he sighed and lifted one as if it were a brick. He resolved to get through the work so that he could review his guards. That at least would pass the morning. He did not know what to do with the rest of his day. Perhaps when he next visited Falco, he'd ask for suggestions. He was far more accustomed to laziness than anyone he knew. Even Curio kept himself busier.

By the time he had picked up enough momentum to get through all the reports before him, a tentative knock sounded from the door. He looked up, eyebrows raised, and saw a shadow spreading across the entrance.

"Enter. I don't want to speak to you through the door."

His rotund house slave stepped into the entrance. He at least had learned her Roman name, Fadia, though he did not know more. She wore her hair tucked under a pale blue cover, and gray spread along her temples. Her accent was unfamiliar to him, though she seemed Iberian.

"Master Varro, there is a visitor at the gate. A woman with a small child. She claims to be a relation, master. The guards refused to open to her without your permission."

Varro stood, sweeping all the wax tablets to the side of his desk.

"This should be interesting. I don't have a female relative with a young child. Let's go see what trickery awaits me this morning."

He followed Fadia through the sun-bright atrium and out the front door into the main villa. His front yard was larger than his ancestral home had been, but did not approach the scale and grandeur of the Scipio estate where he had spent an entire summer. The bar remained across the gate and his newly hired guard stood atop a ladder to see over the stucco wall.

After dismissing his house slave, he regarded the man atop the ladder. He was a few years older in appearance than Varro, with sharp cheekbones and a thin nose. A sword hung from his hip and a round wood shield slung across his back. Varro noted the hem of his gray tunic was stained and frayed.

"There's a woman to see you, sir. Says she is a relation of yours."

Varro ordered his man off the ladder so he could see for himself. As he waited, his jaunty attitude faded as he considered what might await him on the other side of the gate. He had been relieved to escape the cubiculum and his tedious responsibilities. But now he climbed the ladder and each rung higher quickened his heart and tightened his chest.

Now, he remembered faces he had long put out of mind.

He paused just before reaching the top imagining that if he never looked across the wall, his worries would vanish. Somehow, he found it easier to cross swords with the fiercest enemies of Rome than to face his past. Hanging on that shaking ladder he would rather cross into besieged Pisa than greet whoever awaited him.

With a deep breath, he stepped up and looked across the wall.

The woman and her child stood in the shadow of his villa walls. The woman hung her head as if in shame, and her pale hand stretched back to a young girl who seemed ready to flee. She wore a plain stola of sea green and a wooden comb held thick brown hair in an elaborate style. She did not look up, but the child spotted Varro. The girl began to wail and pull her mother's arm as if to seize her last chance to escape.

"Arria, is that you?"

The woman, his sister, at last raised her head. Shrouded in shadow and obscured by the distance, she did not appear as he remembered her. But her voice matched the echoes still living in Varro's memory.

"Marcus, I have nowhere else to go. Please, open your gates to me and your niece."

He descended the ladder, his legs trembling and stomach churning. Suddenly he wished to be back in his cubiculum with his face buried in wax tablets. A thousand memories dredged up from the recesses of his mind. He and Arria had never enjoyed a close relationship, but neither had they been at odds. They lived as normal brother and sister. After joining the legion, she had become a specter of the past, a memory that faded behind more intense experiences. He had been glad to leave it as such.

But now he lifted the bar from the gate, his guardsmen belatedly assisting him. The past had come forward to the present, and he did not know what it would bring.

The guardsmen swung open the gate, the wooden planks dragging across the dirt path. Light spilled through the opening and illuminated his sister. She stood only a dozen yards from him, yet it felt as if a vast ocean lay between them. He stood with his arms hanging uselessly at his side, his expression caught somewhere between a smile and a scream.

Arria returned a tentative smile. She was four years younger, but even at this distance she appeared more like his mother. The years had been unkind, etching deep frown lines between her brows where once there had been smooth skin. Her cheeks no longer glowed and needed red makeup to restore the vigor of youth. But her brown eyes sparkled and her smile showed straight teeth.

"Thank you, Marcus. I was afraid you would keep the doors barred and turn us away."

Varro glanced awkwardly to his guard, who stepped back and turned aside as if he heard nothing.

"Why would you think that? Did you hear something about me?"

Arria's daughter now hid behind her skirt. Her terror was Varro's answer, but his sister tried to pull her forward.

"I just thought that you had become so wealthy you might not care to associate with..."

She let her words trail off, but Varro could not complete the sentence. She appeared tired and up close he could see her stola was ragged and stained. Whatever her story, she had not had an easy time of late.

He did not know how to fill the silence until the guard beside him cleared his throat.

"Don't stand out there," he said. He decided at that moment he had a duty to his sister. He had to put aside his own worries for hers, even if she was as a stranger to him now. "Come inside and introduce me to my niece. I hope all that you heard of me is that I'm a poor host, and nothing worse. Anything worse is a lie."

Arria laughed, and it took Varro back nine years. It was a sparkling clear note that carried across time. This was his sister. He had a family, history, and a clan. All that he put aside for nine years to dedicate to Rome's service. Now he had to remember his family.

At least one member of it.

Arria and her daughter crossed beneath the gate and into the yard. The guard dragged the door back into place while Varro led his sister toward the main house. He ignored the child for now. Young children made him feel awkward, probably because he could not address them as soldiers. The image of shouting at his niece as if she were a legionary made him smile. It was such a ludicrous thought.

"I'm sorry," he said. "I hadn't been expecting you, or I'd have been better prepared."

"Marcus, you couldn't have expected me. I am thankful for your graciousness. I just showed up at your gate, begging for help."

She muttered the final words and lowered her head once more. Varro tucked his down as well. What to say to his sister estranged for nine years? He didn't know. Nor was there anyone around to fill the silence as they crossed to the main building. Again, he wished to return to his wax slates and close the door of his cubiculum.

Fadia greeted them and Varro ordered a meal to be served in the garden. While he did this, Arria and her daughter stared wide-eyed at the clean frescoes and mosaics decorating the atrium. Certainly, it was nothing Arria hadn't seen before. Perhaps she had seen nothing as new as this. The floor hadn't even endured a year of traffic. Yet she continued to gawk at his home as they passed through to the garden.

"Marcus, you have done incredibly well for yourself. I can't imagine how you did it. This is all from serving in the legion? Guards and slaves, too?"

"Something like that." He then gave her and his unnamed niece a quick tour of the small garden. Senator Flamininus had arranged architects to design his villa, patterning it after the estates of the wealthy. He assured Varro everything was in keeping with the latest trends. To him, it seemed a bit overdone for a countryside estate. It was not as if he would be entertaining Rome's elite. But Arria, and eventually her daughter, both restated their amazement at the villa.

Tables and couches were set amid freshly planted rosebushes. The late morning sun painted the grass green. It was a cheerful scene as Fadia organized the one other house slave, a young boy who apparently could not speak. Varro had bought him more out of pity than usefulness. He seemed an earnest young man who probably did not deserve his fate. He dragged couches around while Varro and his sister remained in awkward silence.

At last, Arria led her daughter forward and presented her to Varro.

"She is Lucia." She then gave the young girl a gentle push forward. "This is your uncle Marcus that I told you about. He is a great hero of Rome. He has been away at war all these years, fighting so that we can enjoy our lives at home."

Lucia had lustrous brown hair worn in a braid. She squinted as if looking into the sun and revealed delicate teeth all aligned. It reminded him of his mother, who also had a beautiful smile with straight teeth. The similarity made Varro wince, but he steadied himself. The poor girl was not responsible for her grandmother's actions.

"But Mama, you are always crying."

Arria grabbed her back as if she were about to fall off a cliff, causing Lucia to shout in surprise and Varro to step back.

"Mind what you say, or else your uncle will become worried." Arria's pale skin reddened at the cheeks as she smoothed out Lucia's white stola. She smiled apologetically. "She exaggerates everything. You know how children can be."

Varro smiled at Lucia, uncertain what to make of the girl. He appreciated her frankness, but wasn't ready to delve into his sister's problems.

Instead, they chatted about the recent earthquakes and the trouble in the north. He mentioned his and Falco's participation in the vaguest terms he could invent.

"We were adjutants to the consul. Quite boring but safe enough."

To Varro, it felt as if Fadia and her assistant might never finish setting up the table. So he was delighted when they stepped back to allow Varro and his sister to approach.

They lay back on their couches as Fadia set out plates of fresh fruit. Varro elongated the small talk, and Arria latched onto it like a drowning woman. Lucia reclined beside her mother and accepted the grapes she doled out. Once the meal of fish and leeks came out, Varro used it as an excuse for silence. Arria filled the gap with useless chatter that revealed nothing more of her true situation. When they were done eating, both had to confront the reason for Arria's visit.

"You said you had nowhere else to go." Varro dabbed at the corner of his mouth as he regarded his sister. "Have you always known where to find me? I had no idea where you went when I came back from Macedonia. Old man Pius was gone, and so was our home and the farm and the neighbors. Everything vanished in a few years."

Arria lay back on the couch while her daughter fidgeted with barren grape stems left over from their meal. The silence was filled only by the sound of birds in the distance and the muted conversation of guards at the far end of the garden. At last, she looked up with tears in her eyes.

"Word came that Father was killed in battle, and that you followed him not long after. Mother and I were heartbroken. We didn't learn that you are still alive until a few years ago. My husband had a friend who claimed he served with you and Falco. At first, we didn't believe him. But I saw you once in the city. It's where I lived, and Mother –"

"I don't want to know anything about Mother. I don't care."

Varro's voice carried authority cultivated over many years as a centurion. It set both his sister and her daughter sitting upright in surprise. Lucia once more hid behind her mother on the couch.

"Marcus, I don't understand. Mother has been..." Whatever Arria saw in Varro's face caused her voice to trail off. "I suppose you have your reasons. I won't press you for them, but we are family and you can talk to me if you want to."

"That's very kind. But we have more pressing things to discuss." Varro discovered his fist clenching and forced it open. "Your husband? I assume he is gone?"

Arria nodded then set her hand on Lucia's shoulders.

"He died in Iberia last year. We only got the news some months ago. Both of his parents are dead, and his brother is also away at war. They called him to Pisa earlier this year. There is no one to take care of me. I had heard that you and Falco both built magnificent homes outside the city. One of my husband's legion friends told me. My money is running out. I don't know what to do. Mother has her own concerns. Her husband doesn't care for me. He has his own daughters from another marriage. You're my only family, the only man I can go to for help."

Varro's posture softened and he looked from his sister's dejected face to his young niece, who slouched under her mother's trembling hands. If both needed his help, how could he turn them away now? No matter how he blamed his mother for tricking him into Servus Capax and hiding his father's secrets, Arria was innocent. As a woman, she had little choice over her life. She went where their father sent her, in this case to a man destined to die in the legion. Who else could she turn to now? By the laws of tradition, Varro had responsibility for her.

He also lowered his head. "I'm sorry if I was rough. I know you see a fancy villa and me in clean clothing, but I assure you it is all new to me. I'm better suited to being a soldier than being a brother or even a passable host. Of course, you and Lucia are welcome here. To be honest, this place might benefit from a woman's presence. You can remain with me, at least until I can find a suitable match for you. That may take some time, given how often I'm away."

Arria stood up from the couch, the weariness of the years lifted from her and relit her face with a youthful glow. "Thank you, Marcus! I will not be a burden, nor my daughter. I would do anything to earn my place here. I won't let you regret it."

Varro waved away her gushing, feeling a warmth on his cheeks. "There would never be any regrets. It has just been a hard nine years. I have forgotten that I am a brother as well as a soldier."

He watched Arria's eyes trace the scars etched into his face. She lingered on the one over his eye, but her smile never faltered. "I am so pleased to have a brother again."

Arria surrounded him with a hug. He hesitated to return it, but it seemed she wouldn't release him without reciprocation. She was warm against him and her thick hair smelled fresh. Wet tears touched his shoulder. But he was uncertain how glad he was for this reunion.

Arria and Lucia were now his responsibility. He had the money to care for them, but what else could he offer? He had a higher duty to Servus Capax, one that would take him all around the world and put him in constant danger. Now, when he risked his life, he had to consider what would happen to his sister and niece if he died. He had responsibilities beyond himself now, something he had been avoiding for years.

The past had crept up on him and draped him in chains.

All he could do in answer was smile at his sister and niece, then introduce them to his household.

2

The late afternoon sun cast long shadows across the yard. Varro stood with arms folded behind his back, wishing only for a vine rod to clutch in his hands. Five men lined up at attention, their eyes narrow and fixed on a point beyond the villa walls. Crows settled on the eastern wall as they did at the end of every day. They sidestepped and squawked amongst themselves like miniature optiones preparing their troops for review.

Siculus stood off to the side. Though he was Varro's steward, he was also a slave. Still, he regarded the men he had recruited with an appraising eye. He raked his fingers through his thick, black beard as he watched.

Varro had reviewed the condition of the men and their equipment, and had been satisfied. Now he addressed them as if they were still enlisted with the legion.

"I'm paying you men well, so I expect the best. When I'm away, you will look to Siculus for direction and your pay. While I'm here, I expect your obedience in all matters. Keep your weapons fit for action and yourselves in good condition. I will not tolerate drunkenness or any disorder on my estate. You can expect legion standard punishment if you break my rules. If you keep my rules, then you'll be paid better than the legion ever did for you. You'll also be paid bonuses for risking injury or death. If the worst happens, your salary and bonus will be paid to whomever you designated in your will. Do you have questions?"

The guards' eyes did not shift, though one glanced at the others as if looking for a cue. When no one spoke, he returned to staring ahead like the rest.

"Good," Varro said. "I am also expecting additions to your numbers. My patron is looking for suitable candidates. It shouldn't be long, and I'll require flexibility from you as I adjust duty and leave schedules. I'll also be assigning a guard captain once I have all the guards required. Perhaps he might be one of you? There will be extra pay for that. So work hard to impress me, boys. Now, if there are no other questions, you are dismissed."

The five guards broke up in silence. They had been employed during Varro's time at Pisa and had formed friendships in his absence. Even though Varro was master of the estate, he felt they regarded his sudden return as an intrusion. One was already asking for leave, according to the brief Siculus provided earlier. All were young former soldiers who needed work. Like so many others, they had returned from foreign lands to find their farms empty or the property of another. Their parents, if they still lived, turned them out to fend for themselves. Guard duty was the best employment for such men.

Siculus approached, watching the five returning to their posts.

"They've not been tested yet," he said. "And I think they're disappointed. I told them we had already been attacked once. I even showed them my leg."

He raised the hem of his gray tunic over his thigh to reveal the scab-crusted wound Varro had bound for him. He had taken it when Paullus faked a raid on the estate before leaving for Pisa.

"They're naive to think we won't be tested out here. Falco's villa is the nearest to mine, and we're otherwise alone. We're a fat target for brigands or worse. I'm sure they will crawl out of their mountain hideouts to probe our defenses."

Siculus scratched the scab on his leg and growled in agreement. "Leave a spear behind for me, master. I wouldn't mind pinning a brigand to his shield."

"Like old times?" Varro raised his brow and grinned. Siculus had been a pikeman in the Macedonian army, but Varro suspected he understated his rank. He was too easy with command for a simple infantryman. He seemed to flourish with the range of freedom Varro had granted him, whereas his old master was a drunk who abused him.

"Your sister is charming, master, as is your niece. Having other women in the house will certainly be a relief to Fadia."

"Has she complained about that?"

Siculus shrugged. "Just an observation, master. You do run the estate like a military camp and I'm sure Fadia feels it. But she is a slave and could have a far worse life. I only mention this since you asked."

"The military life is all I know. The guards seem disciplined. I'm pleased with your choices. I am counting on you, perhaps overmuch. I've been promised a swift return to the field. The Boii are a threat that cannot be ignored. You will have to oversee the integration of the additional guards while I'm away. Are you up to that?"

Siculus inclined his head. "I live to earn your trust, master."

"And your freedom," Varro added. His slave bowed deeper.

Varro completed his day with an inspection of the fields. He planted barley after the work his father had done. He knew nothing else, and the demand for it was always high. Even so, he did not absorb as much knowledge as he should have in his youth. He relied on the skill of his foreman, also a slave, to guide the others in their work. Traditionally, he would labor alongside them. However, his arrangement was far from traditional.

As a boy, he thought nothing of slaves being the principal workers. It was commonplace on every farm but for the poorest ones. Now his fortune rested on their shoulders. He was loath to mistreat them for fear that they might ruin his harvest, and therefore his investment. Of course, as their owner, he could do as he pleased with them, including punishment for failed harvests. But no amount of punishment would save a failed harvest.

Satisfied that the slaves were hale and working to their capabilities, he commended the foreman. He appeared startled by it. Varro's father had always said a well-treated slave yielded more than a beaten one.

It seemed hypocritical to Varro that his father would care for the welfare of his slaves and then aid the rich in stealing farms from his fellow citizens. Yet Varro determined it was sound advice, and so far his fields were full. It would be a good harvest.

Before he retired for the night, he returned to his cubiculum and the wax slates he had abandoned. He fished out one from the bottom and held it to the light cast from his bronze lamp. Siculus had been thorough enough to conduct an accounting of all supplies. Varro would've simply scanned through it, but he was still learning how much he could trust his slave.

He decided to take the report at face value and do his own accounting. It would have to wait until tomorrow, but he decided to stop by the storehouse before bed.

He took the bronze lamp with him for light, as the sun had set, and his guards now lit torches by the gates they watched. They nodded to him as he passed through the yard toward the storehouse. One seemed to take an interest in his path. Varro stared back until he turned away.

For too long he had overseen soldiers who hid infractions from their superiors. This one had such an air about him. Varro hadn't yet learned their names, much less their mannerisms. He marked that face and would question Siculus about his history. Yet as soon as the thought arose, he puffed his breath and laughed.

"Relax, Varro," he muttered to himself, standing at the storehouse door. He realized his arrival had changed their routine, and they probably feared his judgment. They were citizens, of course, but he provided their meals and pay. He held as much sway over them as his slaves. Of course they would watch him carefully.

Crates, sacks, and amphorae filled the storeroom. Granted, it was a small space. He remembered his architect warning that he would need a larger storehouse if the estate grew. At the time, he hadn't anticipated needing more guards and certainly hadn't thought of taking in his sister and niece. In the dim light of the wavering lamp, Siculus's neat script filled with shadow. A short comparison between it and the stock revealed nothing unusual, but Varro wanted a stricter accounting.

Realizing he couldn't make any progress in the dark, he closed the door with a soft thump and crossed back to the main home. Fadia and her mute assistant waited for Varro's dismissal, which he gave. Siculus had a room of his own, something prestigious for a slave. But as he was steward as well, Varro wanted him to feel a sense of ownership. His door was already closed and only darkness showed around the jambs.

He knocked on Arria's door beside his own. He heard his niece whining, then a hush from Arria before she opened. She dressed in a simple white gown, her hair loose about her shoulders. With her makeup wiped away, she appeared even older. He saw his father's features in her high-boned cheeks that caught the shadow. She gave a weary smile.

"Marcus, I can't thank you enough for this room and for taking us in. I will find a way to pay you back for this."

"I awaken before dawn, and I am afraid I will disturb you. It's best if you accustom yourself to my schedule while I am here. I do run things more like a military camp than a farm, or so I've been told. I doubt I'll be able to change soon. Old habits, you know."

She assured him everything would be fine. Varro looked past her into what had been an empty room this morning. His young niece wore a gown to match Arria's and sat upright in the bed, rubbing her eyes and clutching a cloth doll.

"You arrived with no baggage, but I see you have retrieved some of your belongings already?"

Arria blushed, the red spreading down to her chest.

"I hope I wasn't too forward, but you are so busy that I didn't want to disturb you. I spoke to one of the guards and asked him to retrieve my baggage. I hid it behind those cypress trees that grow along the path. I didn't want to show up with bags under my arms. How would that look?"

She tittered and again her blush deepened. Varro waved it off and returned to his room.

Once he settled into the darkness, he realized he could hear Arria and her daughter through the wall of his room. He thought to block his ears and allow them privacy. But he also realized that his sister was a stranger. What did he really know of her? Nine years was a long time to change a person. In truth, he had never taken time to know his sister. She was closer to their mother and of little concern to him. Still, he would not listen at the wall in his own home. If he had questions, then he would ask her directly and expect a forthright answer. As he drifted off to sleep, the murmured conversations between mother and daughter pecked at his consciousness. Before sleep overtook him, he thought young Lucia complained about a man.

The next two days were a lesson in patience and understanding for Varro. While Arria and Lucia did their best to remain out of the way, it seemed to him that they were always in need of something. Of particular note, were bathing arrangements. He hadn't considered his sister's privacy, especially with so many male guards about. While he was wealthy, he did not boast the same magnificent villas as the patrician classes. There was one bath and all shared it.

He had hoped Arria might bring a fresh taste to Fadia's cooking. He had put home cooking out of mind for so long, that it wasn't until his sister's return before he remembered it. He missed his mother's cooking, even if he never wanted to see her again. Unfortunately, Arria cooked meals that pleased her former husband, a man who must not have had demanding tastes. Still, anything he ate in his villa was better than what he ate for rations in the field.

Despite his original fervor to review supplies, he let the distractions of his sister's arrival delay him until today. He was glad to let her mend his clothing and even assist Fadia with washing them at the nearby stream. Siculus had arranged for a loom to be delivered from a nearby carpenter. Arria would need to contribute something to the household, and making cloth and clothing was a woman's traditional duty. Varro looked forward to the arrival of the loom if only to have something to occupy his sister's time that did not require him to make conversation.

Now he and Siculus crawled through the storeroom, each holding a wax tablet and making careful counts of the supplies. A vellum sheet detailing the expected inventory sat atop a barrel and was held down by small rocks. Thus far, they had not uncovered any discrepancies. However, Varro squatted beside a clay amphora. The seal had been punctured and fresh wine stains streaked down the side as if poured out of the hole in the seal. As Siculus counted across the room, Varro ran his finger over the stain. It came away wet.

"Who was on guard duty last night?" Varro licked the wine from his finger. The sour taste mingled with the grit from his skin and he puckered his lips.

Siculus popped up from behind a stack of crates, his brows furrowed in thought.

"I think it was Lars, master. Of course, there was more than one on duty. But he was at the western gate, and so closest to the storeroom. Is there something wrong?"

Varro extended his finger, realizing Siculus could not see the wine stain.

"A hole in the amphora and wine poured out. I don't think rats are responsible for this. Someone has been tapping the wine. Who is the heavy drinker in the group? Is it Lars?"

Siculus's face darkened. "None of them, master. I was very particular about that in selecting them, and I've been watching to be certain I wasn't wrong."

"Well, someone was drinking last night, maybe even early this morning. There's only one way to find out. Gather all the men in the yard. We're going to do this the legion way."

While Siculus gathered the guards, Varro went to his room. It didn't take long to find the scourge amongst his legionary gear. He ran the leather lashes through his hands, the edges of iron teeth rapping against his skin. He snapped it tight, then folded the lashes against the rod and strode back out to the yard.

All the guards saw what he carried, and their faces blanched. It seemed as if one of them were ready to run, but not the one Varro expected. His eyes settled on the man called Lars. During the intervening days he had scant time to learn their names. He didn't pretend to know all of them, but Lars had caught his attention that night when he first examined the storehouse.

He held up the scourge for the men to see.

"You all know what this is. I'm sure since you've served in the legion, you've seen it put to good use. I'll tell you a story first. When I was a young optio, my centurion thought I needed to toughen up. I had to flog a man for insubordination, though it was my officer's duty to do so. I thought I would vomit before I could carry out my order. But I did it. Since then, time and practice have hardened me to the task. I won't flinch from using this today."

The five men looked at each other as if wondering whether to run, attack, or cry. Varro realized that if they united against him, he had no chance at all. He wasn't even carrying his pugio. But men seem to fear confidence more than a bared blade. So, he stood with feet wide and the scourge held behind his back. He lowered his eyes at the men, skimming across them and pausing at Lars.

"One of you, and I pray only one, was in the storeroom last night. An amphora of wine was punctured, and the evidence of it being poured out was still fresh this morning. Now, whoever was foolish enough to do this step forward. If you do, I will go easy on you. If you don't, all of you will be discharged. So, which is it? Will you surrender yourself or expose the thief? Be sensible. There's no reason to jeopardize your employment for someone you only recently met."

Varro narrowed his eyes as if supremely confident in his position. In reality, he might become a victim of his guards. It wouldn't be the first time subordinates attacked a difficult master. Yet he had a general sense of the men, and while they were young and anxious for a fight, none of them seemed murderous. Still, a desperate group might be pushed into desperate acts. The scourge, he realized, overplayed his hand. Originally, he thought to flog each man in turn until one revealed the culprit or he stepped forward himself. Of course, the moment he raised his scourge he would be jumped by the five men. Instead, he opted for the dismissal of his entire guard force. He could not trust men who lied to cover each other's crimes.

His words seemed to sink in faster for some than others. He watched Lars in particular, expecting a sign of guilt. Yet he seemed more relaxed than the rest, and the sign he gave was to glance down the line at another man. He was the one who met Arria at the gate, with narrow cheekbones and eyes that now appeared to be hiding secret.

"Well, the grass is growing beneath my feet, boys. Don't look at each other, look at me and tell me which one of you has been stealing extra rations of wine?"

To his surprise, Lars stepped out of line and pointed to the man he had initially glanced at.

"It was him, sir. Proculus was on duty last night, through this morning. It couldn't have been anyone else."

All eyes turned to Proculus, who raised both hands. "It wasn't me, sir. I haven't been to the storeroom at all. I don't even know what's in there."

The other men now took a more skeptical look at their soon-to-be former companion. One of them grabbed Proculus closer by his tunic and sniffed. He shook his head and stepped back, waving his hand before his nose.

"Proculus, you've gone too far now. It's on your breath."

Proculus's eyes widened and he stepped back again. "I just ate breakfast. Wine with breakfast, is that so unusual?"

Yet another of his companions circled behind, flanking him in case he should run. His voice was full of threat. "I knew you for a drunk from the day I first met you. I've just been waiting for you to expose yourself."

Proculus seemed to realize his time was up. He took three steps toward the gate, which was barred in any case, before his companions seized him. They dragged him to Varro then tossed him on his knees into the dirt.

Varro crouched to Proculus's eye level and put an arm on his shoulder. He could smell the wine, and even saw a fresh purple stain on the hem of his frayed tunic.

"You stole from me, and you were drunk on duty. How can you carry out your responsibilities while drunk? We're out in the countryside, prime targets for brigands and opportunists. I need alert and watchful men. And you're not one of them."

With the others in full cooperation, Proculus was dragged to a post set up in the yard. Varro had intended it as a stand for sword practice dummies. But now his guards secured Proculus to what had become a flogging post.

Varro worked out the scourge as the other men stepped back from their former companion. Proculus now cursed and screamed for mercy. Fadia and her mute slave had come to the door to watch. Thankfully, Arria and Lucia were not present, either too busy or wisely avoiding the spectacle.

"You can't do this to me!" Proculus struggled against the rope binding his wrists to the post. "I'm a Roman citizen!"

Varro ignored the plea as the others stepped back in grim satisfaction. Siculus returned to Fadia and guided her young assistant away into the darkness of the house. Varro faced Proculus's exposed back.

"Three lashes, the minimum punishment under legion code."

He decided three would be sufficient punishment. He would strike lighter than usual, as he had no doctor standing by like he would in the legion. "I'll send you off with your full month's pay. It's more than you deserve."

Varro snapped the scourge across Proculus's back, the iron teeth ripping open his flesh. He howled in agony and collapsed against the post. Bright red blood ran down into the tunic folded at his waist.

"One of three." Varro spoke in measured, almost bored tones. He swiped the scourge in the opposite direction, creating a deep cut that now formed a cross on Proculus's back. He shuddered and howled.

"You can't do this! It wasn't me!"

"Three of three." The scourge raked lightly across Proculus's shoulder. He had to complete the stated number of strokes, but Proculus had already endured enough for his crime. Still, the iron teeth did their grizzly work. Another cut opened in the flesh and Proculus collapsed, sweating and sobbing against the post.

"Siculus," Varro called out. "Do what you can for this man's wounds, then pay him his salary before turning him outside the gate. I don't want to see him again."

Siculus returned from the villa, and with the help of Lars and two other men, they carried Proculus away. Varro shot grave looks to the other men, then retired to his room to clean the scourge. During that time, he sat alone, listening to the shocked stillness of the estate. Now it was a military camp, and Varro was not sure how he felt about it. An innocence had been lost this day, but he did not know where it would lead. He hoped Senator Flaminius called him soon. For if he remained in the villa long, he might ruin all he had started to build.

3

Varro sat at his desk in the cubiculum, transcribing notes from a wax tablet Siculus had left for him regarding the outcome of their inventory. One full amphora of wine had been drained from among the six he had in stock. From what he could tell, after stealing the wine the thief replaced the broken seal with a fresh one. Proculus had made a mistake with the last one, forgetting to replace the punctured seal. Varro shook his head, then pinched the bridge of his nose. At least he was now rid of the man.

His stylus scratched across the vellum sheet held down with his free hand. He wrote in careful script, certain to document his actions should Proculus decide to take his case to the magistrates in Rome. It was an unlikely outcome, given his youthful poverty. More likely, he would spend his monthly salary on medical attention. Furthermore, he would have to hire enough men to wrestle Varro before the magistrates. Nevertheless, it was a good habit to document everything that transpired in his villa. He didn't know what was useful or necessary; therefore, a complete record was his best option.

His door hung open to allow the afternoon sunlight bouncing off the atrium reflecting pool to enter the room. Being at the center of the house, the cubiculum was always dark. To Varro, it was a prison.

As often as he had cursed the woodlands, now he preferred them to four walls pressing on all sides. As he scratched away at the vellum, someone stirred outside his door. It was not Fadia, who used to hesitate there when Varro was working. She soon learned he welcomed any interruption to this tedious work. Instead, the shadow was smaller, and he heard a thin shuffling of small feet.

He set the stylus down and folded his hands. "Lucia, is that you?"

The shuffling feet stopped, and a long pause ensued. Varro called her again, and then he heard more shuffling toward the door. She paused again, needing further encouragement to enter.

"Come talk to your uncle. I would enjoy the company."

He would rather have had Siculus to distract him, perhaps wheedling an old war story out of him. It was a measure of how desperate Varro was to escape clerical work that he called in his niece.

Lucia appeared in the doorway, wearing the same sea green stola that she had since arriving. Varro noted it was clean and well maintained, so perhaps she only owned the same design. If only Lucia knew that when her mother was a child, she would never have worn the same clothing two days in a row. She held both her hands at her lap, interlocking her fingers until her knuckles showed white against already pale skin. She looked up at him with a gap-tooth smile. Yet she hung back as if ready to bolt.

"Were you looking at the death masks? There is one for your great-grandfather and your great-great-grandfather. Unfortunately, there isn't one for your grandfather. That's my fault."

Varro hadn't thought what to say to the girl but felt it was time he recognized her as part of his household. After all, unless he found Arria a new husband, his niece might well come of age under his roof.

Lucia nodded her head slowly, too shy to verbalize a reply.

Varro waved her inside and gestured to a chair pushed into the corner. It was for visitors to his estate, but thus far no one had ever sat on it. She carefully placed herself on the wooden chair, her feet dangling above the carpeted floor.

While she did have some of Arria's features, particularly the nose, she must look more like her father. The shallow family resemblance made it harder for Varro to accept her as kin. This was not her fault, and so he put on a smile.

"How do you like it here? Are you comfortable?"

Lucia nodded, without speaking in return.

"Your mother will be getting a new loom soon. You should sit with her and learn. That will be a lot of fun."

And so, Varro's tortured conversation with his young niece continued with him making idle comments and her offering one-word replies or shy nods. At last, he had found something to make his clerical work more appealing. Talking with children was not suited to him. Yet as it seemed their chat neared the end, Lucia sat upright in her chair and tilted her head.

"Mother said you are a great hero like my father was. Did you know him?"

Lucia's sudden animation and the bright hope in her eyes made Varro feel compelled to say he had. But what good would it do to lie?

"Your mother overestimates me as a hero. But I do not doubt that your father was a hero. I never met him, unfortunately. Though I would have been proud to know him. He gave his life in great service to our city and our way of life. Rome is the best in the world. I have traveled the breadth of it and have seen nothing better. So your father is most certainly a hero, for he has helped build the greatest city anyone will ever know. Never forget that, Lucia. It is not the senators and the orators in the forum who are Rome's greatest men. It is your father. That he should bleed for his city and make the ultimate sacrifice shows what a hero he was."

Both Varro and Lucia sat back at his unexpected eulogy for a man he had never met. But he was sincere, and it must've been conveyed in his manner, for Lucia now sat up straighter and smiled with genuine love.

"Do you think so? My father is the greatest hero in Rome?"

"Certainly, his name must be written beside the greatest of our city."

Lucia giggled and Varro swelled with pride. Not for Lucia's departed father, but for his finding common ground with his niece. It was the sort of rousing speech he would give to his soldiers. Already he felt more comfortable speaking to her.

"Mother said you were shy as a boy but grew into a strong man. She said you would take care of us."

Varro gave a solemn nod. "We are family, even if only newly met. I will take care of you and your mother. You can be sure of it. Now, your uncle is derelict in his duties. I've got this boring work on my desk, and I cannot continue to ignore it. So, go find your mother and I will see you for dinner."

Lucia slid off her chair, more at ease than when she had entered. She seemed to hesitate, and Varro realized she might expect a hug or some other sign of affection. But Varro simply nodded and smiled, looking toward the door.

Before she left, he recalled the muted conversation overheard through his bedroom wall.

"Lucia, is there anyone troubling you and your mother? I've heard you mention a man to her. You didn't sound happy about him."

Like so many children, Lucia had not yet learned to conceal her feelings. Her expression shifted, once more appearing as if she had been caught stealing. "No, Uncle. There is no one."

Varro pressed her twice more, each time her performance improving. He realized this pressure simply trained her to become a good liar. So he let it go and watched her leave.

After completing his desk work, he spent the rest of the day wandering his estate and looking for something to occupy his time. Perhaps he had hired too many slaves and servants, for he had little to do that wasn't better handled by someone else. Siculus told him as much just before dinner that night as they returned from the fields.

"Master, you have only been idle for a few weeks. Yet you cannot seem to rest. You have staffed the villa to run without your constant oversight. I know that is forward of me to say."

"I've grown used to your insolence. It's a wonder you have not had all your flesh flogged from your bones by now."

Siculus gave a satisfied smile. "I know who I can trust, master. Besides, I speak only for your good. Please rest before your master sends you into danger again."

He stopped at the edge of the field, watching his slaves gathering their tools as the sun slipped behind distant mountains.

"Perhaps you are right. I cannot find peace here. This is not yet my home. I've not had a home in nine years that wasn't a tent."

Beyond his fields and across grassy hills lay Falco's villa. He knew the answer to his problem.

"I will be away for a few days," he said. "I'll be at Falco's villa, not far. But it would do me good to speak with him. I'll let Arria know tonight at dinner."

With his decision made, his heart already felt lighter. He and Siculus crossed back to the open gate and into the villa, where the smells of roasting meat were already in the air. With Arria's help, Fadia had prepared duck and assorted vegetables for dinner. It was not salty enough for Varro's taste. After so many years of salted meats, nothing tasted right without a heavy dose of it. But he smiled through the meal and proclaimed it delicious. Arria seemed suspicious of his good mood and narrowed her eyes at him.

"I will be visiting Falco for the next few days," he said. He sat up from his couch and wiped grease from his lips with the back of his wrist. "He is not far. Both you and Lucia are well protected. Siculus is a good man. I'm certain he'll see to your every need."

"I haven't seen Falco in years." Arria also sat up and clasped her hands together. A bright smile creased her face. "I want to go with you and see what Falco has done with his good fortune."

Varro looked away and saw Fadia and her mute slave bringing buckets from the kitchen to collect their dishes.

"We have important business to discuss. Unfortunately, you can't accompany me this time. Perhaps another."

Arria argued the point until Varro held up his hand and hardened his voice. He didn't have the heart to tell her he needed to escape them as well as this villa, but her pestering brought him perilously close to doing so.

The next day, Varro had packed his gear, strapped on his sword, and rode his horse beyond the limits of his property.

Freedom at last.

Or at least, that's how he perceived it. The villa and all its responsibilities would be his forever. Any man would kill to have his burdens, and he understood his good fortune. Yet, he was unfit for the tedium of administration. Certainly, the legion created plenty of administrative duties for him like casualty reports, guard duty shifts, and logistics. All that was far more interesting, and in his opinion, more important than how many sacks of grain sat in a storeroom.

Never one to run away from his problems, he felt ashamed as the miles increased. At the same time, when the walls of Falco's villa came into view, he grew excited again. He kicked his horse into a trot.

"Come on boy, I promise you will make plenty of new friends in Falco's stable."

He guided the horse into a dip in the field, eager to surprise Falco this afternoon. Would he also be excited to see him, he wondered?

The terrain between his villa and Falco's was mostly empty fields too rocky for farmland. It was better pasture land, but currently owned by no one. Atop his horse, he enjoyed the cool breeze rushing over his skin. The air was crisp and fresh, unlike the stagnant dimness of his cubiculum. The blue sky framed solitary clouds overhead. Varro wished he could ride on like this for days, free of his cares and responsible only for himself. It was wishful and selfish thinking, he knew. But out here no one had to know his inner thoughts.

His horse picked its way up the slope toward a stand of cypress trees. These grew wild everywhere, and eventually led to the steep hills to the north. It was nothing like a woodlands, especially the forests of the north and the wilds of Iberia. Yet as his horse drew nearer to the clump of trees, its ears picked up.

Varro understood what it meant. He halted just below the trees and studied the bushes growing like a wild beard around the trunks. It might be an animal that caught his horse's attention, but he suspected worse.

He scanned the length of the trees and realized he could bypass them on the left. Yet the moment he turned his horse, two men burst out of hiding.

Unfortunately for them, Varro was riding his cavalry mount. The animal did not spook at the sudden and violent charge, and Varro didn't either. He drew his sword and smiled.

Both ambushers raised long spears, and the smile faltered. He carried only a gladius, not ideal for fighting from horseback. Neither had he taken his shield. One attacker moved to cut off the horse from the front while the other raced to flank Varro. They knew their business, as it would be harder for the horse to turn and flee. They were forcing him onto their spears.

"We only want the horse," shouted the lead attacker. He was a thin man, balding too soon for his youthful face. His friend, however, was thick-necked and lumbering. He was the anvil to the balding attacker's hammer.

Varro kicked his horse toward the leader. "And I only want your head."

His charge left ended all banter. The balding leader skirted aside as Varro charged. His spear stabbed up, but only the shaft glanced Varro's calf.

He swiped down with his own sword, too short to reach the enemy beneath him. But he had broken free of their trap, which he had spoiled the moment he decided not to pass through the stand of trees. The trap had been set either out of foolishness or desperation.

Now free of danger, Varro turned his horse and kept his sword held out the side. The two men rushed for him with lowered spears.

"Don't be fools. Flee or else I'll have no mercy."

Their faces were red and their eyes haunted. Shabby, patched tunics flowed back. Only the bronze edges of their spears seemed to have enjoyed any care.

He kicked his horse to the left, easily maneuvering around them. This time his swipe nicked the head of the balding man, cutting a deep gash and sending him spinning aside. The burly one plunged his spear for Varro's heart, a mistake. The strike couldn't reach but

Varro kicked him in his head as he passed. His toes sparked with the pain of the blow.

But once he turned his horse again, he found both men fleeing over the hill. The balding one clutched a hand to his crown, blood flowing out from beneath it as he howled in rage and pain.

Varro considered running them down to question them. If they worked with a larger group of brigands, then he wanted to know their hideout. His eyes reflexively shifted to the distant mountains. Of course, he knew where they made their lair. But he also felt the throb on his leg where a spear shaft had struck him. Without a shield and a cavalry sword, he would be pressing his luck. Cornered men could be desperate, and their long spears nullified the advantage of attacking from horseback. He let them flee.

Once they reached the crest, he urged his horse to follow. At the top, the cypress trees and other vegetation along with the rolling fields obscured them from sight. While they might be near, they vanished.

Varro sneered at them, but wondered if he might meet them again. For now, the brief excitement had been refreshing, for him at least. He was unsure about his horse, and the balding thief certainly would remember the encounter for years to come. So he turned his horse aside and guided it down the slope for Falco's villa.

The villa was much like his own, though Varro thought this one better situated in the terrain. While his had been built on a flat plain to be closer to his farm land, Falco's sat atop the highest ridge in the area. It did put distance between the villa and farm, but was a far more defensible position. The same architect had designed all of their villas. The only differences might have been in the plants growing in their gardens or the mosaics in their atriums.

He announced himself at the gate, and after a delay was allowed inside. The servant who met him had overlarge eyes, reminding Varro of a fish. But he was well dressed and polite.

"The master is in the garden, sir. I will announce you, if you would but wait a moment."

Varro inclined his head, stifling back laughter at the pompousness. He never imagined the day would come when someone had to announce his arrival to Falco. Formalities aside, Varro eventually joined him in his garden. A quick glance around showed he had planted the same flowers. He never did have much imagination.

Falco sat at a small stone table, his tunic pulled up over his burn-scarred shoulder. Another man sat with him, hunched over Falco's arm and apparently writing something on it. He used a long bronze needle, and a half-dozen more wooden ones lay atop a black cloth. A clay pot of ink sat beside these. Falco's Servus Capax pugio also lay on the table, positioned so the pommel faced the man working intently on his shoulder.

Falco looked up with a grin.

"Your timing is perfect. I'm getting that tattoo we spoke about."

"Hold on," Varro said, his stomach tightening. "We are not supposed to do that until Senator Flamininus approves it."

Falco snorted and shook his head. "He doesn't get to say what I tattoo on my body. Well, I suppose he could if he wanted to. But he didn't! He just needed to think if we could get rid of the pugio once the tattoos are finished. I'm just taking a bit of initiative."

Varro didn't wait for an invitation to sit but pulled up to the seat next to Falco. The tattoo artist laboring at Falco's shoulder glanced up.

"I'll give you both a better price if he gets one too. Same design, I take it?"

"Deal," Falco said, slapping the stone table with his open palm. "Before you complain, Varro, this was your idea. So get one, and we will both visit Curio and get him one. Then all three of us will have matching tattoos. Better than getting married!"

"I'm not sure. Senator Flamininus seemed strange last time we spoke. I don't know if it's wise to irritate him now."

"Well given all the news, and Paullus's condition, how should he feel?" Falco tapped the side of his head. "Your mind is getting too suspicious. He's got to tell Scipio that he turned his nephew's mind to puls. You'd be irritable too if you got that job."

Varro mimicked Falco's hand-waving. "Can you blame me? Being more suspicious would've served us better in recent days."

Both men laughed and fell into idle conversation as the tattoo artist completed his work. They both agreed that neither could rest and wore their new status uneasily.

When the artist completed his work, he patted off Falco's shoulder with a cloth, causing him to wince. He then instructed Falco on how to care for the tattoo while it healed. Varro glanced at it, and it was a perfect representation of the stylized owl head that represented Servus Capax. Now, both men looked to Varro.

Without another word, he rolled up his tunic to expose his shoulder.

Falco sat back and smiled, then tapped the tattoo artist on his arm. "Put a star beneath his owl."

Varro just laughed himself. When Senator Flamininus saw their tattoos, he was certain to be displeased. But as Falco said, he did not own them.

As the artist cleaned off his needle, Varro described his encounter with the brigands just outside of Falco's villa.

"I think we have a bigger problem than it seems," Falco said, his voice lowering. "I've spotted dozens of them, scouting my villa from a distance. Flamininus can't send us more men soon enough. I'm afraid the brigands might know how weak we are out here."

Varro rubbed his chin, considering his recent encounter. They had been hardscrabble, dirty men who wanted to steal his horse. They might have been wanderers, though they had fled toward the distant mountains.

"Well, now they might know I'm away from home. That could mean trouble."

The tattoo artist shifted beside Varro and touched his needle to his skin.

"This will burn, but I expect a hard man like you has experienced far worse."

4

Varro scanned the skies above, searching for signs of rain in the iron-gray clouds. The air smelled like horse and damp grass, even though there had been no rain for days. His horse picked a patient path through the rolling fields and seemed cheered to have Falco's mount beside him. Given the attack and Falco's recent observations, Varro sat straight in the saddle and scanned the horizon for danger. He didn't expect anything would happen on this leg of their trip. This was all farmland, and old villas dotted the landscape. Banditry had been all but eliminated yet was making a resurgence.

They proceeded slowly, careful not to lose the tattoo artist who followed them into Curio's villa. He was a young man, seemingly in constant high spirits. He lagged a dozen paces behind them, whistling merrily. Varro's shoulder burned where he had worked his art. He could not tell from the angle how accurate the owl's head appeared, but Falco's was a perfect recreation. If Senator Flamininus disagreed with their decision, then he could easily hide the tattoo beneath his tunic. He only folded his sleeve up to prevent it from irritating the puffy flesh.

The salty taste of snails still filled his mouth after lunch. Falco's slave had far greater ability than his own. The snails were a delicacy and expertly prepared. He had teased Falco about becoming a fat and lazy countryside equestrian. Falco thumped him on the head in reply.

Now they ambled over the last rise that separated Curio's villa from Falco's. They could see it now, the same familiar design and layout as theirs only with scaffolding along the northern wall. He was still repairing earthquake damage from earlier in the year.

Falco at last slouched in the saddle, then called back to the tattoo artist that they were near their destination. Then he turned to Varro.

"I bet Curio will be surprised to see us both together."

"He'll probably be disappointed. Of the three of us, he likes his privacy the most."

Falco chuckled. "Well, he can get fucked. We better get some good hospitality. I wonder what you'll think of his slave's cooking. Seems like you've set a little contest between the three of us."

"That wasn't my purpose in visiting you. I just wanted to get away from everything at the villa. Now look at me. I've got a tattoo and I'm jealous of your slave's cooking."

Their horses swished gently through the grass as they navigated toward Curio's villa. The red tile roofs were still bright and fresh. The cream-colored stucco on all the walls reflected the weak sunlight. Despite the earthquake damage, the villa was the best it had ever looked. Farther afield, the buildings grew faded and cracked after generations of use.

When they were a few hundred yards from Curio's gate, Varro cleared his throat.

"I should probably tell you that my sister, Arria, and her young daughter are now living with me."

Falco whirled in the saddle, his heavy brows drawn tight over his shadowed eyes.

"Are you trying to knock me from my horse? Your sister? What happened?"

"If I want to knock you from your horse, I'll punch you in the fat head of yours. She had nowhere else to go. Her husband didn't come back from Iberia. That should tell you everything you need to know."

Falco fell silent at the news, giving a grim nod. He seemed to search his thoughts as their horses gained a well-trodden dirt path to the main gate.

"Well, that changes things. Is this a permanent arrangement?"

Varro shrugged. "At least until I can find her a new husband. But only the gods know when I'll have time to do that. Don't forget, we will be back in action soon. I'm dreading it now."

"There's no need for that," Falco said. He waved his hand at the concern. "You make sure she's in your will. You need to write one of those now. We all do. Your sister can inherit your property. I guess Curio and I better find some sons."

Though Falco laughed, Varro knew the truth of it. He did not want to think of it, but he had to consider what happened to his wealth and property when he died. Unknown uncles and cousins could fill in, but to him they were strangers. Arria was the closest relative he would consider leaving his fortune to when he died. He shuffled the thought aside, something Falco had already done as he chatted happily.

"Well, I'll have to visit your sister. I haven't seen her in ten years. How does she look?"

"Like a woman who had to raise her children while her husband was at war. Do you want the truth? She looks like a stranger. She's..." Varro cut himself off and growled, rubbing his face. "Oh, don't listen to me. The whole affair has me upset. I just need time to adjust."

Falco reached across the gap and swiped at Varro's new tattoo.

"You'll do fine. She is family, so hard can it be. Come on now, get that smile back. We are about to surprise Curio."

Their arrival at the gate went much like it did at Falco's villa. A servant had to properly introduce them to master Curio, who would meet them in the garden. Both Varro and Falco shared sly grins, then led the tattoo artist behind them. Varro was once more struck by the similarities between Curio's home and his own. It seemed as if he had returned home but all the servants and slaves had been exchanged for new ones.

They both waited patiently, sitting on a wood bench with a stone table between them. Varro complained about how his tattoo itched, and the artist explained it would go away with time.

"Just like any other wound," he said. Varro looked at the owl's head again. He hadn't thought of it as a scar.

Curio appeared, wearing a clean tunic of sky blue. His hair was tussled and his face red. Having known him for so long, Varro recognized the stress in his eyes. It caused both him and Falco to exchange confused glances.

"What are the two of you doing here? I thought we wouldn't see each other until the senator summoned us."

Falco sniffed and folded his arms. "Well, it's good to see you too. I take it you've been sleeping with a cucumber up your ass."

The insult caught Curio short, and he stopped just before reaching the table. His youthful face was uncharacteristically clouded and aged with a deep frown.

"That's not funny. Now, have we been summoned?"

Varro leaned forward, selecting his words carefully to soothe his prickly friend.

"It's a purely social visit. Apparently, we arrived at the wrong time. I apologize, as this is all my fault. I just was growing impatient at home. I went to visit Falco and the two of us got our Servus Capax tattoos. So, since we are getting a deal, we thought to bring the artist here. Next time, I will be more careful to arrange my visit in advance."

Curio's eyes at last shifted to the tattoo artist, who seemed to be looking for a way to vanish beneath the table. But once called out, he stood and introduced himself.

Curio's frown softened but he remained irritated. "I thought we were to wait for Senator Flamininus to approve a tattoo."

Both held their shoulders forward to display the owl head tattoos. Falco pointed to Varro's. "He got a star on his to show rank. You can add a cucumber to yours."

It seemed Curio was about to explode in anger. Varro held up both hands for peace.

"We are here now, as inconvenient as it may be. We won't stay long, and you don't need to get a tattoo. When we're summoned, I'll be sure to send a messenger straightaway."

At last, Curio's temper eased at Varro's measured response. "All right, I'm sorry. You did catch me at a bad time."

Varro was about to ask after the reason but then saw Curio's house slave escorting a young woman in a sky-blue stola, a match to Curio's tunic. She was lithe like a willow branch and hung her head demurely as she passed through the garden in a rush. Her dark hair flowed freely down her back, indicating she did not have the time to fix it properly.

With his back turned to the scene, Curio did not realize his secret had been revealed. Varro thought it best to remain silent, so obviously Falco would think otherwise.

His eyes went wide, and his heavy brows shot up. He pointed across the garden at the two women. Curio followed, and when he saw them vanish into the villa, he put both hands on his head in surprise.

"That's why you're in a foul mood. We showed up and you couldn't finish up. Oh boy, I am sorry, Curio. I thought you'd be fixing your walls, given we've got brigands in the hills. But it seems like you're focused on plowing the fields, eh?"

Again cutting off Curio's anger, Varro guided his friend to the table and acted like the host. Curio appeared shocked, and looked at his feet.

"I am sorry for visiting unannounced," Varro repeated. "I'm glad you're enjoying your rest."

Falco chortled and slapped the table. "Oh, I don't think he's resting much."

Varro glared, warning him to be silent.

"Whatever you do in your own home is your own business. Falco just likes to give you a hard time. Now, I recommend you get that tattoo. We're getting a special deal for all three of us, but don't feel pressured. You're right that the senator must approve it first. In my opinion, these are just ordinary tattoos that any soldier might get while serving in the legion."

Curio at last studied Varro's tattoo, then frowned at Falco's.

"You put it over your burn scars. It looks like a burned pigeon." He then looked apologetically at the tattoo artist. "That's no criticism of your style, sir. Varro's is exceptional."

"No need to apologize," the tattoo artist said through a stiff smile. "If now's a good time, just roll up your sleeve and I can get to work. I had a lot of practice with this design, so this will be the best one."

With a nod to both Falco and Varro, he rolled up his sleeve. The tattoo artist set out his bundle of bronze and wooden needles, and then searched his pack for a pot of ink.

Before he could set it on the stone table, the same servant who had escorted Curio's female guest rushed back across the garden. She wore a plain stola of brown cloth, and her bony features were haunted by shadows. As she bowed to Curio, she clutched both hands to her chest. She spoke in Latin with a thick Macedonian accent.

"Master Curio, there is a messenger from Rome. The guards have closed the gate to him, but he is insistent he speak with you now."

Curio let his sleeve fall then stood up. He shared confused looks with Falco and Varro.

"A single messenger for me?"

Varro realized Curio did not expect visitors of any sort today and that questioning the servant would go nowhere. Instead, he guided the situation. "See for yourself who is there. The two of us will go with you if you like."

The three of them went to the gate, but only Curio climbed the ladder to look beyond the stone and stucco wall. After some back-and-forth that was beyond Varro's hearing, Curio ordered the gate door open. One of his guards, a short man with a potbelly, lifted the wood bar away to reveal the visitor beyond.

He sat atop a chestnut riding horse. A cavalry sword hung from his side in a well-worn scabbard. He had no shield nor any other armament and appeared unsteady in the saddle despite his haughty glare. His eyes scanned across the opened gate, unsure where to settle.

"Which one of you is Camillus Curio?" The visitor at last settled on Falco, likely because he was the tallest man present. But Curio answered to his name as he clambered down the ladder. The visitor raised a brow and appeared to sneer.

Curio, however, had not noticed this and stood before the visitor's horse. The horse shied away from him, and the rider struggled briefly to control the animal. Curio appeared even shorter beneath the horse.

"Dismount and I'll have your horse looked after. We will speak in the garden once you have a bath."

He was following custom with the offer of a bath and meal to a weary traveler, especially one dispatched from Rome on official business. While Varro had not heard the details of their exchange across the wall, he knew Curio would not make the offer for any other visitor.

The rider, however, shook his head and did not try to dismount.

"I have an urgent message and no time for bathing or other pleasantries. I must speak with you privately and as soon as possible."

Curio's face shifted from irritation to astonishment, and he looked to Varro as if asking for help. But he could only shrug in reply. He was not the master here and had no say over how Curio ran his home. When he did not answer, Curio nodded to the rider.

"All right, but you must get off your horse. At least let me water and feed him. He's a bit of a shy one." He reached for the horse's reins and again the animal sidestepped as if unaccustomed to normal handling.

The rider dismounted and allowed Curio to hand his horse off to his servant. Varro and Falco went to find the tattoo artist still in the garden. While they waited for Curio to conduct his business in the privacy of his cubiculum, they agreed to pay the tattoo artist for the work he had done and that he should return to Rome. They would bring Curio to him later. The artist agreed and packed up his needles and pot, but he would travel with them to Falco's villa. Now all three waited in pensive silence.

They didn't wait long, for Curio emerged from the house and

escorted the visitor back to the gate. Within minutes, he joined them in the garden. He shook his head as he strode across the grass.

"Senator Flamininus has requested I meet him in Rome as soon as possible." He held out a rolled papyrus sheet. "At the usual place."

Varro's eyes shifted to the tattoo artist, who once more seemed to fade even as he sat between them. They could not speak openly while he was present. He nodded to the artist beside him when he addressed Curio.

"Could you find a place for him to relax while we discuss this message?"

Once Curio's servants escorted the tattoo artist away, they huddled around the stone table and stretched out the papyrus between them. Varro rotated it to face himself.

"It's a straightforward request," he said as he ran his finger beneath the neat script. "But I don't know why he sent it in writing. Usually, a verbal message suffices. What did his messenger have to say?"

Curio looked back toward the house as if the messenger were still hiding there.

"He didn't say more than what was written here. I took him into the cubiculum and closed the door. I thought he'd have something secret to share. Honestly, he seemed angry with me. He restated the contents of the message, then got my assurance I would meet the senator at the inn we met at last time."

Falco now turned the papyrus toward himself and frowned at it.

"Just you? Did this messenger have anything to say about us?"

Curio described a brief and tense encounter with his visitor, who appeared as eager to leave as he had been to enter. Curio did not ask about the others joining him in Rome. He was keen to free himself from his discomforting guest.

Falco sat back and folded his arms. "There's nothing else you've kept hidden from us. You know, like that girl we just saw."

"What would I hide? I only see the senator when you do. There's no secret agreement between us."

Falco nodded. "You used his name in front of the tattoo artist. You should be more careful."

Curio bowed his head and pinched his nose bridge.

"I know. This wasn't the day I was expecting. I'm not thinking clearly."

In the end, they decided all of them would go to Rome. Curio would pack his gear and accompany them to Falco's villa to spend the night. They would then gather at Varro's before all three set out for the city. While they might not be invited to Curio's meeting, nothing prevented them from visiting Rome at the same time.

Before setting out, they gathered at the gate where Curio excused himself. Leaving his horse's reins in Varro's hands, he went into the house. Both Falco and Varro understood he had a woman living with him, and they would learn more about her in time. Only Falco was crass enough to comment aloud.

"So, you are saddled with a sister and now Curio has a lay waiting for him at home. Seems like I'm the only free man left."

Varro yawned and mounted his horse. "Keep talking like that and you'll be the first among us to lose his tongue."

"Oh, Varro, you talk like you can best me in a fight. The truth is, you will lose your tongue first. You trip over it often enough." He then mounted his horse and tilted his head in challenge. Varro just chuckled and soon Curio emerged from his house.

They reached Falco's villa before sunset and found a messenger waiting. While he differed from Curio's, he shared the same attitude and message. He did not want to linger and was satisfied to travel alone at night.

They discussed the strangeness over dinner. They could not understand why an official messenger would prefer to risk his life camping outdoors rather than accept hospitality. In the end, they decided these messengers had other duties in the area. Falco had suggested they were paid by the delivery and wanted to make them all in the shortest time possible.

The following morning, they paid the tattoo artist for his work, and then a little more for his discretion. As it was Falco's villa, he escorted the artist to the gate and gave him a gentle warning. "Just remember you came out here to do two jobs, and it was all boring with nothing interesting happening."

The three of them reached Varro's villa by midmorning.

Varro expected to find the third messenger waiting there. When they found none, he left Falco and Curio in the yard and entered the home. He met Arria waiting in the atrium where weak sunlight sparkled on the reflecting pool. She carried a papyrus that still had a wax seal.

She extended the papyrus to him with a shy smile. "A messenger arrived while you were away. You came home sooner than I thought. When I told him I was your sister, he left this for you."

As he unrolled the papyrus, already seeing the now familiar note, he asked Arria for details of the messenger.

"He was just a normal messenger. He didn't want to delay, saying he was only paid to deliver the message and not for a social call. Honestly, he was rude and I was glad to see him leave."

Varro rolled up the papyrus again. He only scanned it, as it contained the same terse request to report to Rome. "Well, I'll be leaving again. But before I go, I have a surprise for you. Falco is just outside."

Arria immediately ran her hands over her thick brown hair. She looked toward the open door and leaned to the side as if she might glimpse him. "Really? I wasn't ready to meet him yet. Let me prepare. Oh, and don't let Lucia meet him before I have."

His sister rushed off to her room, leaving Varro in the atrium shaking his head.

Back outside with his two friends, he held out the papyrus.

"Something is not right about this," he said. "Even with secretaries to do the writing for him, this is a waste of time and effort. Normally, he contacts me and asks that I gather you two. It's more efficient that way."

Falco bent his lips, then gave a grim nod. "Something is not right with these messengers, either. It's as if they were instructed to act like asses."

Varro sucked his teeth and looked down at the papyrus. It was an expensive material to use for a message that should never have been written. Someone summoned them to Rome, and he was uncertain Senator Flamininus was behind it. Yet he could not think of who else would want them to return to the city. He shrugged in exasperation.

"In any case, we must go. His seal is on the message. But let's keep our wits about us. There's more to this than just a meeting with our patron."

Curio plucked the papyrus out of Varro's fingers and looked it over.

"Do you suspect a trap?"

Varro's bitter smile was his answer.

5

Arria appeared in the doorway to the villa as Varro led his friends across the yard. He could see that Arria had fixed her hair and makeup. She wore the same cream-colored stola as she had the day she arrived. She folded both hands at her lap and kept her eyes lowered. Varro almost laughed when he saw the blush on her cheeks.

Yet when he glanced at Falco, he grew serious. His mouth slackened and his heavy brows lifted. It took a moment, but he realized his friend was gawking at his sister. He whispered to Falco.

"Dear gods, am I misunderstanding what I see?"

"Your sister has grown up, Varro. Are you sure she's her?"

Curio squinted as they crossed the final distance. "That should be her. She's got Varro's nose. There aren't many like it in this world."

"What?" Varro put his hand over his nose, feeling its bony length then rubbing the flexible tip. "No one has ever said anything about my nose before."

Curio laughed then slapped Falco's back. "Shut your mouth, you fool. An eagle could nest in it."

Varro found introductions suddenly stiff and formal, as if he were introducing higher ranking officers to each other. Falco muttered his introduction, saying something about how long he had been gone and how much Arria had changed. For her part, Arria tilted her head with a giggle so fake Varro looked aside in embarrassment.

"Well, now you've met my sister." He turned Arria around and guided her into the atrium. Then he gave a look to Falco. "We've got business to attend to and not much time to prepare. I will introduce you to Siculus. You should find a man as good as him to run your villas."

They did not need a tour, as the layout was the same as their homes. Instead, he took them to meet Siculus out in the fields. He bowed low to them. "Master cannot go a day without mentioning the greatness of his two friends. It is an honor to meet both of you, sirs."

The guards were less enthusiastic, and Varro suspected memory of the flogging was too fresh. He warned Siculus and his guards of brigands in the area. He also informed them he would be gone for an unspecified period, and that they should expect reinforcements soon.

Varro endured a soup lunch that Arria had prepared. The soup itself was passable, but the banter between his sister and Falco spoiled his appetite. Curio did not help the situation, praising the meal as if it were fit for the gods and proclaiming how happy her future husband would be to eat like this every day.

"Her husband just died. Have some decency." Varro's snap chastened Arria and Falco, but only made Curio smirk.

Throughout it all, his petite niece lay quietly on the couch by her mother's side. She stirred her soup bowl as if searching for something within. Varro considered how frightened the girl must be to meet so many strangers in so short a time. Worse still, she had just lost her father. He had no skill in judging a child's mind, but he believed Lucia understood how precarious her future was.

Eventually they finished the meal, and Varro was the first to stand up from the table. He dismissed his friends to the yard while he claimed to need only a few moments to ready himself.

"But the horses haven't rested enough," Falco said. Behind him, Curio put a hand over his smirking mouth.

"We are taking a cart. Our horses will rest here and be ready if we need them. The two of you are already packed, and I only need a moment to gather my belongings."

They did as he asked, and he fled to his room to prepare. He debated what to take, eying the mail armor on its rack. Arms and armor were forbidden inside the city, and while the others had brought their own, they were offloading their gear here as a collection point should they need it. Varro's villa was closest to the city.

Just as he finished, Arria appeared in the doorway.

Her face was flushed, and her mouth hung open. Varro looked at her nose, long and thin, then resisted the urge to touch his own. What had Curio been talking about?

"Marcus, I know you must leave soon. But when will you return?"

Varro shouldered his pack and looked past Arria into the atrium. His servants and slaves waited for him there, with Siculus at the fore.

"I am not sure. If the reason for my summons is what I believe it is, then perhaps a month or more. We will stop here to collect our gear and horses, in any case."

Arria made a sharp intake of breath, but covered her dismay with a trembling smile.

"Does this happen often? I mean, does your patron summon you for a mysterious purpose and with no idea how long you will be away?"

Arria's question was sensible, but not until she and Lucia became his responsibility had he ever needed to answer it. It angered him, and he struggled not to express it in his tone.

"I cannot time the needs of Rome to my convenience. If there is a war, such as there is now, then I am called to serve."

"But you already served six years. Isn't that enough?" Arria again smiled with faint sincerity. She knew the answer to her own question. Everyone understood all men were required to serve six consecutive years and then ten more as required. If Varro had his way, he would never stop serving in the legion.

"Siculus will see to your care and safety. I cannot lie to you and say that I know him well. But I've learned to trust my judgments over the years, and he is a good man. You can depend on him. But be warned. Don't mistreat my slaves, him in particular. I wouldn't find another equal to him, at least not easily."

Arria closed her open mouth, evidently holding back something. Varro guessed what she intended to ask.

"I will put you into my will. If something should happen to me but the others survive, I'm certain they will take care of you." An image of Falco and his sister holding hands against golden sunlight came unbidden into his mind. His lunch nearly rose into his mouth. "If something should happen to all three of us--always a possibility--then you will own all my possessions. It will not be hard to attract a man with a fortune in the offering."

"Marcus, don't speak of such things. I know you will come back to me safely. Besides, that's not what I wanted to talk to you about."

Varro raised his brow, unable to guess what else could concern her. "Is it about Falco?"

Arria clucked her tongue and closed her eyes.

"No, Marcus, you should know something before you leave. Our mother is ill. If you are in Rome, then--"

"I told you I do not want to hear about her." Varro hitched his pack on his shoulder and pushed past Arria. Yet she grabbed him by the shoulder, tugging the sleeve of his tunic and exposing his fresh tattoo.

"Why? She is your mother."

Varro tugged out of her grasp. "She is the concern of another man. When she dies, I will do what the gods require. But until then, I serve her best by staying away. Perhaps you should ask her about our father and what she knew of his crimes. Then you might understand why that is so."

In the atrium, he gave last-minute instructions to his slaves and servants. Siculus would once more assume stewardship of the villa.

The last person he spoke with before joining the others in the yard was Lucia. She waited by the door, clutching her gray cloth doll to her chest. She looked sheepishly at him, an expression Varro could not read. He set his pack down before her.

"You and your mother are safe here, even if I am away."

Lucia nodded as she looked at the mosaic on the floor. It depicted a black bull in mid charge. Varro did not know if it symbolized anything special, but he liked the design. He glanced at it alongside Lucia.

"Remember what I asked you? If there is someone bothering you, tell me."

Yet his niece simply shook her head. "Are you going to the legion?"

"Something like it. I go to serve Rome and keep it safe for you."

Lucia offered a fleeting smile, then hid it behind her doll. Varro stood, collected his pack, then patted her on the shoulder. He exited into the yard, satisfied that he had arranged everything as best as he could. Falco and Curio were already in the cart, and one of Varro's farm slaves would drive them into the city.

They left Varro's guards watching from over the wall. The journey to Rome would take most of the afternoon. They crossed undulating fields of knee-high grass, and the purple hills of Rome stood high in the distance. Each carried only minimal supplies, expecting to receive orders to head north and then return to the villa. Each also carried his own thoughts and spoke little during the trip. Varro listened to the cart squeal and clatter as the slave drove a single, tired horse along the dirt road.

When they were nearer to the city, Varro could not resist the silence any longer.

"Look, Falco, you seemed smitten with my sister."

Falco's brows shot up and his eyes widened. "What you're talking about? I was just surprised to see her changed. She was just a whiny little girl last I saw her."

Curio leaned back in his saddle and laughed. "You didn't see anyone else the entire time you were there. You can't fool us. We know you better than your own mother."

Varro tried to hide his words by looking toward the distant city as he spoke.

"I need to find a husband for her. But you would only solve half of the problem. Instead of worrying for myself in the field, I will fumble over you all the time. The gods know how often I've had to risk my life to save you. I can't imagine what it will be like if you are my brother-in-law."

Falco's face contorted into a grimace.

"Husband? Brother-in-law? I don't want to get married. That's for fools, like Curio. Or presumptuous idiots like you."

Curio howled with laughter. "Presumptuous? You're already talking like a boring married man. Shouldn't you have said something like 'I ought to break your skull, Varro'?"

He dropped his voice in imitation of Falco, then swung his fist into the air as if punching.

"It's a good idea," Falco said. "But his skull would release all the foul air in it and spook the horse."

Since Varro had misunderstood Falco, he dropped the issue. They swayed on the bench as the slave crossed into the traffic headed for Rome. All the while, Curio would snicker to himself, and Falco would shout at him for silence.

Before reaching the gates, Varro halted his slave then all of them jumped off the cart. They would go on foot from here, flowing into the city along with the late afternoon traffic. The slave then turned the cart and headed back toward the villa.

Varro always found Rome to be exciting, mysterious, and grand. However, it was also always better in his memory than in reality.

The streets were narrow and winding, and though the day was at its end, the sun was still bright. Yet, the streets hid in shadows. A myriad of people thronged within those shadows, some calling out to passersby and others ignoring them as they carried on with their own business. He had smelled Rome long before entering, and now the odors of the city assaulted him. He had grown too accustomed to life in the field. As he led the others through the streets, at points he put his finger to his nose.

He silently cursed Curio as he did, for now he could not stop feeling the length of it and wondering what made him so unusual.

They arrived at the taberna they had used for their clandestine meeting with Senator Flamininus. The sign above the entrance depicted a black crow, and it was known by the same name. It stood at the end of a long street, dominating the corner of a small square. It was a prime location, as dozens of people crossed the square in all directions. The Black Crow also had three floors, with the top floor reserved for special guests.

They ducked through the doorway. People filled the tables inside, laborers mostly. It was not in one of Rome's finer neighborhoods. Servers carried steaming plates of food and red clay jugs of wine to and from the tables. Conversation and laughter filled the room as Varro pushed toward the rear. He recognized the owner from his last visit, an old fellow legionary with watery eyes and a fierce red scar that ran crosswise over his face.

Varro fished a denarius from his purse as he approached. The owner tilted his head back in wordless challenge. He was expecting to be shown the Servus Capax pugio, but Varro simply held up his sleeve to display his shoulder.

The owner stared at this a moment, then shrugged and extended his palm. Varro slipped the coin into it and then made for the stairs with Falco and Curio following. They tramped up two flights of creaking wooden stairs until finding the room they had used only weeks ago.

They sat on hard chairs around a wooden table. A small window high in the wall cast weak light across it. Varro expected a servant would arrive with wine and a lamp before long.

Falco tugged up his sleeve and displayed his tattoo to Curio.

"See how useful that was? We didn't even have to expose our weapons. Not that he would say anything. I'm sure he's got a weighted club stashed nearby."

"I will get one after Senator Flamininus approves." Curio folded his arms and sat back in his chair. Falco rolled his eyes and the two of them debated their freedom of choice. Varro rested against the back of his chair and waited for the wine to arrive. It came just when he was about to go downstairs and ask for it. A mousy woman delivered three clay cups and a small jug before escaping.

Falco poured the wine for all three, was the first to drink. He set it down with a frown.

"I guess they don't expect the senator to be here. This is a grade above goat piss."

"They only gave us three cups," Curio said. He sipped from his, then stuck out his tongue. "This is vinegar."

Based on the other's reactions, Varro let his cup sit. This was only the second time they had used the Black Crow as a meeting place. So, it was feasible the owner did not understand why they were here. Yet as Falco and Curio continued to drink despite their opinions, Varro counted the hours.

"He didn't specify a time," Falco said in answer to Varro's doubts. "Maybe he meant this morning and we're too late."

"It's possible," Varro conceded. "But if that were so, then he would've left instructions. The owner would have had a message for us. All of this is strange."

Curio lifted the clay jug and refilled his and Falco's cups. "Well, we don't know why Senator Flamininus called us. And it's not like we've done this more than twice. Maybe this is just the way of things. We've got to wait."

While Varro agreed, it was unlike the senator to leave a loose end.

"I will go to his home and see what is keeping him. Other business might have delayed him. The two of you wait here, in case he shows up or sends a message."

Falco drank deeply from his cup before answering. "I can go with you. Rome's a dangerous place."

"The two of you are getting drunk as it is. Just stay here. I won't take long."

"He lives on the other side of the city. If he shows up while you're away, you'll miss the whole meeting."

"Then pay careful attention. And for the love of Jupiter, stop drinking. This isn't a celebration. This is the start of a new mission. So, act like it."

Falco gave him a half-hearted salute, and Varro descended the creaking stairs to the bottom floor.

Only a handful of men now sat around a single table, laughing and joking with each other. The tavern door hung open to show the square beyond, where people flickered across the gap. The owner had moved to the door and sat on a stool in a posture of dejection. When he saw Varro, he straightened himself.

"You haven't received word from anyone regarding the three of us?" He kept his question deliberately vague, aware that even if the taberna was now half-empty he still had to be discreet. The owner shook his head. His voice was deep and gravelly.

"No word and no business. Other than the regular crew for this time a day. Don't know why everything slowed down suddenly."

Varro then slipped out to the square and began a long walk to Flamininus's home. As Falco had said, it was across the city. Going on foot through the crowds and up steep hills made for an even longer trip.

As he walked, he considered all of this represented what he had fought for all these years. It pained him to see maimed beggars lining the sides of broad streets as others passed them by. Every street and every corner were home to at least one of these unfortunates. He could not be certain all were former legionaries, but many carried the familiar scars of battle. Some were old and some young, and it bothered him to pass without giving each a coin. Yet even all his fortune could not satisfy those condemned to a life on Rome's streets. He reminded himself that not every unfortunate was a former legionary. And so, he pushed on until reaching the summit of a steep hill where Flamininus maintained one of his homes.

The home was one of many walled villas that dominated the Palatine Hill. Each home he passed increased in grandeur and beauty. Beyond the walls, he saw carefully tended trees growing in private gardens. He heard gentle laughter from some and pleasant music from others. The horribly maimed homeless did not dare climb into these rare heights.

While Varro did not expect to knock on Flamininus's door and have him answer, he hoped a servant would help explain the delay.

Yet when he arrived, he found a half-dozen of Flamininus's other clients waiting at the door.

He recognized most of them, having met them either in the legions or more recently. He hailed them as he approached, and they opened their small circle to welcome him in. They exchanged greetings and pleasantries, and Varro felt awkward to ask what they were doing outside the home.

One client, Manius, answered his question. He was a stout man with a broad head and thickly curled hair. He was a fellow Sabine and so Varro felt a level of kinship with him.

"We're waiting for him to return from the Senate. What else would we be doing? The others will escort him home, and we will greet him. Of course, living out in the countryside you wouldn't know this, would you? To be a countryside equestrian must be grand!"

Manius's remark drew thin laughter from the others, but soon his mirth faded. "What's bothering you, Varro? Do you have business with the senator?"

Others spoke up about this, claiming they also had business and were here earlier. But Varro held up his hand and shook his head.

In his other hand, he clutched the papyrus message and the broken wax seal. The surrounding men faded as his mind cast back over the last two days. A new picture emerged in his mind, one that did not include a summons from Senator Flamininus. Nothing but the senator's seal seemed authentic to him, from the way they had been summoned to the careless arrangement in Rome. Then he thought of the Black Crow and the owner's dismay at the sudden drop in business. And Varro thought about the so-called regular crowd. He wished he looked harder at them, for they appeared nothing more than laborers finished with their work. Yet, more than one of them had paused in their laughter to stare at him when he came downstairs. At the time, he thought they were surprised to find they were not alone.

But what if they were surprised and confused to find one of their targets leaving?

Varro's hands turned icy, and he realized this had been an elaborate plan to lure them into the city and away from the protection of their villa walls.

Now Manius and the others had fallen silent and were staring at Varro as he emerged from his thoughts. They looked at him with furrowed brows.

"It is a trap," he whispered. "And I left Falco and Curio in the jaws of it."

6

Outside of Flamininus's villa, the setting sun cast golden light across the shoulders of the clients huddled around Varro. They pressed closer, asking if they had heard correctly that Varro was in danger. Beside them, the red door to the senator's home was firmly shut. Varro stared at it. He was shut out from all help just as the door kept the world away from Flamininus and his family.

"Say that again." Manius put a firm hand on Varro's shoulder. "Do you need our aid?"

"I need a horse immediately. I must get back across the city. The others are in danger and don't realize it."

The six clients debated where he could find a horse in short order. But Manius had the answer.

"We'll take the first we can find. Look, it may not be a cavalry horse, but there is one hitched to that cart. It seems lithe enough to travel fast. Don't worry about paying the man. I will cover for you. I know you will pay me back."

Varro dashed the short distance, the others following behind. The horse pricked up its ears but did not seem alarmed. However, the two men unloading a heavy barrel in the cart stood up at their approach.

Being middle-aged men, the clients did not make for a threatening sight. However, Varro led them with his hand held high, drawing the laborers' attention.

"I need this horse. These men will compensate you, and I will return it to you shortly."

The men set down the barrel and the one still in the cart raced Varro to the hitch. "Hold on, this is my horse. You will not--"

Varro leaped into the bed of the cart and easily shoved the man over the side. He thudded to the ground with a shriek. In the meantime, Manius helped him untether the horse.

"You can ride without a saddle?" The broad-faced man seemed astonished as Varro climbed onto the horse's back.

"I learned it in Numidia. Pay the man for me."

Horses might be herd animals, but Varro knew each had their own personality and opinions about their riders. Once freed from the cart, Varro grabbed its mane and kicked it forward. At first, the horse resisted him. He had learned from the Numidians to negotiate with the horse rather than attempt to command it. He remembered his old mentor, Baku, being so frustrated with his riding skills. But if he could see him now, speeding downhill through crowded Roman streets in the shadows of the dying day, he would howl in delight.

Once more, Fortuna had blessed him. His horse was far more daring than a common draft animal. He must have dreamed of this moment, when he could charge through the streets, causing men and women to leap aside in terror. Varro shouted for pedestrians to yield as he thundered past them. Some onlookers laughed and others cursed as he crashed through the lower neighborhoods. Fortunately, at the end of the day people were in their homes and not wandering the streets. It made for easier passage.

All the way, he hoped guessed correctly. The ambushers had probably questioned the owner after he left. They would expect his return when he discovered the senator was not home. Whoever organized the ambush must have wanted all three of them at once. So he prayed they waited for him to return in order to bag all three targets in one swoop. Otherwise, he might be returning to an empty taberna or worse.

He reached the square where the Black Crow stood in silent watch over the vacant space. Although it was evening, being Rome, more people should've been present at this hour.

He slipped off the horse, patting its neck and thanking it. It heaved and its sides were lathered with sweat. The horse was free to roam since he had nothing to tether him. Varro hoped he had not blown the horse, who had served him like his own mount.

Expecting his ambushers watched him, he strode confidently across the square. His Servus Capax pugio was strapped to his inner thigh. As he approached, he feigned scratching himself and withdrew the blade just before entering.

He did not know what to expect, imagining the laborers gone from their table and the owner lying dead on the floor.

Instead, he walked into the same scene he had left. The owner gave him a bland smile.

"You look like a phalanx of pikemen has charged you. Are you all right?"

Varro narrowed his eyes at the owner.

"Have those regulars moved from their table? Have either of my friends come downstairs?"

The owner glanced toward the stairs, then across the empty room to the laborers still chatting over their drinks.

"Only flies have visited this room since you left. Those fools will drink until they can't pay me. Your friends have stayed upstairs, quiet as usual."

"You know why we're here." Varro lowered his voice, causing the owner to lean in. "Did a representative of the senator arrange for a meeting?"

The owner stared back at him with a blank expression. He shook his head. "I remember you three and that owl symbol from the last time. Wasn't that long ago. I figured you needed the room again. No one let me know this time."

His eyes drifted down to the dagger in Varro's grip. He raised his brow, then gave a chiding look.

Varro awkwardly slipped it back into the sheath and glanced at the laborers drinking around their table. None of them appeared interested in his conversation with the owner.

"And you've seen nothing strange from anyone? Those men over there are familiar to you?"

The owner's expression flattened. "The strangest thing all day has been you."

Satisfied the owner knew nothing, Varro nodded his thanks and turned to the only occupants of the room other than the mousy serving woman who sat in the shadows while waiting on the laborers. He narrowed his eyes and approached them.

His sandals tapped lightly on the wooden floor as he crossed to them. At first, the laborers were so drunk none of them noticed Varro's arrival. But soon a bleary-eyed man frowned at him, and Varro drew closer to the table.

"Sorry to bother you, but I was expecting to meet a woman here tonight. She would've been wearing a red cloak. Have you seen such a woman enter since you've been here?"

The drunk laborers frowned and joked with or cursed Varro for his interruption. But Varro was only concerned with studying the six men around the table. None of them seemed suspicious, but then he knew better than to rely on appearances. They all seemed drunk and bemused at his interruption. But Varro cataloged their distinctive appearances in his memory. He couldn't be sure he would ever need the information, but his suspicion was still high.

After having a good look at all six and finding something about each that stood out to him, he raised his hands and begged forgiveness. "I fear I've missed her tonight. Sorry to have bothered you."

He crossed back toward the stairs leading up to the room where Falco and Curio waited. He had been certain of a trap. Yet as he looked back a last time before mounting the steps, he saw only the owner shaking his head at him and the laborers returned to their drunken conversation.

"I was sure of a trap," he said to himself as he bounced up the wooden steps.

When he reached the second floor, he suddenly realized his mistake. It was no ambush.

"The wine." He bit back on his words and charged up the stairs. He had been the only one to refuse the wine. The other two had drunk it and complained of its foul taste.

Poison!

His heart slammed into the base of his throat as he took two steps at a time to reach the third floor. He stood in a short corridor with a door on either side and at the end a high window that refused light from the setting sun. Their room was to the left, and the door was closed.

He slammed it open, his dagger once more in hand. It nearly fell off its hinges from the force, and he swept inside then poised for a strike.

Yet, he found Falco leaning over the table where he had left him. He pressed the point of his Servus Capax pugio into the wood with one hand and spun the blade with the other. Across from him, Curio had his head down on the table. Varro's raucous arrival only caused him to turn and look at him with bleary eyes.

"How much of that wine did you drink?" Varro pushed completely into the room, then snatched the clay jug from the table and dumped the dregs onto the floor.

His manic actions drew little reaction from either of his friends. Falco stopped playing with his dagger and frowned.

"Calling it wine is generous, but you can see we didn't waste it." Just as the owner had done, Falco's gaze settled on the pugio in Varro's white-knuckled grip. "And here I thought you were just mad at the door. You planning to stab me?"

Curio at last sat up and rubbed his face. "That wine was too much for an empty stomach. I feel sick."

"And how do you feel?" Varro placed his dagger on the table then sat beside Falco. He leaned close to study his friend's eyes, which gazed back at him in irritation.

"I feel like punching you in the mouth. If I'm being honest, I get that feeling a lot."

Varro sniffed inside the clay jug, finding it vinegary but not like anything poisonous. He slapped his palm on the table, then released a long sigh.

"No poison and no ambush." He thumped the table again with the clay jug.

"And no senator," Falco said, gently removing the jug from his hand. "You must have a story to tell."

He nodded and then explained what had happened. When he finished, both of his friends seemed more alert. Falco rubbed his jaw and tilted his head.

"Senator Flamininus probably had pressing business at the Senate. You know, the Boii are still a threat. Maybe they've attacked. He was probably so frantic that he forgot to send word to us here."

Curio nodded. "That's right. He knew you would go find him. He probably realized his oversight when it was already too late."

Varro held both sides of his head as he leaned on the table, struggling to reconcile his instincts with reality. "But the strange messengers and the wastefulness of it all. None of it seems like something Senator Flamininus would do."

"Maybe he is just using a new messenger service." Falco sniffed the wine jar, then recoiled, muttering something about poison. "Every good man in the city has been called into the legion. It's not surprising he has only fools left to do his business."

"That may be so," Varro conceded. His head sank lower into his hands. "I stole a man's horse. I hope the poor beast is fine. I rode him so carelessly."

They continued to debate the various reasons for Flamininus's absence and the slipshod nature of his messengers. In the end, Varro had only his hunches to support his position. Falco summarized it for him.

"You see everything you don't understand as a threat. It's a shame, really. You used to be a good boy and would walk right into my waiting fist. Now you see an enemy hidden in every shadow."

Curio, who had again set his head down, spoke in a muffled voice.

"But that caution is what makes him our leader. If you were in charge, never mind walking into fists. We wouldn't be alive today to walk anywhere."

"Whatever the reason, Flamininus is not here, and I think we've done enough to jeopardize our secrecy. Let's spend the night elsewhere, and tomorrow we will go see the senator." He fished out the papyrus from his tunic. A portion of the wax seal had vanished and what remained had deformed from his body heat. He spread the message open on the table again, hoping to find a missed clue to the actual author. "The senator will want to know who wrote this."

"If only to get his money back," Falco said, collecting the papyrus from Varro. "Or else he wrote it himself. Maybe he felt like hiding in his office away from everybody while he wrote three unnecessary letters. Don't think too much about this."

They collected their bags, and Varro swept away the crumbs of wax spilled on the table. They left the owner with a simple nod of thanks. He welcomed them to return anytime. Outside, the air was fresher, which was something considering the stagnant odors that hung over the city. The sun would soon vanish and the streets must be cleared by that time. Fortunately, they knew another inn nearby.

They made it in time to rent a single room. The proprietor offered to vacate other rooms when he realized Varro could pay. But he preferred they all remained together until he spoke with the senator.

Once again, they had a room on the third floor. A servant had left them a clay lamp after leading them to their quarters. The wavering orange light revealed a space large enough for Falco to lie prone. A straw mattress that smelled faintly of rot covered a narrow bed. None of them wanted to sleep on it, but finally Curio took it.

"I feel like I'm going to throw up. So, it's better if I'm on the straw."

Varro and Falco would take the floor, and all their gear stuffed beneath a small table in the corner. Falco noted the room was not much larger than a field tent on the march. Both Curio and Falco unstrapped their hidden daggers and set them on the table.

Varro remained leaning against the wall, wondering how he had misunderstood. The threat had felt so real. Perhaps Falco was right about his state of mind. So many years of searching for enemies, seen and unseen, had left him suspicious of everything. The words stung for their truth. Everything he did not understand was a threat.

As Curio climbed into the bed, he suddenly clutched his stomach and vomited onto the straw mattress. A foul odor bloomed in the room as he ejected his stomach contents to splash across the bed and flow onto the floor. Falco, who stood behind him, leaped back and bumped into the wall with a thud.

"Jupiter's balls! You threw up more than you drank. How is that possible?"

Curio tried to answer but only vomited again, a disgusting squelch drowning out his words.

Standing up, Varro slipped to the door to avoid the spreading pool of odious fluid.

"That's a proper mess. We won't sleep here, not for what we paid. I'll go talk to the proprietor about a new room while he gets this one cleaned up."

Falco waved him off. "Hurry before we drown."

Curio wanted to reply, but only leaned forward and heaved another stream. Varro left the disgusting scene, glad to be the one in charge of negotiating prices. The room was already stifling before Curio made it unlivable.

He clambered down the stairs. The main room was still full of patrons at the end of the day. Many were preparing to leave, and others to retire to their rooms. Their animated voices echoed up the stairwell. As he approached the bottom, he ducked down to see if the proprietor was still present.

When he reached the bottom, he froze in place.

Across the room by the entrance, blocked by dozens of people settling their bills and saying their farewells, stood a familiar face.

It could be no coincidence.

One of the drunken laborers from the Black Crow, a fit man with short and sandy-colored hair, argued with the proprietor. The laborer wore a plain brown tunic, with short sleeves that revealed strong arms. His muscles flexed as he pointed across the room toward the stairs and argued with the proprietor. Whatever they said, it seemed he wanted a room and the proprietor declined him.

Varro had to capture this man. Without a doubt, he had followed them and now sought to get a room beside theirs. And for what other purpose, he wondered, other than to kill them in the night.

He moved calmly, slipping in between men clasping arms and promising to meet again. All the while, he kept his eyes fixed on the laborer, if that's what he really was. Varro was inclined now to think of him as an enemy assassin, and damn whatever Falco said about his suspicions. The laborer had no business here other than to stay close to his targets.

An enormous barrel-shaped man rose out of his seat and staggered into Varro's path. Each step he took to avoid the tottering giant followed the man's path. He stuck his arms out to keep his balance, and Varro tapped him aside. Unfortunately, it caused the man to trip.

For his size, he screeched like a child and grabbed Varro's tunic as he collapsed with a blubbery thump. Varro stumbled forward, drawing curses and shouts from the patrons surrounding him. They shoved back, and the barrel-shaped man thrashed on the floor like a speared fish, trapping Varro as if in a net.

When he recovered his footing, he locked eyes with the laborer who had turned toward the chaos along with the proprietor.

He felt a chill, as if looking into the eyes of a cobra. The laborer had sandy hair and light hazel eyes that seemed lit with feral purpose. He was too far away to grab, and the enormous man on the floor kicked at Varro's legs and hindered forward progress.

The laborer turned and sprinted out the door.

Varro leaped over the fallen giant, only to have his undersized friend seize him by the collar.

"See here! You can't go knocking over people and just run off."

Varro spun around, looping his arm over the man who held him in place. He too screamed like a child as Varro pressed against the outside of his elbow. He immediately released his grip. Varro brushed past others in his way then fled out the front door.

The streets were in shadow as the last light of the day retreated behind Rome's walls. A dozen people crisscrossed the streets in all directions. For an instant, Varro feared he had lost his target. Then, he heard men cursing to his left and turned in time to see a shape in a brown tunic vanishing into a narrow street.

He dashed off in pursuit, shouting for those in the streets to give way. The offended group of men outside the street entrance saw Varro charging and drew up in a line. They were young bravos not accustomed to being pushed around on what they must consider to be their own territory.

Impatient with nonsense, Varro lowered his shoulders to make a direct charge. Four stood against him and had one of their numbers not lost heart they might have bounced him. But Varro targeted the second from the left who flinched. His shoulder collided with the youth, pushing him against the others and breaking a hole in their line.

He now sped down the sloping street into darkness, glad he was not wearing caligae or else he might skid out of control. The four men behind him cursed and promised revenge, but Varro was not listening carefully. Instead, he searched for his enemy.

The narrow street tumbled away in the darkness, with only a single old woman in a tattered gray stola plodding uphill. Varro rushed to her, startling the woman so that her eyes shined white in the dark.

"Did you see a man in a brown tunic fleeing down this hill?"

The old woman blinked, then gathered her stola tight around her neck. She pointed at an alley to the left.

He wasted no time in pursuit. The alley barely fit him, slowing him as he shoved across rough stucco walls and over slick trash underfoot. The confines of the alley were dark and smelled of waste and rot. But a bright orange light wavered at the end, and he saw the fleeting shadow of a running man.

Turning the corner at the end of the alley, a brilliant fire burned in an outdoor forge tucked into a hidden yard. No one tended the flames, but tools were laid out on a nearby bench. He again paused, searching for signs of passage. The ground was unpaved, and the forge light cast shadows in every direction. If his enemy left any footprints, they were lost in the confusion.

Breathless, he scanned three exits, all narrow alleys leading back out to different streets.

He growled in frustration. He would have to pick one at random and hope Fortuna smiled on him once more. It's not how he preferred to work, but he had no other choice than to surrender.

He picked the alley closest to the forge, guessing his enemy would take the nearest path. The heat caressed his right side as he passed into the cool darkness of the alley.

A dozen steps in, and something heavy hit him square in the back.

He sprawled forward, stretching out his arms to break his fall. He landed hard on packed earth and refuse. The thick paste smeared his face and arms as he struggled to regain his breath.

A hand snatched the back of his tunic then yanked him over. Still dazed, Varro fumbled to reach the pugio strapped to his thigh.

Curving, muscular lines defined the silhouette that hovered over him. He raised something like a pair of iron tongs in his free hand.

His voice was reedy and contemptuous.

"You were supposed to be the dangerous one." He coughed a laugh. "Well, your skull will break easily enough."

The shadowed figure heaved back the metal tongs to bash Varro in the head.

But he had recovered his wits and drew his Servus Capax pugio.

The silhouette extended back to put as much strength into the blow as possible. In that moment, Varro slashed the point of his dagger across the extended torso.

The attacker doubled over in shock and pain, his improvised weapon clanking to the ground with a puff of air beside Varro's head.

He then reversed the grip on his pugio and drove the pommel into the shadow's face, hoping to capture him alive. It connected with something hard, then slipped across to spin his attacker's head around. He fell backward into the light that reached the top of the alley.

Scrambling to his feet, Varro had gained the upper hand and now prepared to jump atop his enemy.

In the same instant, the four young bravos he had plowed through appeared in the yellow light of the forge.

"Here he is!" one of them shouted, and the rest rushed into the alley.

Howling in frustration, Varro backed up as they surged around the prone body of his attacker. One of the young men still tripped while the three others filled the alley. One raised his fist.

"We'll teach you some respect."

But Varro's rage was stoked, both at his enemy's luck and the audacity of the bravos. He plunged forward, sinking his pugio into the flesh wall before him. One bravo gurgled a curse, then collapsed to his knees. Fists pummeled Varro, but his muscles were hardened, and he suffered little from their unskilled blows. He again stabbed into the chaotic press, drawing another curse as hot blood sprayed across his hands.

"He's got a sword!"

It was all the surviving bravos needed to know, and they turned to flee the way they had come. Varro was uninterested in pursuit. Somewhere in the darkness at his feet a young bravo groaned and cried for his mother. Varro left him to his fate. Instead, he went to where he had defeated the laborer and found only a discarded pair of iron tongs.

Light from the forge illuminated the top of the alley, and Varro searched in the muddy blood for any clue to his attacker's identity. His fingers found something hard with a sharp edge. He pried it up and held it in the light. It was a broken front tooth stained with fresh blood.

"Well, I've marked you twice. I'll find you yet."

~

~

7

Varro sipped the wine from a delicate clay cup decorated with Greek-style patterns. It was sweet and warm, and he hoped enough of it would wash away the humiliation he felt from the prior night. Beside him, both Falco and Curio enjoyed their wine. They waited in Senator Flamininus's cubiculum, with a slave in attendance. The young boy minded their cups, refilling them as fast as they drained them.

Falco tilted his head in appreciation as he set his cup down. Then he offered Varro a sympathetic smile and nudged him under the table where Varro had set their letters, wax seals, and the broken tooth he captured.

"We're on a mission. Don't drink so much."

Varro ground his teeth and looked aside as Curio chuckled. "You're enjoying this."

"And why not? What goes for me goes for him."

He had already drunk more wine at breakfast than was prudent, and now indulged in the senator's kind offering of food and drink while he finished up his other business.

Varro's account had equally enraged and amused both Falco and

Curio. Curio was especially glad that his stomach ailment had produced valuable results.

"It makes sleeping with that stench worth it," he had said. Thanks to Varro's exploits, they never got a new room or anyone to clean up the vomit.

Now Varro admired the Greek vases and statuary that decorated Flamininus's office. A Macedonian general's helmet and armor were displayed on a rack and polished enough to reflect Varro's face. He turned away from this as well, unable to look at himself.

At last, Senator Flamininus arrived with his secretary following. He wore a bright white tunic with purple trim to denote his status as senator. Though years had passed since he had been Varro's consul, he was still muscular, and his soulful eyes reflected keen intelligence. He had been the youngest consul Varro had served under, and the youngest in recent memory.

All three of them stood, but Flamininus smiled and gestured to their stools.

"It is I who should stand in the presence of two grass crown holders."

Varro was glad for the senator's cheerful mood, particularly since he had to reveal his tattoo during their meeting. For now, the red and puffy tattoo remained hidden under his sleeve.

Once they were all seated, Flamininus dismissed his secretary and the slave. Notably, he sent away the wine and cups as well. While he saw the various evidence Varro had set out, he ignored it and instead folded both hands on the table.

"Manius told me of your recent horse purchase, Varro. And I understand you had an eventful visit to the city last night. So, let's hear the story."

"Yes, sir." Varro then carefully laid out the entire story, starting from their strange summons and ending with his fight in the alleyway. All the while, Flamininus revealed no hint of his thoughts. He examined the papyrus message, then picked up the broken seal that Varro had tried to assemble into its original shape. When he reached the end of the story, his hooded eyes fell on the broken tooth.

"That's the entire story, sir. Someone tried to lure the three of us into the city and then planned to murder us. It must be the same group that Paullus worked with to eliminate Consul Minucius. It seems they want revenge for foiling their plans."

Flamininus remained still, his hands now hidden under the table and his face expressionless. He once more picked up the broken seal pieces, then flicked them away in disdain.

"A copy of my signet ring, passable but not anything to hold up against scrutiny."

Regardless of whether it was intended as a reprimand, Varro lowered his head and apologized. "I should have studied the seal better, sir."

Flamininus flipped away Varro's concern. "But why would you? You were expecting my summons, and the only unusual thing was the manner of it. It stands to reason you would be more interested in the messengers than a wax seal."

The four of them then debated possible culprits. All agreed that whoever carried out the ruse knew their process. Yet they did not know enough to re-create it perfectly. They concluded that a spy was among them. Flamininus's eyes narrowed as he seemed to search his thoughts

"It will be up to me to learn who the spy is. It could be someone in my household, or maybe even one of our own."

Varro cleared his throat. "Or it could've been information Paullus shared with his accomplices, sir."

"Paullus ain't talking these days," Falco said. But the senator nodded in agreement with Varro.

"Speaking of the man, I've done my own investigation into his activities prior to joining us. I've not yielded anything fruitful, but I know he had spoken to his uncle about Servus Capax. So, it is possible he had provided intelligence prior to his recent incapacitation."

All of them fell silent, and Varro considered the depth of Paullus's treachery. What promises could have driven him to such treachery? Also, Flamininus had just connected Paullus to the enemy from the night before. Their situation held no room for coincidence. This mysterious organization was well developed and hidden in shadow.

"That would explain how they copied your family ring, sir." Varro swept the broken pieces of wax into a pile as he spoke. "If Paullus wakes up, then he will have much to answer for."

Flamininus's frown deepened. "Leave Paullus for me to handle. The Scipio and Paullus families have favorable impressions of you that I'd rather not sully with you asking uncomfortable questions."

The senator set his jaw and looked like he did when leading the legions into battle.

"No matter how it was done, this forgery was a direct attack on me and my family. While I cannot prove anything yet, I deeply suspect this is all entwined with the events at Pisa. Therefore, I'm assigning the three of you to bring this man to me for interrogation."

With his mood fouled, Flamininus's scowl seemed to drain the light from the room. Varro knew what sort of interrogation he planned for his enemy. It was not the type he would likely survive.

Varro and the others affirmed their commitment to capturing Varro's attacker. Flamininus sat up straighter and looked once more at the papyrus letter. He tilted his head.

"The three of you must be far closer to the truth than you realize. They went to elaborate lengths to gather you in one place. But if it was just for murder, then they would've been better served ambushing you along the road to Rome. Therefore, you should be careful in the city. There is a reason they drew you here. Why they did is still a mystery. I trust you will solve it along with our other questions. Interesting times ahead, boys."

That Flamininus referred to their enemy in the plural chilled Varro. He might be dealing with a handful of traitors, but given the scope of their activities, he was far more likely to be dealing with an expansive organization. For all he knew, Falco, Curio, and himself were all that Servus Capax had.

"I will support you in every way possible," Flamininus said in a brighter voice. "You have never once disappointed me. You've surprised me, certainly. I expect before all of this is done you will surprise me again. I look forward to speaking with Varro's attacker. The moment you capture him, send word directly to my front door. Keep your captive well guarded while you wait for my instructions."

Flamininus placed both hands on the desk with a gentle bump of his fingers, signaling the end of their meeting. Varro looked at Falco, who nodded imperceptibly.

"Sir, there is one more thing you should know." Varro and Falco rolled up their sleeves then displayed their shoulders in unison.

At first Flamininus appeared not to understand, but then his frown returned.

"I told you to wait for my decision before acting. It seems you misunderstood me."

"Sir, it's only an easily hidden tattoo. We still have pugiones if you require us to carry them. We left them with your servant."

Varro watched the thin muscles of Flamininus's jaw twitch as he regarded their tattoos. He gave them a scowl, then settled on Curio. "Did you get one?"

"No, sir. But I think they look great on Falco and Varro." His words were weak and trembling under Flamininus's glare.

"Good for you. You'll have to take care of your friends once I have those tattoos skinned from their shoulders."

Flamininus stood, suddenly appearing twice as tall in Varro's mind. The rest of them stood as well and saluted. The senator held the silence a heartbeat longer than he should have.

"Retrieve your weapons from my servant. I'm certain you will need them, given the murderous intent of our foes. Be careful about revealing weapons in the city. Now, you have your orders. Don't waste time, for you can be sure our enemies are already making new plans."

A servant opened the door with a call from the senator and then Varro led the others out in a file. Within moments, they had their daggers returned, and they were once more outside of the senator's home and in the streets of Rome.

Curio rubbed his shoulder. "I warned you. Now he's going to cut your shoulders off."

Falco groaned. "Don't worry about it. Remember, he's a senator and a hero of Rome and Greece. When was the last time that man had anyone say or do anything he didn't want? He's upset, but I'm sure he'll get over it. He has bigger problems to worry about."

"It didn't seem like he was joking." Curio mimicked a knife skinning his shoulder. "If they shave it off in one piece, maybe you can have it cured and hang it in your cubiculum."

Varro interrupted Curio's gleeful imitation of their impending mutilation.

"The senator was right. We can't waste time while our enemies are using the moment to regroup. This man we're searching for must still be nearby. He'll be a lot easier to identify now that I knocked out his front tooth and cut him across his belly."

Falco rubbed the back of his head and grimaced. "Are we going to ask everyone we meet to smile and raise their tunics? Seems like a sure way to get into a brawl."

Rolling his eyes, Varro gestured south of the Palatine Hill.

"He was drinking with five other men last night at the Black Crow. I noted all their faces, and that's why I recognized him in the first place. We'll start there and expand the search as needed."

They followed the same road Varro had taken yesterday, but now he had time to see the surrounding neighborhood. Stately homes gradually turned to businesses, which then turned to common homes and businesses. People clogged the streets, and he was relieved he did not trample anyone in the prior day's mad charge.

At last, they came to the square where Varro had suspected its emptiness the night before. The Black Crow sat across the way, its door open and people flowing in and out.

They entered and found the proprietor was not present, which suited Varro. He did not want any interference. Smoke filled the main room and flowed from the kitchen along the ceiling. The room smelled of tangy scents of food, sour wine, and sweat. Men and women sat at tables to drink, while others reclined on couches along the walls and enjoyed a meal. Servants sped back and forth across the room with full or empty trays held in both hands.

Falco leaned close, his voice fighting against the loud chatter. "From that blank expression, you don't recognize anyone?"

"There are more people than I expected. It's also early yet. We might have to wait for the others to finish their day's labor."

Nevertheless, they pretended to search for seating in the crowded room while Varro studied the patrons as they circled. After a few rotations, an irritated serving woman blocked their path. "Are you three blind? You've twice walked by that empty table. Have a seat or practice marching someplace else."

Not wishing to call more attention than they already had, the three piled into the corner table. A dark-eyed man reclining nearby stared at them before returning to his meal. They ordered wine and Varro slipped an extra denarius onto the table. "We just need time to rest and talk. Bring us cups and a jug then leave us be."

The silver coin scraped off the table and vanished into the serving woman's hand. "Whatever you want."

They sat in silence, and shortly Falco and Curio grew bored. However, Varro paid rigid attention to the front door. Falco made disparaging remarks about being on guard duty, drawing chuckles from Curio. But he could not risk one of last night's enemies peeking inside and finding him first. He might bound away like a frightened doe and warn their enemy. So, he studied every person entering the door until his eyes stung with tears.

Hours passed and still none of the laborers appeared. The proprietor returned but did not notice them in the general confusion of a full room. He seemed especially pleased with his business compared to yesterday. Curio had set his head on the table as if to nap, while Falco balanced his head against his palm and thrummed the table with the other.

Another hour later, Curio snored lightly, and Falco now slouched forward, as if ready to join him. Even Varro's ironclad patience was crumbling. He inhaled, ready to surrender the vigil, then one of his marks appeared in the entrance.

He was of medium build, dark and stocky from laboring in the sun. A streak of white ran through dark hair, the landmark Varro had noted the night before. Additionally, he wore the same faded brown tunic from the prior night, and a prominent stain marked his collar.

Varro kicked Curio under the table and nudged Falco with his elbow. Both men sat up and turned toward the entrance. Curio yawned.

"The one with the streak of gray?"

They watched him approach the table he sat at the night before. He looked around as if expecting someone, then pulled up a stool. After a speaking with a server, he relaxed and waited for his jug.

But Varro and the others already surrounded him at the table.

The man looked up with a scowl. "Excuse me, do I know any of you?"

Falco slipped onto the stool beside him and Curio blocked him from behind. No fool, the man attempted to stand, but Varro now sat on his left side. He deftly drew his pugio beneath the table and set it against the man's kidney. His eyes flicked wide and his mouth opened as if to scream. But Varro pressed harder.

"Relax, we just have some questions for you. Walk with us for a bit."

The man's mouth cycled wordlessly until he finally spilled out something. "Look, I promise after I'm paid this week, you'll collect everything I owe. This time, it's for real. No tricks."

Falco stood as Curio put his hand on the man's shoulder. Varro increased the pressure on his blade.

"I'm not here about that, friend, but maybe I can help you. You share information with me and I might ease your financial burdens. Just get up from your table and follow the man behind you. We will go someplace more private and have a mutually beneficial conversation."

The four of them made for an awkward group as they exited the Black Crow. Curio led them toward a quiet alley across the square, while Falco held the man by his arm. Varro kept his dagger pressed against his forearm, prepared for trouble.

Yet they reached the shade of the alleyway, and their captive trembled enough that Varro feared he might collapse.

"You were drinking at the Black Crow last night with your friends. One of them had hazel eyes and sandy hair. He wore a brown tunic." Varro plucked the man's tunic. "Much like this one. He sat directly across from you and beside another with a mole on his cheek. What is his name?"

The man blinked rapidly, his head swiveling between the three men surrounding him.

"I... I know him. His name is Marcus Longus."

Falco snorted a laugh and shook the man.

"Come on, give his real name, not the name of every other man in Rome."

"But that's the name he gave us."

Their captive's face paled, and when Varro produced his dagger, it turned so white it glowed in the shadows.

"How long have you known Marcus Longus? Tell me everything you know."

His brows furrowed in confusion, and he glanced out the alley where others rushed past. Varro sensed he might call out for help, and set the dagger point against his belly.

"Don't make me hate myself for your death. Answer my question."

The man backed up to the wall and raised both hands.

"He's only been with us for a week or so. At the Pilus olive oil warehouse. We load the carts coming in and going out. The foreman threw him in with us. He's just like the rest of us. Works hard, plays dice, and drinks at the Black Crow. I don't know anything else. He doesn't talk about family or anything."

Varro glanced to the others, and both shrugged to his silent question. This man seemed genuine, though truth might only be confirmed with the application of pain. Fortunately for his captive and his own conscience, he couldn't risk it in daylight Rome.

"So a new man with no history joins your team and you ask no questions?"

The captive looked between Varro and the street, his face now gleaming with sweat.

"I don't go prying into other people's lives. That'd get him mad in a hurry and I've got to work with him every day."

"And he has been at work every day this past week?"

"Yes. He's been making us all look bad, showing up earlier than everyone else. He's fast and cuts his breaks short, too. But he didn't show up today."

"Did anyone else not show up?"

"Just the new guy was absent. The rest of us can't afford to miss a day without pay and risk losing our job to a replacement."

Varro searched the sweaty, white face before him. He withdrew his pugio and again hid it against his forearm.

"You must have some idea where he lives."

The man's expression brightened and he pointed with one of his raised hands. "Pilus has a worker's dormitory. Look, he's probably there now. The foreman said he took a spill last night and broke his tooth. He's probably keeping himself drunk against the pain. I know I would."

Falco and Curio pulled the man's arms down, holding him in place while Varro sheathed his dagger then fished in his purse.

"What do you owe your creditor?"

Again, the man blinked rapidly before realizing his fortunes were shifting.

"Fifty denarii."

Falco hissed through his teeth. "You must be gambling with some rich friends to owe that kind of money."

The man hung his head. "It's the interest that does it."

Varro dug out three denarii, more than a laborer would make in a week. He set them on his palm and extended it.

"You weren't that helpful. But this should pay for your inconvenience and your silence. Forget us and everything we discussed. If you see Marcus Longus again, you can arrange through the proprietor to meet us at the Black Crow." Varro then looked to the others. "Let him go."

Their captive snatched the denarii into his sweaty fist and bobbed his head in gratitude. Seeming to realize he had his freedom, took three steps backward toward the street, then fled.

"Marcus Longus. What a fake name." Falco stood beside Varro, watching their former captive push through the crowds. "Do you think he's working with him?"

Varro sighed. "There's only one way to know. We should follow him. He probably lives in the same dormitory."

"I can trail him," Curio said. "Though he'll be hard to see over all these people."

"Let's put him aside for now. We've got daylight still. Let's see if we can increase our crimes today from mere kidnapping. I think we will break into the Pilus olive oil workers' dormitory next."

8

The sun had turned red by the time they found the workers' dormitory in the Suburra district. Though it was a dormitory and should've been on the private side of the wall dividing the neighborhood, the building stood close to the warehouse on the public side. The warehouse was a long and low building with gaps in the tile roof.

The narrow dormitory stood three floors tall and leaned to the left like it needed help from the neighboring building to stand. Gray and crumbling stucco seemed to threaten imminent collapse. Small windows dotted the walls and black streaks ran from the sills. The only relief to the depressing facade was a red and white striped awning set against the lower floor wall.

"Honestly," Falco said upon seeing the building. "I know he is trying to kill us, but I feel bad for him living there."

Curio pointed down the street. "Don't feel too bad. Look at all the prostitutes and gambling houses. Not to mention all the happy drunks."

While Falco shook his head, Varro scanned the neighborhood. Being the worst area in Rome, he was glad to be armed. Crowded into narrow buildings and narrower streets, the poorest and most wretched of Rome's inhabitants lived here. As Curio had noted, drunks staggered amongst prostitutes and the homeless. Suspiciously clean men with faces shaped from hard brawling stood among them like hawks stalking a kill.

"Well, if you wanted to lie low, this would be the place," Varro said. "It doesn't seem like there's much money in the olive oil trade."

The three of them loitered on the sidewalk, where people in shabby tunics passed them without a second glance. They were just one more group of thugs in an entire district full of them. The street smelled of urine, though Varro could not find a source. The odor permeated the air.

"What's the plan?" Falco folded his arms and regarded the building. "We could probably knock it over and shake out everyone inside."

"I forgot multiple floors. I'm so used to countryside life," Varro said. "I don't know how we will search three floors without arousing suspicion."

Now Curio sniffed the air and covered his nose before speaking, turning his voice nasal.

"Well, do you think he's even there? He's probably gone by now. So, we just need to ask who has moved out recently."

"I agree," Varro said. "He's probably gone, and I doubt anyone knows. But you just gave me an idea. Let's go."

They crossed the street with a dozen other people. After sunset, Varro expected the streets should clear. However, he realized life in this district would differ greatly from the others in Rome. They would have to be careful about drawing attention.

Three men lingered outside the door to the dormitory. They wore the same faded brown tunics, and their hair was thin and graying in advance of their years. Hard labor had sapped their youth and replaced it with scars and hollow cheeks. They paused their conversation to stare at Varro as he stepped forward.

"We're looking for Marcus Longus. He should've just moved in a week ago. I heard he's hurt."

The three men looked at each other and then folded their arms. The one closest to Varro narrowed his tired eyes.

"And who are you? His doctor?"

The other two laughed, and Varro concealed his impatience with a thin smile.

"Oh, we're not doctors. We're the exact opposite. I hope none of you are trying to hide him from us. We have business to discuss with him."

The lead man remained defiant, but behind him, his two friends unfolded their arms and shrank back toward the flimsy door.

"Well, this is our dormitory. We don't just let anyone inside, especially if they're going to make a mess of the place."

Varro's smile widened. "Sorry, I just started with Quintus. He runs his gang differently than the ones I'm used to. Maybe you've been seeing someone else before we showed up. Now we're responsible for making sure Marcus pays his debts. He's missed a payment. Quintus doesn't care where the money comes from. So if you don't want to let us inside, you can pay instead. If you won't, and you also won't let us inside, then we have a problem with you. I wonder how you'll do your jobs without thumbs."

The bravado melted away and all three men stepped aside, one even opening the door that would be challenged to block a strong breeze.

"He's on the third floor. He's a rich man. That's where the private rooms are. He hasn't come out all day. I don't know what his situation is and don't care. But if you need to get physical with him, can you do it someplace else?"

Varro patted the man's shoulder as he passed. "We're just here for the payment. He pays, we leave. But we'll be back next week."

The interior of the dormitory was dark and stank enough to sting Varro's eyes. The bottom floor was a common area where exhausted and hopeless men stretched out on the floor. Each one guarded a narrow patch of floor territory but otherwise seemed at peace. They murmured and stared as Varro led the group up thin stairs that threatened to break underfoot.

Falco leaned in as they climbed to the third floor.

"Quintus?"

"I can use common names, too. It doesn't seem like Marcus Longus has made many loyal friends in his week here. They gave them up easily enough."

The stairs led into a long hallway on the top floor. A threadbare carpet ran the length of the hall. It might have been red once, but now it was a dusty brown. Five narrow doors on each side lined the walls. Ostensibly, the doors should provide protection and privacy. But as Varro moved down the hallway, the ill-fitting doors revealed glimpses of the inhabitants behind them.

"Which one?" Falco was so tall he nearly reached the ceiling of the small hallway.

Varro scanned the doors and found one dark around the jambs. He pointed to it.

The three of them fell silent, each drawing his pugio in preparation. Varro listened at the door, and despite its flimsiness, he heard nothing behind it. He gave it a gentle push and found it was not barred.

He remained still a heartbeat longer, then shoved the door open. Using it like a shield, he swept inside and kept his pugio ready to strike.

The room was empty and lit only with a thin light that spilled in from a tiny window. Varro felt a cooling breeze rolling in through it. He shoved the door back against the wall to make certain no one hid behind it. It thumped with an empty echo and creaked back toward him.

The private room was as tiny as expected. Only one man could fit comfortably. Someone had ransacked the place and had flipped the bed, such as it was, scattering mattress straw everywhere. Remains of several meals mixed with the straw, creating a chaotic scene. Varro stood in the doorway, and his shoulders drooped.

"Well, either someone got to him first or he wrecked the place before leaving."

Falco leaned in across his shoulder, looking at the narrow window high on the wall before them.

"From what you described I don't think he could fit. So that means he slipped out when no one was looking."

He led them inside, using his feet to shove through the straw and scraps scattered on the rickety wood floor. The gaps were wide enough that straw fell through to the apartment below. As the three of them tramped about looking for any sign of so-called Marcus Longus, residents directly below thumped on the floor and protested the noise and trash raining on them.

The three of them had no room to turn around in the small apartment. They bumped into each other as they kicked through the trash. They found fat drops of sticky blood all over the apartment. Clearly Longus had returned here after Varro wounded him. But otherwise, their search proved fruitless. He had left nothing useful behind.

Varro laced his fingers behind his head and sighed in frustration.

"The trail goes dead here. Who knows where he could have got to."

He scanned the dim apartment again, and when Curio turned over a worn-out carpet, he revealed a hole to the apartment below. Varro could see shadows of a man beyond it.

"You bastard, stop jumping around up there! You and your friends have been nothing but trouble since you arrived. I don't care what the foreman thinks about you. You carry on, and I will come up there and beat some manners into you."

Varro smiled. "Looks like the trail is not so cold after all."

Back in the third-floor hallway, other residents had come out to investigate. They hid halfway behind their doors, four men in total. One ducked away when Varro met his eyes. But he turned to the man directly across from Marcus's apartment.

"Have you seen where this one went? Has he had visitors?"

The man was bone thin and bald, though he had a long black beard stretching to his chest.

"I don't know what he does. I only sleep here. He's got friends he goes drinking with. Maybe sometimes he comes back with them to keep drinking after everyplace closes. I don't know anything. Just leave me out of it."

The other residents seemed to understand Longus represented trouble, and they closed their doors. Varro heard bolts slide into place, though the doors would not stand against a determined break-in.

Rather than force them to speak, Varro led the others to the second floor and found the apartment directly beneath Longus's. He rapped on the door and didn't even need to speak before it swung open to a brightly lit room.

A red-faced man with thick and curly black hair glared at him. Another man sat on the floor against the far wall, a clay jug beside him. He pulled his knees up to his chin as if recoiling.

"You're the bastards who were banging about upstairs. What do you want?"

Varro stepped forward and the man blocked him, but relented when he noticed the pugio in Varro's grip.

"What do you mean carrying that in here? We've made no trouble for anyone."

Falco and Curio squeezed into the small space and filled the room to capacity. The man on the floor grabbed his wine jug as if fearing it might be taken.

"We both don't like the neighbor above you," Varro said, pointing the tip of his pugio toward the ceiling. "You can hear everything he says through the holes in the floor. Who has he been speaking with?"

Rather than look up, he stared at Varro's pugio and its carefully tended white edge. He swallowed.

"All of us are trying to sleep here. I'm not trying to listen to what he's talking about. He has only been here a week, and three times someone has visited him late at night. Stuff falls through the ceiling all the time. It drives me mad, especially when straw and other stuff lands on my face while I'm trying to sleep. At times, I felt like killing him. He came home last night and trashed the place before he left again. He hasn't been back, though I thought you were him and his friends."

Varro and the others examined the ceiling. He saw dark gaps, many stuffed with cloth that hung limp. The hole that Curio had revealed was too big to be stuffed, and it seemed someone tried to pin a hide sheet over it. But two of the pins had fallen out and caused the sheet to hang like an open trapdoor.

The man clutching his wine jug on the floor saw Varro staring. He pointed at the sheet.

"I need different nails. The wood there is too hard." He dared to remove a hand from the jug and wiped his face as if dusting the sheet away. "That hide fell right out of the ceiling."

Varro's eyes widened and before he could ask, Falco snatched the sheet down and flipped it over.

"Oh, you're going to like this."

Falco passed him what now appeared like a uniform sheet of vellum. It was marred only where he had torn it from the ceiling nails. At first, Varro thought he held it upside down, for he could understand none of the writing. But once rotated, it still made no sense.

Now both residents, along with Falco and Curio, gathered around Varro, their shadows blocking out the bright light of their lamps. Varro had to hold it higher to read.

"A secret code," Falco proclaimed.

Curio stood on his toes for a better view. "Before I learned my letters, all writing looked like that to me."

Varro chuckled, understanding why Curio could not identify it but amused with Falco's assessment.

"You don't recognize this script? We saw it everywhere in Numidia. It's Punic."

Falco grabbed the vellum sheet, his heavy brows drawn tight. "A message from Carthage?"

"Who's saying it's from Carthage? It could be from anyone, or he could be a Carthaginian." Varro tugged it gently from Falco's grip, then showed it to the two residents. "You don't read Punic, do you?"

Both residents now backed away, hands up as if in surrender. The red-faced one, previously so bold, now seemed ready to hide behind the opened door.

"We don't have any business with Carthage. My father fought against Hannibal. My uncles too."

"Don't worry," Varro said as he sheathed his dagger. "I was joking. The three of us will rent your room for the night. And I'll pay you to forget we were here. You can come back after work tomorrow, and everything will be just as it is now."

The red-faced man regained some of his earlier bluster, stating the room was not for rent. Then he re-examined the three powerful men before him and appeared to change his mind. Varro picked four obols from his purse and gave two to each resident.

"Is there another way into this building besides the front door?"

The resident with the jug, which he clutched to his side like a child, nodded. "There's the back delivery entrance. We use it all the time, but not everyone does."

Varro waited until the two residents left before turning to his friends. Falco begged for an explanation.

"You see what we have here?" He held up the vellum sheet. "I don't know what it says, but it seems to be a continuation from a prior page. You can tell from how the script flows. And did you notice this?"

Varro's finger slid down the vellum to the last line and the last character. This was not a Punic letter, but a symbol.

It was a snake, just like the one Paullus and his accomplices carried. It seemed to be an ink impression rather than drawn.

"By the gods," Falco said, grabbing the vellum away. "He's working with the same people Paullus was. They used their amulets to mark the sheet."

Varro retrieved the vellum again, then folded it in four before stuffing it into his belt. "He will soon realize the sheet is missing, probably dropped while he was wrecking the apartment. I expect he will return tonight. This is too important to leave behind. When he realizes it's not upstairs, he'll come down here. And we will be waiting for him."

Curio mimed grabbing an unseen figure. "And then we'll know what he's up to. It can't be anything good if he's writing in Punic. But why do we have to ambush him in this room?"

"Because he'll be wary of entering his own room, and he'll hear us inside. This entire building is hardly better than a cloth tent. But he won't think anything of sound coming from this apartment. Though he will be ready to kill when he arrives. Even so, I believe we can overtake him."

Curio smirked at Falco. "See? It's good that he suspects everything. You didn't think of that."

Falco sniffed, then glanced out the door into the hall. "I don't bother with thinking when he's around. It's a waste of time."

"Let's complete our ruse," Varro said. "We'll go out the front door, speak to the three fine men who let us in, and let them see us walk away. We can't be too careful. They might work with Longus. We will circle back to the delivery entrance. But we need to be fast. The sun is already down."

Following Varro's plan, they left by the front door just as the three men were climbing the stairs to find their own rooms. They pressed against the wall to let them pass, and Varro commented Longus wasn't home but left some interesting things behind. They then circled back to find the delivery entrance, which was an equally flimsy door that did not withstand Falco's shoulder.

Now that night had fallen, they huddled in the second-floor apartment beneath Longus's and listened to the night. Dogs barked and shouts echoed in the distance. Far closer, he heard the coughing and low notes of laborers speaking in the rooms beside and below him. If someone rolled over on his mattress, Varro could hear it.

They waited with their daggers drawn and in silence. After the first hour, Varro feared Longus might not return. Then he heard feet padding down the hallway above.

In the darkness, he saw Falco and Curio look up. Feet shuffled across the floor and the boards creaked, releasing powdery dust that settled on Varro like a mist. He itched to rush up the stairs and corner Longus. But he knew better than to try. He would not underestimate his enemy. The best plan was the patient one.

As Varro controlled his patience, Longus above them lost his. He heard muttered curses and thumps. A light flared up, and Varro guessed his enemy was now on hands and knees searching the floor by lamplight. He even saw fingers testing the cracks.

Then the light went out, and he heard footsteps bouncing away.

"Be ready," Varro whispered and got to his feet, pressing against the wall opposite the door. Flanking the entrance on either side, Falco and Curio waited with drawn daggers.

Time seemed to stretch while he waited. For a moment, he wondered if Longus had decided he lost the vellum elsewhere. Then he saw the shadow at the door. It was a deeper black against the darkness of the hallway. He heard the door rattle as Longus tested it. Varro kept it unbarred to encourage his enemy inside. Such was Longus's desperation that he swept the door open, covering Curio behind it.

It was the same muscular silhouette that had threatened to bash Varro's skull with iron tongs. He crouched low, and metal glinted in his right hand.

He lingered in the doorframe, searching the darkness and poised to strike. But Falco acted first. He bounded out of the corner behind Longus and grabbed his weapon arm.

Varro seized him by his other arm and hauled him forward while Curio slammed the door shut.

The room was utterly dark, and Varro only knew that all of them fell into a pile on the floor. He maintained position above Longus. Elbows and knees banged into bodies as the four writhed on the floor. They struggled in silence, no one emitting more than a grunt or groan. Kicks and weak punches landed on Varro's ribs. He supposed some of them were from Falco and Curio. For his part, he knew he had Longus's head in his hands. His thumb sought an eye socket, pressing into yielding flesh.

Now Longus screamed and ceased struggling.

"It's over, Longus. Release your weapon, and you can keep your eye."

Varro hissed the words into Longus's ear. He heard a metallic thud on the floorboards and Falco confirmed he now held the weapon.

"You came back for the letter," Varro said, still pressing atop his enemy. "We have it now, and you have a lot to explain. I'm certain it will prove interesting reading. I'm going to stand you up. Don't do anything foolish or I'll give you a match for that broken tooth."

In the crowded space, getting Longus to his feet was as much a struggle as it was to pin him. In the darkness, Varro could not see more than outlines. Once Curio opened the door again, the faint light did little to help. Longus did not struggle in Varro's captivity and kept strict silence.

Falco exited the room first, with Varro leading his captive next and Curio to block the rear. If anyone else had heard their struggle, they kept their apartment doors shut. A narrow window at the end of the hall was the only source of light. Varro could now make out a faint smile on Longus's face.

He also realized blood smeared his tunic. Initially confused, he realized the struggle must have reopened Longus's wound.

Their feet shuffled over the threadbare carpet as they headed for the stairs. Falco ducked to enter the black opening. Varro shifted to move Longus ahead of him.

In the next instant, he slammed against the hallway wall, clutching his throat and barely able to breathe. The strike had been so fast that all he knew was the pain of it.

"Sorry, boys. I've got another appointment."

Longus then ran for the stairs. Varro snatched at him but was out of reach.

"Falco, look out!"

But Varro's warning made no difference. Longus did not head downstairs, but leaped onto the stairs to the third floor. The planks creaked as he dashed up and out of sight.

Scrambling to his feet, Varro and Curio both raced up the stairs in pursuit.

They spilled out into the third-floor hallway, expecting to see Longus entering his room. Instead, they caught him kicking in an apartment door to his left. He glanced back at them before dashing inside.

Varro followed him through, nearly tripping on the two occupants who cowered in shock. Directly across, Longus had hopped into a wide window, the ones that faced the front of the dormitory. He leaned out, holding the sill for support.

"You won't survive the drop." Varro stopped short, Curio pushing him from behind.

Longus glanced out the window, then turned back with a smile.

"You won't survive Rome."

He then tumbled backward out the window, leaving only yellow moonlight behind.

9

Varro stood outside the dormitory with Falco and Curio flanking him. The red and white striped awning had collapsed under the force of Longus's fall. Its colors turned gray in the moonlight. The wood pillars all collapsed toward the center, folding over the canvas awning. He toed it, lifting it up as if he might find Longus hiding beneath it.

He craned his neck up to the third-floor window. Everything had been built to be more appealing to the front. The back apartments all had tiny windows, a detail he did not notice before. Now sleepy residents opened their shutters and looked down at them.

Falco weighed the plain dagger in his hand. He bounced it then spun it around to examine the pommel in the light of the moon.

"No special markings on this one. So this serpent society ain't copying us, at least."

Varro let out a long sigh and lowered his head. His neck was sore from staring up at the window where Longus had made his escape.

"We had him but for only a moment. He's as real a snake there is."

Curio also lifted the edge of the canvas, admiring the distance Longus had fallen.

"It's like he planned it."

While Varro could accept Longus was crafty, he did not believe tonight was a setup.

"We surprised him, or we wouldn't have caught him. My mistake was in not binding him. But we didn't have more than bedsheets to tie him with. I thought the three of us could contain him."

Falco cleared his throat. "It was too crowded in there. I couldn't get back to help you in time. No room to turn, and the little bastard knew it. He knew the awning would break his fall. And if it didn't, he probably had a way to kill himself. I don't think we'll get anything out of him unless he makes it to an interrogator alive."

Varro turned his back to the dormitory to face the empty and quiet street.

"We will not capture him tonight. But not all is lost since we captured this."

He patted his waist where the vellum was folded.

His palm echoed on plain skin.

With his hands turning icy cold, he plunged them beneath his belt and found nothing.

"It's gone. I must've lost it in the room during our struggle."

The three of them headed back into the dormitory and charged up the stairs. Along the way Varro studied the floor, finding only litter swept to the corners of the hallway. In the room itself, they found nothing. Falco had commandeered a lamp from across the hall, and its light confirmed what they all knew.

"Not only did he get away," Varro said through gritted teeth. "But he took the letter as well. We didn't capture him. He let us in close so he could retrieve the vellum. He knew I'd have it and I gave myself away in the dark by talking to him. So he plucked it out of my belt, and surrendered only long enough to enact his escape."

Falco groaned. "You're right about him being a real snake, and not just a sneaky bastard wearing an icon of one on a chain."

Defeated and exhausted, they returned to the halls. Though the building had come alive from all the action, every door remained sealed as they found Longus's old room. While Varro did not expect him to return, he still set a watch schedule. If not Longus, perhaps an accomplice or a curious laborer might turn up in the night.

They awakened the next morning to the sound of residents grumbling and shuffling around their rooms. In the morning light, Varro took stock of his bumps and bruises. Other than sore ribs, he had not endured any damage. However, he discovered a strip of vellum still hanging from his belt.

Curio yawned and stretched, and Falco complained of having a boring third watch. But Varro was now wide awake and jumping to his feet. The shred of vellum had moved along his belt and stuck at his back. In the darkness and their weariness, no one had seen it. Now, he spread it out into the light.

His heart thudded with anticipation, hoping an important detail remained visible.

But it was mostly blank vellum. The original page had not been filled with writing, and only the bottom half had torn away. He was left with a scrap of Punic writing, and the incriminating serpent symbol pressed in ink at the end.

Falco, rubbing the back of his neck, leaned over the blank vellum.

"You still have some of those squiggles on it. Maybe Senator Flamininus or someone on his staff can translate it."

Rolling up the thin vellum, Varro shook his head. "It's not even a complete sentence. I doubt it has anything useful to us."

Curio was still rubbing his eyes and sitting on the floor.

"But it has that serpent image. That's more than we knew yesterday."

Varro agreed, but still regretted his foolishness. He had thought he respected his enemy's intelligence, but instead had underestimated it. When he caught him next time, he would be certain to bind him by hands, neck, and feet.

They exited the dormitory along with the Pius olive oil warehouse laborers. No one met their eyes, and all of them stayed away. Falco joked about how fast news of their adventure got around. But to Varro, it meant they had announced themselves too clearly. Anyone working with Longus would now be alert.

Whatever their situation, they were glad to leave the Suburra district and climb the Palatine Hill to Flamininus's home. They did not stop for food or drink, and Varro had developed a fierce thirst. Falco said it best.

"We might not have the best news for the senator, but we're still going to get an excellent breakfast out of it. So it is not all bad."

Yet when they arrived at the senator's home, a dozen of Flamininus's patrons were standing guard around the red front door. They shouldered clubs, which were not strictly identified as prohibited weapons. One man in a white tunic stood out among the others in brown or faded green.

Varro closed the distance with the group, nodding to the man in white.

"Is there trouble, Manius?"

Thickset and curly-haired Manius narrowed his eyes as he looked at some unseen point higher on the hill.

"A senator has been murdered. Word came to Senator Flamininus this morning as we were about to escort him to the Senate. He asked us to guard his home while he conferred with his peers."

An icy trickle of fear ran down Varro's back. He looked at both of his friends, and their expressions mirrored his own suspicions.

Varro grabbed Manius by his tunic. "When did it happen? Was it this morning?"

Manius shook his broad head.

"We didn't get the details. I'm sure the senator will have news for us when he returns." Then his frown turned into a thin smile. "We must settle on the price of the horse. Those men were not happy with you, even after I explained the need. Anyway, I expect once the senator returns you will be off on a new adventure."

Varro and the rest mingled with the other clients, and none of them gleaned more information about the murder. So, they waited close to an hour before Flamininus and another group of his clients returned.

Overwhelmed with questions from his clients pressing on all

sides, Flamininus raised his hands and addressed the small group assembled before the red door of his home.

"As you must understand, I cannot provide you with details at this time. Someone murdered Senator Facilis in his home. The Senate has adjourned for the day while we investigate." Now his eyes scanned across Varro and the others. "I appreciate everyone standing guard over my home. However, currently, I do not believe I am in any danger. So I will ask you to go about your business as usual. Please meet me here tomorrow morning, for the business of the Senate must continue and I will require an escort."

The clients pressed him for more detail, several asking if they could remain on duty in case the senator was mistaken. But Flamininus firmly sent them away, except for Varro, Falco, and Curio. He instructed them to follow him inside.

As they traversed his modest front yard and headed toward his garden, servants trailed behind. Flamininus ordered wine and bread but otherwise said nothing until they were seated on stone benches around a marble table in the shade of his garden trees.

His soulful eyes were now filled with righteous fury.

"It was a terrible business. Poor Facilis was stabbed in the kidney and then had his throat cut ear to ear. His wife discovered him in the hall after his blood leaked beneath the door to her room. The poor woman is now mad with grief. And he has two young daughters who had to see their father face down in a pool of his blood."

Flamininus closed his eyes against the horror of what he described. Varro assumed Facilis was an old friend and his murder pained the senator. But then he seemed to shake away his grief when the wine and bread arrived.

It was hot black bread, soft and steaming in the late morning air. The servant delivered wine in silver cups, making breakfast feel more like a feast. The senator paused and allowed them to sate themselves before continuing.

"Facilis was still a junior senator. He didn't have time to make the kind of enemy that would do something like this. Unless, of course, he was involved in something criminal. But a murder in his own home is a message to all other senators. Perhaps that was the only purpose of his death."

Distracted by the sweet wine and delicious bread, Varro simply nodded. Instead, Curio spoke up.

"Sir, I don't think so. He must've been part of the same society Paullus belonged to. They're removing anyone who could reveal them."

Flamininus at last joined them in breakfast, tearing off a hunk of black bread. He chewed thoughtfully before making his reply.

"I suppose it is possible, but I don't think so. However, that group may be involved."

Varro finished his wine, then set it on the marble table with a silvery chime. "Sir, I should tell you about last night. Perhaps there might be some connection to the murder."

He explained all that had occurred and how Longus had slipped through their fingers. Flamininus listened carefully, nodding and asking clarifying questions until Varro had brought him up to date. When finished, he slid the torn vellum out of his belt and presented it to the senator. He took it in both hands, frowning at the foreign script.

"Had it been Greek, then I could tell you on the spot what it means. I'll have to get someone to translate this. But it is undoubtedly Punic, and that causes me great concern."

He rolled up the torn vellum, then massaged his temples in thought.

"But let us address one problem at a time. Senator Facilis was killed in the early morning. How the killer entered the home and escaped still needs to be determined. But it could well have been this Marcus Longus fellow. He would have had to race to the home, no doubt delayed by you three."

Varro straightened up on the bench. "Sir, I would like to see the murder scene before others move things about."

Flamininus shook his head. "I'm afraid his widow is too distraught, and of course, blood must be cleaned away. I don't think it's wise to disturb her today."

"Sir, it's unwise to waste time." Varro leaned forward to emphasize his words. "Every moment that passes some key piece of evidence will be lost. Every hour that passes gives the killer space to cover his tracks. As uncomfortable as it might be, someone needs to investigate immediately."

Flamininus's brows furrowed, and he paused as he considered. "Of course, you're correct. But why should it be the three of you?"

Varro looked at both Curio and Falco, who seemed equally interested in the answer. He hoped his disappointment did not show, for he believed the three of them were better than anyone else for the task.

"Sir, if it was Longus, I know how he got in and how he got out. I could tell someone what I know, and they could search for the same clues. But whoever that person is, isn't your person, sir."

With his frown turned to a sly smile, he gave Varro an appreciative nod.

"I will provide you with an official pass. But there is something you should know. Facilis was a protégé of Senator Flaccus. I expect he will be there to personally oversee the investigation. So, tread carefully. In the meantime, I will have this vellum translated. It may not offer much information but is worth checking."

They finished their breakfast and were soon back on the streets of the Palatine Hill and headed for Senator Facilis's home. Varro clutched a signed note on a clean vellum from Senator Flamininus. As they walked in the morning shade, Falco and Curio debated whether Flaccus would even know Varro had mangled his nephews.

"That's not the problem," Varro said. "If he wanted revenge for them, then he would've had it by now. Flamininus was warning us because Flaccus is Cato's mentor and friend."

Although Cato was still in Iberia, by now his frustrations must've reached the ears of his closest friends, particularly Flaccus. Varro hoped he would discover otherwise.

They threaded streets that were far less crowded on these lofty heights. The citizens here dressed in finery and wore jewels openly. This emphasized thoughts of Cato in Varro's mind since it was just the sort of gross display of wealth he despised. Even if he was still in Iberia as proconsul, he had the reach to trouble them if he chose.

For a junior senator, Facilis lived in a home that rivaled the richest senators. High walls surrounded an estate filled with dark green cypress trees. A line of pigeons stood guard atop the ridge line of his tiled roof. More practically, a handful of his clients stood guard around the home.

It took a bit of wrangling with men unsuited for guard duty. They were too young to have served in the legion or else had forgotten their discipline. Eventually, they allowed passage, citing the official letter from Flamininus.

Sunlight filled the atrium, sparkling on the reflecting pool where a young girl stared listlessly at her reflection. A servant hovered behind her, hands folded tightly at her lap. She studied the girl so intently that she only spared a glance for Varro and the others. Not knowing where to go, Varro followed the sound of male voices on the other side of the house. It led to a short flight of stairs.

At the top, he found a group of five men in white or gray tunics. One man had a purple stripe on the hem of his. When Varro and the others mounted the stairs, the group fell silent and stared. The senator was no taller than Curio, but his bulging eyes radiated power and his bearing was full of strength too great for such a small body. A halo of white hair surrounded his head like a grass crown. He glared at Varro.

Without a doubt, he stood before Senator Flaccus, the most powerful man in Rome after Scipio.

"You're not the men I sent for. What business do you have here?"

The senator's eyes flicked to the folded velum sheet in Varro's grip.

"We have been sent on behalf of Senator Flamininus, sir." He presented the note, careful to show no fear or disrespect. Flaccus's bulging eyes bored into his own as he accepted the note. He held Varro's gaze a moment longer than was comfortable, then scanned the sheet.

"He thinks you can identify the murderer?" One heavy brow, nearly a match to Falco's, cocked as he returned the velum.

"I do not know his motives, sir, but I know his work. My friends and I would only need to do a quick review to confirm what we suspect."

The men surrounding Flaccus drew closer, less imposing but no less skeptical. Flaccus tilted his head, studying Varro as if to commend him or kill him on the spot.

"Since you're Flamininus's boys, I'll allow you a moment. What is your name?"

Varro did not flinch, expecting the question. He announced himself, and then introduced the others before all three stood to attention.

That gesture seemed to please Flaccus, who had once been a consul. In his experience, Varro understood these men never left their military careers behind. It helped to play to that memory when dealing with them.

A thin smile spread on Flaccus's creased face. The similarity to Cato was striking, and perhaps the shared countenance had grown from long association. Still, Varro remained at attention.

"Familiar names," he said. "Heroes of Iberia, or so I have heard. But also traitors and deserters before that. And newly rich, too. Such complex men to have at my service."

Wary of blundering into a trap, Varro held his silence until at last Flaccus relented.

"You may conduct your search, but Crassus will accompany you."

He indicated one of his entourage, a tall man with dark circles under bagged eyes. Lank hair clung to his narrow skull. If Varro didn't think Longus was the culprit, Crassus certainly appeared capable of filling the role.

"Thank you, sir," Varro said without delay. "Would someone be able to describe the position of the body?"

Flaccus seemed to have already dismissed him from his thoughts, and scowled. "Crassus will answer your questions. Do not take too long and do not disturb Senator Facilis's widow. Her room is locked and don't dare to knock on the door."

They followed Crassus deeper into the house, eventually stopping in a second-floor hallway that ran to the number of rooms. All the ornate doors were firmly closed, light seeping beneath them. He heard weeping to his left behind one of the doors.

The blood stains on the floor were fresh and obvious. A long carpet had been rolled up and set into a corner at the far end. Varro turned to Crassus and pointed to the spot on the floor.

"What was the posture of the body when discovered?"

Crassus had dull eyes that lacked any spark of intelligence. He shrugged and mimicked a man lying face down, with his arms stretched out as if to break a fall. Varro knew he was making it up. So he tried a different tactic.

"Which way was his head facing?"

Crassus seemed to consider the question, then stood in the approximate spot where Facilis had been discovered. "I think he was going to his wife's room. So his head pointed this way."

Varro turned in the opposite direction to find the door directly behind where Facilis had died. Curio stood before it, arms folded as he stared with intense interest. Falco stood beside him, a bemused smile on his face.

Entering the room between his two friends, Varro crouched to examine the floor. It was a bedroom, possibly for his daughter. The room smelled sweet, and clothing for a young woman was set on the bed.

He searched the floor, finding telltale drops of blood puddled by the entrance. He then looked at the bed. It was far enough against the opposite wall that the killer could've crouched in the doorway without disturbing the sleeper.

"It was Longus," Varro said, standing from his crouch. "He hid here, as you can see from the blood dripping in a tight pattern. He didn't go farther into the room since he was waiting for Facilis to show his back. If you stand here, you can see the door to his wife's room clearly. It would've been dark, and Facilis would not have expected him."

Falco gave an appreciative nod. "How did he get in and out?"

"Crassus, does anyone know how he gained entrance?"

He narrowed his eyes as if straining to think. "We don't know how he got in the house."

Varro again stood in the hallway and examined the possibilities. Longus had established himself as being quite acrobatic. He could've scaled any of the house walls using the vines or trees that grew close to it. He was more interested in where Longus had escaped. To determine this, he asked Crassus to help him replace the carpet.

They reset it so the bloodstains on the carpet matched those on the wooden floor. As they worked, he heard sobs from the wife's room turn to murmurs.

"He would've made a swift exit. He clearly did not realize he was bleeding as badly as he was. But when waiting for Facilis, he would've realized it. Without time to clean up his blood trail, the best he could do was to move fast and leave as little evidence as possible."

Varro examined the carpet and found thick drops that were not splatter from opening Facilis's throat. He followed the dark and thick drizzle down the hall to a door on the right. He opened it, revealing another empty room, one that from its unadorned appearance seemed for servants rather than Facilis's family.

He found two fat drops of blood on the bare floor, and both pointed to an open window. He discovered a thin, bloody handprint on the windowsill. While he couldn't be sure, it seemed to be the size of a man like Longus.

Leaning out the window, he confirmed what he suspected. It looked out on the garden, and heavy bushes grew directly beneath the room.

"If we go down there, we will find more of Longus's blood on the leaves. His cut had reopened in the struggle with us earlier in the night. I saw the blood on him after our fight."

The four of them threaded back through the house and into the garden, where Varro found fresh blood on smashed bushes. The others fanned out to see what else they could find. Curio located a puddle of blood by a tree that grew close to the wall. He called them over, and when they gathered, he offered his opinion.

"He is hurt worse than we thought. All this jumping out of windows has done him in."

Varro stared up at the twisting trunk. "Planting a tree here is a bad idea. Anyone who reaches the lower branches can climb in and out. That's how Longus entered and escaped. There's probably more blood around the exterior wall. But it won't lead anywhere before the trail is lost."

Falco patted the tree trunk as if testing its sturdiness. "He's agile for a big man, I'll give him that. But now he's bleeding bad."

"I agree." Varro stared into the dark leaves brightened with the morning sun behind them. "We won't be seeing him again for a while. He needs to heal before all else. I expect whoever he works for will shelter him. But there is a chance he is on his own, like we would be if given a similar assignment."

He looked at Crassus for a reaction, hoping he had not said too much. But he stared vacantly across the garden at two serving girls carrying baskets across the garden.

"So our next step is to find doctors who wouldn't ask questions for the right fee. There will be many, I expect. Rome is a big city. Still, I think we could start in the Suburra district."

Crassus at last announced their time was up. How he had tracked time while daydreaming, Varro did not know. But he marched them back to where Senator Flaccus had been. Fortunately, he had left on other business and his cronies were uninterested in what Varro had to say.

They hastened back to Senator Flamininus and were surprised when a young boy servant whisked them inside and led them to the garden. "The master said you have an important visitor."

Varro could not understand the urgency or the boy's discomfort. But the moment he entered the garden, fear like a gout of flame spread through his belly.

Siculus paced back and forth between the stone benches and the marble table. His head was bandaged.

He stopped at the sound of their approach and clasped his hands together.

"Master," he said in a trembling voice. "I didn't know where to find you. Thank the gods you are here. Something terrible has happened."

Varro stopped in mid-stride, wishing he could turn back and reenter to find the garden empty. But Siculus lowered his head.

"It's brigands, master. They've overrun the villa."

10

Even as Varro sat in the sunlit garden, he could not help but shiver at Siculus's recounting. Falco and Curio both listened in solemn silence as Siculus held back both rage and tears. Behind them, servants waited on their call. But none had a stomach for wine or food after hearing how Varro's villa had been sacked. The only blessing was they had not set it to the torch. Instead, they had moved in and fortified it themselves.

"I am glad that I lived long enough to bring you the news, master." Siculus knelt on the grass rather than sit. The bandage around his head was stained brown from dried blood. "Now that I have done so, you may end my miserable life."

Varro swallowed hard, trying to imagine what had happened in the days he had been away. Rage welled up in him, but nothing specific to Siculus. He was as much a victim as Varro.

"If you are to die," he said. "It will be during the fight to reclaim my home."

Siculus bent deeper on the grass, nearly touching his head to Varro's feet.

"I will gladly fight for you, master. But they have claimed your land for their own, and there are none to stand against them."

Falco cleared his throat. "And you've no news from my estate? If my men are still there, then we will stand against them."

Siculus shook his bandaged head. "I could not spare the time to learn more."

The four of them fell to silence again, the vague sounds of Rome drifting over the walls to invade the quiet. In stark contrast to their mood, birds sang in the trees nearby.

Varro's rage instead focused on the brigands and his sister. Now, she was a hostage, and Siculus had brought their demands for ransom. If Arria had not come to him, then he could have dealt with this problem as a military affair. He had the wealth to raise a mercenary force to oppose the brigands. But now, they wanted almost all that same money in ransom.

Falco stared at him as he thought.

"Of course, we're going to rescue them. We've done harder missions before. A gang of countryside brigands is nothing to us now."

"Harder yes, but not where my family is involved." Varro cupped his head in his hands, then scrubbed his face to refresh his thoughts. Siculus still knelt in the grass. "Sit up, please. Let's go over the details of how this happened."

Siculus hesitated to sit upright again. Varro did not doubt he was once an officer in the Macedonian army. For even now, in slavery and defeat, bandaged around his head, he still had an air of self-possession and confidence.

"It happened the night you left. It was as if they were watching for your departure. It was Lars who betrayed us. I didn't think anything of it at the time, but after firing Proculus I had a gap in my watch schedule. He was supposed to be on gate duty that night. Lars volunteered to take that shift, and I let him."

Siculus stopped and closed his eyes, seemingly pained at speaking aloud his mistake.

"He opened the gates to the brigands. Since they counted on Lars's betrayal, they didn't even carry torches to light their way. They only had to find the open gate. Lars killed the other guard on duty with him. From there, twenty brigands invaded. We were caught completely unaware."

He then described the carnage that followed. With the doors thrown open to their enemies, the guards fought or surrendered. In either case, they were killed on the spot. The slaves in the villa itself were allowed to join the brigands or flee. Later, the ones living outside near the farms were given the same offer. According to Siculus, half joined the brigands and the others fled.

"Only Fadia remained loyal, master. I think she is fond of your sister, though they only just met."

He was recognized as the leader and therefore captured alive. They forced him to hand over any silver or other valuables. At the same time, they dragged Arria and Lucia into the main yard.

"I could not accept defeat, master. I presented them with the small chest of denarii you left in my care. It distracted them long enough. That is when I ran to your sister and niece's aid. They had only a single man to guard them, believing them helpless girls. But your sister joined me in the fight."

This was a detail Varro had not yet heard. He raised his head from his palms and listened carefully as Siculus described the struggle.

"I wrestled with the brigand for his spear. Thanks to your good treatment, master, I am strong enough still to challenge a younger man. But it was your sister who guaranteed victory. She kicked him between the legs as we wrestled. He released the spear, and I turned it on him. Forgive me for saying this, but it felt good in my hands and felt better buried in the brigand's guts."

Falco grunted in assent. "No forgiveness needed there. You're killing the right Romans. If the scum was even once a citizen."

Siculus bowed lower. "I wish I could've done more. But I was one spear against many. The brigands had followed me out of the house, and in those brief moments had closed the distance. I grabbed the young girl by her arm and tried to do the same for your sister."

He shook his head and paused as he seemed to relive the moment behind his damp eyes.

"They had left the gate open, and it was still dark. Your niece moves with great speed. But your sister did not take my hand, and the gate closed behind me. I led Lucia to safety among a stand of cypress trees. Then I returned to learn what I could. There were already guards on the wall, and they had lit torches. I stepped up as close as I dared, praying they hadn't armed themselves with bows. They spotted me and I warned them you would return. That is when they demanded ransom for your sister."

Varro now sat up straighter, his eyes wide in surprise.

"Lucia escaped with you? Is she here?" Varro turned around, and only the servants waiting against the walls stirred in response.

"I did not know where to go, master. You have mentioned Senator Flamininus. But I did not know where to find such a great man. However, Lucia knew where her grandmother lived. I took her there, and that is where she is now. Her grandmother then told me how to find this place. I came as fast as I could."

"Her grandmother," Varro said in a whisper. His eyes narrowed as he tried to imagine his mother and her reaction. He then remembered what Arria had said about their mother's health.

"Did--her grandmother--appear ill?"

"She lived in a fine home with a small garden. I was met by a servant who did not want us to enter until Lucia's grandmother appeared. She did not seem ill to me, though I did not linger. Lucia was happy to see her grandmother and so I felt confident leaving her there."

All the while, Siculus had carefully avoided naming her as Varro's mother. He was unsure how his slave had learned of his strained relationship with her but appreciated his discretion. Varro felt everyone's eyes on him. He also felt his mother's eyes on him. Somewhere in the city she now sat with Lucia asking questions about her long-lost son. She would look toward the Palatine Hill, and maybe wonder if she should seek him out.

He shook his head to clear his thoughts.

"You've done well, Siculus. I'll owe you much after this. There are still open questions. How did Lars cooperate with the brigands? You hired him in this city, not from the countryside. Yet it seems he was one of them from the start. Also, what has happened to Falco's and Curio's estates? It seems unlikely that both were left alone. But then who knows how many brigands there are?"

Curio at last sat back and let out a long sigh. "We don't have as much to worry about. First, we need to free your sister and push the bandits out of your home."

"Where are the men that Senator Flamininus promised me?" Varro looked about as if expecting to find a century of legionaries at his back. "I will need four times however many he picked for the job."

Falco groaned. "More like ten times. Don't attack a fortified wall without twice the strength in your favor."

"We don't have the luxury of military logistics," Varro said. "This is a private battle."

The reality silenced all of them. Varro knew Falco was correct, and that digging out twenty men from his estate would require at least forty more to do the job. However, that was only true if he planned a direct assault.

"I know the weaknesses of my villa. Lars may know as well, but I am betting he is spending his days drunk and happy. If they didn't have my sister, I would wait until the supplies ran out. As it stands, I will have to free her and then deal with the brigands."

"They're a bold lot," Falco said. "All the years we've lived here, and I've never heard of anything like it. I guess our families guarded their lands a lot better than we did."

The tension began to flow out of Varro as he focused on his next steps. He was not good at sitting idly by and waiting for others to act. The brigands had ceded initiative to him, and they would never get it back. He began to sketch out his ideas, and even Siculus now joined them around the marble table.

They did not even realize Senator Flamininus returned with his adjutant and secretaries fluttering behind him.

Once they realized his presence, they stood at attention. Varro introduced his slave, and the senator gave a shallow nod before asking his servant to lead Siculus away to rest elsewhere while his master was busy. Then he asked for details of their investigation.

It seemed like events from another time to Varro, but it had only been hours ago. Given his new problems, he rushed through his explanation of their discoveries. But he did confirm for the senator his belief that Longus committed the murder.

The senator listened, sitting between them and keeping his adjutant standing behind. He only interrupted Varro twice with clarifying questions. When the summary of the morning's investigations ended, he produced the scrap of vellum with Punic writing.

"I believe you are correct that Longus murdered Facilis. But I'm afraid he has only just begun. This scrap confirms it for me. I had someone translate it while you were at the crime scene. What it says is alarming. Though only a fragment of a sentence, it completes the thought that started with Facilis's murder."

He spread the vellum on the marble table, holding it down with his tapered fingers. Varro noted how clean and trimmed his nails were in comparison to his own. The senator never got his hands dirty. Now, he intoned the words scratched out on the vellum.

"Until all five are dead."

Even the singing birds in the trees above them fell silent. Varro stared at the angular writing. The ink had bled into the vellum, blurring the neat and uniform lettering. The pressed image of the serpent amulet was less clear, but the coiled snake seemed to stare out at him.

Falco leaned over the vellum as if verifying the accuracy of the translation. "Do you know who the five are?"

Flamininus glared in answer. "Of course not. And I've not shared this with anyone else yet. Longus, if that is his real name, has a list of targets. Your highest priority right now is finding him and stopping whatever plan he has in motion."

Varro looked between the others, hesitant to bring up his problems. Instead, he focused on the senator's concerns.

"Of course, we will do everything possible to bring him down. But you see the seal at the end of this sentence. Stopping Longus might mean nothing when he has the backing of this organization."

"For all you know, Longus could be the entire organization. You do not need to think so deeply about why I have given you orders. You only need to carry them out perfectly."

It had been many years since Varro had seen Flamininus so agitated. His face had reddened, and his eyes flashed with all his old consular authority. He was on the verge of baring his teeth.

"Of course, sir." Varro leaned back, fighting a reflex to look to the others for their reactions. He held Flamininus's gaze to the edge of impropriety. Then he lowered his gaze and spoke softly. "Excuse my disrespect, sir. My slave has brought me dire news."

The senator also softened his stance and indicated he should explain. Varro then laid out all he had been told. When it was done, he spoke more forcefully.

"I must act now to save my sister. There is no telling how long they will hold her before they lose patience."

He searched Flamininus's face for a reaction, and his heart sank when the senator's soulful eyes were not touched with any emotion.

The silence grew uncomfortable enough that Falco cleared his throat and rubbed the back of his neck. "Sir, we will make it swift work. They're just countryside brigands. They'll be no trouble for us. We won't lose any progress with Longus."

"I don't believe you will," Flamininus said evenly. He drew a breath and gave Varro an apologetic smile. "I sympathize with your troubles. But you can pay the ransom and I will send men along to guarantee the exchange is made. However, I need you to focus on Longus. You know what he looks like, something no one else knows. Now, while he is injured, is the best chance to capture him. We cannot allow the moment to slip by us."

Varro glanced once more at Flamininus's trimmed and clean fingers. He wondered what he meant by referring to "us."

"Sir, if it was just a matter of my home, then I would not even trouble you with this news. But she is my sister, and I have promised to protect her. Now, within days of making that promise, she is in grave danger."

Flamininus again gave a thin smile. "As are five senators of Rome.

We need to arrest Longus as soon as possible. Who are the names on his list? What damage could he do if allowed to carry out his plan?"

"Sir, you simply need to alert your peers to the danger they face. Each man must protect himself, even a senator."

He had spoken from anger, though he had kept his tone respectful. Still, Flamininus seemed to grow larger, and his face darkened.

"Shall we announce all we know to the Senate? Can you be certain some of my peers are not behind this plot? We cannot simply reveal everything and expect our enemies will not adjust. Indeed, they are probably expecting us to do just that. Varro, of all people, you should know not to do what the enemy expects you to."

"He would not expect me to leave Rome and return to my villa."

His words were like drawing a sword against Flamininus. He sat up from the bench, so suddenly his adjutant stumbled backward. His fists balled tight.

"Do not spar with me." He spoke through gritted teeth, his face a mask of rage. "I see that I have been too indulgent with you. You are forgetting your station and mistaking my good nature for equality. Last we met, you addressed me as if we were on even terms, and I let it go because of our history. Next, you dare to show up with that tattoo on your arm, then tell me it's a simple design. Now, you put your personal problems before your duty to Rome and then speak back to your commander."

As he spoke, he thrust his finger at Varro as his words battered him back on his bench.

"I am giving you a direct order, Varro, and it shall not be disobeyed without consequences. You will find Longus and bring him to me alive for interrogation. This is your immediate and urgent duty. If you defy me, I will treat it as the gravest form of insubordination. Do I need to remind you of the social and physical punishment that entails? Rome needs you. So, you will do your duty as you always have. Likewise, you'll remember who your commander and benefactor is and address me with utmost respect. Are you clear on this?"

The lines on Flamininus's face twitched and filled with shadow.

He searched between Varro and the others as if daring any of them to so much as blink. The adjutant behind him lowered his eyes and looked aside. Varro felt like doing the same but knew better.

"Yes, sir." His voice was like that of a humiliated child. He hated the sound of it but had no choice.

Flamininus gave a curt nod. "Excellent. Now, let's discuss the plan of action. You will need a base of operations. I know a home in the center of the city with easy access to anywhere you need to go. As your slave his here, he can care for your daily needs. Don't fret about meals and such. Just focus on apprehending Longus."

His rage ebbed and his flush drained from his cheeks. He paused before dressing Varro.

"I understand your conflicted loyalties. But it is more than just Facilis's murder. Five senators are targeted by this mysterious group. Minucius was one. I could also be among those names. And if that's not enough, we have the Boii to the north stirring trouble. What would happen if the Senate were cast into turmoil while these northern barbarians are pressing the city? Would they achieve what Hannibal could not? It is not an outlandish question."

Varro let out a sigh. "No, it is not, sir. I know my duty, and I will not fail you in it. Longus will not escape me again."

Tilting his head back in satisfaction, Flamininus seemed at ease again.

"Now, you can arrange the ransom with my adjutant. I will see that it is safely delivered and your sister is returned to my home. She will be an honored guest, and the brigands will be dealt with in time. How much do they demand?"

"Fifty talents of silver, sir."

Flamininus stepped back as if punched in the gut. "That is outrageous. Clearly, they don't intend for you to pay it."

"It is what they demanded, and nearly all I have left after investing in my villa. I can only assume that investment is destroyed now. I will be utterly without wealth after paying that ransom. Since I will be focused here, the brigands will escape with it. But at least my sister will be safe. Of course, assuming they have not killed her already. I suppose I won't know until after I pay the ransom."

He had started with enough contrition to keep Flamininus sympathetic. But his frustrations crept into his voice by the end, leading Flamininus to once again narrow his eyes at Varro.

"You will not pay them fifty talents. That is a ransom for foreign princes. You can negotiate with them. Greed will win out in the end, as it always does with these types. They have simply asked for all you own, but don't expect it. Send them twenty pounds of silver, one pound for each. It's more than those scrubby bastards will ever own. You will make that up in your next harvest."

Varro thought to remind Flamininus that the brigands likely destroyed his harvest out of spite. Nor was twenty pounds of silver a trivial amount for him. But he had driven the senator to his limits already and simply nodded in agreement.

Flamininus composed himself and turned to his adjutant with orders to relocate Varro and the others to this new base of operations. Once he had established those details, he was smiling again.

"Don't waste any time in your search for Longus. Rome is a big city, but there are many eyes in a big city. Someone will have seen something, and I trust you will discover who did. Now, I have other business still pressing me. Between the Ligurians and the Boii, we will have no peace and no end to my work."

Varro stood as did his friends and saluted before Flamininus turned away. His adjutant asked them to wait for him to return. For the moment, it was only the three of them and chirping birds in the garden standing around the empty marble table.

Falco let out his breath. "I thought he was going to slice that tattoo off your arm right now. He's in a foul mood."

Varro nodded, staring after the senator as he vanished into his home. "He's afraid for his life. Until he knows who's on that list, he assumes his name is at the top."

"Well, it probably is," Falco said.

Curio stepped in front of Varro, his youthful face dark with concern.

"What are you going to do about your sister? What if the silver you send is not enough? They might do something terrible."

"I know," Varro said quietly. "That is why I'm going to save her."

11

Their new base was a small home in the city's heart. It was at the top of a steep hill, and three floors high. Falco wryly noted that there were no striped awnings beneath the narrow windows. They claimed the top floor for their sleeping quarters, the second floor remained empty, and the bottom floor was given to the kitchen and Siculus.

Varro stared out the thin slits of the window, watching as people milled about the streets in the golden light of early evening. All around the building, he heard the mumbling city vibrating through the walls. A pigeon cooed on the roof above him, its talons scratching on the wood.

On the top floor, they were treated to a small round table and two stools where Falco and Curio sat. Red clay lamps lit the room along with the narrow shaft of light from the thin window.

Falco slapped his palm on it to draw everyone's attention.

"All right, Siculus is off buying vegetables or meat, hopefully both. It's just the three of us. So let's straighten out this business. Varro, I've known you my whole life, so you don't even need to say what you're going to say next. It's all bullshit, anyway. You cannot disobey the senator. He is not joking. If you go after the brigands, you may as well never come back."

"He's right," Curio said. "You'll be flogged to death, even if you did everything else he asked."

Varro chuckled, watching a man wrestle with his mule on the street below. It decided to stop in the middle of traffic, drawing curses and threats from all sides.

"You're both right, of course. He is forcing me to decide where I stand." He turned from the window, the room appearing darker for the shift in light. "Even a mere week ago, I would not hesitate. But then Arria returned and reminded me I have a family. She's even caused me to remember my mother. She has no one else to protect her. Her husband gave his life in Iberia. I am her oldest male relative and responsible for her."

Curio lowered his gaze, but Falco closed his eyes and shook his head.

"That's all great. But you won't be much help to her or your mother, or anyone else for that matter, if you're dead. That will be the price of your disobedience. That's what we would do to our soldiers if they were so grossly insubordinate. We can't expect anything less from our commanding officer."

Curio thumped the table. "But are we even in the legion?"

Varro shrugged. "It's an idle debate. We are Flamininus's men, and he runs things like he is still consul."

"Then it's decided," Falco said, sitting up straighter on his stool. "Varro will keep searching for Longus."

"I am going to rescue my sister and those servants who remained loyal to me. I will not abandon her now." He looked out the window again, and the mule had finally surrendered to its driver. But the crowd around his cart blocked the way ahead.

"You're going to do what the consul commanded you to do," Falco said with patient finality. "And I'm going to do what he didn't command me to do."

Varro spun around from the window and stared at Falco. He sat leaning on the table with one arm, and the other resting on his knee. He gave a crooked smile.

Curio looked on in confusion. "I don't know what you mean. Wasn't he commanding all of us?"

Falco shook his head. "He was furious at Varro and gave him a direct order to pursue Longus. He wasn't looking at us."

Varro held up both hands to slow down his friend's runaway reasoning.

"You'll anger him just as badly as if I had disobeyed. You think you're poking holes in his orders, but you're just poking your finger into a snake's den."

"Don't be so dire." Falco flipped his wrist at Varro's concern. "I'll be in and out with your sister before the brigands know what is happening. I'll bring her here, and Flamininus needn't be any wiser. As long as you and Curio continue searching for Longus, he will be satisfied. Besides, everyone knows I'm only around for muscle. If he could spare anyone of us from this duty, it would be me."

Varro shook his head. "I cannot let you take this risk for me. She's my sister, and my responsibility."

"How are either of you going to do this alone?" Curio asked. "Is Varro's sister skilled enough to slip out unseen with you?"

"We'll figure that out when the time comes." Both Falco and Varro gave the same answer. They looked at each other in surprise, then everyone burst into laughter.

At last, Falco stood up and put his heavy hand on Varro's shoulder.

"You catch Longus and let me figure out what to do with your sister. Anyway, someone needs to see the situation at the villa before deciding what to do next. I might need to go back to my home and gather reinforcements. I just regret leaving all our gear at your place. A sword would be nice, but a pugio will do."

Varro looked into his friend's dark eyes and knew he was right.

"I will send Siculus with you. He knows the villa well enough to guide you to its weak spots. I doubt the bandits have taken the time to discover them. Don't do anything stupid and come back if there is no way in. I'll be sending a ransom in any case. It might make a good distraction for you."

Falco straightened his shoulders and beamed with confidence.

"Delay sending the ransom. Your sister will be safely back in Rome before you know it."

∼

∼

FALCO WAS grateful for the rain. While it was not pouring, travelers in and out of Rome all wore hooded and oiled cloaks. He and Siculus could pass out of the city unmarked by any of Flamininus's men, joining the flow of merchants and wanderers spreading into the network of roads connected to the city. They traveled in groups of ten to twenty for mutual protection. Falco and Siculus trailed a group of a dozen travelers in a cart headed along the same road.

The rain pattered over his hood, and the cold water ran into his face. He didn't know Siculus well, but since Varro respected him, then that was good enough. Besides, he had shown great loyalty in rescuing Lucia and finding Varro. He was a good man for a Macedonian.

The cart ahead bobbed along the muddy road, which would soon become a track. Falco had driven it often enough in his youth, always in the company of his father. The sounds of clacking wood planks from the cart bed and the familiar road he traveled took his mind back to simpler times. He remembered his father, the old drunk. Much like Varro, he preferred to forget his family. His father had lost their farm to mismanagement, and Varro's father had kept it going on his behalf. Now Falco had his own villa and swore to run it better than his father had.

"Sir, Master Varro said you would have a plan."

Falco's thoughts snapped back from the hazy past to the gray of today. The cart had drawn ahead, its riders huddled under their cloaks. Siculus's voice was weak against the rain slashing across the muddy road. Gritty rainwater sloshed through Falco's sandals as he increased his step to keep time with the cart.

"Usually, it's your master who does all the fancy planning for these sorts of things. But there is one thing I've learned after watching him all these years."

He grinned at Siculus, who hid his face beneath his tightly drawn hood. He pulled it back to give a quizzical look.

"I've learned that plans don't mean shit. I can't think of one time they ever went as we expected. It's been true a hundred times before and will be true today."

Siculus seemed a thoughtful man, and he did not answer immediately but continued to splash through mud puddles as they both chased the cart ahead. At length, he spoke.

"But there must be a plan, sir. Even if you accept it will be abandoned, you must have an end in mind. Master Varro's sister is depending on you."

Falco frowned at the heavy-bearded Macedonian.

"Is that a nice way to say I don't know what I'm doing?"

Siculus laughed, an unexpected response. Falco was used to slaves who cowered at the first hint of dissatisfying their betters. But this one carried himself with dignity and confidence. While admirable, it tested the limits of social acceptability. He understood now how Flamininus felt the day before.

"Sir, I am ready to give my life to correct my mistakes. But I'm not ready to throw it away, if you understand what I mean."

"Of course I understand. It's what I tell Varro all the time. And this isn't your mistake. You and Varro were deceived from the start, apparently set up. There was no way around that. But what we need to focus on now is getting Arria out alive. I wouldn't mention this in front of Varro, but I don't believe any amount of ransom will make a difference. I think they're going to kill Arria after..."

He found himself unable to voice the fate he feared for Varro's sister.

He remembered her as a young girl, being all hair and little else. She competed with Varro for being the biggest whiner he ever knew.

She never figured into his thoughts as a youth. By the time he was old enough to be interested in girls, Arria was still not someone he would have looked at twice.

But she changed. He did not want to admit it, even if the others had guessed it. She was a beautiful woman, and he felt an attraction he would never have expected. In his estimation, being Varro's sister was a benefit. He knew she came from an excellent family, never mind what Varro might think of his parents. Certainly, his father had been involved with shady business associates. Yet there was no reason to lump Arria into the same group. Varro was the bravest and noblest person he ever met. Shouldn't it also be true of his sister? They shared the same upbringing, after all.

"I understand what you mean, sir." Siculus broke into his thoughts, returning him once more to the muddy track they followed into the countryside. "She is probably the finest woman those scum will ever encounter."

"Yeah, let's hope she's just been their honored guest for a few days." Falco swiped the rain off his face and tried not to imagine Arria's fate.

They trudged behind the cart until arriving at the fork that skirted the farmland ahead. Their leader was thoughtful enough to pause and ask if Falco and Siculus would be fine for the rest of their journey. They exchanged pleasantries, shared wine and gossip beneath nearby trees, then parted ways. He stood at the fork and waited for the cart to vanish into the gray rain before turning toward Varro's estate.

Through the rain, Varro's estate appeared at peace. It rose out of golden fields of barley on the verge of harvest. The rain sapped everything of brilliance, but a streamer of white smoke from a hearth made it seem homely and welcoming.

"If I didn't know better, I'd think Varro was home and getting a meal ready for me."

Falco crouched in the barley fields abutting the villa. As far as he could tell, the brigands had not ruined the harvest, nor had they damaged the buildings. He could not see much else through the rain, yet he feared sharper eyes than his own might spot him. So, he and Siculus crossed the distance in a crouch, following the paths slaves took to work the fields.

He halted when details of the cream-colored stucco walls came into focus. He still did not observe anyone on the wall. Yet at this distance, he heard an errant shout of men calling to each other across the yard. He and Siculus now huddled on the soft earth, their eyes skimming above the tops of the barley.

"At least someone is home," Falco whispered. "I don't know what I thought we'd find, but I expected something more terrible."

Siculus shrugged. "I do not know what the brigands intended, sir. They asked for a ridiculous ransom, and perhaps they believe they will get it."

Falco examined the walls and the two entrances to the villa. Normally, men stood on small platforms by either gate on watch. But either the rain or laziness kept the brigands inside. The hearth fire and the sounds of voices over the rain meant they were still occupying the home. Therefore, Arria was still their prisoner. Otherwise, Falco guessed they would loot the villa and then escape after burning it behind them. That was the way of bandits.

"I know the layout of this villa. It's exactly as my own. But what is the weak spot Varro mentioned? Can I use it to get in and then escape with Arria?"

Crawling closer, as if to get a better look, Siculus pointed to the corner of the west wall.

"There is a crack there from the earthquake earlier this year. The men I hired to repair it knew I was a slave and did shoddy work thinking they could cheat me. I discovered it too late, but it is just a poor stucco job over a wider hole in the stone. You could break it open and use it as footing to scale the wall."

"Something about standing up in front of twenty armed brigands doesn't appeal to me. And I don't have rope, either. Remember, I've got to sneak Arria out. Could I widen the gap around the base?"

Siculus raised himself higher and considered. The rain continued to speckle over their cloaks, the gentle thumping filling the silence.

"The rain should have softened the earth around the base. After the sun sets, we could dig a hole wide enough for your shoulders, sir."

"A simple plan, but the simpler ones are, the more likely it is to succeed. I hope Varro's sister doesn't mind getting muddy. I will get inside, find Arria, and meet you outside the walls. It'll be like a stroll around the garden."

Siculus sat back behind the waving barley, his heavy beard now flattened with rainwater. He gave a broad smile. "You laugh at danger, sir. That is very admirable."

"I think the word is stupid. It takes a certain kind of stupidity to succeed as a centurion. The sensible ones are all standing in the rear ranks and not dying. Anyway, I will need you on the outside to watch for threats."

"I thought I would accompany you, sir. It will be dangerous inside, and I am a competent warrior, sir."

"Weapons beat competence anytime." Falco glanced at Siculus's belt. "I see you are unharmed. I know what Arria looks like. Everyone else is an enemy. Just tell me, does Varro make his bedroom upstairs?"

"No one sleeps upstairs, sir. But I can grab a weapon from inside. I want revenge, as well."

Falco appreciated the eagerness, but he could not work with anyone other than Varro and Curio. He feared bringing in an unknown element, even if Varro trusted his slave.

"Revenge is for another day, when we can come back with an army. Even if Varro doesn't use the upstairs, that must be where Arria is held." Falco now stuck his hand beneath his tunic and felt for the wooden whistle hung about his neck. He drew it out and handed it to Siculus. "You keep a watch on things outside the building. If the brigands are alerted, blow on that whistle as hard as you can, then escape back here. If you can't, then head to Rome and tell Varro I need help."

Siculus examined the plain whistle, even testing it against his lips but not blowing into it.

"Why do you carry this?"

"Well, I use it when commanding my century. I haven't had to do that in a while, but I find it comforting. It brings me good luck.

Anyway, it will be our signal for trouble. I'm counting on you to watch my back."

Siculus fitted the cord about his neck and adjusted the whistle over his cloak. Then he examined Falco.

"Sir, you are quite tall and strong. You will stand out no matter where you try to hide."

Falco patted him on the back with a smile. "In Numidia they called us the ghosts, and not because we walked around moaning. I've had a lot of practice hiding myself over the years. A bunch of mountain brigands will be no challenge. Getting Arria to follow along will be the hardest thing I have to do. But once we're outside, they'll never catch us."

They hid in the fields until the sun went down and the rain petered out. Falco pulled his cloak tight overhead and leaned over to doze. It was a light sleep, but refreshing enough that when Siculus shook him he was prepared.

Under the cover of darkness, both men slid out of the barley field and toward the villa wall. Either out of supreme confidence or foolishness, the brigands did not light the walls. Falco followed Siculus as he tapped along the western wall and searched for the hollow space. When his knuckles rapped against emptiness, he used the stone to chip away the fresh stucco. It revealed a crack at the base as wide as Falco's head.

They excavated beneath the wall with flat stones they had dug up earlier from the edges of the field. The muddy earth was easy to clear away, and soon Falco had exploited the gap to create a hole wide and deep enough to fit him. He was now glad he did not have his armor and shield as he originally hoped for.

He slipped on his belly in the cold mud and fit beneath the wall. Sharp broken stone scraped across his back, but he popped up inside the villa yard. He slithered against the wall, now glistening with mud that only served as camouflage. At least outside the villa. He helped Siculus through, and the two of them sat motionless while searching around for enemies. When neither spotted danger, Falco leaned close to whisper.

"Don't leave this spot. Use the whistle if needed. Give two quick blows if trouble is headed toward me and one long blow if our escape route has been discovered. In either case, I am ordering you to get back to Varro. Someone must tell him the situation here."

Siculus bobbed his head, then held up the whistle in the wan light of the evening.

Falco put his hand over the sheathed pugio at his hip, then bent at the waist as he crossed the yard toward the house.

He had two points of entry, either through the garden and kitchens or the front door and the atrium. He could not see the front door, but a dull orange light flickered around the gaps in the garden door. As the layout was his own, he knew the stairs were at the center, just behind the cubiculum where Varro conducted business. No matter which entrance he used, the stairs remained the key challenge. He was on the wrong side of the house to observe any light from the bedroom on the second floor. He regretted prioritizing rest over examining the villa. Had Varro been in charge, he would not have made that mistake.

Now he sloshed through the rain-covered grass, which had been beaten to muddy patches by the tread of many feet. In the garden, he saw fresh lumps of earth that had worn down. They were fresh graves, and likely held the remains of Varro's loyal guards. The one called Lars would still be among these brigands, and if any of them should be killed night, Falco hoped it would be him. He detested traitors, particularly those who put the lives of his friends in danger.

Finding himself pressed against the house wall by the garden door, he had unconsciously selected it as his entry point. At least, it would be a direct escape route. He searched the darkness for Siculus and only found him crouched by the wall because he knew where to look.

He listened at the door, but heard only the faintest mumbling from deep within. For twenty brigands, they were as quiet as old maids. He wondered if the place was so quiet even when Varro lived here. He knew his own home was not. Nevertheless, danger lurked inside and he kept his palm clamped on his pugio as he pushed open the door.

Someone had left a clay lamp lit on a table by a basin. The bronze basin shimmered with water. He noted it rippled, warning him of motion nearby. He realized footsteps came from behind the opposite wall.

Rather than risk a fight so early, he ducked back out the door and closed it as the footsteps drew near. His heart thudded against his chest as he listened at the door. He heard feet scraping across the wood floor, and then the door shook in its frame.

Falco swept back just in time with the door opening. He pressed against the wall, his pugio now drawn and clasped against his thigh. The cold bronze edge prickled his skin as he waited for the man inside to act.

Whoever he was, he had only opened the door for fresh air. Falco heard him rest against the frame and draw a breath of cool night air. If the brigand stood there, Falco was pinned in place. He searched around and confirmed the yard was empty still.

Sweeping into the doorway, he confronted a man of roughly his own size leaning against the frame, a clay mug in one of his hands. He had no time to study details, glimpsing only terror-widened eyes as he yanked the man out of the door and onto his blade.

The mug tumbled out of the brigand's hand and bounced off Falco's foot. Warm wine spread between his toes as he dragged his victim out of the doorway. The pugio had sunk to the hilt into the struggling man's stomach. Blood drizzled on the ground as Falco dragged him out of sight into the yard. He now clamped a hand over the brigand's mouth as he struggled. He had to twist the blade, then drive it sideways in a sickening cut before he went still.

Now, with the corpse at his feet, the urgency of his mission doubled. He wiped away the blood on the nameless brigand's tunic, then peered inside the door. The clay lamp now flickered wildly with the breeze from the open door, but the reflections in the bronze basin were still.

He swept inside and gently closed the door behind himself. He rested until his breathing returned to normal, letting only his eyes move as he studied the layout. It was exactly as his own and he remembered it perfectly from his last visit.

The stairs lay ahead of him.

But he had found most of the brigands.

They slept on the floor, scattered around the stairs and covered in blankets. Others slept in the small rooms off the atrium. The murmuring he had heard outside the door had been snoring.

He stared ahead, and realized he would have to thread them to reach the stairs, then hope the wooden planks did not creak loud enough to warn his enemies. Then, even with success, he would have to do it all in reverse with Arria as well.

He gave a bleak smile, wondering what he had been thinking when he volunteered to do this alone.

12

Even as he stood undetected against the door, surrounded by nearly twenty snoring brigands, Falco held his breath. The corpse just outside the door was like a weight against him, pushing him toward action. The brigand must've been on watch and would soon be missed either by the man who would relieve him, or another guard set outside.

He noted that at least the brigands left enough space between them for him to pass. They covered the wood flooring, sprawled out beside Varro's cups and emptied wine jugs. The interior smelled faintly of sweet smoke and sour sweat. The humid air emphasized the pungent notes.

Seeing how the common brigands had sprawled out in a drunken stupor all over the bottom floor, he knew Arria and the leader would be upstairs. She was probably a prisoner in his bed. The thought of it set a fire in Falco's belly. You don't have to suffer much longer, he thought.

Yet the moment he stepped forward to thread the maze of slumbering enemies, he saw a light flicker from the top of the stairs and a shadow falling before it.

He slid deeper into the kitchen and crouched behind a table. It was a poor hiding spot, but in the darkness his unsuspecting enemies would likely not see him.

The stairs barely creaked as someone descended. Falco watched intently. The shadowed figure of a man trotted down the stairs, and then stepped among his companions. While he skirted the sleeping bodies, he did not take care to hide his passage. Of course, he was one of them. Yet he had come from the top floor and Falco guessed he might be the leader.

He suspected this development. Why had the leader come downstairs? He headed around the stairs and through the atrium before passing out of Falco's sight. It was unlikely he would stand guard duty, if he was indeed the leader. Falco felt a tug toward the man who had just exited the house. But he also realized it was not the mission. Arria might be left unguarded, and this was his moment to save her.

Again, he stepped out of hiding and threaded the figures sleeping on the floor. He set his feet down as if the wood might shatter like ice on a mountain lake and then plunge him into chaos. But the brigands slept soundly as he danced between them for the stairs. Only a handful seemed fitfully aware of his presence, turning their backs and pulling their blankets tight.

At the bottom of the stairs, he listened both above and ahead. The cubiculum walls blocked the atrium and front door. He strained to hear anything, but only snoring and the occasional shift of the blanket met his ears. He set his muddy sandals on the steps and climbed up into the darkness.

Taking two stairs at once, he emerged on the second floor into a brief hallway, then he turned right to the room he had used as his own in his villa. Even without a bed in the room, Falco knew an arrogant brigand would claim the largest room on the top floor as his own den. Arria must be held within.

The door was ajar, proving to him that the leader had just been inside. Behind him, past the stairwell, was another room with a window that overlooked the yard. That door was likewise open and unoccupied. Varro seemed to use it as some sort of storage space, given the number of crates and sacks stacked within.

Cursing himself for being a fool, he could not resist the draw of the window. He crouched low and crossed the short hall into the storage room. He slipped up to the open window and leaned just enough to see the yard below.

In the vague darkness, he saw the front gate was opened. Yet he did not see anyone having entered. If the brigands had been receiving reinforcements, even in the darkness, Falco would've expected a sign of them. Instead, he glimpsed two figures standing framed against the opened gate. The leader had apparently gone to meet someone at a prearranged time and out of sight of his own men.

Falco knew this was somehow important. He had long ago ceased believing in coincidence. The gods moved men around their game boards and then watched what happened. Tonight must be a game to entertain the gods.

He bit his lip and pulled back from the window. If the gods were at play tonight, then they favored him. He would not squander their goodwill. He crossed out of the room and down the hall to the opened door.

Experience had taught him to be careful about assumptions. Arria might be inside, or it might be quarters for the brigands' elite guards. Armed only with his bloodstained pugio, he held it ready as his other arm gently opened the door. It creaked on iron hinges, as loud as a horn sounding into the night. Yet he exposed only deeper darkness, relieved by faint light streaming in from a window to his right. It painted a veneer of gray over the many crates and barrels pushed into the corners of the room. Varro had left it mostly empty.

But in the center, a figure rose from a pile of blankets. The folds appeared as jagged shards of black against the weak light. From the hair alone, the rest of the body being lost in shadow, Falco knew he had found Arria. His heart lifted since no one else guarded her.

He was about to whisper her name, but she spoke first and in barely hushed tones.

"That was fast. What did he have to say? Is it done?"

Falco froze in place, his foot poised to enter the room now flattened against the wood floor. It was Arria's voice, but he could not see any other detail.

He didn't know how to respond. Arria's shadow remained still, her head tilted as if expecting an answer. He realized she believed he was the brigand leader since the darkness shrouded his features.

"What happened? Did something go wrong?"

Arria's voice rose in concern, and her shadow stirred as if she were about to stand.

Preempting another question, Falco held up his palm. Arria's posture relaxed, but she remained staring at him.

He wondered how long before she realized he was not whom she expected. He also wondered when the actual leader would return.

"Why aren't you answering me?" Arria's voice held a note of irritation. She was not acting like a prisoner.

Falco never considered himself as smart as Varro. He never figured out the difficult problems they faced, leaving it all to his friend's keen intellect. But even a dumb brute like himself understood Arria was not a captive.

She was a conspirator.

It was too much for him and he stuck to the floorboards as if he had stepped in tar. What could he do now? He had only moments to decide before Arria unmasked him or the leader blocked his escape.

"Lars?" Arria's voice softened and grew smaller, frightened.

He garbled his voice, dropping it low in his throat and grumbling. He shook his head. "Not Lars, girl. But he sent me up to fetch you. It's time to go. We're not safe here anymore."

He did not know what he was doing. But Arria acted as he expected.

Her form slouched forward, and the outline of her messy hair vanished into the dark. She let out a long sigh. "That's my brother for you. Wait. Who are you?"

Falco lunged forward, his pugio extended out of reflex. He pulled back at the last moment. He wanted her answers, not her death. It was that distraction that allowed Arria to slip away before he reached her.

"Who are you?" She now shouted at him and showed only as faint gray from the blankets covering her nakedness.

He snapped the pugio back into its sheath, but Arria heard the click and darted into the hallway before Falco could cut her off.

Then he heard the shrill note of a wooden whistle, one long and terrified note that told him Siculus had been discovered. Worse yet, two sharp and short notes warned him of trouble headed toward him.

And he had thought the gods favored him this night.

The dire warning dissolved the shock of discovering Arria as an accomplice to the brigands. He heard her shouting as she bounded down the stairs. Additionally, below, he heard deep voices cursing and mumbling.

He regarded the open window with a bitter smile. Was he as good as Longus? He had no choice but to find out. He could not reasonably charge into twenty men with only a pugio to cut his way through them. Such a feat was impossible even wearing a full mail coat and carrying a scutum. Shouts now floated up the stairwell. He could hear Arria's voice among them.

In three strides, he reached the window and pulled the shutters wide. He looked outside, but there was nothing to break his fall. Further, he faced the back wall where the smaller gate leading to Varro's crops was bolted shut.

As heavy footfalls echoed behind him, he crawled into the window one leg at a time, then dangled from it. He kept his eyes closed, fearing the height. Even hanging off the side, he might still break an ankle in the drop.

But he heard voices now clamoring for blood echoing through the second floor.

He released his grip, and his stomach lurched up into his throat.

He hit the ground with both heels, then rolled backward into the mud. Keeping his body loose, he avoided any serious injury. When he opened his eyes, he saw the window above as if it reached the moon that barely shined through thick clouds. It was a trick of his sight, enhanced by lying prone in the cold mud. But he leaped up with a groan, the mud sucking against his skin.

Siculus would have slipped out through the hole under the wall. The slave was on his own for now. He looked at the barred gate behind him. It seemed his only chance was to remove the bar and drag the gate open himself.

He scrabbled through the mud, his mind racing with all he had uncovered. When he reached safety, he would have to figure out the puzzle before he told anything to Varro. This was too much to accept. Too much for him, and definitely too much for his best friend.

Now he slapped his hands on the rain-soaked bar and tried to lift it off. Normally, one man would manage the bar, but somehow it defied him. The bar refused to budge in the wood brackets. He cursed as he hauled up on the bar, rain water spilling over his feet as he did. Then he realized the rain had caused the wood to swell and jammed it in the bracket.

The precious moments cost him. He heard voices shouting from Arria's room and glanced over his shoulder to see a yellow light now flickering along the ceiling. Changing tactics, he identified which end of the bar was jammed and hauled it up with both hands. It gave a satisfying pop as it flipped away and splashed into the mud.

He slid the bar aside with his foot, then hauled open the rear gate. The fields of barley spread out before him, and using the vague moonlight he could find his way through to safety. He would worry about Siculus later.

The squishing splash of running feet warned him to turn in time to receive a charge. A hulking, dark figure rammed into him, plowing his shoulder into Falco's body. The impact sent him skidding back in the mud, and he flopped onto his back. The figure now hovered over him.

"What do we have here?" The voice was rough like stone on stone.

Falco heard the rasp of metal on a wooden sheath, then the moonlight gleamed on its edge. He kicked up at the hand bearing the blade, his heel connecting with flesh. The gravelly voice shouted in pain, and the blade vanished into his shadow.

Reaching for his own pugio, Falco slithered away from his

attacker. The muddy earth squelched beneath him as he freed his blade.

But his attacker recovered and staggered forward with his dagger held high. Moonlight scraped along its honed edge as he swiped down at Falco.

The strike fell short, and Falco used the moment to scramble to his feet. Now he squared off with a man about his size who also blocked the way out.

Now that he had shifted position, he saw his enemy clearer in the paltry moonlight. He stood in a crouch, his narrow dagger ranging ahead of him defensively. But Falco was certain he stared at the man called Marcus Longus.

Longus did not allow him time to confirm his identity and struck for him again. This time, the blade nicked him across his knuckles, causing him to release his pugio. It tumbled out of his grip and plopped into the mud at his feet.

Grunting at the pain, Falco still connected a left-handed punch to Longus's jaw. His head snapped back and he staggered aside, unable to capitalize on his wound to Falco. He slipped and crashed to his side.

Shadow and mud conspired to hide Falco's pugio from him. He had no time to get on hands and knees, for the shouting above had faded and resumed on the ground floor. All the brigands would soon overwhelm him.

The gate bar was a handier weapon, and he pried it out of the mud just as Longus got to hands and knees. With both hands, he hefted it overhead, then stepped into a downward strike, groaning with the effort.

The heavy wood bolt slammed onto Longus's head, bending his neck at a violent angle. He heard bones snap and Longus collapse face first into the mud.

Tossing aside the bolt, he scooped up Longus's prone body. He was vaguely aware that he might have killed him, but still hoped he would live long enough for questioning. His body was warm and loose as he hefted him over his shoulder. At the same moment, the brigands rounded to the back of Varro's house.

Falco raced out of the back gate with Longus bobbing over his shoulder. His own hand ran red with blood, and he felt something hot trickling down his back. Despite Longus's weight, he ran as if unencumbered. He had no illusions about his fate if the brigands captured him. Even with Arria among them, he could not depend on her to save him.

Now he bounded into waist-high barley, and his pursuers followed. They shouted for blood, and when he looked back, he saw dozens of black shapes spreading into the crops. Fortunately, none had brought so much as a torch in pursuit. Falco took the paths between fields, careful not to leave trampled barley in his wake for them to follow. Soon he had put enough distance to slow to a jog.

He let Longus slide off his body, leaving a streak of mud and blood over his tunic. Falco used the moment to examine his knuckle and cursed yet another scar. At least he had not taken a serious scar to his face like Varro had back in Macedonia. He would need to clean this cut and wrap it before forgetting about it until it healed.

The brigands' search had petered out, with only shouted promises of revenge echoing into the night. Falco at last collapsed onto the wet ground beside Longus.

His head lolled over his shoulder, and his face had turned blue. Still, Falco rolled him onto his back and straightened his lopsided head. His fingers sank into a sticky softness on Longus's crown.

"Shit. You're not answering questions now."

Falco searched for a pulse in Longus's broken neck and confirmed what he already knew.

"You're dead, and I will be soon." He patted Longus's shoulder like an old friend. Once Flamininus discovered he had killed the man they were to capture for interrogation, he counted his own life in days. The senator could probably kill him with his bare hands. Longus was their only lead. Now that he was dead, they would have to wait for their enemies to act before they learned more.

He shuddered while catching his breath, staring up at the thick clouds masking the moon. What was he going to tell Varro? Was Arria really in league with the brigands, or was there something else he didn't understand about the situation? Maybe she was going along with them to save herself.

That thought encouraged him, and if he got to pick what he believed, then he would anchor on that. Arria was just being sly. It was his fault for not identifying himself. She couldn't see him in the dark, and of course suspected a threat.

He shook his head, then rapped the knuckles of his uninjured hand against his skull.

"You've been spending too much time with Varro. Everything is suspicious. Why did you think she was one of the brigands, you dumb ox? She was just going along with them to save herself."

As he sat beside Longus's corpse, staring up at the woolly clouds that glowed with moonlight, he considered his next steps. Arria remained a prisoner, and Varro was still on the hook for a ransom. If he sent the ransom, would Lars release Arria if he believed she had joined him?

He was too exhausted to consider plans tonight. He must still rescue Arria, and next time he would be clear about his identity. Certainly, once given a real chance at rescue she would drop her act.

Now he shifted to Longus's corpse. It occurred to him that Longus must have the vellum sheets. If he could at least recover these, then Flamininus might not gouge his eyes out in rage.

His hands swept across Longus's body, but found nothing like vellum. He carried a pack of supplies, and Falco helped himself to salted pork and diluted wine. It was a standard military kit, and suggested Longus had been a legionary. That in itself might be good information. Falco was not sure and would rely on Varro to make sense of it.

However, his hand scooped up a leather cord which held an iron amulet about the size of his thumbnail. He pulled this free, easily snapping the cord, then examined it. He held it forward into the weak moonlight, running his thumb over the raised image on it.

Based more on the feel than what he could see in the dim light, he realized it was the relief of a snake coiled and ready to strike. It was the same as what Paullus and his fellow conspirators used to identify themselves.

He tucked the amulet away. At least it would be confirmation for Flamininus that this shadowy organization was still actively attacking senators.

As for Longus's body, he regretted leaving it on Varro's estate, but he had no will or strength to dig a grave. Let his companions find him by the flock of crows feasting on his body come morning.

At last, he dragged himself up from the muddy ground and went in search of Siculus, considering his plan for the next day.

Arria was still in danger, and his mission was not yet complete.

13

Falco spent the rest of the evening trying to sleep in his soaked and muddy tunic beneath a stand of cypress trees. He must have dozed at some point, for he did not realize the sun pushed at the eastern horizon as a vague white stripe. The realization set him bolt upright.

A warm hand against his chest pressed him down. "Do not move so sharply in sight of the villa."

Falco turned to Siculus, who sat beside him among bushes and rocks crowding the tree trunks. His black beard was restored to its vast thickness now that it had dried. Light brown mud flaked off his clothes and stuck to the back of his head. Falco was aware of the clammy and uncomfortable shell of mud clinging to himself.

"Well, you seem to have had a good night's sleep."

"Not at all, sir. I spent most of it searching for you. But I'm used to little sleep. I've never needed much, ever since I was a child. It disturbed my mother's sense of things. Everyone had to sleep and awaken at the same time. Uniformity was key to her view of life."

"Nice. I don't even remember my mother. Well, I'd rather not remember my mother or my father."

Falco brushed away the mud on his arms and felt a bright sting of pain when he scraped across the cut on his knuckles and disturbed the scab. Blood still oozed from the deepest part of the cut.

"Did you learn anything more after escaping the villa?"

Siculus peered down at the villa and Falco followed his gaze. Rose-colored light skimmed across the roof of the main house as the sun climbed into the sky.

"Lars leads the brigands and is working with another. He met an outsider at the gate. I watched as he waited then saw him listen before opening the door. It seemed they had some sort of arrangement, and both continually gestured toward Master Varro's home. I wish I could have heard them. But I did not dare move from my spot."

"Well, they found you anyway." Falco examined the seemingly peaceful estate down the slope from where they hid among cypress trees. "Thank you for sounding the warning signal. I had made my own mess, but it was good to know I wasn't leaving early."

Siculus inclined his head in thanks. "They came toward me as if they knew where I hid. But I am no ghost, like you claim to be, sir. They spotted me immediately, and when I slipped through the hole, I realized they would wake the others. So, I warned you, in case."

Falco again thanked him, then explained all that had happened the night before. When he was done Siculus could not accept it anymore than Falco could.

"Mistress Arria and her daughter were very kind. Fadia took an instant liking to her. I cannot believe she would conspire against her own brother. Besides, she fought against them when they took her captive. She must be pretending to join them, sir, just as you said."

"She couldn't recognize me in the dark and my mind has grown suspicious over the years. So of course, I thought the worst. Then everything went to shit, and I had a jump out the window. And fuck me if I didn't kill Longus as well. The night was a complete disaster. But I retrieved Longus's pack and it holds his rations. So, at least we have breakfast."

"An adventure that ends with breakfast is no disaster, sir."

Falco laughed as he revealed the meager contents of Longus's pack. He fished out hard bread wrapped in a clean cloth along with a half-empty bronze canteen. "Now that is a quote, Siculus! I see why Varro likes you so much. You have the same knack for language that he does. But this isn't even your native speech. Impressive."

After they shared the bread and the last of the thin wine, Falco wiped his mouth with the cloth, then tucked it into his belt.

"There's a nearby stream," he said, looking through the gentle hill that masked it from his sight. "I need to clean and bandage this cut. Both of us need a good wash. We don't want to be mistaken for brigands, do we? We'll have to be careful, since they could use that stream as well. But based on what I saw last night, I don't expect to meet them there in the early morning."

Falco's body ached as he crawled away from their hiding spot. The fall out of the window lingered as a painful echo in his ankles and knees, worsened by a night spent on wet earth. But as they crossed the fields, he worked out the stiffness in his joints. By the time they reached the stream, he felt limber again.

They bathed in shifts, each taking a watch toward the villa. While Falco scrubbed the mud out of his hair and thin beard, he raked his mind for a plan. This was always Varro's strength. At one time, he might have been better at thinking ahead. But the long association with Varro had softened him, much like the way his legs lose strength when he cannot march regularly.

Once they finished and sat drying under the morning sun, Falco touched his empty scabbard.

"Now we're even for weapons. I dropped my pugio back at the villa. With luck, Arria will see it and maybe recognize it as one of ours. Fortunately, losing it doesn't matter much since one dagger against twenty swords is useless."

"Sir, another assault on the villa would be madness. They'll be eager for revenge, to say the least."

"It takes all my strength to resist that idea, but you're right. So, we will have to lure them out of the villa. I can think of a few ways, but all of them would endanger Arria."

His mind roved over various schemes, all involving fire. Varro might be mad at him for burning down his estate, but the brigands would not leave of their own accord.

"Sir, it seems as if they're waiting for a sign, or perhaps news from the outside. Otherwise, they would have looted the villa and retreated to their hideout in the mountains. But they are poised here, close to Rome. Perhaps they plan something larger than we expect. Do you know the state of your villa, sir?"

Falco shrugged. "I don't, but I have considered going there to rearm and resupply. I think Arria will be fine for a day. But even if I returned with my men, we still cannot directly attack the villa. That's why we need to divide their numbers. If we can get them down to a skeleton force, then we might stand a chance with a handful of our own men. Otherwise, we'll have to pry them out with a proper siege. It wouldn't take much to ram down the door and storm the villa. Trouble is in raising enough men to do it and keeping Arria safe as well."

Falco determined he had to return to his own villa before attempting anything at Varro's. Arria had secured her safety, at least for the moment. If he could return with his own guards, he would at least have some hope of success. He would have to take a chance with Arria's safety, but she had proved herself resourceful.

They set out for Falco's estate, traveling close to the ground and hiding in the folds of the land. Varro had been attacked on the same route, and it seemed likely brigands were still patrolling the area. He wondered at their numbers. If twenty occupied Varro's home, then how many more remained behind? It couldn't be as many. There had just not been enough brigandage in the area to suggest large numbers of them.

They arrived at his villa by late afternoon. He had selected a high hill to dominate the landscape and provide line of sight to approaching enemies. His home appeared at peace, with a white strand of hearth smoke stretching in the breeze.

Still, he did not want to walk up to his front gate given recent developments.

He cursed his well-placed villa, finding no easy approach in open daylight. But he was encouraged that the one guard on the wall sounded a warning horn at his approach. Assuming it was his own man, he had done a fine job.

"Did I say I was a ghost?"

Siculus lingered just behind him. "Ghosts are still visible by daylight, sir. It seems the best way to approach your walls is from the opposite side."

"Then let's hope any brigands had the same trouble we did."

He continued to the front gate but kept both hands in the air. His guard continued to watch him steadily, but he did not have a javelin ready. Falco took it as a good sign, and when he came within shouting distance, he called out.

"It is your master, Caius Falco!"

He doubted brigands would be clever enough to lead them inside and capture him, instead preferring to spear him while he stood defenseless beneath his own walls. But he recognized the face of his guard peering down at him. He was a gaunt man who had an expression of continual shock. Falco had interviewed him about his time in Iberia, and the man had served with distinction.

"Open up, Titus. You recognize me."

To his relief, the gate door shook as the bar lifted aside, and another of his guards dragged it open.

"Welcome home, sir." Gaunt-faced Titus saluted him as he and Siculus passed beneath his gate.

He had six guards in his employment, and expected Senator Flamininus would send reinforcements. For the first time in his memory, the senator had not made good on his promise. They had all prepared themselves for battle after Titus had sounded his horn. They seemed relieved at his presence, and were only curious about Siculus.

"Gather up, men. We've got a lot to discuss."

The yard was still muddy from the prior night's rain, so they moved inside the villa. Servants greeted Falco and offered him food and wine, which he ordered for himself and the others. Even though it was his own stock, he felt as if he were enjoying the hospitality of another. Much like Varro, he had not come to think of this place as home. It lacked anything that made it so.

The thought led his mind back to Arria. Would she enjoy living here? But the moment the thought arose in his mind, he waved it away. His men looked at him strangely, forcing him to explain.

"Sorry, I've got too many distractions. Tell me, while we wait for the wine, has there been any activity since I've been gone?"

His men looked at each other, then turned to Titus. He still wore an expression like he had discovered something too horrible to describe. Falco knew it was his natural condition, a different kind of scar inflicted by the horror of war, but he found it hard to overlook.

"We were attacked by ten brigands, sir. They came the day after you left, but we saw them from afar. We used javelins to send them off. Four of them are buried just beyond the barley fields, sir. We then held down the gates, and sure enough, they returned with ten more. This time, they brought fire and threatened to burn us out. But we wouldn't have it, sir. They couldn't get close enough while we had javelins. Good thing they didn't know we are almost out of them. So we dared them to do their worst, but they did not move. After a man on horseback arrived, they retreated. He seemed like a leader and called them to some other purpose. We've been wary ever since, sir."

Now Titus set his wide eyes on Siculus.

"We hoped that you would return with the reinforcements you promised, sir."

Falco drew a long breath. Fortunately, his servants arrived with wine and disrupted their conversation. He grabbed the moment to drink deep from the cup, searching for the right excuse.

"I can't be sure when those reinforcements will arrive. Everything is a mess in Rome. We've got the fucking barbarians to the north causing all sorts of trouble. The Senate has grabbed everyone out of the city and pressed them into the legion. You are all lucky to be here, strange as that may sound. Otherwise, you'd be mucking around the north and chasing barbarians."

He drew polite laughter from his men, but they all hid their faces behind their wine cups. They sat in the atrium, a black and white mosaic of hunting dogs pursuing deer spread out beneath their feet. The clear water in the reflecting pool shimmered behind them. They were good and loyal men, but they were losing confidence. Falco knew when he was looking at potential deserters.

"You did a fine job. Of course, there will be a bonus for your bravery."

His offer of a reward did not draw the reaction he had hoped. Titus gave a weak smile.

"If the brigands return, sir, then we are out of javelins. There is scarcely a dozen left, and I am not sure when more will come. There are enough brigands out there still to overwhelm our defenses."

Falco ground his teeth as he thought. He could already tell the men had no heart to defend even his villa, never mind march to the aid of Varro's.

"Have you had any news from Curio's estate?" When the men looked between each other in confusion, he realized they didn't know the names of their neighbors. "Curio is to the north and Varro is to the south. I come with bad news from the south. Varro's estate has been overrun and brigands now occupy it. It seems they tried to do the same here, so it stands to reason they also hit Curio. I just need to know if they succeeded."

He realized too late that his artless revelation undermined his intentions. His six guards lowered their wine cups in unison, each one with an expression that pleaded for Falco to admit he was joking. But he drew a long breath and nodded his head.

"So this attack happened a few days ago, and the brigands were called away before they could achieve anything. That tells me they won't be back."

"How so, sir?" Titus's voice carried an edge of challenge, and his expression of shock drew closer to one of anger. "They may be gathering for one big sweep of this entire region. It wouldn't be the first time brigands have overrun countryside farms, especially wealthy ones. Without the reinforcements you promised, we are too weak. The brigands understand that, too. They will be back, and we cannot stand against them."

The rest of the guards grumbled in agreement, frowning at the mosaic floor. None of them dared to look at Falco, and he sensed their imminent resignation. He needed these men to rescue Arria, though he did not know specifically how they could aid him. Yet, alone, he stood no chance.

They sat in uncomfortable silence while Falco gritted his teeth in thought. His next words might cost him his men, and so he had to be careful.

"It seems a strategic withdrawal is in order."

Titus raised his head, his expression of shock now apparently genuine.

"Sir, we would risk much outside the walls. We would be exposed to their attacks."

Falco held up his hand and cautioned his men for silence.

"First, as far as we know they have withdrawn as well. They might have someone watching us, but Siculus and I walked up to the gate without issue. Second, the brigands want this villa, and we would only be secondary prizes. We are fighting men and not some easy slave bait lost in the countryside. They don't want to get hurt any more than we do."

It might not have been the most solid logic, but Falco judged his words found his audience. Titus blinked and nodded.

"But we would have the slaves and your strongbox, sir. That would make us targets."

The limits of Falco's patience buckled, but he forced a smile. In the meantime, a plan was coming to mind, one that would make Varro envious. Unfortunately, it required him to lie to his men.

"It might, but I have not told you my entire plan. We are withdrawing to Varro's estate. Before I came here, I sent a runner back to Rome. Our reinforcements, plus the reinforcements slated for Varro's estate, will meet us there. Once we are combined, we will be a match for the brigands holding Varro's villa. We will hold up there until we can arrange for more men to retake this villa."

This fiction brought great hope to his men, and their faces brightened, and postures straightened. To his relief, Siculus smiled and nodded beside him as if everything he had said was true. Titus and the rest agreed to collect everything necessary and prepare to march out the next morning.

They then moved to the garden and enjoyed the hastily prepared meal of salted fish and vegetables. When all were through, Falco dismissed his men to their duties while he and Siculus remained.

"Sir, would you explain your plan to me one more time? I believe there are details to address."

Falco bowed his head in contrition but could not hide his smile.

"They wouldn't dare leave otherwise. Look, I only partially lied to these men. I know Varro much better than you do. Let me tell you what he is going to do next. Lacking any news from me, he is going to conclude the worst. He always does. So, he is going to dispatch the ransom, which will require at least a dozen armed men to escort it from Rome. When they arrive, we will coordinate the rescue, if that is necessary."

Falco sat back, satisfied with himself, then looked around the garden. The sun was now setting, and birds gathered on the roof of his house.

"But they demanded fifty talents of silver, sir. Unless Master Varro sends all he owns, they may not accept it. Why would the escorts then be persuaded to attack them?"

"And who are these escorts?" Falco smiled, feeling like Varro must when he reveals his plan in stages. "They are former legionaries and mercenaries, men known for trading acts of violence for pay. They will carry their pay for attacking the villa. We will need to work out the details, but it would only be a distracting attack. I will reenter the villa to get Arria out. After that, we can pull back and meet in Rome to discuss what happens next."

Siculus gave a weak smile behind his thick beard. "Your plan depends on many factors out of your control. Are you certain Master Varro will send an escort with the ransom?"

Falco patted the slave's knee.

"It is as certain as night following day."

14

Two nights followed two days, and Falco was out of time. He and his six men huddled in their camp a half mile from Varro's estate. The third night was about to begin, and a light rain misted the gray twilight that settled over the wide field. He strained his vision, searching the distance for any sign of traffic coming from Rome. Except for a small group of merchants spotted yesterday, the road had remained empty.

His men huddled together while Falco leaned against a lone tree. It was thin and bent as if it had barely survived the seasons. He now turned toward the direction of the villa. But the rolling fields concealed it from view, and all he saw was the purple stripe of rugged hills behind it.

Siculus approached him. The guards had not accepted him as one of their own, and seeing he was a slave ignored him. Yet, Falco saw him as an equal even though he knew otherwise.

"Sir, it will not surprise you to know the men will not remain here by morning. Your plan has failed, as much as I hate to admit it. By now, Master Varro would have dispatched the ransom. In the meantime, your soldiers have endured more than I would have expected from them."

Falco gripped the cold tree, his fingernails digging into the bark.

"We must go back. There isn't anything left to do. I can't get Arria out of there on my own. I've just wasted time and maybe endangered her even more. We'll return to Rome at dawn." He sagged against the tree, then struck it with his injured fist. "I squandered my only chance to rescue Arria, and now Varro will have to spend his fortune to clean up my mistake."

Siculus did not answer, and Falco had only the courage to stare at his sandaled feet. They were cold and dirty.

"Tell the others for me. I'm going to take a short walk. It's hard for me to accept defeat. Fuck, Varro is going to kill me."

He heard Siculus swishing through the grass, and he walked in the opposite direction. The knee-high grass tickled his skin as he left the camp behind. A heavy sword swayed on his hip, not his own, but a battered and nicked gladius recovered from one of the slain brigands. He had paid his men in advance, then they buried his strongbox in the garden. The servants, slaves, and horses remained at his villa. He prayed the brigands would not realize it was undefended. Releasing them would be more dangerous than allowing them to hole up behind solid walls. Falco did not know what else to do.

He and the others had made displays of wealth that had drawn the brigands to this place. Then they failed to protect it with enough men, instead spending their money on fine gardens, mosaics, and slaves. If he could do it again, he would have hired three times as many guards and dispensed with the finery. He was no equestrian, but a country boy. Flamininus was a patrician and approached building their estates like his own personal project. If Falco didn't know better, it's almost as if the senator wanted them to lose everything. He should have advised them to look to their defenses before all else. Yet again, being from the countryside, Falco should've realized this himself. Perhaps, in the end, he could blame no one else.

"It's a good night for beating yourself up."

He spoke in a whisper, even though the camp was now far behind. He had wandered in his self-pity almost to the road. If he followed it, he would reach the fork and then Varro's villa. He prayed Arria remained safe. He did not want to think about what she might have to do in Lars's bed to maintain her deception. If he could do anything to save her, he would.

That Varro had sent no one after an entire week also worried him. Not even Curio had come with a message. He couldn't be pursuing Longus, since that scum was long dead. So, it meant something else happened in his absence. He was not naïve enough to believe the delay indicated anything good. Nothing good happens when they separate. Of course, the separation was his own doing, and he rapped his good knuckles against his head in frustration.

He heard shouts from behind. It was distant and followed by the clang of sword on sword.

His camp was under attack.

Turning to the bright clash of swords, he could see flashing blades in the distance. How had he wandered so far? He sprinted back to aid his men, drawing his sword as he did, but the ground seemed to stretch out before him. The grass seemed to force his legs back. The screams and curses of combat washed against him like ocean waves.

Now he was on the outskirts of the battle. A dozen brigands armed with dull swords and battered round shields surrounded his camp. Several had their backs to Falco, and his first instinct was to run at them while they were unaware.

His men were quick to throw down their weapons after Titus fell. Falco watched him take a sword through his neck and back at the same moment. Falco stood frozen and unseen. He did not see Siculus, but the ring of brigands obscured his view.

The fight was effectively over, with only two of his men still standing. The third was gravely wounded on the ground, and one brigand inverted his grip on his sword and then stabbed into the man's chest. His back flexed and he groaned before collapsing into silence.

Falco backed away, hating himself even more for retreating, but realizing he could help no one as a corpse. He doubled back the way he had come.

Reaching a safe distance, he crouched into the high grass and observed his enemies. They took two of his men captive, placing them in chains that rattled like old bones. The drizzle coated everyone in a shimmering light from the last rays of the sun. In minutes, it would vanish behind the western horizon and throw the land into the darkness.

The brigands upturned the campsite, laughing and shouting as they did. Once they had looted whatever they could, they turned the captives around and marched them toward the road.

Crouching in the wet grass, Falco rubbed his temples. He couldn't go back to Rome. Not now. He had led his men to their deaths for no reason, and two of them would become either slaves or be forced to join the brigands. Both fates were the same in his mind.

He had to save them and Arria, and he had to do it tonight.

Once the brigands had gone far enough from the camp, Falco swept out of hiding and returned to it. Keeping low, he examined the faces of the dead. He did not count Siculus among them and sat up to search the darkness for him. But he found no one and decided the slave had finally reconsidered his service to Varro and his crazed friends. He couldn't blame him. Better to risk life as a renegade slave than certainly die as one.

He avoided looking at his slain guards, but not out of squeamishness. They were dead on account of his foolishness. He had tried to be clever like Varro. But he had miscalculated, even after Siculus had warned him.

While he kept watch on the retreating brigands, he searched the camp for the one item he knew could help him. His men had packed gear that would be useful in the field. One had taken his trenching tool, a holdover from his time in the legion. The brigands did not find any use for it, and he discovered it in a puddle of blood that had leaked from beneath one of the bodies.

He wiped away the gore with his tunic. He found the body of its former owner and offered a silent prayer of thanks. Then he looked at the three men in postures of defeat and death.

"I'll return to give you a proper burial. You didn't deserve this. I swear that I'll take revenge for you."

Now he raced off, parallel to the brigands' path. He sprinted as fast as he could, counting on his intimate knowledge of the land to avoid danger. Yet he could not account for every rock or dip that might trip him, so he prayed to the gods for their favor. His plan would need it.

His pace did not flag, such was the power of his fury. His original plan had focused on being clever, which was not his strong point. Indeed, his brawn was his strength. So, his plan would rely on it for success.

Now he reached the villa but had to double over and catch his breath. He had outpaced the slower-moving column of brigands herding their reluctant captives home. This time, torches were lit at the front gate as if expecting their return. The rain continued as a thin drizzle, causing the firelight to twirl and shudder against the purple night. Notably, the rear gate was dark. Falco grinned.

He recovered as much of his breath as he could, then raced around to the back gate. All the while, he had done the calculations in his head. He had estimated a dozen men had attacked his camp. Based on what he had seen previously, that meant less than half of their number remained behind. Perhaps there were only ten or fewer manning the villa defenses. Based on the position of the torches, they were all stationed in the front yard.

Of course, he could be wrong. He had been wrong about so much leading up to tonight. Yet, he believed the front gate would fly open and the returning brigands would be greeted with cheers. Lars would be there to inspect their catch. While he was focused on victory and celebration, he would forget Arria. Falco would be there to whisk her away.

The brigands had a week to plug the hole under the wall, but he wondered how well they had done so. The ground was muddy and the crack in the wall needed expert repair. They might have filled the hole with mud and hoped for the best, perhaps placing a stone to plug the gap. He couldn't get Arria out that way, and his captured men might be too disoriented to do anything other than follow him.

So, they would have to go out the back gate.

He now stood before that gate. It was dark and unguarded, and only high enough for the top to be just beyond his reach. He backed up and hefted the trenching tool so that its pick edge faced out. Then he ran at the door, raising the trenching tool high overhead.

While the brigands celebrated at the front gate, Falco leaped into the air and slammed the tool high into the rear gate door. He bounced against the wooden planks, striking his knees hard. But the tool split the wood and sank deep. He released his grip and slid to the damp earth.

He pulled back and admired his work. If the brigands hadn't been occupied, he would've made enough noise to bring the entire villa to him. Instead, they continued cheering at the far end, just as he had hoped.

Now, he had a handhold to pull himself to the top of the gate. He reached up, tested the hold, and then used it to climb high enough to reach the top. His fingers latched onto rough wood that bit into his flesh as he hauled himself over the wall. For an instant, he expected a javelin or spear to greet him on the other side.

But he thumped down into the mud on the opposite side of the gate. His hand immediately reached for the gladius at his side, but he was alone in the darkness. The brigands had decided they were secure here, or so it seemed to Falco.

His heart thudded in his chest, and he looked up to the window where he had recently fallen from. To his surprise, a light fluttered there. He studied it for a moment and thought he detected a shadow moving in the room. It was too vague to be certain, but someone was there.

If he dared to enter the house, he might become trapped again. But if Arria was still a prisoner, although one who shared a bed with the brigand leader, then she would be left behind while the others went to the gate.

It would've been better for him if she had come down with the rest. He imagined leading her away from the rear of the group to freedom. But it seemed the gods would not give him that boon tonight. He turned back to the gate, then lifted the bar away from its brackets. It was drier now, and smoothly released. He set it carefully to the side, then searched for a stone in the muddy earth to toss at the window.

Three stones later, the knocking around the window drew someone to it. In the wavering light of a lamp, Arria appeared. Her hair was disheveled, and her face was hidden in wavering shadows. She leaned forward as if struggling to see through the darkness.

Falco found himself breathless. His plan was working, and only moments away from success.

"Arria, it's me, Falco."

He spoke as loudly as he dared and looked across the garden to where orange torchlight flickered as the brigands celebrated in the front yard. It seemed he remained unheard.

"Falco? What are you doing here?" Arria leaned out the window, still straining to see him. He wondered if he was that skilled at hiding or if she had a vision problem. Nevertheless, he waved to make himself more visible.

"It was me the other night, too. You just had me confused with that business about Lars. I understand everything now. Look, we don't have time. Hang out of that window. It's a short drop. I'll be here to help break your fall. Just don't land on top of me."

He sheathed the gladius, then positioned himself beneath the window and gestured with both hands as if he might catch Arria.

But she shook her head.

"I can't jump out the window. I'll break my legs."

"Dangle and drop. Don't jump. Hurry, this is the perfect moment. I've got to get you out of here. Varro is worried sick about you."

"Is he? Then I would have expected a ransom instead of this."

Falco shook his head in impatience and emphasized with both hands that he would catch her. But Arria withdrew out of sight, only to stick her head out again.

"Someone is coming. You better get out of here now."

"Jupiter's balls, girl! Jump and we'll escape."

Once more, she ducked into the room, and then the shutters snapped shut behind her.

To Falco, it felt as if massive bronze doors had been slammed into his nose, breaking it along with his entire face.

"This can't be happening," he said to the darkness. Yet, the moment had passed, and if he intended to get her out tonight, he had to act fast.

He hadn't come so close to surrender now. Cheers from the celebration still echoed at the front yard, so perhaps only Lars or one of his lackeys had come to fetch Arria. He again drew his sword and ran toward the kitchen door. This time, he did not hesitate, but slammed it open and prepared to face whatever greeted him.

The first floor was empty. At a glance, he saw bedding and belongings scattered around. It seemed as if some other damage had been done, noting broken pottery and other scraps on the fine mosaic floor. But the way to the stairs remained open.

He bounded up, taking two steps at a time. As he reached the top floor, he found Arria's door open and light spilling out from it.

Someone was inside with her, or so she had reported. He did not sense anyone in the room, but where else could she have gone? In two strides he entered, then spun toward the door side expecting an ambush.

Instead, something heavy slammed against the back of his head. His face crashed into the door, and he lost grip of his sword. He heard it clatter to the floor but remembered nothing else before his vision went black.

He could not have been unconscious for long, for he felt himself bumping along the stairs. Someone grabbed him by his ankles, and his head thumped on each step. The warm hands gripped him like iron manacles, but he worked Falco down the steps with some care.

"Who the fuck are you?" Falco tried to grab the walls that slid past him. But in the darkness, and with his vision swimming, his palms simply glided against the smooth wood. "Where's Arria?"

The shape dragging him down the stairs grunted some sort of

reply. But Falco's head was still ringing from the blow this brigand had probably given him. He resisted, twisting in the narrow stairwell and finding no purchase to prevent his descent.

At last, he slid onto the cold tile floor, then the shadowed figure dragged him around the front. Another man was there. Falco couldn't be sure how many more had come. When the man reached beneath his arms and hauled him up, Falco thought he would vomit.

Now with far less care, they shoved him into a room on the bottom floor. He crashed against furniture in the darkness, and before he could stand, they slammed the door on him.

"You are all as good as dead." Falco raised his fist to the darkness but dropped it when the brigands outside laughed. "You'll see. Everyone learns it the hard way."

He wasn't sure of what he was saying, but rage coiled in his heart. All these brigands would die by his hand, or so he imagined in the hollow darkness of the small room.

The celebration continued outside, and he heard louder voices shouting in the atrium beyond the door. The villa was once again full of brigands, their loud and boasting voices hurting Falco's head. He had crawled atop a bed, maybe the same one Varro used. He lay on his side, fearful that he might vomit still. The brigand had struck a hard blow, and when he touched the back of his head his fingers came away wet.

"Thank the gods you don't have any brains to lose."

He tried to discern what the brigands said, but it all sounded woolly and vague through the walls. At last, the celebration died down and Falco guessed they were returning to their beds. He wondered where they kept his men. He would've expected them to protest imprisonment or beg for freedom. But he heard nothing more than shuffling feet and low conversation.

After lying on his side for a stretch of time, his eyes began to flutter and sleep threatened to overtake him. But before it could, the door rattled as whatever they had blocked it with came away. Then it opened and the brigands shoved a figure inside.

He sat up in bed, expecting it to be one of his guards.

Instead, Arria cursed under her breath as she got her feet. Falco could smell her sweet scent and feel the warmth of her presence. But in the stark black of the room he could see nothing.

"I wish you hadn't come," Arria said, her voice full of anger. "Now look at the mess you've made."

Falco flopped onto his back and put both hands over his eyes, hoping to sink into utter darkness and be forgotten by the world.

"I will find a way to make it right. I swear it. We will escape."

15

Falco slid off the edge of the bed and stood up in the darkness. He didn't know what else was in the room and didn't dare move far for fear of tripping.

"There's a bed in here," he said to Arria. He couldn't see her but felt her presence. "You can have it and I'll sit on the floor."

He lowered himself carefully and heard Arria's feet shuffle toward the bed. A soft thump against the frame was followed by Arria's cursing. "I think I broke my toe."

"Why did they stick you in here? Did Lars figure out you wanted to escape?"

The bed creaked as Arria settled atop it, and she gave a short and frustrated sigh.

"Well, you've made two failed attempts to rescue me. By now, Lars has a good idea that I would've escaped with you. So, he is making this room a prison cell. It looks like you'll be my company for a while."

Falco lowered his head in shame. He crawled backward until he found the wall to prop him up. It was cool and hard against his skin.

"Lucia is with your mother," Falco said. "Varro was arranging your ransom when I left Rome. It shouldn't be long now before it arrives. You'll be free soon. For myself, it's no loss to anyone if I rot here."

"Well, I pray to the gods he hurries with that ransom. I don't know how long I can endure this place."

Falco's brows drew together, and he tilted his head. It seemed odd that she did not ask more about her daughter. Perhaps it was stress at being caught in her lie and imprisoned. Even stranger, he felt angered that she did not console him. He had spoken a bit dramatically, he realized, but he also risked his life twice to free her. Would it be so hard to thank him, even if he had failed both times?

"Your ransom was set to the same amount as King Philip's son. Lars and his brigands either don't know how much fifty talents are or have vastly overestimated your brother's wealth. In either case, you might not be getting out as fast as you think."

The jab did not have its intended effect. Arria simply hummed at his comment.

"Then how much does Marcus actually have? This villa is grander than anything I've seen. The mosaic floors, slaves, gardens filled with bright flowers, it's like the home of a senator."

"I've seen the homes of senators," Falco said. "This still looks like a poor man's shack in comparison."

Again, Arria simply hummed as if weighing the truth of his words. He heard her shift and then lie down.

"What is this secret organization you and my brother have joined? Is that why you are suddenly so rich?"

"Well, it's a secret organization," he said as if speaking to a child. "So I can't speak about it. We got rich in the legion. I know it doesn't happen to many, but we are clients of Senator Flamininus. We were with him for his victories, and he was very generous to his best soldiers."

"Best soldiers?" Arria giggled, a sound out of place for their situation. "Marcus wouldn't raise a hand even in self-defense. You used to beat him black and blue. But no matter how much anyone told him otherwise, he swore that he would never commit an act of violence against another man. And now he is an exceptional soldier?"

Falco found himself leaning forward and his fists balling tight. "He is an exceptional soldier. I happen to be one myself. So I should know one when I see him."

"I still can't imagine Marcus doing secret missions for the Senate. That's what you do, right? Is it just Senator Flamininus who gives you orders? How many others have you met in this secret group? There can't be that many exceptional soldiers still alive. I would think the bravest ones have all died in battle."

Falco's mouth hung open at her implication. Either she was purposefully cruel or woefully ignorant. Given what he remembered of her, he expected the latter. Yet the tone in her voice sounded more like the former.

"When did you become the judge of a soldier's worth?"

Arria did not respond, and he heard her flip over on the bed. That simple, curt action communicated more than she could say. He remembered that her husband had died in Iberia. The pain of that loss must still be fresh for her, and the stress of her current predicament probably weighed just as heavily. He felt shame burning on his cheeks. When the silence became too much, he spoke softly.

"I'm sorry. I'm out of sorts tonight. Being hit on the head and all. I'm sure your husband was very brave and also an exceptional soldier."

She did not respond, but he at least heard the sheets shifting as she moved on the bed. Then he heard the frame squeak under her weight.

"He served under a less generous leader than you and Marcus. I'll say that much."

"We've been fortunate," Falco admitted. "Senator Flamininus has been good to us from the beginning. He brought us into Servus Capax."

The bed creaked again, and he imagined Arria now sat at its edge. He could feel her leaning closer in the darkness.

"So it is true. You do belong to a secret organization. Is the senator the only one giving you orders? It seems amazing to me that my brother and his oldest enemy are both in the same secret society.

What are the chances? There can't be more than just you and a few others. Or are there more?"

"I would not know about that. We've been doing the senator's work since Macedonia. There's never any rest, never any time to enjoy all the wealth you think we have. I don't know what comes next, but if your brother is with me, then I have no fear. We were never enemies, Arria. We just didn't know how to work together like we do now. If he was here, you would've escaped, and we would be back in Rome with your daughter. I'm sorry it was just me this time."

"So what is Marcus doing in Rome?"

"He's looking for a man I've already killed. It's too much to discuss tonight. Look, I know you have questions. But let's get some sleep, and tomorrow I can tell you more if you want."

Arria did not respond, and he heard her lie back in the bed. Falco now slouched down the wall until he was prone on the cold floor. He wished Varro had spent money on rugs.

When he had drifted to the edge of sleep, Arria spoke again.

"Did you really kill the man Marcus was looking for?"

"He was here with the brigands. I broke his head in a fight at the back gate."

Arria chuckled, then her sheets rustled as she turned over.

At last, sleep overtook him. He had dark and confused dreams, nightmares of Iberia where warriors three times his size chased him through its primal forests. When he awakened, his pulse still throbbed from the terror of the nightmare. Light now streamed in from around the doorjambs, and he heard voices outside. The bass tones vibrated through the walls as men grumbled amongst themselves. He heard bumping and sounds of heavy objects scraping against the mosaic floor.

Lying flat on the cold floor, he touched the back of his head. He felt a soft lump and a scab. Between his hand and his head, he had acquired a few new scars from his adventure. With the new day came a new realization that he was now part of a ransom deal. Had the brigands wanted to kill him, they could have dragged him into the yard and made a spectacle of his death. Perhaps they still intended to do so. But they likely realized who he was and his value as a hostage.

Whether that would give him the time to escape was another matter. Of course, he could ransom his own life and not bother Varro or Curio for it. He wondered what price the brigands would place on him. If they set it as ridiculously high as Arria's ransom, he might have to borrow money from his friends.

Thinking of her, he sat up. His vision swooned from rising too fast, and he steadied himself with both hands on the floor. When he recovered, he turned over onto hands and knees, then used the bronze bed frame to stand.

The bed was empty.

He looked from the crumpled sheets to the door and back again. He blinked in amazement. Had he slept through the brigands taking her away? Again, he felt the lump at the back of his head and realized it might be so. But he had slept right in front of her bed. They would have had to straddle him to reach her. He would not have slept through that.

Now he pressed his ear to the door and listened. The bass voices vibrated through the walls, and the hard, cold wood pressed against his cheek. Their speech remained indistinct and low, just like men going about their business. If Arria was nearby, she was not making any sound.

Had Lars come to fetch her? Would she be subjected to new torments now that her treachery had been uncovered?

He collapsed onto the bed, pressing the heels of his palms into his eyes.

Then he heard the sound of a female voice. It was in the room next to his. The wall was thin, and when he pressed against it the voice was clearly Arria's.

Someone had moved her into another room. They had probably realized that the two of them might conspire to escape if left together. But in the morning, when Lars had his wits about him, he realized the mistake.

Just as he was about to strike the wall for her attention, he heard Arria speak.

"He wouldn't tell me more. He's not the smartest, and he is stubborn. If you had given me a little more time, he might've told me everything."

A male voice grunted before speaking.

"I can't let you out of my sight for that long, my darling. He has told you enough for our purposes. Between your ransom and what we will make working with the snakes, we'll never have to worry about money again."

The two of them broke into laughter.

Falco recoiled from the wall as if burned. He crashed against the bronze bed frame and toppled into it. The mattress absorbed the blow to his wounded head. He clamped his hands over his ears as if blocking them would change what he heard.

He could not doubt it any longer.

His first instinct had been the right one. He had persuaded himself otherwise and justified everything he had seen and heard to fit what he wanted to believe. But the truth was painfully obvious.

She didn't even ask after her own daughter. Was Lucia even her daughter? Her only care about Varro was that he bring her ransom immediately. When he tried to rescue her, she had used herself as a lure to capture him. Then she pretended to be imprisoned with him so she could pump him for information about Servus Capax.

He thrashed on the bed as if physically tortured, trying to think how all he revealed could be used against him. He had said more to her last night than he had said to any other person. No one knew Flamininus issued their orders, at least outside the Senate. How that was valuable, he didn't know. But she had been eager to learn where they got their orders and their numbers.

What was worse, Lars mentioned working with the snakes. It took little to connect Longus to the brigands. He had that strip of vellum with the Punic writing and the impression of the snake amulet. Whatever this was about, it was not just for Arria's ransom. Something bigger than what he could conceive was going on.

He only hoped killing Longus had ruined their plans. Arria had asked specifically about it. Though, it seemed a strange thing given that they would have buried his body. Falco knew a corpse from an unconscious man. The door bolt had shattered the top of his skull and bent his neck. No one survives a wound like that.

At length, he stopped struggling and settled in the bed. Hoping to distract himself, he looked around the small chamber. Anything of value had been removed, leaving only a bronze bed frame behind. He doubted he could use it as a weapon, but might use it as a distraction.

He had to warn Varro of what he had learned. Even if he could escape the house, he still had his men to free, as well as getting beyond the villa wall. A plan would come to him, if only he could relax enough to discover it.

So, he settled back on the bed and closed his eyes, imagining what Varro would tell him if he were in the same position.

"Come on, Varro. Speak to me. Tell me how to break out of your house."

16

Varro and Curio followed their escorts up the Palatine Hill. It was early evening, just before the streets would clear out and citizens returned to their families to celebrate the end of another day. They rushed about on their errands, ignoring the five men moving purposely up the wide roads. The hood of Varro's cloak cut his field of vision to just what was before him. Two of Flamininus's messengers went ahead hiding thick clubs against their sides and beneath their brown cloaks. To his right, Curio pulled his hood over his eyes. The third messenger hung back to be certain they were not followed.

Why they had to conceal themselves was a mystery to Varro. The messengers had arrived with Flamininus's summons and extra cloaks for them to wear. He had tried to pry information from them, but knew the senator would not have told them more than they needed to know. In this case, they were to follow the escorts to the senator's home and await his instructions.

As they passed beautiful houses and vibrant gardens, Varro wondered if Flamininus had finally tired of his failures. Perhaps he had learned of Falco's mission to save Arria and would punish him for it. He hadn't heard from him or Siculus in nearly a week. But he did not expect Falco to return in a day, as he had so jauntily promised. It would take time to develop a strategy and then execute it.

Of course, if Falco tried to devise any strategy that did not rely on brute strength, he would shortly become part of the ransom price. Varro would not consider other possibilities for his silence, as these would distract him from his single-minded purpose.

Longus had vanished from Rome, or so it seemed. His trail went cold after the laborers' dormitory. Varro had pursued leads he considered clever, only to learn nothing of use. He blamed his ineffectiveness on the constant nag of her sister's imprisonment and his niece staying with his mother. No matter how he tried to convince himself Falco had all in hand, worry still tugged at the edges of his mind, particularly during the night when nightmares plagued his sleep.

Throughout, Curio had tried to keep him focused and assure him that Falco would succeed. He kept pace with him now, mounting the final distance to the villa. Leaning out of his hood, he gave Varro a meaningful look. He was just as mystified at the secrecy.

Their escorts negotiated with servants at the door, and soon Varro and Curio found themselves once more in Flamininus's garden. With the onset of twilight, it was lit with hanging lamps. The soft glow of yellow light enhanced the flowers waving all around them. Birds chirped in the bushes and landed on the rooftops. It was a pleasant backdrop to what Varro expected to be an unpleasant meeting.

Two men in togas emerged from the main house. A group of servants trailed them, each looking attentively to their masters. One was Flamininus, leading his small entourage toward Varro and Curio. The other was Senator Flaccus.

Varro stood bolt upright, as did Curio.

"This isn't going to be good," Curio whispered.

With only a moment to nod in agreement, Varro now came to attention before the two senators. Neither were consuls any longer, but among themselves, they were still military leaders. They dismissed their followers to the back of the garden, then both folded their hands at their laps.

The stout, bulging-eyed Flaccus raised the corners of his mouth in a vague smile. But it was Flamininus who allowed them to stand down.

"Sorry for the extra caution, but it was necessary given recent developments."

Varro inhaled to ask questions but saw the scornful look on Flaccus's face and instead held his breath. Flamininus looked at him with a hint of approval. But he quickly shifted to one of irritation.

"It seems you have not paid your sister's ransom yet, preferring to send Falco to his likely death. I do not understand how you can continue to defy orders. I'm beginning to question your loyalty."

He felt himself shrink to Curio's size, and Curio beside him likewise seemed ready to shrink behind the marble table they stood beside.

"Sir, I'm not disobeying your order to pursue Longus. I have slept mere hours in the last week and focused all my attention on searching for him."

Now Flaccus tilted his head back and sneered.

"But you haven't found him. Instead, my men have."

Varro's mouth fell open, and suddenly he grew to his normal size again.

"Your men? You mean Crassus, sir?"

Flaccus dropped his smug smile and let Flamininus answer.

"It doesn't matter who. What matters is Longus has made another attempt to kill a senator."

All eyes shifted to Flaccus who closed his bulging orbs in acknowledgment.

"Had my men not been ready, I would've had my throat slit just like Facilis. At least that monster did not break into my home. He caught me in a rare moment when I was away from my clients. I had paused to admire Greek trinkets set out on the side of the road. My mistake. I should've been surrounded by my protectors, but I insisted and so nearly lost my life. It was in broad daylight, on a street filled with people."

"I'm glad you survived, sir." Varro would not regret the senator's death and hoped his true feelings did not show. "You say your men caught Longus?"

Now Flaccus's gloating sneer faded, and his bulging eyes looked aside.

"They haven't caught him. But they did foil his attempt on my life. It was only yesterday. Once I recovered from the shock, I thought to share this horrid news with my friend."

He gestured to Flamininus, who was not strictly friends with Flaccus as far as Varro understood. But the world of senators and their flexible alliances made no sense to him.

Attention now shifted to Varro. He felt as if he were backed against the garden wall.

"Sir, why would Longus seek to harm you?"

"Harm me? You are a master of understatement." Flaccus's sneer returned in full force. "I do not know why I should become his target, other than I also have been conducting an investigation into Facilis's murder. Perhaps I'm closer to the truth than I realize. But I must concede, I have not determined more than you have. This Longus fellow and his accomplices are well hidden."

Varro's chest tightened as he considered the possibilities. "Sir, there may be others in the Senate who are involved. It can be the only answer, particularly when you consider the evidence."

Flaccus's brow arched, furrowing the deep lines on his forehead.

"He is speaking of Paullus," Flamininus explained. He then folded his arms. "That is a sensitive situation, and one I have been pursuing. But I doubt we will turn up anything fruitful in time."

All of them fell to silence, and Varro felt the pressure to speak. Yet the words clogged his throat. Nothing made sense, and he could not connect Longus to any wider plan.

"Longus and his patron have only targeted senators." Varro felt the germ of an idea. Normally, he would explore this with Falco and Curio. But under the circumstances, he felt compelled to provide something. "To me, it means some faction wants to overthrow another faction in the Senate. I don't understand how it all works. But there must be a connection between the targets and the assassins."

Flaccus rolled his bulging eyes, then turned away to sit himself on a stone bench. Flamininus, however, was more patient.

"That much seems obvious. But there are no factions, as you say. Certainly, some senators are more aligned with the values of others. However, there aren't enough differences between us to warrant murder."

"Particularly murder in such a spectacular and public fashion." Flaccus straightened the folds of his toga as he spoke. "We don't have time to waste speculating on what is already known. We need the rest of that vellum sheet, the one with the names of all five targets. Until we know them, all of us must be on constant alert."

When Flaccus drew a breath, Flamininus inserted himself.

"While the Ligurians are under control for the moment, the Boii are not. Perhaps they are still seeking an alliance with each other. In any case, the Senate can ill afford to be distracted with so many barbarians active to the north. So we mustn't create panic, leading senators to spend more time looking after their safety rather than the good of Rome. For now, they believe Facilis was murdered for some other reason. We've let speculation create a narrative. But had Flaccus or another on that list been killed, the Senate would turn itself upside down."

Flaccus shifted forward on his seat and spread his hands wide. "And perhaps that is the goal. Many consider me powerful, second only to the great Scipio."

He spoke modestly, but Varro heard the proud note within. He kept his expression flat as the senator continued.

"Had I been so easily dispatched in broad daylight, could you imagine the panic it would cause among my peers? Each one would raise a private army to defend himself. It would be madness, particularly when the gods send earthquakes to wrack the countryside and stir the hearts of barbarian tribes against us. The people would suffer."

Varro nodded solemnly but thought Flaccus overestimated the impact of his death.

"This is all well understood, sir. Curio and I have been pursuing every lead and every possibility. But he is a master of hiding in plain sight. Did your man pursue him after his attempt on your life?"

Flaccus again sat back, folding his arms like a child who had his toy taken away.

"I'm glad you understand the seriousness of the matter, since your results do not reflect it. We have brought you here in secret because Longus or his spies are surely watching Senator Flamininus's home."

Varro felt Curio stir at his side, likely holding the same doubts as himself.

"Sir, those cloaks might hide our faces from those unfamiliar with us. But it would not fool Longus or anyone he trained to watch for us."

While Flaccus's frown deepened, Flamininus smiled.

"That is what we hope for. Let him believe we are foolish enough to think those cloaks would disguise your identity. By now, he must be confident in his abilities to evade us. That creates hubris in a man, which can be turned against him. He has seen you enter my home, but he will not see you leave it."

Flaccus unfolded his arms and shifted on the stone bench.

"You asked if my men pursued Longus. They did and chased him into a building at the bottom of the Palatine Hill. But he vanished within. I had my men watch it all night, and it is still empty."

"There must be a secret exit Longus knew about," Flamininus said. "That would mean the building is owned by someone allied to him and his serpent society. I will find out who that is. But in the meantime, while the trail is still fresh, I want you and Curio to investigate that building. You will learn how he escaped and where he went. You will leave with Senator Flaccus, hidden in his carriage. Hopefully, Longus and his cronies will remain watching my home for your exit while you are busy learning his tricks. By now, he must know you return here for instructions. Since he has tried to eliminate you previously, I expect he still intends to do so."

"Then I am also excellent bait for a trap, sir."

Varro saw from the corner of his vision Curio turn toward him, but Flamininus and Flaccus both smiled.

"He might expect that as well," Flamininus said, rubbing his chin as his soulful eyes sparked. "But if we lull him into believing we are less capable than he expected, it might be our next step."

Flaccus gave an alarmed look to his peer.

"But Longus might ignore him completely. It's the senators he's after, and it's the senators we must protect."

"Agreed. But you're not familiar with how we work out our plans. The two of us were talking through options. Of course, they will first focus on that building."

With their next step determined, both senators seemed to relax. However, Varro and Curio remained standing. At last, Flamininus dismissed them to prepare.

"I'm uncertain what you will find inside. Take your daggers, of course, and speak to my adjutant for anything else you may need. A search by daylight would be easier, but less discreet. Unfortunately, you may take nothing brighter than a small lamp into the building. We can't risk attracting attention to your activities."

They waited by the red front door to Flamininus's home. The yard was as wide as the hill would allow, gently sloping to one side where bushes of violet flowers bloomed. The sun now hid behind the hill, not yet below the horizon. Varro looked up to the indigo sky where faint stars blinked. Curio followed his gaze.

"Do you think he's up there?"

Varro chuckled. "Seeing how we've searched everywhere else, it's possible."

Curio now looked toward the door, and then pressed his palm against it as if testing the bar.

"The senator thinks he's watching this place. Do you think he is, and that he'll be fooled? He's been a bit of a tough nut to crack. As far as tricks go, it's a simple one."

"The senator has been off the line for a while now. Besides, the kinds of traps he is used to setting are battlefield puzzles. Nothing like what we are facing today." He looked to the door, then to where servants watched them from the edge of the yard. "Do you know where I think Longus is? I think he is still in that house."

"Do you think he's setting a trap for us?" Curio then mimicked drawing his pugio and stabbing forward. "Because if he is, we're going to stick him good. Just enough that he doesn't die."

"We will only know once we get there."

As if summoned by Varro's words, Senator Flaccus and his three staff appeared. Flamininus accompanied him to the door, where they parted as if they were dear old friends.

"This should be easy enough," Flaccus said, looking Varro and Curio over. "The little one is a bit short but shouldn't be noticeable for the brief time you will be visible. Now put on these tunics."

His servants produced two tunics, both bulky and long. But Varro immediately understood these matched Flaccus's servants. They then slipped on the tunics over their own and fastened their belts loosely about their waists. The servants adjusted the length of the hem. Varro had naturally worn his higher than a civilian would. They needed to look like servants and not soldiers. The two actual servants would remain behind with Senator Flamininus for the evening.

Flaccus did not say more to them but indicated they should help him into the carriage waiting outside. It was a wide and ornate affair, and covered with cloth veils to hide the passengers. The two drivers were muscular men with hard lines framing their grim faces.

Once inside the carriage, Flaccus stared at Varro. Rather than return the senator's pointed stare, he listened to hooves clapping against the street.

"You had better get results," Flaccus said in a low voice. His only servant suddenly appeared to be dozing. "Flamininus speaks highly of you, but I've yet to understand why. You've done nothing but run in a circle and put me in grave danger."

Varro inclined his head as if complimented. "Thank you, sir. It has been my honor to serve the senator these years."

Now Flaccus stretched and yawned as if tired.

"Oh yes, I know about your service. You seem to have also left quite an impression on Consul Cato. I suppose he has you to thank for recovering his stolen silver." Now he smiled without mirth, none of it reaching his eyes. "Unfortunately, he is still busy in Iberia, otherwise I'm certain he would love nothing more than to join you on this investigation. It's just the sort of thing he excels at."

"Certainly, sir," Varro suddenly felt as if he and Curio were stuck in a box with a cobra. He needed to remain still and silent if he wished to survive.

"Oh yes, quite an investigator. Do you know he uncovered financial mismanagement when he served under the great Scipio? It left a lot of bad blood between them, as you can imagine. Perhaps Scipio believed he did not need to manage his treasury so carefully if he was victorious in battle. That is not so. But there is a lesson to be drawn from that experience. No man, however great or highly regarded, is above the law. No man can hide behind his titles and friends when he has done wrong. Even someone as glorious as Scipio Africanus. So, you must always consider yourself first, and keep good friends."

"Certainly, sir." Varro remained as still as if the cobra was ready to strike.

But Flaccus fell into a self-satisfied silence. They did not speak for the rest of the trip, instead listening to hooves beating against pavement. They rocked and shuddered to a halt, and then Flaccus's servant awakened from his pretense of sleep.

He instructed them on how to reach the building and where Longus had entered. All the while Flaccus studied them with hooded eyes. They removed their white tunics, revealing dirty brown clothes. Varro was suddenly ashamed of his appearance; his tunic having become soiled after a week of relentless searching.

"Bring back that list," Flaccus said. "Do not fail this time."

Once the carriage pulled away, Varro and Curio slipped off the empty street into the shadow of buildings along the side. In the distance, two figures crossed the street to vanish into the warm light of an open door. Otherwise, despite standing at the heart of one of the biggest cities in the world, they were alone.

Varro patted Curio's shoulder, who still glared after Flaccus's retreating carriage.

"Forget him. We've got an assassin to catch."

17

Varro and Curio clung to the shadows alongside the street to the bottom of the Palatine Hill. The dark houses to their left echoed with the joyous laughter of their inhabitants. He thought it strange to hear so much happiness but then realized this was one of the richest neighborhoods in Rome. Of course, who would not be happy here? Perhaps only the slaves, but some lived lives better than most citizens.

Guards stood watch outside some of the larger homes, and they cast suspicious looks at Varro and Curio as they glided past. Dressed in their shabby tunics, and keeping to the shadows, they appeared as conspicuous criminals. Varro realized belatedly they might have been better served walking confidently to their objective.

The building Senator Flaccus had described stood at the corner of a dark and narrow street. It was two stories high and clearly abandoned. Part of the west end showed signs of old fire damage. The windows had been boarded up and were dark. The fine home beside it was a stark contrast, being three stories high and surrounded by red walls. Garden trees stretched toward the abandoned building, their branches waving gently in the breeze. Green tiles on the roof reflected the twilight sky. White trim around its windows seemed to glow.

"I bet the owner of that house must hate his neighbor for leaving the place a wreck," Curio said.

Varro smiled, then gestured that they approach the abandoned house by its damaged side.

After they crossed the street, they both pressed into the shadow and checked their surroundings. The luxurious home next door was dark and quiet, suggesting the owners were in bed or not home. He was grateful for it since he expected to confront Longus in this abandoned building tonight.

"Flaccus claimed his men watched all day," Varro whispered as they slid along the rough wall. Flakes of white stucco fluttered away as he scraped down the side. "No one exited. Therefore, Longus is hidden inside still. But where exactly?"

They reached the door that Flaccus's men had kicked in during the pursuit. Varro tried to imagine Longus vanishing through the door as he looked over his shoulder at his pursuers. Flaccus's men could not have been close. Otherwise, he would not have had time to open the door and then bar it. The door now lay in ruins, the bar cast aside. The faint light only illuminated a small arc of the interior.

"So, they chased him inside," Curio said. "But they wasted time breaking down the door. Longus knew exactly where he was going. He would have had time to escape out the other side. Maybe he isn't here after all."

Varro shook his head. "Look here. Footprints on the pavement lead to either side. You can see them if you squint. They understood Longus might flee through the other side and so surrounded the building. They would have seen him, but didn't."

Curio crouched by the door and then ran his finger through the thin footprints left behind.

"Good eyes. I didn't see this. Are you sure it's Flaccus's men?"

"After the rain we had earlier this week, there is a lot of mud about. You see it on the street. So, these prints are recent. They'll be gone with the next rain. Of course it was them who made these tracks."

Both entered the first-floor room. It smelled of mold and dust, yet the wooden floor was well kept with only debris accumulated in the corners.

"He has been using this place for a while," Varro announced. "He doesn't want to leave tracks through the dust."

"But his pursuers didn't care." Curio pointed to the flurry of footprints that spread out into the dark interior.

With the windows boarded up, no light from the streets reached the interior. This forced them to spend precious minutes sparking a clay lamp. Once the flame grew strong enough, Curio shielded it as they moved through the bottom floor.

Prints of any kind vanished into the wood, which creaked as they crossed from empty room to empty room. Someone had regularly swept the floor despite the house being abandoned.

Curio held the lamp higher and looked at the wooden rafters above. "Do you think he escaped out of the roof?"

"It's possible he could have gone that way when Flaccus's men quit their vigil. Of course, he could have walked out the door in that case. We'll still search up there."

Yet their investigation of the top floor yielded nothing of interest. The fire damage was worse here, and rain had entered through a hole in the wall to stain the floor. Tellingly, the wooden flooring here was covered in dust except where the recent rain had washed it away.

"That's all," Varro said. "While that lamp is still burning bright, we need to search downstairs again."

After another scan of the bottom floor, they descended a ladder into a cellar. Once both piled into the room, they found it appeared smaller than it should have given the length of the building above. Curio's lamp cast a guttering orange light over rotting barrels and shattered clay jugs. He heard the chittering of rats from a corner, and Curio's light caught them just as they vanished into cracks in the stone walls. Moisture from the recent rains shined on the stone walls and flagstone floor.

"It smells awful here," Curio said while extending the lamp ahead and covering his nose with his free hand. "No one could get used to this."

"This is where he is," Varro said. "Set that lamp down. We're close now."

"I know he's good," Curio said as placed the lamp on the remnants of a shattered crate. "But he can't turn invisible."

Varro drew his pugio, confident he had cornered Longus in his hideout. The small cellar suggested the existence of a hidden space. Longus would've had little time while being pursued but could've easily reached this position before the door gave way. Certainly, Flaccus's men would have searched this cellar, if only briefly.

"One of these walls is false," Varro said. "It must be the answer. Knock on each one until you hear something hollow."

Both used the hilts of their pugiones to tap the stones, pressing their ears to the slimy and hard surface and listening for a telltale echo. But after a painstaking search, they found nothing.

The lamp was now guttering, indicating nearly an hour had passed and they still had not determined Longus's hiding place. They stood together in the center of the warm lamplight, both staring at their feet.

"It can't be," Varro whispered. "He never went upstairs, only his pursuers did. He ran inside this building, went down that ladder, and vanished into this cellar. He's probably still here and listening to us. Do you hear me, Longus? Are you laughing at me? I'm going to find you yet."

Curio tilted his head and offered a sympathetic smile. "Or it could be he escaped some other way. It's all right, Varro. It was a good guess, but maybe too clever even for him. He probably just waited for everyone to clear out, then left by a window."

"How did he disappear inside this house?" The words came out stronger than he wanted, and Curio's smile wavered as he shrugged.

He continued to stare at his feet but saw nothing as his mind sorted through possibilities. None made any sense unless Flaccus's men had lied. He was about to concede that was the case, since he could not figure another way for him to escape. But something at the tip of his sandaled toe caught his attention.

Stepping back, he then grabbed the clay lamp and brought it down to the floor. Curio crouched beside him as he angled light over the rough flagstone floor.

He touched his finger to a thick drop of dark red. The fat drop was mostly dried but broke apart at his touch and marked his finger with sticky blood. He held it up for Curio.

"He was here," Varro said with a triumphant smile. "I gave him a nasty cut across his body that night we met. He has been too active since then, and he keeps reopening the wound. Imagine, he had just tried to kill Senator Flaccus and then had to run for his life. He reopened the stitches, and blood dribbled out."

"He must've given himself the stitches," Curio said.

Varro had already guessed that Longus might have visited a doctor to tend to his cut. But after meeting with every doctor he could find, it seemed none of them had treated such a wound recently that matched Longus's description.

"So, if he dripped blood on these flagstones, then where did he go? He ran down that ladder." Varro now stood and reenacted what he imagined were Longus's steps. "His pursuers were right behind. There's nowhere to hide here. So, he wouldn't corner himself like this."

Again, Varro stepped to where he had discovered the blood, then knelt to search the flagstones. Next to the fat blood drop was a smaller one. It had dried but told Varro the answer to his question.

"Look here. This blood drop is split down the middle."

As Curio leaned in beside him, Varro angled the lamp, so the yellow light slanted across the rock floor. Just as he thought, it revealed a hairline shadow running in a straight line through the flagstones.

Both he and Curio sat back in amazement. Right beneath their knees was a trapdoor, expertly meshed with the flagstone design.

They both ran their fingers along the hairline crack, feeling for anything unusual. Curio then lifted a section of stone that acted like a handhold.

He stood up and prepared to open the trapdoor. Varro could feel his limbs shuddering with anticipation. Both communicated through gestures, Curio positioning himself to open the trapdoor while Varro held his pugio ready. Once both were in position, Varro gave the nod.

The door opened upward, creaking on rusted hinges. It appeared heavy in Curio's grip, but he flipped it aside. Varro expected Longus to leap out of hiding and fight his way to the ladder. Instead, he looked down at darkness that smelled sour and stale.

He hung over the blackness, finding another narrow ladder.

"Do you think he's curled up down there?" Curio pointed with his pugio. "I'm smaller. So let me go first."

"I'll go first. Don't let him get out no matter what happens."

But Curio was faster and slid past Varro then dropped down onto the ladder, clenching his pugio between his teeth. Varro protested, but Curio disappeared into the shaft. So he instead knelt and extended the lamp into the darkness.

He expected a shout or clash of weapons, but once Curio reached the bottom of the ladder he simply turned around in the weak circle of orange light.

"He's not here," he said. "But you want to come down. He has definitely lived here."

Cursing, Varro sheathed his pugio, then carried the flickering lamp down the short ladder. It bounced and groaned under his weight, but he soon stepped off onto a packed earth floor. He spun around the cramped space, bumping Curio's shoulder as he did.

It was a crudely excavated room, the walls held up with wood bracing. Likewise, heavy beams supported the ceiling. But the room was only wide enough for a man to lie flat and have extra space to stash his belongings.

Curio was already picking over the remains of a straw mattress. The thick scent of rotten straw filled Varro's nose. He used the lantern to scan the small area, settling on a pile of ash in one corner.

It had been a tiny fire, contained in a depression in the earthen floor and surrounded by small stones. He could imagine no one cooking on it. The ashes were cold, but dry and flaky. The fire had been recent, otherwise, the dank air would have caused it to clump.

He stirred it with his finger and found what he most feared.

The strip of vellum was still legible after most of the sheet had been burned. He recognized the fragments of Punic writing. As he tried to read it, Curio spoke from behind.

"There's a broken chinstrap here. Looks like it frayed and was about to snap when the owner cut it free. Also, there are a few worn-out hobnails in this mess."

Varro nodded as Curio kicked through the straw mattress behind him. Instead, he focused on the remaining strips of vellum. Longus had burned these in haste, not remaining behind to ensure everything important had been erased.

Another fragment, just longer than the length of his thumb, had Latin writing.

It was the list of names, at least what remained of them.

These were written in Latin: Facilis and a name that started with the letter M. The next letter could have been I or E. He could not determine it in the low light and soot damage.

He sat back and growled in frustration. "He burned the letter, and the only part of it to survive has the names of targets we already know."

"No matter," Curio said brightly. "The interrogators will get it out of him. He'll never complete his mission. Have a look at this."

Varro joined Curio over the remnants of the straw mattress. He had set aside the helmet strap and bent hobnails but had scattered the straw and blanket. It revealed a mess of bloody bandages stuffed into the corner. Some stains were dark brown, and others were fresher red. But Curio fished out one and held it forward.

"You can smell the pus from here. Longus is going to die from infection. You killed him, just not fast enough."

Now that odor he had mistaken for mold smelled like an infected old wound. Curio spread the bandage to reveal the vile fluids that stained it.

"Then either he is going to step up his pace or pass the mission to another. In either case, we are running out of time. He can't die before the interrogators get him."

Curio shoved the hobnails around in the dirt with his toe.

"He had a military kit down here. He replaced his hobnails. That means he wants to pass some centurion's inspection. Seems like Longus is joining the legion."

Varro nodded, then looked again at his list. The initial M and the next letter were his only clues. He had to identify two more names, and the initials M and E or I confused him. It could be Minucius, but he was not sure of it.

"Let's get out of here before that trapdoor slams shut on us," Curio said, staring nervously at the ladder. "It would be just our luck to get locked in here."

Without another word, both shot up the ladder back into the cellar. Varro was not ashamed that his heart thundered in his chest at how vulnerable he had left himself.

Once again, in the safety of the first floor, he and Curio tried to puzzle out the initials. Both settled on the letter E, indicating a name he did not know. They would have to confirm their guess in better lighting.

"How did Longus get out of here unobserved?" Varro looked around the darkness beyond the shallow globe of their lamp.

"Well, he was dripping blood," Curio said. "Let's follow it from the trapdoor to the cellar."

"You know, sometimes it pays to think simply about things. Of course you are right. He was taking care not to leave a trail, but his wound had to betray him. Let's get to work."

Now understanding what they needed to do, Varro and Curio both scoured the floor in search of blood. They found stains that might have been traces of his blood, but these did not lead anywhere. At last, Varro found a trail that held promise. Drops half the size of his smallest fingernail fell at regular intervals and led them upstairs.

They proceeded cautiously, careful to not lose the trail in the hall of the second floor. Varro noted how the bloodstains were undisturbed by the footprints they had fallen over. It proved that Longus had hidden in the secret room and waited for his pursuers to disband. Then he escaped.

Varro already determined where the trail was leading.

"You follow the trail," he said. "But I know he is in the home next door."

Halfway up the steps, Curio turned around in confusion.

"And how do you figure that?"

"It's the same way he got into Facilis's house. You saw it when we came in. This trail goes up to the second floor. There's a hole there where the rain came through and it's big enough to fit a man. He jumped across that opening and grabbed onto the tree branches extending from the home next door. And now, he is there. If he is as injured as I believe he is, then he cannot have gone far."

Curio seemed to consider, then looked up the stairs into the darkness beyond.

"Then we don't need to follow the trail. We will not be so foolish as to separate now. Let's go together."

Both turned around in the stairwell and drew their weapons as they spilled back out to the bottom floor. Curio was close behind, and he whispered across Varro's shoulder.

"If he's in that house, do the owners know?"

"He could hide there with the owner's permission, or the owners are not home. No matter the situation, we are getting inside and confronting him. He needs to rest before he can go further. His attack on Flaccus was a desperate attempt."

The front door to the neighbor's home was barred, and no one answered his pounding and shouting. Curio watched for signs of activity, but soon realized this fine home was as abandoned as the wreck beside it.

Varro gave Curio a lift over the wall and soon removed the bar from the front gate.

His youthful face was creased with worry as he stood in the doorway.

"Rich people don't take well to intruders. They hire big, strong guards to keep out fools like us."

"But no one is home." Varro rushed in beside him, eyes roving over the small yard and house. He saw the tree that leaned across the wall to touch the burned building. Even when injured, Longus was supremely agile and could have reached the branch.

They were soon pounding on the door to the main home, getting nothing but echoes from within. It was also barred, and Varro put his heel to it. A few strikes later the door slammed open.

He could smell the festering wound long before he found Longus.

Across the atrium, in a cubiculum much like his own, Longus sat at a desk. He wore a clean green tunic and seemed to glow with health despite his injury. He gave a wide smile, displaying his broken tooth.

"Good job, both of you. I didn't expect you to find me here."

With their pugiones in hand, both Varro and Curio dropped into a fighting crouch. Varro led them across the atrium.

"You are hurt, Longus. There is no escape for you now."

But Longus gave a patient smile.

"I am hurt, and I'll repay you for that. But it's not me who has no chance of escape."

Varro heard a door snap shut behind him, and its dim light cast the atrium into darkness.

18

Falco had spent all day either lying on the bed or pacing the small room. He heard brigands all around, their voices vibrating through the exterior wall or the door to the atrium. The room where he had heard Arria and Lars speaking this morning remained quiet. The brigands had only opened the door once and thrust a spear into Falco's face. Had he been more aggressive, he would have impaled himself on it. But they were only keeping him at bay to shove through a mug of wine and stale bread. After being struck on the head, and suffering Arria's betrayal, he had no appetite. Yet he forced himself to eat, realizing he would need the sustenance to seize any opportunities.

As the day drew on, those imagined opportunities faded. With no natural light in the room, he depended on what leaked around the door to count the hour. For all his pacing and straining his imagination, he could think of nothing other than bull-rushing the guards at his next opportunity and praying for success. He had to admit, he could not plan like Varro. Nor had Varro visited his thoughts and revealed a hidden truth about his home. He remained trapped.

When light receded from around the door, he heard the brigands cheering in the garden. They were celebrating something. It made

Falco roll his eyes in disgust. His stomach growled, hardly sated after the hunk of bread he had eaten that morning. He set his cut hand over his belly and patted it.

"Don't worry, Falco. You'll be eating at Senator Flamininus's table again. I promise you. You're too handsome to die at the hands of these ugly bastards."

He sat on the edge of the bed, probably where Arria had mocked him in the dark. What was he going to say to Varro after he escaped? His sister had deceived him, attempting to turn his best qualities against him. She played the role of a helpless sister held hostage to brigands. Of course he would run to her rescue. She knew it and knew he had the money to pay for her release.

Only that money would flow into her lover's hands. What would happen then? Would she find new ways to drain the last of her brother's wealth? His hands turned cold when he realized the alternative. She and Lars might assert themselves as the new owners of this villa. They would have Varro's money and already occupied his land. They could take the ransom and change nothing other than leaving Varro destitute.

Falco pressed both hands to his head but then gave a wicked smile.

He realized that Arria didn't know her brother anymore. Nine years of living at the edge of death had changed him. He was no longer the boy who endured punches without raising a hand in defense. Now, if you could even land a punch on him, he would return the violence threefold. He might whine about it later and carp about making amends. But he was far more a killer than the agent of peace he once aspired to become.

Arria and Lars would pay. He wasn't sure how Varro would handle his sister. He would probably do something stupid like forgive her. But he would mark Lars for death.

No matter how consoling the thought, it availed Falco nothing in the current moment. He still perched on Varro's bed, imprisoned in his room, and wished for a way out.

At first, Falco believed he was listening to the sound of rats scratching inside the walls. But the villa was too new to have a serious problem with vermin. He leaned closer and held his breath. It seemed as if the scratching came from the door.

At length, he was certain of it. "Someone there?"

A muffled voice replied, "Are you Falco?"

"How many other Falcos are being held in this place?"

The voice at the door fell silent, but Falco now stood and pressed against it to make himself heard through the wood.

"Of course it's me. I've been here since last night. But I've got nothing more to say to anyone other than you're all going to regret this."

He heard shifting at the door and could see shadow blocking light around the cracks. With his ear still pressed against it, he heard the man grumble before answering.

"Regret, eh? I've got a life full of those already. Most recently, signing up with Marcus Varro. But I've got an issue with Lars as well. I owe that man revenge."

Falco pressed harder against the door, testing it to find it still blocked.

"I deal in revenge, friend. I've got a problem with Lars as well. So, it seems we could work together. Let me out and we will create a plan."

The door rattled as the shadow in the doorjambs shifted. "It's not so easy. But some of us are unhappy with the way Lars is running things. We don't need your help to take him down. But we need your help to get away. The shit here stinks. We don't want to get caught up in it. I only care about taking the hide off Lars's back. After that, I want to be left alone. Same with the others. So, you are Varro's friend, or so I've heard."

For the first time in years, Falco hesitated to recognize Varro as a friend. It seemed he would risk his release if he did.

"He's my best friend, and if you have any trouble with him, then you have trouble with me. I don't care if that means I'll never get out of here otherwise."

The voice on the other side chuckled. "Now that's friendship.

Listen, we'll get you out of here, but once we're out, you'll keep Varro from coming after us for revenge."

"Agreed," Falco said, pushing up against the door. "Now, open the door and get me a sword. Do you want to be the one to cut out Lars's heart or leave it to me?"

"Everyone is gathered in the garden, my companions as well. But you've got to swear to the gods you'll keep Varro away from us. Then, I'll let you out."

"By Jupiter, greatest and foremost, I swear to keep Varro away from you if you let me out." He stressed each word by slapping his open palms against the door. He waited for it to open, but he only heard vague scratching through the wood, as if someone in a mail shirt brushed against it. "What are you waiting for?"

"Hold on."

Now Falco heard voices calling out behind the one at the door. He pressed himself harder against it, wishing he could somehow pop out the other side. The voices were rough and commanding.

"Proculus, what are you saying?"

"Fuck off. I was just having some fun with him."

Voices drew closer, but somehow, they became more garbled. Falco resisted the urge to bang at the door and instead pressed his ear until it sucked against the smooth wood.

The voices dropped low, and he heard them shuffling away from the door. Light now spilled through the cracks where his rescuer had been standing. It was the orange glow of a distant fire in the garden. He wondered what mischief Lars and his brigands were up to. He called out for a reply, but none came.

When the voice no longer answered him, Falco returned to the bed and collapsed on it again.

He had aid on the outside, but it seemed they were as cautious as he was about escaping. Now that he knew Lars did not have full command of his men, he had an opportunity to exploit them. He would still need to rescue his two captured guards. He assumed they were held in rooms across from his own. If that were so, then all of them could fight their way out of the front gate. It would be a near thing to escape this way. Yet, his options were limited. Night offered the best cover and chance of a successful escape. During the day, enemies could easily bring them down at a distance with a well-cast javelin or aimed arrow.

When Proculus did not return, he realized escape now lay with him. Once he broke out of this room, those who resisted Lars would join him in revenge. He would have to capture his own gear, perhaps now fortunately stored nearby. It would be worth good coin to prospective buyers in Rome, and so he doubted anyone had claimed it other than Lars. He likely piled it with his claim of the loot. But once Falco had his sword in hand, no one could prevent him from taking revenge.

Yet he remained behind a barred door. He eyed it, wondering if he had the strength to bash it down. These doors were not designed to withstand repeated assault. They only built these doors to provide privacy. However, the brigands had reinforced it, and it would need several attempts to break open. By that time, the brigands would have covered his escape.

He remained lying on the bed, looking up at the rafters supporting the second floor. Did Varro realize he had built his bedroom as a prison cell?

Inspiration struck him, causing him to leap up in bed.

The walls between rooms were flimsy enough for him to hear Arria and Lars speaking. Certainly, the material was thinner than the door. It had been a way to reduce expenses during construction. Rather than build stone partitions, the builders had erected little more than wood panels between rooms.

And so, he had found the weak part of Varro's home.

He slipped off the bed, now excited for his plan. Granted, it remained a vague and hopeless plan. But it was his own and played to his strengths. No more subtleties. He was strong, and he was lucky in battle. Anything needing more finesse than that was beyond his capabilities.

But a direct approach did not mean a thoughtless one. Falco realized any attempt to break through the wall would draw attention. So, he decided to draw the attention on his own terms and mask his efforts. He clapped his palm against the bronze bed frame.

"You made a fine choice for your bed, Varro."

He slipped off it, and then angled it so it touched the door. Climbing back atop the mattress, he walked to the door and began to kick and scream at it.

"Help! There's a snake in here! By the gods, I think it's venomous!"

He beat on the door with balled fists, hoping to draw someone. It didn't take long for an irritated voice to shout at him through the door.

"You've been a quiet one until now. What's your problem?"

Falco now waddled off the bed and positioned himself behind it. He had one foot on the bed frame and then aimed his shoulder for the interior wall.

"I think there's a snake in here! I'm terrified!"

He then kicked the bronze bed frame so that it slammed against the door. At the same time, he threw himself against the wall. He hoped the thud against the door covered for his attack on the wall.

"A snake?" The voice outside the door broke into laughter.

"Dear gods, it's in here somewhere!"

He kicked the bed frame into the door again, hoping it sounded as if he were attempting to break out. This time he crashed against the wall and heard a satisfying wooden split. It bowed beneath his shoulder as he struck it.

"If there's a snake in there, then you better catch it," the voice said through his laughter. "It's the best meat you'll get."

Falco again kicked the bed frame, sending it crashing into the door with extra force. Then he burst through the wall into the neighboring room.

He stumbled through the splinters to emerge into a dim room like the one he had just escaped. Falling onto a bed, he rolled off the mattress and thumped to the floor. He sprang up as if he had landed on hot flame.

Outside, he heard the brigand shouting at the door to the other room. "What's going on in there?"

In the dim light that fluttered through the half-opened door, he saw the glint of bronze piled in the corner. It was all their gear, his, Varro's, and Curio's. Helmets and greaves, shields and pila, and most important their swords all lay bunched amid two chests and three sacks.

Without questioning his fortune, he grabbed the first sword available, then pulled open the door and dashed into the atrium.

Across from him, the door to the garden hung open and cast a bright yellow light from a fire. Shadows flickered before it, and he heard animated voices beyond the exit. To his right, the brigand at the door of his former prison had just pushed open the door after removing the makeshift bolt they had created to imprison him. The brigand leaned inside with his spear pointed forward.

In one sweeping motion, Falco glided across the wall, then shoved his former captor into the room. The brigand fell atop the bed and Falco pounced on him with gladius raised. He stabbed the shaggy-haired man through his kidney, and with his free hand pushed his face into the bed to stifle his dying scream.

The fine mattress absorbed an ever-widening pool of blood. Falco cursed the brigand as he shoved him completely into the room, then closed the door. He reset the bar, then pressed flat against the wall.

His heart thundered in his chest. The atrium held no one, and grime covered the fine mosaic floor depicting a charging bull. The water in the reflecting pool smelled stale to him. At the far end, Varro's cubiculum hung open, and he could see that someone had thoroughly ransacked it.

He slid back down the wall, reaching the room where Lars had stored his loot. The sword he held was not his own, feeling awkward in his grip. It was the mark of a recruit when any sword would do. A veteran valued his weapon as much as his own life. Now that he had opened the door all the way, more light filled the room and revealed his own shield and helmet. He had no time to wear his chain shirt, which might be tangled beyond use now. He grabbed his helmet and scutum, and trusted he would return to liberate the rest of their gear later.

Spinning around, he once more emerged into the atrium.

And he stopped short, leaping back into the doorframe and raising his shield in defense.

Arria stood before him, dressed in a green stola. The light behind her turned the edges of her wild hair glowing white. Her face was lost in shadow, but he heard the smile in her voice.

"Falco, please say you are not leaving without me."

Realizing that she appeared alone, he lowered the scutum enough to reveal his face. But he held his gladius to its side and pointed it at Arria.

"It seems you found a comfortable new home. I didn't think you wanted to leave."

She stepped closer, but Falco warded her back as he too stepped forward. She held her hands over her chest as if in shock.

"But you came here to rescue me, and now you're going to flee without me. What will you tell my brother?"

"I'd tell him that his sister is a treacherous bitch. I heard you speaking to Lars and figured out your plans. The walls are thin here."

Arria continued to back up toward the reflecting pool. As she did, the light from the garden beyond caught the side of her face. She was smiling.

"Aw, Falco, we're old friends. You should know me better. Of course, I have to side with Lars. He is in power here. What choice do you think I have?"

"Where are my men being held?" Falco looked behind her at the two doors, where he hoped his men were imprisoned. The two doors lacked makeshift locks like his.

Arria followed his eyes, then turned back with a wider smile.

"They're dead. They knew nothing useful, other than telling Lars that your villa is unprotected as well. I imagine by now it is overrun."

Falco swallowed hard at the thought of his two men being interrogated then killed. He didn't want to know the details. Whatever happened, they didn't deserve it and he was to blame. But he also refused to reveal his emotions and instead looked toward the garden.

"Well, are you collecting our villas just to burn them down? What's going on out there?"

Arria did not follow his eyes this time but held his steady.

"They're taking care of the traitor. I think Proculus came to visit you. He blames Lars for my brother flogging him. Misguided fool; it wasn't Lars who took the scourge to his back."

He couldn't believe the shift in Arria, both in personality and appearance. Where she had once seemed radiantly beautiful, she now appeared twisted and evil. How had he found this attractive? Likewise, how could she be so different from Varro in every way? Perhaps this is how Varro's father acted in life. He was a criminal, after all.

"And who is Lars, anyway? Does he lead the brigands or is he just an opportunist? How did you end up in his bed? Don't tell me you're just an innocent captive here. Your smile tells me everything. You fucking love this. You came here planning to steal your brother's money. Why? You know he would've given it to you if you asked. He's stupid that way."

In the dark atrium, her laughter sounded bright and out of place.

"He is foolish. I will agree. But is he generous? For years, I never heard from him. Then he appeared out of nowhere, flush with riches. Did he look for his family? Did he care what happened to me after our father died? After we lost our farm? Did he take responsibility as the oldest man in the family? Before you make excuses for my brother, let me tell you that he failed on every count. Can you blame me if I don't believe he is as generous as you say?"

As Arria spoke, her voice had grown louder while her fists balled tight. Each word seemed to take her deeper into the anger coiled at her heart. Now, she stepped forward as if to threaten Falco behind his heavy shield and helmet.

"All right, he could've done some things differently. But that does not justify robbing him of his home and murdering his servants. And you don't know everything he has been through. It's not like we were off having a grand time. You weren't the only one to suffer."

Arria lifted her chin, and he saw the familiar defiance in her eyes. She appeared much like Varro did when challenged.

"It's not fair. My husband served and gave everything to Rome. I suffered alone to raise my daughter. What did I get? No fine homes or piles of silver. No slaves to tend my fields and gardens. I deserved better. What did Marcus do to deserve so much? He did not give his life!"

Falco realized Arria was too absorbed in her jealousy to listen to reason. Instead, he looked toward the door to the front yard. It opened to the darkness, stained orange with light reaching from the garden. If Lars and his brigands were occupied with tormenting Proculus, then he was wasting his moment.

He tipped up his shield, creating a bridge between himself and Arria. She looked down at it in confusion before Falco shoved the edge into her stomach. With a surprised squeal, she tripped back and splashed into the reflecting pool.

"Your brother will set you straight," he said as she splashed around trying to regain her footing. "I'll be back with him and we'll bring swords rather than silver. Better be gone before then."

Arria used words Falco never expected from a woman. But he now ran for the door to freedom.

But before he could reach it, the brigands swarmed in from the garden while others cut off the front exit, leaving him still trapped in the house.

He drew up short, holding his scutum ready but exposed on all sides. The brigands likewise paused, but were more like hunters closing in on an injured boar. Some held shields against his and took tentative steps forward.

Falco bellowed a war cry, then rushed the enemies in front of him.

19

The doors slamming shut behind Varro echoed through the empty house. Before everything collapsed into darkness, he glimpsed Longus. He sat at a cubiculum desk, grinning in a posture of relaxation. He wore a gray tunic, and the bandage around his torso showed as a bump.

Curio shouted beside him, and Varro heard footsteps rushing toward him in all directions. The sudden shift in illumination deepened the black of his vision. His eyes had no time to adjust to whatever scant light remained. He felt a threat to his left and whirled to face it with his pugio ready to strike.

But he had miscalculated. Instead, someone grunted behind him, then two arms wrapped around his torso and wrestled him off balance.

He collapsed to the floor with his enemy holding him from behind. The cold mosaic stones scratched against his skin as he struggled to break free. But whoever gripped him was his match in strength. He smelled sweat and felt the wiry hair of a man's beard on his neck. His assailant had control of his pugio hand, keeping it pinned flat to the floor.

"Hold him still."

Over his cursing, Varro heard Longus's voice as he positioned himself.

He also heard Curio struggling with his assailant. In the darkness, with his face pressed to the floor, Varro sensed Curio drifting from him. He heard feet shuffling across the rough floor, and then the clatter of a blade dropping atop it. A thud followed, and Curio's cursing ceased.

At the same moment, another set of hands seized Varro by his ankles. There had to be three other men hidden in this house, which he had thought abandoned. All of them worked for Longus, who Varro sensed hovered over him.

Now a fist connected with his head, bouncing it off the hard floor and stunning him. He went slack, and his enemy shifted to pin him to the floor. He felt someone standing close.

"It's not what I want to do," Longus hissed. "For now, you are going on a little trip."

Strong fingers grabbed him by his hair and lifted his head while another fit a bag over it. The rough material cinched around his neck, tightening over his throat just enough that he could breathe. Longus patted him on the face through the canvas bag.

"Don't cry out," he warned. "Or I might forget my orders. Wouldn't that be a shame for you?"

He heard chuckling around him. Still woozy from the blow to his skull, he did not resist as brawny arms lifted him to his feet. They supported him like old friends, but Longus jabbed him from behind with the point of a blade. He forced Varro to step forward, which he did, but only a single step. Another jab was more urgent and less forgiving. He felt blood dribble down the small of his back.

"Don't play games. You don't know where you are and who you're facing. Be nice and I will let Curio live. Give me shit, then I'll let you carry his head the rest of the way. Do we have a deal, Varro?"

Varro nodded, his head scratching against the canvas bag. With Longus's blade still at his back, he let his enemy steer him through the house.

He heard someone striking iron, and then a vague light bled

through the thin material of the sack. He couldn't see anything other than an orange point. They had tied the sack leaving no gap.

Deprived of his sight, and his ears ringing from the blow to his head, he stumbled forward like a drunk. Longus forced him through the house, and eventually outside. He heard rustling trees in the garden and felt the cool night air on his arms. Longus and his accomplices murmured to each other, nothing more revealing than simple directions.

He crossed through the garden path then Longus shoved him against a stucco wall.

"Time for your ride," he said. Varro could hear the smile in his voice. "Normally, a cart at night would draw a lot of attention. But it's a short ride. Just be a good boy and I'll keep my promise to not hurt Curio."

Varro heard hooves against the street outside the villa. Longus poked him in the back and forced him onto the bed of the cart. He climbed beside him along with another man. But he did not think Curio accompanied them.

He knew that if he asked about Curio or any other question, Longus would not reveal anything. But now that he had calmed down and was confined in the cart's bed with Longus, Varro could smell the sour scent of his wound.

"That wound isn't healing properly," Varro said. "Your master doesn't care about your life. Otherwise, he wouldn't let you die of infection."

He heard hobnails drag against the boards of the cart bed and expected a kick to follow. Instead, Longus merely adjusted his position.

"I'll allow you that one comment, Varro. Another word, and I'm going to smash out all your teeth. You don't need your teeth for what comes next."

Instead of provoking Longus, who was clearly held at the end of his leash, Varro lay flat as the cart shuddered and lurched down the hill. He closed his eyes and tried to imagine the path the cart followed. But he had not familiarized himself enough with Rome's streets to know where they were headed. He listened to the horse trotting and the carriage wheels clacking over the pavement. The wagon took several turns, each sliding Varro left or right. True to his word, Longus did not take him far. The cart rolled to a halt, and the other man groaned as he slipped out of the bed.

"You've been good," Longus said, leaning close to Varro's ear. "It's too bad I am a man of my word. Curio aggravates me. He looks like a little boy playing the role of centurion. But you stayed still and so he lives. For now."

Longus once more patted Varro's cheek through the rough canvas bag. He helped Varro stand, first dragging him to the edge of the cart and then grabbing him up by the arm. Longus's hobnailed caligae chimed against the stone as he guided Varro away.

A fresh set of hands took him into custody, rough and sweaty against his arms. A dagger pressed into the small of his back again.

"We say goodbye here," Longus said. "It has been a pleasure to watch you fumble through the city searching for me. You did come close, especially in that dormitory. But after that, you lost your way. Got boring by the end. Anyway, the chase is over, and you have lost. All of you have lost. I wish I could see your face after tonight. But I have a greater calling to attend."

The words bounced off Varro. Instead, he focused on what he could determine from Longus's voice. He did not speak with a foreign accent as he might have expected. Yet he could read Punic. Furthermore, he did not speak like the thug he expected, but like an educated man. Perhaps even as an equestrian or patrician might speak.

A new, gruff voice from behind disrupted his analysis. "All right, you come with me."

The blade against his back prodded him forward. He heard Longus's hobnails clacking as he receded, apparently leaving the horse and cart behind.

Varro considered he might escape from a single man. But he was being led somewhere for a purpose, and his curiosity got the better of him. Curio was allegedly safe, though Varro could not be certain how long the guarantee applied. So, he allowed his guide to lead him through a door and into a warm interior. His feet slapped against wood flooring, which suggested a poorer house than the one he had been captured in.

His captor guided him around furniture and past the source of heat. He imagined passing through a kitchen. Along the way, his hip bumped against tables and other furniture. This was certainly a dwelling, though he heard no other voices besides his captor's.

"We're here now. I'm going to take off the bag. Don't turn around and don't be stupid. Just go down the steps and you'll know where to stop. After that, you're not my problem."

The blade at his back lifted away, and he heard it slip into a sheath. Then two hands wrestled with the tie around his neck, cursing its tightness as he worked it loose. Then, the bag popped off his head and fresh air rushed against his face.

He looked down at narrow wooden stairs that led into darkness. He felt the pressure of the brute behind him, and his shadow loomed large over Varro's. The temptation to turn around was strong, but he heard the blade drawn once more.

"Very well," Varro said, while raising his hands. "I'll take the stairs. Where do they lead?"

"How the fuck do I know? It's not what I'm paid for. Now go."

It seemed the thug was hired muscle who was paid not only for his strength but also his discretion. Even if Varro could make him speak, he wouldn't know anything about his employers. So, he set his foot on the top riser. It was surprisingly sturdy and took his weight easily. After three more steps, the door slammed behind him. He heard two bolts slide into place and the door rattle. At last, he turned around and saw only faint light seeping through the edges of the doorway.

Ahead of him lay only darkness and the promise of another light at the end of a passage.

At the bottom of the stairs, he found a narrow corridor lined with fitted rock. It seemed to carry on forever, with an orange light glowing at the end. The air was still and stale, smelling of wet earth. Black streaks stained the stone in places. Only a single man could travel the path, and so he followed it until coming to a door on his right. His captor had said he would know where to stop. The passage continued, and the sturdy but aged door did not yield to his touch. It remained steadfastly locked.

He determined the path sloped downward at a gradual angle. When he reached the end, he peered into a large, torch-lit room that smelled of burning pitch.

"Hello?" he called into the open room but only heard an echo in reply.

He stepped inside to discover it was a vast and circular room with a pounded earth floor. Smooth plaster covered the walls, depicting faded frescoes of gladiators and beasts locked in battle. Halfway up the walls were rows of seats like a theater.

This was an arena, he decided. He noticed an archway directly across from him, with a grate drawn shut over the darkness beyond. He spun around, expecting another grate to fall across the archway he had entered. But it remained open, though he did see in the shadows of the archway the tips of a grate like retracted fangs.

"Come to the center, Varro. I would speak with you."

The voice startled him, causing him to lurch around and reach for a gladius that he did not carry.

The ring of torchlight cast strange and conflicting shadows. His motion sent exaggerated shadows flying across the high domed ceiling. He did not see the source of speech as he circled in place. The unfamiliar voice sounded old and dry. Yet it carried a note of privilege, like that of a patrician.

"Up here," the voice said. "Please, you are testing the limits of my patience. I did not expect to meet you tonight. Fortunately, I could make it in time."

Varro now turned to the source, looking up between the torches lining the edge of the arena walls. A figure stood among the bench seating. He wore a loose-fitting toga and stood with both hands limp at his sides. An actor's mask concealed his face, bearing an expression of deep sadness. Gray hair fringed the top and caught the wavering light. He appeared alone but might have others hidden with him in the gloom.

He stood close to the edge, and Varro saw the glint of something metal leaning against it by his right hand. A weapon, he thought.

Scanning the darkness, he could not see any threat other than this old man. Yet he warily approached the center of the arena expecting a trap. The enigmatic figure stared at him through its dark and sad eyeholes.

"Stop there." The figure held up a bony and gnarled hand. His palm was smooth and reflected the yellow light of the torches.

He stopped on command as if he were about to tumble off a cliff edge. Cool and fresh air circulated here, but he could not see the source. His palm itched for the welcoming weight of a gladius or pugio. Instead, he had to stand with empty hands flexing at his sides.

"Who are you? What do you want from me?"

The masked figure leaned back in laughter, echoes resounding through the circular arena. It sounded as if he were surrounded, even though he faced a single old man.

"Such unimaginative and foolish questions. I would expect better from you, Centurion Varro." The old man placed a blue-veined hand over his chest as if needing to steady his laughter. But the sad mask seemed to glare down at him. "Would I wear a mask if you should know my identity? As for what I want from you, I shall make that as clear as possible."

"You are Longus's employer. So far, you have only wanted me dead. I can't imagine what else you have planned for me." He extended both arms to indicate the arena walls. "I am to be your entertainment tonight?"

"You have been entertainment all along," the old man said. He stepped closer to the edge of the arena, both of his thin hands on the banister. "But now, tonight, you will become more than entertainment. Tonight, you will seize your destiny or cast it away."

"Only the gods make a man's destiny. All I see here is an old man too frightened to reveal his face."

Varro searched for a way out other than the door he had entered or the portcullis across from him. He expected at least one other exit in the seating area, otherwise, his masked enemy would have had to climb up to reach his seat. At his low angle, however, he could not see to the rear. Also, he was not alone with his enemy. Someone had lit the torches in preparation for his arrival, suggesting hidden servants or guards.

The masked patrician ignored the jab and dusted at his toga.

"What do you know of Servus Capax, Centurion Varro? Do you think you serve some noble purpose? I will tell you what your patron will not dare say. You serve a faction of the Senate. A faction of Hellenes and empire builders. They have charmed you with the belief you spread Roman values and prosperity to the world. But you have seen firsthand what is delivered. Do the Iberians prosper? Do the Numidians celebrate their servitude to Rome? I needn't instruct you in Macedonia and the quarrelsome Greek Leagues we have left behind. Flamininus proclaimed the Greeks free. But you know as well as I that the legions will return to finish what has been many years in the making."

Varro wanted to block out the poisonous words of the masked patrician. How could he trust someone who would hide his identity and coerce him with violence? Yet, he could not deny a kernel of truth amid the distortions. At least, a hinted truth. He had long suspected Servus Capax might not be completely for the benefit of all Rome, and more for the benefit of certain powerful men.

"You speak to me of truth but hide your face." Varro pointed to the closed portcullis. "You keep me prisoner and will shortly threaten to harm my family and friends should I refuse whatever offer you will make. Laugh at me for my simple questions. That laughter rebounds upon you. I have been made this offer once before, and I will refuse it again. Deliver my regrets to Consul Cato."

He had attempted to guess at the power behind this man. But the masked patrician again leaned back in laughter, this time full and genuine.

"You could not be more off the mark than to name Cato, of all men. Listen, I have brought you to this place for a purpose. For understanding and communication. Where else can we speak without distraction? Were I to meet you in public you would be constantly thinking of a way to escape, or a means to capture me. Here I am assured of your attention." He tapped a bony finger on the wooden mask. "I wear this only as long as necessary. If you will cooperate, then there shall be no secrets between us, unlike your current patron. If you refuse, of course I will threaten your family and friends. It is expedient. But also, completely avoidable."

Varro narrowed his eyes in hatred. His fingers burned for a weapon and his legs quivered to launch him to the top of the arena wall. It was a body length over his head, yet such was his fury he might make the jump still.

"You could have chosen any mask. Yet you chose one for melancholy. It tells me you already know how this must end."

The masked patrician folded his arms as if weighing his thoughts.

"You are a rational man, Centurion Varro. It is one reason we are speaking tonight rather than simply removing you from the game board. I appreciate you do not enjoy games. Yet you placed yourself upon the board, and it is no one's fault but your own if you did not realize that."

"I have my mother to thank for it." Varro muttered to himself, but apparently the arena carried his voice.

"It is a weak man who blames his parents for his own misguided decisions. Throughout these many years, your actions reinforced your choice. You have emblazoned the very symbol of your mistake on your arm. Do not point to your mother and lay blame on her."

As if summoned by this accusation, the tattoo on his arm itched. He resisted the urge to hide it beneath his hand.

"And so you believe your new offer will be more to my liking? You imply that my mistakes can be undone tonight, of course, by accepting whatever criminal and underhanded offer you are about to make."

The masked patrician withdrew his hands behind the banister and stood straighter. The enigmatic and expressionless stare lasted until Varro could no longer stand to look into the dark eyeholes of the mask.

"Centurion Varro, you have performed excellent work for Senator Flamininus. Indeed, you spared him from a ruined career back in Macedonia. Had he lost both Prince Demetrius along with the war indemnity to his own tribunes not only would it have ended his career, but history would mark him as a fool forever. Instead, he received a triumph upon his return. What a different story his life has now, thanks to you and your companions. He was right to reward you so richly. But now that reward binds you in servitude to him. I know you feel it, heavy chains of silver around your neck. All the trappings of wealth and prestige now weighing upon your young shoulders. There is no one to guide you but him. No one to protect you but him. Indeed, you are a slave, and your freedom is an illusion. But you will insist neither is true. A man finds no better deceiver than his own self."

The patrician stared down through his mask frozen in an effigy of sorrow. He folded his hands neatly on his lap as if concluding his argument.

Varro shook his head. It was all true. He felt the chains and the bond they created.

But it did not mean he was ungrateful.

"Mistake or not, I have made my choice. You've presented me with nothing better. So, if you have taken me here for a lecture, then your time and mine are both wasted. My head still throbs from Longus smashing it against a mosaic floor. Nothing you can say will make me forget that. Flamininus offered me accolades, riches, support, and leadership. You offer nothing but pain for disobedience. Don't bother with the rest of your argument. Move along to the punishment you have prepared. And don't be so sure that I won't yet remove that mask from your face. You know my history and should know that's no idle threat."

He wished his actual confidence matched his tone. Predators like this masked patrician had a way of sniffing out one's true fear. He only hoped he had learned to conceal it well.

The masked patrician seemed to toy with something behind the arena wall as he considered the threat. At length, he tilted his masked face backward.

"Perhaps if you understood the truth as we do then you would not be so stubborn. Centurion Varro, the death of the Republic is at hand. You cannot see it from your vantage, much like you cannot see all of me from where you are standing now. But that does not make it less true."

Varro cocked his head. "Well, you're targeting senators and consuls for murder. But that won't end the Republic."

"Don't be clever with me." The masked patrician leaned against the railing as he emphasized his words. "What you are failing to see, or perhaps willing to disregard, is how constant war erodes the Republic. The countryside is filled with destitute legionaries who turn to brigandage for survival. The Senate only demands more of them and pushes the entire world into war. Why? So certain men may advance their own glory. Flamininus is a perfect example of this, delaying the Macedonian war as he did and extending the suffering of his soldiers. Wars bloom all around us, each season bringing new threats requiring new legions to defeat. With constant warfare and more destitute soldiers filling the streets, the public will weary of the uncertainty and demand stability.

"All of it will lead to a dictator who will not step down even if the crisis ends. The people will not want him to but instead cling to the false security he will offer. His name will be from one of the great patrician families. His lineage will be pure and glorious. The republic will become an afterthought. One day, sooner than you realize, there will be a king in Rome once more."

"But you are going to prevent that, of course," Varro said with a crooked smile. "And you need me to help you do it. What sort of fool do you take me for?"

The masked patrician's bony hands balled up and he glared down in enigmatic silence. When he spoke again, however, his voice was measured and calm.

"Just as some work toward this future, others work against it. I represent the defense of the Republic. You are a patriot, Centurion Varro, and you are better aligned with me than Flamininus. We have chosen the snake as our sign because we are medicine and healing for an ailing government."

Varro stepped back, laughing.

"Defense of the Republic by murdering senators and consuls? How do you imagine that helps anything?"

The patrician slammed his hands on the arena wall hard enough that his mask shifted. "By hastening the end, you fool! What we have today is rotten, and can no more be made whole again than one can restore spoiled meat. The end must come now so that men of vision can remake it as it should be."

Even beneath his mask, the patrician seemed to gaze into the future as he continued to rant.

"Otherwise, it is a long and painful stumble to destruction and by that time a new king will secure his rule beyond challenge. But if we act today, and push through the hard times swiftly, then the Republic will be reborn more glorious and solid than before."

"Madness," Varro whispered in shock, his mockery and scorn subsumed into complete disbelief.

The masked patrician drew himself straighter.

"Join with me, Centurion Varro. Bring your friends to the cause, and we will save the Republic. Yes, it will hurt, as good medicine often does. But we will spare our beloved society from a far worse fate. Better a mercy killing than a long and agonizing death. Just as the snake sheds its dead skin to reveal a fresh and repaired one beneath, so must we do for Rome."

Varro shook his head and turned back to the open archway behind him. If he ran now, he might reach it before the grate sealed him inside the arena.

"The answer is not behind you, Centurion Varro. Look at me and choose your fate."

Without another thought, he spun around and made a running leap for the arena wall.

20

Falco charged with blind rage consuming his vision. Carrying a scutum on his left arm and holding a gladius tight in his right fist filled him with battle lust. Never mind the rage he felt at Arria for her treachery and betrayal of her own brother. If he died fighting these brigands, then at least he would end his days doing something worthwhile.

These scum deserved death.

He had not properly strapped the bronze helmet, and its leather liner shifted as he charged the brigands entering the front door. One dark-skinned man held up a round shield that his mates hid behind. The greater threat, Falco knew, came from behind where the brigands had more space to surround him.

He heard Arria screaming and cursing as she splashed in the reflecting pool. But that vanished under the thunderous sound of his scutum crashing into the lead brigand in the doorway.

Enraged as he was, he plowed the thin line of brigands back through the opening. Indeed, the scutum was like a door slamming on the attack from the front. Unfortunately, this left his back exposed and prickling with expected wounds. He could not contain the men to the front while also protecting his rear.

Fortunately, surprised shouts erupted behind him.

He could only afford a glimpse over his right shoulder. But he heard men calling for Lars's head and the sudden eruption of violence that followed.

With his hope rejuvenated, he shoved forward through the door. "Follow me to victory!"

Whether his battle cry would generate any élan amongst his erstwhile enemies, Falco did not know. The enemies to his front crumpled under the weight of his brawny push. He spilled out into Varro's front yard and a semicircle of hesitant brigands.

He knew enough to eliminate the shield bearer before the others. This makeshift unit looked to him as their leader. So, he punched out with his scutum and connected with a body. He heard the satisfying thump of it and felt the triple-layered wood shudder on his arm. Then the shield bearer flew aside as he created space for his next attack.

Angry faces greeted him on the right, a mistake for them to strike so hastily. If these men had once been legionaries, they had forgotten everything they learned. Perhaps they had never learned.

Falco pivoted on the ball of his foot, now lining up to a man on his far right and covering the others with his massive shield. The brigand struck out with a pugio that had seen better days. The strike narrowly passed his side, and only a lucky step spared him from injury.

His opponent, however, did not fare as well. He rammed his gladius under the man's neck, breaking through the bottom of his jaw and driving the blade into his brain. The hapless brigand's eyes rolled back as he slid off the blade, spilling blood down its length before collapsing into the open doorway.

Someone leaped upon his back in a desperate bid to overwhelm him and lower his shield. But Falco simply leaned forward with the momentum, and the barest bucking of his shoulders sent his attacker into the next man to challenge him.

Now he found himself unopposed, with the shield-bearer sprawled out in the dirt, another dead in the doorway, and two others entangled with themselves. The front gate was a sprint away, but it was barred shut.

Inside the house, a fierce battle raged between those who sought to depose Lars and those still aligned with him. Around the corner, a bright orange bonfire glowed in the garden. No more shadows flickered before it. All the brigands had turned upon themselves, as was often the case with lawless scum. Falco fled before any more of the brigands came for him.

Reaching the front gate, he found the bar spiked in place. He slammed his scutum against it out of frustration. Likewise, the lookout platform was empty and its ladder was taken down. It seems Proculus and his rebels had intended to deny any means of easy escape. Unfortunately, it left him trapped as well.

He dug at the iron spikes holding the bar in place. With no time pressure, it would be a simple matter to free the bar. Yet, looking over his shoulder, he found the two brigands had untangled themselves and rushed for him with drawn swords.

Cursing his luck, he spun about to face them with his scutum up. This time, at least, he had the gate against his back.

"Come on, you fuckers! I can fight here all night!"

Their brash charge slowed at Falco's challenge. Though he felt pinned to the wall, and on the verge of death, his enemies likely saw an impenetrable shield, glittering bronze helmet, and a keen-edged gladius. The two were not brave enough to challenge that strength.

They skidded to a halt, spreading out into fighting crouches and brandishing their short swords. Sweat gleamed on their skin from the fire blazing in the garden.

Falco took satisfaction in halting their attack, but that feeling died as fast as he would if he turned his back on them. If Lars's faction prevailed, then he would be overcome eventually. Even if the rebels secured victory, they might not side with him. They did not know the arrangement he had made with Proculus.

Yet the gods were not interested in that scenario.

Behind the two brigands, Falco saw a woman in a green stola

emerge from the house. The fighting there had ended, and Arria appeared entangled in Lars's arms.

He held a knife to her pale throat. Her stola was plastered to her body and challenged Falco to look aside even under these circumstances. Her eyes were wide with fear and she struggled against Lars as he shoved her ahead.

"Oh fuck," he muttered under his breath. He understood immediately what Lars wanted.

The two brigands facing off against Falco mistook his expression and encroached on his position with sly smiles. Yet they froze when Lars called out from behind.

All the brigands that remained now gathered in the yard. Despite the din of their battle, it did not seem to Falco that many had died other than the ones he had eliminated. He estimated at least twelve remained and could not tell who the rebels among them were. At this point, it might not matter with Proculus dead.

Lars guided Arria before him like a body shield, leering as he pressed his knife into the side of her neck. His other arm wrapped around her body just beneath her breasts. Arria's normally voluminous hair now clung to the sides of her narrow head. Robbed of her fashion and styling, she looked like a feminine version of her brother.

"It seems you've been locked in with the rest of us," Lars said, tilting his head toward one brigand who shied away. Falco now at least identified one rebel.

"You have a problem with loyalty," Falco said. "And they are right to question you. You led them into a fucking mess. You can't hold what you've taken. Varro will send a private army to mop you up. He's got the money for it."

In the gloom, Falco was uncertain how the brigands in the rear reacted. But several up front gave him a hard stare as if trying to determine whether he spoke the truth.

However, the threat seemed to bounce off Lars.

"You've got a more immediate problem, Falco. Besides, who says I'm waiting around? I guess Arria's big brother doesn't care much for her. But I wonder if you are a better bet for a ransom payout than his own sister."

He hooked the short knife higher so that it pressed into Arria's flesh. If she faked her panic, it was convincing. Her eyes were about to pop from their sockets, and they gleamed with tears that streamed down both cheeks. Her mouth trembled defiantly, and tight lines were drawn down either side. For a moment, Falco forgot her treachery and his heart ached to see her in such distress.

Then he blinked away the illusion.

"Do I look like some fucking fool? She has been sleeping with you this whole time. You've both plotted to get her brother's money. Now you expect me to surrender myself in trade for Arria's life?"

Lars's grin faltered, and his nostrils flared.

"Well, that's the offer. I'll let her go free, and you can take her place. I bet Varro will send your ransom immediately. He doesn't care about his family. That's obvious. So, time to make a better trade."

Falco snorted a laugh.

"My eyes were closed before. But they're open now." He looked at the others surrounding Lars. "You all got a fine take here. Now it's time to head back to the hills before you die for a few coins more. None of you were ever going to get all Lars promised you. You can't expect Varro to drain every obol to free me or his sister. He will not do it. If he would, then you would have had that ransom a week ago. Instead, here I am trying to free his sister on the cheap."

"Falco," Arria's voice was small and frightened. "This isn't an act. Give up, or he will kill me."

Lars dug the blade deeper to emphasize the threat, and a thin line of blood flowed down from its point. Arria squealed and struggled before Lars pulled her tight.

"The gate behind you is barred and nailed shut. You're trapped against a wall. I can take you alive and make a fair trade for good ransom, or I can trade your dead body. You're probably worth more alive. But I am assuming Varro still wouldn't want your head rotting in the yard of his own home. So he'll probably still pay something for your corpse. Now, wouldn't it be more practical to trade yourself and let Arria leave alive?"

"Please, Falco, I know Marcus will pay your ransom. Forget what I said earlier. I'm sorry. Please, think of my daughter at least. Who will raise her?"

Anger welled up in his chest.

"You remember that you have a daughter now?" Falco narrowed his eyes at her. There was nothing Arria could say that he would believe at this point. Even the small runnel of blood on her throat was a small price for all the wealth she could gain through continued deception.

Instead, he noticed the man he had marked as a rebel staring intently at him. He seemed to indicate a willingness to fight Lars, motioning with his eyes toward his former leader and keeping his sword ready. Other brigands seemed to subtly creep closer. They would fight if he would. Perhaps Proculus had guaranteed their freedom from retribution beforehand.

"Come on, it's not a hard choice." Lars stepped forward with Arria held tight against his body and twisted the blade against her throat. She cried out as more blood ran down her neck.

"You don't have to cut her up," Falco said through his sneer. "I appreciate your commitment to the act. But it's just a nick that bleeds a lot."

"Falco, please." It was all Arria could say before Lars pressed the blade again, causing her to shout in pain.

"I won't be duped a third time."

He met the eyes of the rebel beside Lars, who had grown too fixated on his dreams of ransom to notice his disloyal man. With a barely perceptible nod, Falco agreed to the attack.

The rebel brigand shouted, "Down with Lars!"

Others took up the shout, and the fight resumed in the yard. The brigands turned on each other with weapons raised.

Falco sprang forward with his shield up and gladius poised to strike.

Then Lars rammed the knife into Arria's neck.

It slid easily through her pale flesh, driving through the pulsing artery and plunging into her throat. Her eyes rolled back, and blood flowed from her mouth and poured around the blade onto her chest.

Lars cast her aside like discarding an old rag doll, leaving the blade jutting from her neck. Arria crashed into the rebel attacking Lars from the side, spoiling his blow. She then flopped backward into Falco's path, causing his charge to skid to a halt.

Intended or not, she had defended her lover even in her final moments. Falco stumbled to a halt before her. This allowed Lars to vanish into the glare of the bonfire, skirting the battle swirling around him.

The rebel brigand who had just crashed into Arria now stumbled into Falco. He cursed as he shoved the man back with his scutum.

A pool of fresh blood spread out from beneath Arria, a dark stream of it reaching for Falco's feet as if begging him for help. But he stared into eyes rolled up in death. Her mouth was frozen in mid-scream and her teeth were red with blood.

The sight staggered Falco worse than any blow. He recoiled from the spreading pool of blood and shook his head at the reality before him. Arria had not been acting.

The sharp battle in the yard unfolded in slow motion. He saw dirty and ragged men, their faces crimson with rage, slashing at each other. Some had already collapsed to their knees, clutching their guts as blood flowed through their fingers. Others searched around for new targets.

"He's escaping!"

Falco didn't know who shouted the warning, but it galvanized him to pursue Lars. He avoided Arria on the ground and chased Lars into the blazing light of the garden.

Rounding the corner, he discovered the purpose of the fire. Two brigands, one he assumed to be Proculus, were bound to poles. Lars had built up a fire around them, and their flesh was now withered and blackened. The wind had kept the sweet stench of burning bodies away from the house. He did not understand why he had not heard them screaming in torment. But he had no time to consider more.

The garden had once been beautiful, but now the colorful flowers had all been dug up and scattered to create this miserable scene. Stone benches lay shattered and wood tables overthrown. Much of the home furniture had been destroyed to create the fire that now roasted Proculus and his accomplice.

But Falco had no time to study details. All of this passed before him in a blur as he searched for Lars. The glare and heat of the bonfire drove Falco toward the wall. He could not see where Lars had fled, but guessed he might attempt the rear gate. However, if Proculus and his accomplices had nailed the front gate then they would have done so for the rear. Lars would guess this as well.

Falco knew where to go.

Pressing against the wall, feeling the taut heat vanish behind the scutum on his left side, he found Lars in the garden wall corner. He had dug away the stone that had filled the gap Falco previously exploited.

He looked up, frantic and sweating.

"You can't fit through it in time," Falco said as he approached. "It's your turn to surrender to me."

Lars sprang back from the hole, and rather than answer, flung a hand-sized rock at Falco.

Fortunately, the scutum was like a movable wall. The rock thudded off it and did not delay Falco's approach.

"Throwing rocks like a child? You fucking murderer. I'm going to make this hurt."

Lars retreated, and Falco raced after him. He headed for the rear gate, a gamble that would avail him nothing. If the gate opened, Falco could still catch him. If it was closed, Falco could kill him.

As expected, someone had nailed the rear gate bar in place. Lars strained to pull out the spike. But Falco let a tiny smile flicker as he raised his shield and braced his gladius against it. Lars's eye widened in terror and he pressed his back to the barred gate.

"You can't kill me! I have information you need."

But Falco was beyond listening. The words reached his mind, and somewhere in that primitive darkness he understood Lars was a valuable prisoner. But rage overruled logic. Arria had been deceitful and treacherous. But Varro would have found it in his heart to understand and forgive his sister. Now, she was dead at Lars's hands.

Falco's shadow grew ominously over Lars as he pressed against the gate. The bonfire light danced across his shoulders to cast a fractured yellow light over the brigand leader.

"Don't! There are more of us. Rome is behind this. Let me live. I will tell you everything."

"Too late," Falco said, now squarely before Lars. "Who would believe a fucking word from your filthy mouth?"

The gladius plowed beneath Lars's sternum, and Falco felt it drag against bone. He pushed hard enough to sink the entire blade up to the hilt in his flesh. The tip of it thumped against the wooden gate door, pinning him.

Lars opened his mouth to let his final breath escape in a ragged blast. Falco stepped back, lowering his scutum to admire his work.

"You were right. I probably should've taken you alive. But this feels better."

He didn't care whether Lars heard his cynical comment, since his life now drained into a red puddle at his feet. His body slumped forward, held up only by the gladius sank to its hilt in the center of his torso. Blood and drool stretched from his open mouth and his eyes were vacant.

Falco turned, now bearing only his scutum against whatever enemy remained.

The fight had ended, and men lay moaning on the ground. Between the two burning bodies in the garden and others scattered through the house and yard, Falco predicted only a handful of brigands remained in fighting shape. Now, he would learn which side prevailed, if any.

He returned to the front gate where Arria remained sprawled out in death. One hand seemed to have reached for her neck before she expired. Perhaps she had not died immediately, for Falco did not remember her moving. One leg was bent awkwardly, revealing a dislocated knee from her twisting fall.

Five brigands remained alive in the front yard. He scanned the carnage, trying to remember what this place looked like before it became a battlefield. A pair of white legs extended from the darkness of the front door. Falco remembered killing that one. Other bodies lay in postures comfortable only to the dead. Everywhere, blood caught the reflections of the fluttering light from the unattended bonfire. Falco noted sparks had finally caught the wall on fire. A tentative line of orange flame spread along the painted stucco. Had it not been damp from the recent rain, the fire would spread faster than any of them could escape.

One brigand stepped closer. Falco shot up to his full height and presented his scutum.

"This is just as good for bashing your brains out. Want to learn how it's done?"

The brigand held up his hand for peace. Falco didn't recognize him, but he might have been the rebel who had signaled the start of this brawl.

"We're getting out of here. Do you want to come with us?"

Falco's heavy brows drew together in confusion. He tilted his head as if he had not heard correctly.

"You want me to become a brigand like you?"

He was so stunned that he lowered his shield to get a better look at the five. All of them were cut and bruised, dripping with blood and sweat. Their mouths hung open from their exertions, and none of them could continue in anything more strenuous than a jog to safety.

"Are you going to return to your friend in failure?" The brigand had barely the strength to wave toward Arria's corpse. "The others have also captured your place by now. You've got nothing left."

Again, Falco's shield slipped lower and now thumped against the ground. These brigands had likely never heard of a bank before. He was far from dispossessed. But he felt the pull of Arria's corpse at his feet. He had miscalculated and caused her death. Would Varro forgive him? Would he forgive himself?

"And so you think I'm better off hiding in the hills with you than going back for my punishment?"

The brigands looked between themselves and shrugged. Their spokesman scratched beneath his sweat-matted hair.

"We want no more fighting. Lars got away, and the hostage is dead. This thing is a fucking mess. We could always use a good fighter. You can come with us or go your own way. But we just want to escape before Lars recovers."

"Lars is recovering with his friends in Hades. I nailed him to the back door. Go see for yourselves on the way out. Just take nothing more from the home and leave Arria with me. Her corpse is worth nothing now to you."

The other brigands grumbled at his request, but the wiser leader gestured for them to keep quiet. They would take their stashes of hidden booty, but Falco was more concerned with their gear and Varro's family death masks.

In the end, he collected what he could carry of their gear and Varro's belongings. He strapped on his chain shirt, which had not been tangled despite poor storage. The shields were too large to carry, and the helmets too bulky. Smoke now reached inside the house, and Falco knew he could only take weapons along with a few smaller items.

As the fire on the wall caught, Falco worked with grim patience to fashion his scutum into a sled for Arria's body. Even as the heat pricked at his exposed flesh, and the fear of fire made him wince, he carefully set Arria on the scutum. The other brigands had removed the spikes and bar from the gate, which now hung open to the cool darkness.

Falco left Varro's villa just as the flame spread to the front gate. He dragged Arria across the grass behind him, the shield bumping and rocking on the uneven ground. At times he had to pause and adjust her corpse.

He never looked behind again.

At length, he arrived at the stand of cypress trees close to the villa. Among the gear he had packed was also a spade taken from the garden. He set to work, digging into the soft earth beneath the trees. As exhausted as he was, he forced himself until his shoulders and back burned. His hamstrings screamed in pain. But he dug until he stood shoulder-deep in the hole.

It was near dawn when he completed Arria's burial. He packed the mound with the spade ensuring no animal would dig it up. Once satisfied, he plunged the spade into the earth, then collapsed beneath the cypress trees.

The sky above turned light purple, and the stars glittered as they retreated from the encroaching sun pressing at the eastern horizon.

He wondered how everything had gone so badly. No matter how he retraced his steps, he could not see other choices that made more sense. Even Arria's death. She had been opportunistic and deceitful, and probably would've been fine to let him die if it was within her power. Yet, he did not wish the same for her.

It was not his place to decide her fate. That was for Varro.

Now her death would forever haunt him. His inept actions had cost Varro his home, his best slave, and his sister. He had also scuttled their primary mission by killing Longus. No one would welcome him back with so many disasters to his name.

What limit did Varro have on forgiveness? He was vengeful and suspicious; years of treachery and bloodshed had eroded his kindness to reveal a core harder than anything Falco would've guessed. If he told Varro the truth, would it be the end of their friendship?

And if he would not tell Varro the truth, then what was his own capacity to carry a secret for the rest of his life? And what was his limit on forgiveness for himself?

There were no answers in the dying starlight above him. Instead, he felt warm tears leak from his eyes. He closed them and let a dreadful, black sleep overtake him.

21

Varro's legs took three long bounds before launching him into the air. While Longus and his thugs had disarmed him, they had failed to restrain him. He now leaped up to the arena's edge where torches guttered in a draft from an unseen opening.

His rage and fear propelled him. The masked patrician retreated, his expression hidden behind a perpetual visage of sorrow. Varro's hands slapped against the hard stone of the arena edge.

But one slipped free and his body slammed against the stone wall as he barely held on. Now he dangled by his sword arm, lacking any strength to pull himself up, never mind maintain his grip.

He slid down the cold wall and landed on his feet, before flopping backward onto the packed earth floor.

The patrician now stepped back to his position against the edge of the arena. He laughed.

"A fine display of strength and acrobatics. But you are not the first to attempt a leap up from the floor. This was once a private arena for games to entertain the elites. It has served many purposes over the years since."

Varro's tailbone protested the humiliating fall. But his thoughts were consumed with other fears. He had revealed his intentions and was now at the mercy of his captor. The arena floor felt twice as wide and empty than a moment ago.

"I had hopes you might join us," the patrician said. From Varro's low vantage directly below, he seemed elongated against the dark ceiling. "Perhaps with more time to reveal certain truths, you might have come around. But you forced my hand tonight. It is a pity to waste a precious resource. You are a talented man, and from all accounts beloved of the gods. I must make sacrifices to beg their forgiveness."

A metallic crash echoed behind Varro, causing him to leap in shock. The grate hummed as it settled over the archway where he had entered. He whirled to face the other grate, expecting it to open and a new threat to emerge from the violet gloom beyond.

Instead, the masked patrician now raised something in his hand. He had selected it from the objects Varro had noticed hidden behind the arena wall.

He raised a thin javelin in a throwing grip.

"Let's see if this old man still has his skill. I was unmatched in my youth. Tonight, you will make easy practice for a rusty arm."

Varro had nowhere to take cover and no escape.

The patrician cocked his arm, and Varro realized he had one choice.

He leaped again for the wall, just at the moment the javelin streaked down for him.

Bright pain skimmed across the top of his shoulder as he flew through the air. He cried out in both pain and desperation. The weapon had grazed him and now spun away out of his vision.

Once more, both hands slapped onto the arena wall edge and forced the patrician back as he too howled in shock. Varro's body endured another jarring slam against the stone wall. The cut on his shoulder burned as he summoned all his might to remain in place.

"Laudable persistence," the masked patrician said. He remained out of sight as Varro dangled from the edge, but his voice drew closer.

"Yet ultimately doomed. I see you have gone all these years without the loss of a digit. Let's correct that now."

Varro had expected as much, leaving both hands set out on the stone wall like offerings at a butcher's market. He needed time to gather strength and hook his leg onto the wall. Then he would be across it and on even footing with his enemy.

But he also knew his enemy wouldn't delay.

"At this range, I should just put a javelin through your neck," the patrician said. His shadow now slid over Varro and clammy hands cupped over his trembling grip. "But this arena was constructed for entertainment. I have a sheaf of javelins that won't run out before your strength does."

Varro considered dropping again, but it would be surrendering to death in the open arena. He still was unsure if other guards remained out of sight or what opposition he would face if he reached the arena seating.

The clammy hands clasped over his own pulled away.

"Just one finger will do."

Varro heard the clack of a wooden javelin against stone, and then the hiss of a blade drawn from its sheath. His exposed fingers tingled as he struggled to keep his grip on the edge of the wall. He had a single moment to decide whether to drop or fight, but he could see no way to get over the wall in time.

Then he remembered the torches.

The long shafts were set into holes set at regular intervals along the arena edge. They leaned out to illuminate the floor below. Two flanked either of his hands, and Varro knew immediately what to do.

Just as the cold bronze blade touched his left little finger, Varro hauled himself up and snatched the torch out of its holder.

He now wielded it like a dagger and stabbed it at the patrician hovering over his hand, evidently relishing the moment before Varro's mutilation. Despite his advanced age and his voluminous toga, the patrician skirted aside in time to avoid a blow from the torch. But its flames licked his skin and clothing, causing him to scream in horror as he recoiled.

Now Varro used his momentum to swing his right leg over the edge of the arena wall. With desperation fueling him, he lifted over the edge. He dropped the torch as he hauled himself over the side to land on the floor beside a stone bench.

The patrician batted at his toga, which had caught flame. Barely a thumb-length of cloth burned, but it caused panic nonetheless. His right shoulder smoldered as he patted out the fire.

Varro scrambled back and snatched at one of the dozen javelins knocked to the floor. He snatched one as he used a stone bench to raise himself to his feet. Simultaneously, the masked patrician had stumbled and now lay exposed with his mask halfway up his face. He clawed at it, trying to set the eyeholes right.

Varro took the javelin in both hands like a spear and lowered it at his enemy.

"Now, I will remove that mask as I promised."

The patrician cried out and raised both hands to protect his face, forgetting his mask.

"Help me!"

Two figures detached themselves from the shadows at the rear of the arena seating. They both dressed in black tunics and concealed their faces with black cloth. But Varro saw the shine of bronze swords in both of their hands.

They leaped down between the stair-like seating, spreading out to flank him.

Varro understood he was still cornered, and taking the patrician as a hostage was his best solution.

Yet, in the moment he had turned aside, the masked patrician had scuttled away. He was now out of easy reach and his two guards were fast approaching. Their sandaled feet echoed through the empty arena. For a moment, it was the only sound, the echoes of approaching death.

Varro hurled his javelin at the attacker to his left. The long white missile sailed up into the shadows. The enemy easily dodged but stumbled amid the stone benches.

He snatched another javelin in time for the second attacker to reach him.

Strangely blue eyes met his, and they were filled with hatred.

A javelin was too long for in-close fighting, but his enemy's sword was perfectly suited to it. Rather than engage him, Varro slipped away from a vicious strike and grabbed the attacker by his arm. He then used the enemy's momentum to hurl him over the side of the arena wall. A scream of surprise vanished behind Varro as he turned to meet the other enemy.

He had recovered and bounded down to the edge. Varro's easy handling of his companion did not deter him.

He was a stocky man, and like his companion, wore a black mask that revealed only pale eyes regarding him with repugnance. His blade flashed and drove Varro against the arena wall as he dodged away. But a new strike followed on the first, and he was forced to parry with his javelin.

The sword snapped the javelin in half, leaving only useless wood in Varro's grip. He flung this at his opponent to buy him time. But his relentless enemy charged forward with his sword held low.

Again, he forced Varro to sidestep the murderous blow. The space between the arena wall and stone benches left little room for maneuver. If he could unbalance his attacker, then he might capture his sword. In the same way, a single misstep would cause him to topple.

He jumped up to the first stone bench to gain a height advantage. Of course, without a shield, his attacker could easily nullify this by slicing his legs. And this is exactly what he attempted.

Again, Varro sidestepped but also kicked at the extended sword arm. It landed with a soft thud, but his attacker held on to the blade.

Conversely, Varro lost his footing. He sprawled out on the bench, breaking his fall with his arms as he did. It was a reflex, and now he lay exposed before his enemy with his arm behind.

The black-masked attacker shouted with victory and raised his sword to drive it into Varro's gut.

In the narrow aisle between benches, he had no way to flip aside.

Yet before the blade plunged into his stomach, the masked

attacker arched his back and screamed. Rather than stick his blade into Varro's flesh, he collapsed atop him.

Varro screamed in shock, expecting a sword to impale him. He felt the fresh blood rushing over his chest and neck, but it was not his own. Instead, his attacker writhed atop Varro. His screams blasted into Varro's ears, overwhelming the shouts he heard from beyond.

At last, he shoved the body away, flipping it onto the floor between stone benches. Yet his enemy rebounded, springing back to expose a white javelin buried between his shoulder blades. He then cursed as he reached for the weapon buried in his back, but then slumped in death.

"Are you all right, Varro?"

He sat up to the familiar voice of Senator Flamininus. Racing down the stone benches, the senator led at least ten other men. They dressed in tunics as black as Varro's enemies' but wore them in a soldier's style, high up the thigh. They carried drawn swords and wore bronze chest guards.

Flamininus dressed in a simple tunic of gray, eschewing any armor but wearing his sword harness. His left hand clutched two more javelins and his men likewise carried more.

Varro wiped away the blood that had pooled around his neck and then searched for the masked patrician. As expected, he was nowhere to be found.

As Flamininus arrived, his soulful eyes filled with genuine concern, he seemed to understand who Varro was searching for.

"I'm afraid I arrived too late to catch him. Did you at least get a look beneath the mask?"

Varro blinked at his commander, whose voice echoed through the arena along with the patter of his soldiers' feet. They spread out into the dark corners, searching for hidden threats.

"No, sir. His mask never fell from his face and only lifted high enough for me to see his mouth."

Flamininus nodded, then helped Varro up to where he stood on the higher bench.

"It seems I got here just in time. Sorry for the delay, but I had trouble finding this place."

At first, Varro frowned, not understanding how the senator knew to find him here. Then realization chilled him.

"I was the bait in a trap, sir. But the trap failed to close in time."

The senator lowered his head, and his silence was his answer.

"Is Curio unharmed?"

Flamininus's sullen expression now brightened. "We have him. Other than a nasty knock on the head, he did not suffer much. He is recovering in my home. Your shoulder is cut. Is it bad?"

Varro glanced at the burning line of red on his right shoulder. "It's nothing, sir. Just one more memory to carry on my body."

"I'm sorry about all of this deceit. But I tried to make the ruse as convincing as possible, which would include telling you nothing of it. So, I had you come in a disguise that would certainly attract our opposition's attention. From there, we stayed as close as possible without giving ourselves away. Longus eluded us once more and left Curio behind to throw us off the chase. We might not have achieved our ultimate objective but the night was not a complete loss."

Varro stepped down and leaned over the side of the arena. At the bottom was the enemy he had thrown over the side, but he was dead. The fall had not killed him. Rather, he had taken his own life from the looks of it. Both hands still gripped the dagger he had driven into his stomach and a deep pool of blood under his body reflected the torchlight.

"Then I don't understand, sir. I thought you meant this one would be a good captive for interrogation. Neither of these men seemed like the hired thugs I've been dealing with. I think these two were genuinely committed to their cause."

Flamininus's eyes glittered as he stepped down to join Varro. He glanced over the side at the body on the arena floor. "Taking them captive would've been ideal, but the gods decided otherwise tonight. I am speaking about the list. Curio says you discovered it in that burned-out building."

Varro rubbed his chin.

"Sir, Curio has been hit in the head and is not remembering things clearly. I found a scrap of vellum with names we already know, and the initials of another name we do not. Longus had burned the letter."

The radiant glow on the senator's face diminished but did not vanish.

"Even so, initials might be enough to determine his next victim. Also, we've dealt this group a hard blow tonight. We've exposed Longus, killed more of his dedicated followers, and nearly cornered his leader."

"That is optimistic, sir. I don't feel that we achieved as much as you think we have. That masked man has considerable resources. Just look at this place. He must also control that abandoned house and the home next to it."

"Just so," Flamininus said. "We can trace the owners of those properties to eventually find a clue to his identity. Somewhere he must have revealed himself, even if he worked through agents."

The other soldiers scouring the arena called back to Flamininus to report they found nothing other than an exit. The senator ordered them to follow it and hopefully catch the masked man. But Varro knew they would not catch him so easily.

"Sir, he said many things to me before you arrived."

Varro spoke in guarded language, unsure of what he should reveal. He hoped Flamininus would prompt him, and perhaps even confirm Varro's suspicions without having to directly ask.

Flamininus folded his arms and leaned against the arena wall. "I'm certain he had much to say to you. No doubt, he attempted to turn you against Servus Capax."

"He did, sir. But of course, I have a tattoo now. I can't waste the money I spent on it."

For an instant Flamininus seemed confused, then his eyes drifted to Varro's arm.

"Of course not. Perhaps I should rethink my position on it."

He spoke with a thin smile that another might mistake for sarcasm. But after so many years, Varro had learned to read his expression and understood Flamininus had just made peace with Varro's rogue decision.

"Sir, after everything he said, much of it being madness, I believe I understand his goals. I know what Longus will do next. I need a quiet moment to put my thoughts together."

"Then would the ride back to my home be enough time for your thoughts to congeal?"

"I believe so, sir. That and a cup of wine from your reserves should work."

So, Flamininus left Varro to sit on a bench while one of his men tended the cut on his shoulder. Others recovered the two enemy bodies. These would be examined for tattoos or other telltale marks that might reveal more of their history. Varro knew both were legionaries just from the way they wore their tunics.

The senator had gone with an escort of his men to follow the escape passage, and soon returned shaking his head. It had simply exited into another home and onto a back street. Of course, the home was unoccupied and maintained only as a front.

"I knew this arena existed," Flamininus said when he rejoined Varro. "But I thought it sealed up long ago. Yet another line of investigation for us to follow. Don't worry, I see from your expression you'd rather not be assigned that duty. I'll keep you close to the fighting, where you do best."

"If I keep getting my flesh cut away, I don't know how much fighting will be left in me."

The senator led Varro out of the underground arena, leaving half of his men behind to clean up and remove the bodies. Outside, Varro did not recognize the neighborhood. Stars still filled the sky though it lightened with a hint of dawn. They stepped into a covered carriage and rode in silence through empty streets back to the Palatine Hill and the comforts of Flamininus's home.

He directed Varro to a room off the central atrium. They spoke in hushed voices since the senator's family was asleep upstairs. "I will be with you shortly. Curio is inside."

Varro found Curio stretched out on a green couch. A slave sat in the corner, a quiet and small young man dressed in a clean gray tunic. He stood when Varro entered, but Curio remained lying on his back and staring at the ceiling.

"I've got a lump on my head," Curio said. "What was your prize?"

Finding a chair by a table, Varro dragged it beside his diminutive friend and sat.

"Just bruise and a cut." He checked the bandage wrapped over his shoulder and under his arm. A tiny spot of red showed through it. "It doesn't even require a stitch."

Curio nodded but remained staring vacantly at the ceiling with his hands folded comfortably over his stomach.

"The senator says we were bait in a trap. You were right."

"A poor trap, since Longus got away and we are no closer to catching him. Though the senator feels it was worth risking our lives for."

Again, Curio only nodded in silence. They sat together, Varro collecting his thoughts and Curio letting his eyes close. They had not slept for nearly twenty-four hours. Varro felt not only the pull of sleep but a growl in his belly. He hoped Flamininus would return with something to eat.

His mind turned over all that he had seen and heard this night. This society of the serpent, with its imagery of shedding skin and healing, wanted to destroy the Republic rather than let it crumble. He fished out the scrap of vellum with the names of senators already threatened and the initials that faded into the burned edge. The letters M and E seemed familiar, but he struggled to connect them to a name. He flattened out the wrinkled vellum on his thigh and considered.

The original letter being written in Punic meant that Longus was either a Carthaginian or a well-educated Roman citizen. He assumed the latter based on Longus's accent and word choice. This made sense, considering one of his former accomplices was Marcellus Paullus. Also, Longus had to return to retrieve the lost page of his letter. This suggested he had not committed all the instructions to memory at that time. Once he did, he burned the letter. So, this plan was only recently revealed to him. He wondered if Longus took over the mission from Paullus, meaning if Paullus ever revived he would be a key source of information.

Curio shifted on the couch and snored lightly. Varro envied him but could find no rest until he worked through this puzzle.

Longus and his master created a list of senators they wanted killed to speed the fall of the Republic. While Varro understood the value of killing someone as powerful as Flaccus or as key to Rome's defense as Consul Minucius, he did not understand Facilis's death. Yet there had to be a common thread that connected these three men and the two others still on their list.

He held the scrap up again and skimmed his finger across the burned vellum. He imagined the complete letter, written in Punic script. Carthage was also involved, but to what end?

Then it struck him.

"Curio, do you remember how much Consul Cato despised Carthage?"

Curio's snoring continued, and Varro shook him awake and repeated his question.

"I do," he said. "Why did you wake me up for that? For once, I was having a dream of beautiful women feeding me figs. Not the usual blood and guts nightmare."

"Right, and Cato shares that hatred with his mentor, Flaccus. And Flaccus was a friend of Facilis, who must have shared a similar view. Do you see? They are targeting senators who violently oppose Carthage."

Curio yawned and now sat up on the couch. He glanced at the slave as if to ask whether they should speak in front of him. "Doesn't everyone hate Carthage? Even so, killing Cato and his friends would not end the Republic."

Varro rubbed the back of his neck. Of course, Curio was correct. There had to be more to it than he understood.

"If they are eliminating senators who want to destroy Carthage, then it points to a wider problem. Carthage must be plotting something. Not directly in opposition to Rome, but something that would be provocative enough that hostile senators would call for action against them."

Curio stretched and sat back on the couch. "So, let's go burn down Carthage for good."

The door opened, and Senator Flamininus entered. He paused at Curio's statement and raised his brows in surprise.

Varro stood and held out the vellum scrap.

"I know the names of the senators. And I know how they plan to bring down the Republic."

22

Senator Flamininus handed silver cups to both Varro and Curio as they sat around the table with a burned vellum scrap at its center. It was early morning, but the only light in the room came from bronze lamps shaped like bulls, with the flames rising from their nostrils. The senator had dismissed his slave and left instructions that no one was to disturb them.

Along with the wine, Flamininus had brought a small board of white bread and cheese. But he seemed to hold this hostage to Varro's explanation. It sat to his right, and away from the others. Varro's mouth salivated at the sight of it.

He had explained all he had shared with Curio, and the senator listened intently. He did not ask questions, as was usual for him. But he leaned forward, lips pressed tight against the one question that fought for his voice. Varro at last answered it for him.

"Your name is not on that list, sir. At least, for now. Some senators would seize upon any provocation from Carthage. All of them must be removed before their plot can be enacted. Facilis is the most unfortunate of these. Minucius is safe for the moment. Longus attempted to remove Flaccus before his infected wound overtook him, and now he too is alert. Of the last two names, without a doubt, Proconsul Cato must be one."

Flamininus closed his eyes and nodded. "Of all the men you have named, he is the most vociferous. I agree with your assessment. And the last name?"

"Consul Merula. He is leading the war against the Boii. His initials are on this vellum."

Varro tapped the strip of vellum, and Flamininus dragged it closer to the bull lamp.

"He is not known for strong opposition to Carthage."

"But he is leading the defense of Rome. The same as Consul Minucius. Sir, whatever will happen in Carthage must draw Rome's attention. But what if our attention could not be spared? What if the Ligurians and the Boii unite to overrun the north? What if brigands massing to the east converge on Rome? Will the people care for something happening so far away when facing such immediate threats?"

Flamininus blinked, his eyes widening in realization.

"Hannibal. Carthage will bring back Hannibal."

Varro gave a solemn nod. "Who else could hasten the destruction of the Republic?"

"Well, they are fools to believe we would not respond to Hannibal returning to Carthage." Varro saw the resolution in Flamininus's eyes which caught the orange flame from the bull lamps.

"Sir, I do not pretend to understand the complexities of government. But I know what most men do, that Hannibal is exiled. If he is to return, some among the Carthaginian elite must plan a coup for that to happen. It seems our own are willing to aid in that effort."

"We would not ignore Hannibal's return," Flamininus said. "Unless we had barbarians and brigands pressing us from all sides. By Jupiter, Varro! We need confirmation of this. Do you know Hannibal is currently with the Selucids? They must also be in support."

Flamininus now slid the board of bread and cheese to Varro and Curio, who did not hesitate to eat.

The soft white bread melted in Varro's over-salivating mouth. He crammed as much in as he could, his gurgling stomach eager for more. Curio likewise roused from his sleepiness to wipe out the cheese and bread.

"I know you are both tired and hungry," Flamininus said. "I promise, you may rest this morning and when you awaken, I will stuff you full of figs and olives."

"I was just dreaming of figs," Curio said with his mouth full.

Flamininus chuckled. "Well, after your pleasant dream, you both must ride with all urgency to Consul Merula. From what you described, Longus is likely heading to him."

Varro wiped his mouth with the back of his wrist before answering.

"He was dressed as a legionary when I last saw him. He mentioned a higher calling, and I assume that refers to his plan to eliminate the senators on his list. Merula seems the likely candidate."

"Then you must prevent that from happening, and capture Longus for interrogation. If you can deliver him to me, that would be ideal. But don't let him slip away before getting everything we can from him. If you must interrogate him in the field, then do so."

After finishing the last of the bread and wine, Varro hesitated to mention Falco. He knew they had broken Flamininus's trust by sending Falco to handle his sister's ransom. But he did not want to leave on an important mission without him. He also needed to handle his sister's ransom. Time did not allow for it, but he realized this was his fault.

Their discussion ended with Flamininus assigning them a room and a servant to attend to them. They could sleep until midmorning when the senator would have horses and gear requisitioned for their urgent mission.

"I will prepare a third horse should Falco return in time." Flamininus gave Varro a stern look. "He has been gone overlong, and that cannot bode well for your sister. I pray you made the correct decision, Varro."

Ending on that gloomy note led Varro into dark dreams when he at last fell asleep. Soon, he awakened to Curio shaking him by his uninjured shoulder, and shouted in terror. Curio backed away, giving him a sympathetic smile. They stared at each other in silence for a moment. All of them routinely suffered from nightmares earned from the terrors of war and it was not uncommon to wake each other to end a bad dream.

"I was already awake, so when the servant came to fetch us, I sent him away and let you sleep. But there is good news. Falco has returned."

Varro shot up from the comfortable feathered mattress, nightmares and hunger forgotten. Their room was small in comparison to the grander chambers upstairs. This was still a servant's quarters, even if the appointments were luxurious. He pulled on his tunic and laced his sandals while Curio shared what he knew.

"He was with the other clients at Flamininus's door this morning. I guess he waited all night to enter Rome and came directly here."

"I wish the senator awakened me the moment he arrived. Did he bring Arria?"

Curio turned over both hands and shrugged, then they followed a servant back into Flamininus's garden where Falco waited alone.

He was not facing them, instead he stared blankly into a tall bush of yellow flowers. The late morning sun draped across his shoulders, which slumped in a posture of defeat. He clasped both hands behind his back as if inspecting the flowers inches from his nose.

Varro's stomach tightened, knowing how bad the news must be.

"And Siculus is not with him, either." He whispered the words to himself, but Curio replied.

"Maybe he has gone to fetch breakfast."

It wasn't until they stood an arm's length away from Falco that he turned. His face was puffy and reddened as well as bruised. Varro noted the thin cuts around his wrists, evidence of narrowly avoided blades.

Falco's heavy brows shaded his eyes, but they still glinted with the sun. All three of them stood in silence, understanding what news Falco had brought.

"I'm sorry, Varro. She didn't make it out alive."

Varro had not seen or thought of his sister in nearly a decade, yet news of her death sent him crashing down onto the stone bench nearby. Both Falco and Curio rushed to stabilize him.

"Are you certain?"

Falco swallowed hard, his thick brows furrowing. "I buried her myself. Under the cypress trees along the path to your villa."

Varro nodded, unsure of what he should do. Beyond the garden walls, Rome was full of life. He heard happy voices mingled with the sound of traffic passing along well-maintained streets. Surely, not all of Rome was so idyllic as this Palatine Hill. Yet, it seemed impossible that such horrible news could be delivered in such a beautiful environment.

His voice was hoarse and dry when he spoke at last.

"And Siculus?"

"Gone. I don't know where."

The three of them sat crowded on a single bench. Varro was aware of birds hopping between branches in the trees overhead. He felt as if they were listening in, each one vying for the best position to view his reaction. Maybe they were the gods themselves in disguise, eager to see his defeat.

"It's all my fault," Varro said. "I should have paid the ransom straightaway. Instead, I put a price on my sister's life and then refused to pay it."

He stared at his feet as he spoke, and the birds chirped in response to his self-recrimination. But Falco drew a sharp breath.

"Why don't you let me tell the whole story before you start blaming yourself."

Falco began his story with a long sigh, starting from the first rainy days of his attempt to rescue Arria. All the while, he stared at his feet and never looked up.

The only bright spot in the entire story was learning Falco had at last nailed Lars to his gate door and that the villa burned down. After such carnage, he would never rebuild it in the same spot. His harvest might still be salvageable, but after all else that happened, he could not imagine continuing with the farm.

"So, Lars killed Arria rather than accept a lower ransom?" Varro found the brigand's greed inconceivable. "It's as if he set it so high that I could not pay without destroying my finances."

"He wouldn't budge," Falco said. "And when I told him the same, he simply cut Arria's throat and tried to take me as a substitute hostage. What a fool. If you couldn't pay it for your own sister, then you couldn't pay it for me."

Varro shook his head and patted Falco on his strong shoulder.

"The truth is I could have paid and had it been you I would not have hesitated. I am the definition of greed. I allowed my sister to die rather than part with any of my fortune. How much lower can I sink?"

Both Falco and Curio groaned in disagreement. Curio was swift to fill in Falco's awkward pause.

"Your decision was not unreasonable. No sane person would demand that much. We all expected him to negotiate, given the amount demanded. That's how negotiations work. You start high and work down to what you want."

Curio used his hands to measure the height of an imaginary pile of silver then lowered it step by step.

"Lars was supposed to drop his demand but didn't play the game. It cost him his life."

Pursing his lips, Varro considered the truth of it. Nevertheless, he would not forgive himself. Then he considered Falco and how badly he must feel. So he acted more cheered than he felt.

"I have Falco to thank for that mercy. You avenged my sister. I would never be able to rest if Lars were still out there."

He squeezed Falco's shoulder and he winced as if it pained him. But Varro kept his grip tight, grateful for the courage and persistence his friend had shown.

"I know you did all you could. You are blameless in all this. Arria was my responsibility, not yours. I can't repay you for all you suffered on my behalf."

Falco grimaced. "Well, never mind it. I failed you, after all. And I lost your best slave, too. Then there's your burned-down villa. I think repayment lies with me."

Servants interrupted their meeting, setting out tables and delivering plates of meats and fish along with jugs of wine. Varro was still hungry and tired but felt guilty anticipating the food. How could he feast knowing that he had allowed his sister to die? The three of them stepped back to allow the slaves room to complete their tasks, and at last, they offered couches for them to begin their meal.

When they settled, Varro could see Falco had more on his mind and prompted him to speak.

"Well, there is more bad news. It seems Longus had involved himself with the brigands. I overheard Lars talking about working for the snakes, and then Longus arrived at your villa the day I broke out."

Falco's eyes fluttered and he looked aside while covering his mouth with his hand.

"They plotted together in the room next to where I was held. Your bedroom."

Varro looked at Curio, who stared back in confusion.

"The walls in my room are certainly thin enough to hear conversation," Varro said. "But are you sure it was Longus? How long ago was this?"

"I lost track of the days, for the love of Jupiter. It wasn't recent. Maybe three days ago. When I escaped, not only did I kill Lars but I accidentally killed Longus. Smashed his skull open with your gate bar. I didn't tell the senator that part yet. I figured you'd want to know first."

"That's impossible. Curio and I just confronted him yesterday."

Now Falco dropped his hand from his mouth.

"No, that's impossible. I know a dead man when I see one."

"But do you know Longus when you see him?" Varro chuckled. "Did he have a broken tooth and a festering cut across his belly? Because I gave him both, and the man I spoke with last night was certainly Longus."

Falco titled his head in thought. "I got a good look at him. But I've only ever seen him in bad lighting. So, maybe I was wrong."

He slapped his thigh, his face brightening. "Great news! Well, that's one less thing I've got to worry about keeping straight."

Varro tilted his head. "What do you mean by keeping things straight?"

"Don't pounce on me like that!" Falco shouted, shocking Varro at his outburst. "I just misspoke, for fuck's sake. I thought I had scuttled the mission by killing Longus."

Falco glared at him as if insulted, and if Varro didn't know better, seemed on the verge of tears. When he seemed calm again, Varro gestured to the table.

"You've got to be as hungry as I am. Let's eat. I'm sure the man you killed wasn't Longus at all."

They fell to silence and the temptations of the hot food laid out for them.

Flamininus joined them just after they started. Varro and the others were hesitant to grab too much to start, but hunger overwhelmed them and soon their plates were full. When Varro's stomach bulged and he leaned back on his couch, Flamininus at last spoke.

"I learned the basics from Falco earlier this morning. I'm terribly sorry about your sister, Varro."

All he could do was to nod in thanks. The senator's voice lacked any hint of condemnation, but he felt it nonetheless.

"I must go to my mother and inform my niece. She is so young. How do I tell her she has become an orphan?"

Flamininus's soulful eyes met his, and he patted Varro on his forearm.

"She is not an orphan yet. She has her grandmother and you. As for going to her mother, I will ensure she understands the situation. But you do not have time now. While you were in discussion, I requisitioned gear and a pack horse to be prepared by the east gate. You must leave immediately and protect Consul Merula. Again, I have written a letter introducing your credentials. By now, he might have heard of the attempt on his fellow consul's life. I'm certain he will give you the freedom of his camp, considering the stakes. But you cannot lose time. Longus most certainly departed at dawn this morning when the gates opened, if not earlier by some illegal means. If you can catch him before he reaches Merula, all the better."

Varro acknowledged his orders, but as the shock of Arria's death wore off, he reconsidered his guilt. Certainly, he had made a mistake sending Siculus and Falco in his stead. However, Flamininus had never sent the guard reinforcements he promised. If his villa had been better guarded, perhaps they might have repelled Lars and his traitors. The senator bore partial responsibility for Arria's murder. Yet, he resolved to set aside those corrosive thoughts for now.

He felt the sting of the masked patrician's accusations. It would be imprudent to spoil his relationship with Flamininus.

"You know where my mother is?"

"Of course, her husband is well known to me." Flamininus's face reddened, and he straightened up on his couch. "I should say her current husband. I understand there is some complexity between you and your mother, which I have respected these years. But, yes, I know her residence. I know the same for Falco and Curio as well. At the very least, I must know who to contact if needed."

Now all three of them sat up from their couches with white faces. Falco had always been distant from his family. Curio never mentioned family other than secondary relations that informed his wide social network. But over these many years, it seemed as if Curio had no other family. Yet, Flamininus had investigated all of them. This should not have surprised Varro as much as it did.

"Sir, there would be no need to contact my mother if I died. She belongs to another man and another family now."

Flamininus inclined his head and then waved off the subject.

"You've no time to lose. It is three of you against Longus, who is already suffering a mortal wound. Stop him before he can carry out his final act of treason. Arrange yourselves this morning and leave at once."

With their orders delivered, and their bellies filled, they returned to their room to prepare. Falco had little to do and instead caught up with Varro on all that had happened while he was away. Their moods had improved by the time they said farewell to the senator, then started through the streets of Rome toward the east gate. They had a mission to complete. All else was a distraction.

And Longus was owed revenge.

They met with Flamininus's agents by the gate, and Varro was astounded with the level of preparations. They had sacks of provisions along with skins of concentrated wine, and laborers had just finished packing these on a chestnut horse that also carried their tent and other survival gear. Mail shirts were too personal to acquire on short notice. But the senator had prepared a full infantry kit of black-painted scuta, honed gladii, and unmarked pugiones, along with feathered helmets suited to their rank. Even Senator Flaccus had sent a dozen infantrymen who would serve as an escort through the hills and territory rife with brigands.

They sorted their gear and introduced themselves to their escorts, then departed by the east gate just before noon.

"This is one of the best-provisioned missions I've been on," Falco said, his usual demeanor restored from the gloomier one this morning.

"It's amazing what the Senate can do when they feel personally threatened," Varro said.

They marched at top speed between their escorts, who were young men just returned from the legion. Some had served in Iberia and others in Greece. They understood Varro and the rest were centurions on an important mission. As typical soldiers, they only wanted to know what they must do to collect a generous payday. Flaccus apparently spared no expense on them.

They followed the main roads filled with traffic headed both in and out of the city. Merchants and travelers carried on their business as if the barbarian threats to the north did not exist. Varro thought back to Pisa and its desperate conditions. How easily it could become Rome, and all these confident people would not walk so easily beneath the cheerful midday sun. Their freedom and way of life rested on the shoulders of legionaries and their allies. As he passed these columns, he searched the faces bobbing past him. He didn't know what he sought. Maybe a friend or an enemy? It seemed he could no longer look at others without suspicion. Longus and his accomplices might hide among any of these people, and he would never know. Right now, the cloaked woman riding past him on the back of a mule might be a killer in disguise. She might be the one to tip the Republic into chaos.

They skirted the road that would lead to their villas. Fortunately, their escorts agreed it was faster to take a more direct route to the northeast. Varro had no desire to look upon the ruins of his erstwhile home. While he had not acknowledged it as such yet, he despaired at its loss. His sister had gone there seeking protection and a new life. Instead, she died miserably at the hands of brigands and traitors. Perhaps after handling Longus, he would have the stomach to visit the ruins and the nerve to apologize to his sister over her lonely grave.

At points along the journey, they spotted figures on the horizon watching them. Even by the end of the first day, men shadowed their path, reappearing whenever the terrain expanded their view.

"We better find a defensible position for our camp," Varro said to his escorts. "You're all fresh out of the legion, so you know the procedure. If you don't have stakes with you, then let's use the last light of the day to forage for replacements. Given the urgency of our mission, we won't be sleeping the full night. Still, we must be prepared."

Falco whispered, leaning into Varro while their escorts began trenching at the top of a ridge. "Once I thought they were all the brigands around. Now, there might be ten times what we can see."

Both he and Falco stared across the distance at a dark line of men gathered on a ridge matching their own. Throughout the day, they had not approached, being about equally matched in numbers from what he could determine at this distance. Brigands liked nothing better than overwhelming odds in their favor.

"For now, they are studying us." Varro lifted off his helmet and set it under his arm. "They're wondering if we're worth attacking."

"Or they could be scouts for a larger group of brigands." Falco turned his back and pointed toward the nascent camp. "In any case, we are fifteen armed men in a fortified camp. Unless they come back with fifty of their friends, they'll just be watching us tonight."

Varro continued to stare at the purple silhouettes across the waving grass that swept in a broken carpet to the opposite ridge. The figures peeled away, vanishing over the ridge out of sight.

"And we will watch them," he said.

23

They broke camp in the predawn hours when the sky was dark and starless. Their escorts were not typical legionaries, in that they did not need encouragement to leave their tents, pull up the stakes, and resume the march in darkness. They were eager to earn their payday, and likely just as eager to gamble it away.

Varro led them at the fastest march they could sustain in darkness. When the sun rose and revealed the path ahead, they would reach their full pace. Roman infantry regularly astounded their enemies with their speed on foot. Varro's legs were still in good shape from Pisa, and his escorts were likewise accustomed to long marches. He was confident they would reach Consul Merula in time.

They followed the ridge on the opposite side from where they had spotted the brigands. The twilight concealed them for now, but a keen eye might still spot them against a brightening sky. The guides ahead warned of the upcoming hills and the need for better light to traverse them.

While he expected to reach Merula before Longus could act, he could not delay for ideal conditions and maintained their pace.

While they marched, Falco shared the news of his own villa's destruction.

"I haven't seen it myself, and maybe I don't want to. But all my guards are dead and no one's there to defend the place. Seems like we're going to be starting over or moving in with Curio."

"You're both welcome to stay with me," Curio said, marching directly behind them. "You will find my rent is quite reasonable. And if you can't pay, you can always work it off."

Varro gave a grim smile. "I doubt your villa is in any better condition than ours. The snakes are organizing brigands in this region, encouraging them to violence and likely promising unreasonable spoils. It's part of their plan to create panic and distraction, just like prolonging the wars in the north will do. I'm sorry, Curio. I don't think any lightly defended farm here will remain intact for long."

Curio cursed under his breath, and the three of them fell silent again. After all, their conversation drew sidelong glances from the men they had commanded to silence on the march.

When the sun pushed at the eastern horizon, Varro drew the column to a halt. The so-called hills lay before them, and he wanted everyone rested before navigating the narrow passes to the other side.

He hesitated to call them hills. They were rocky and steep piles of earth that would eventually become the Apennines. Upon clearing these hills, they would take well-traveled passes through those mountains to reach the eastern coast, where they would follow it north to Consul Merula. It was a week-long journey that Varro had to cut down to half that time.

After conferring with his escorts, they sent two men ahead to scout the pass. But it would be a cursory examination. The scouts would probe ahead, then return to signal the advance before heading out again. It was the best they could do, given their time constraints.

The first two rotations went smoothly, and the scouts returned with reports of clear paths. They navigated a twisting pass cutting between the steep walls of the surrounding hills. If ever there was a place for an ambush, Varro determined this was it. Lower ledges protected the high sides, blocking any easy way up. Trees and heavy brush lined the top of the pass, providing cover to anyone hiding there. The pass itself was narrow with uneven ground strewn with rocks and ruts.

Yet their column forged ahead, keeping a swift pace despite the uncertain footing. Falco's caligae crunched on the grit as he plodded along beside Varro.

"I hate to admit it, but I've got a stitch in my side. This pace is going to kill me."

And then Varro stopped.

Curio bumped into him as Falco and those escorts in the lead continued ahead. But those in the rear pulled up short.

He no longer saw the rocky pass, and instead his mind's eye plunged him into memory. Once more, he was back in the hidden cellar and examining pus-stained bandages. He recalled the stink of the wound lingering in that confined space.

Curio shifted around him but slapped his injured shoulder to break him out of his thoughts.

"You look like you lost everything in a dice game."

Falco also turned and called the lead escorts to a halt. Now Varro stood in a ring of men with their brows drawn together over their shaded eyes. Curio nudged his shoulder again, and Varro put into words the fears swirling through his mind.

"It's what you said, Falco. How have I been so foolish? It's this nonstop pace. The news of my sister. I'm just not thinking right."

While he stumbled to find his thoughts, both Curio and Falco now closed around him and kept the escorts to the side. Indeed, Falco ordered them to take a rest period. They found places to sit among the rocks but continued to eye Varro.

"Calm down," Falco said. "What did I say that has you pissing your tunic?"

"The pace is killing you. It's a lot for me and our escorts as well. And this isn't even the start of the real journey. We've got to cut through the Apennines and then march north along the coast. It's at least a week, and to do it in less time will leave us breathless by the end. Do you see what is wrong with this?"

It was a coy trick to buy more time to order his thoughts. Both Falco and Curio frowned at each other, with Curio offering an answer.

"We will be too tired to do anything about Longus at the end?"

Varro shook his head, the feathers on his helmet shaking as he did.

"Longus is dying from an infected wound. If we feel this journey is a strain, then how much worse would it be for him? He can't make it. Merula might be in danger, but not from Longus. He won't ever reach him. We're chasing my miscalculation, and not our objective."

Falco groaned. "Maybe he is traveling on horseback. It'll be faster and easier on him. He might still make it in time."

Varro removed his helmet and let it hang by the strap over his chest. Then he laced his fingers behind his head.

"By the time he reaches Merula he will have to go directly to the hospital. He knows that, and his superiors know that. And we should have known that. Merula would smell him coming. Longus cannot kill him. At best, someone else has that mission. Instead, Longus is organizing the brigands."

Varro felt relieved after openly stating his error, as he could now plan to correct it. Still, he leaned back into his interlaced fingers and stared at the deep blue sky.

Falco turned aside and pinched the bridge of his nose. "Fuck. You're probably right. We left him back at the ridge last night."

"But Consul Merula is still in danger." Curio spoke in a hopeful tone mismatched to the topic. "So, we need to reach him before someone cuts his throat."

"This is where I cannot be sure," Varro said, still staring at the sky and hoping an answer might fall from it. "They have been unsuccessful in all their assassination attempts, except for Senator Facilis. They might have revised their plans. It is possible that is why Longus burned his letter. That attempt on Senator Flaccus felt like a last chance to enact their plan. They have been using a brute force approach, but don't have the numbers for it to succeed."

"If you ask me," Falco said, folding his arms. "Those snakes turn up everywhere. They have plenty of numbers."

"No, they have plenty of resources to buy the help they need. But they don't have many in their core group. If they wanted to eliminate five senators, then all five needed to go down in rapid succession. Doing it as they have has allowed us to interfere. Their targets are now all alert. Perhaps only Consul Merula might not be, but that depends on whether he has communicated with Minucius."

Varro stared between his friends and glanced at the escorts sitting within earshot. He realized they should not know these details, but it was too late now. Besides, for what came next, he would need them to understand everything.

"It all makes sense now," Varro said, finally releasing his interlaced fingers. "They wanted to recruit me and bring you two along. They need help and more than just hired muscle. Longus and his accomplices are nearer to defeat than it would seem."

Curio also removed his helmet, then scratched the back of his head. "One of them gave me a lump on the head. I wouldn't join that crew for anything. Sorry, Varro, even if you join with them."

"Senator Flamininus gave us two missions," Varro said. "One is to protect Consul Merula's life, and the other is to capture and interrogate Longus. It's apparent now that we can only complete one objective. The more important one is Longus. Without the other senators' assassinations, Merula's death will not have the same effect. Still, they may attempt it as a distraction. We cannot ignore it."

"Send the escorts to Merula," Falco said. "And we go after Longus."

"Exactly," Varro said, clapping his hands together. "They've already heard enough. We will select two among them to memorize a message to the consul. I'll hand them my letter from Flamininus. It should be enough to convince Merula to be alert for hidden enemies. In the meantime, we will return to that ridge where we spotted brigands last night. We can pick up their trail and follow it to Longus."

The escorts were already reorganizing themselves based on what they had heard. Varro admired their professionalism and promised to commend them to Flaccus when they returned to Rome. He selected two men and gave them a simple message to memorize. It outlined all the assassination attempts and warned Merula to exercise caution even with those he trusted. Once he was satisfied the escorts understood their message and the mission, he sent them on their way.

"You take the pack horse and all the supplies. We will not be joining you. So be certain to protect the messengers and ensure at least one reaches the consul."

They watched the column navigate the narrow pass until it was just the three of them once more.

"To be honest," Falco said. "I like this mission better than being a messenger. This is the type of work suited to us."

Curio replaced his helmet and rubbed his nose with the back of his wrist as he peered down the pass.

"We're not geared for infiltration. The shields are too big and our helmets are too obvious. Not to mention, you sent all the rations away."

Varro spread his hands wide, confused at Curio's complaint, since they carried their rations. Falco chuckled and slapped Curio on his back.

"I think he means to say we packed the good wine on the horse. But don't worry. When we bring back Longus, there will be plenty of excellent wine for us. We'll be drinking it while interrogators cut off his toes in the next room."

They retraced their path through the hills, grateful for the good weather and sunlight to help them make up for lost time. None of them spoke as they marched. Varro focused only on the objective ahead. Once he pinpointed Longus in whatever bolt hole he had made for himself, he would have no mercy. Longus would beg for the interrogators.

By late afternoon, they had not only retraced their steps but reached the ridge where they had spotted brigands watching them the night before. They had not taken care to cover their passing, and tracks were easy enough to follow across grassy fields and ridges. By evening, they realized where the tracks were leading them.

"Fuck me! I can't believe we're going to infiltrate my own home."

Falco pointed across the distance to the ridge where his villa stood. Campfire light spread out around it, indicating many more men than could fit within its walls.

Curio set both hands on his hips and shook his head. "Well, you had to build your house on a ridge. And that didn't even keep it from falling into the brigands' hands."

"It doesn't matter where we built our homes," Varro said. "We did not properly defend them with enough men."

Falco stepped forward and shielded his eyes against the setting sun. "Well, how would we know a brigand uprising was growing in the hills? If we had, then we would've gone elsewhere."

"Debating what we should've done is pointless now," Varro said. "We've got to scout their camp and determine if Longus is present. I'm guessing from their numbers that he is here."

Now, with an enemy in sight, they bent low to the grass to keep their profiles hidden. Falco plucked the feathers from his helmet, and the others did as well. They then stowed them in their packs, to prevent a reflection from giving away their location.

Varro could hear singing carrying across the distance as they closed. It seemed to come from within the main building behind the walls, and the campsites outside them were less joyous. They went flat in the grass, covering themselves with black shields on their backs. The closest campfire had only three men around it. They dressed in dirty and patched tunics, sitting on stones arranged around their small fire. A tent sagged behind them. It was a hide legionary tent that had seen better days.

They observed the three brigands sharing a drink and muted conversation. The next campfire was a dozen yards to their left, and more disappeared around the corner of the villa walls. Down the other side of the ridge, Falco's fields stretched into the gathering darkness. He growled at seeing his unattended harvest.

"These bastards have cost me half my fortune."

Varro gave a bleak smile. "Well, maybe Flamininus will lose another war indemnity for us to recover. In the meantime, we've got to get closer. My intuition tells me Longus is inside. This must be the main brigand camp. They're waiting for Longus to give them orders to move out."

While he could not know exactly their plan, he expected the brigands would strike at a key moment, perhaps when news of defeat in the north reached Rome or a signal came from Carthage that their coup had started. No matter what, hundreds of brigands descending on the countryside so close to Rome would command the attention of the entire city.

"I'm not sure I want to go inside," Falco whispered. "I don't want to see what happened to my servants. I know the slaves must have joined with them, but it's the girls I'm worried for."

Varro continued to study the three men around their campfire. The sky now faded to deep purple, and stars appeared on the horizon to challenge the fleeing sun for dominance. The brigands seemed content to drink and wait, none of them attentive to the world around them. Longus and whoever commanded in his absence had not instilled discipline in his men.

Yet one stood up from the fire, and Varro craned his head higher in surprise. Curio hissed at him and shoved him down by the shoulder.

"Don't give us away so close to the walls." He squinted after Varro but shook his head. "What are you looking at?"

"Falco, you never saw Siculus again after your men were captured? Because I think that is him."

They drew together, shoulder to shoulder on the grass, and crawled forward for a better look. Falco sucked his breath.

"That little bastard. That beard gives him away. He joined with the fucking brigands."

"More like coerced, I'd say. They probably caught him and offered death or service as his two choices. He may not be a brigand at heart, but he is practical."

Across the field at the other campsite, the brigands there began to shout and argue. Their fight drew Varro's attention, along with the brigands nearest to them.

"Now's the time." Varro gathered himself and looked at Falco and

Curio. "I will create the distraction while you both take out the other two brigands."

He stood from the grass and set his scutum on his left arm, while keeping his palm atop the pommel of his gladius. Siculus and his two companions were straining to see the cause of the argument in the neighboring camp when they startled at Varro's sudden arrival.

Siculus looked at him in confusion. His left eye was swollen and bruised, and a thick scab had grown across the bridge of his nose. The other two brigands seemed equally confused and did not reach for their spears laying in the grass at their feet.

"It is time to choose," Varro said as he stepped toward his slave. "Brigands or freedom?"

In the twisting light of the campfire, Siculus's face contorted with a wicked smile. "Freedom it shall be."

Falco exploded from behind the brigands' pitiful tent. He swept into the nearest enemy, clamping his big hand over the enemy's mouth while driving his pugio into his back. His muffled scream cut short, and his knees buckled as Falco guided him to the ground.

At the same moment, Curio raced to attack the other brigand on the far side. But this one reacted to the danger and already backed away.

Siculus, however, extended his foot behind his erstwhile companion and tripped him in the grass. He collapsed with a howl of surprise, and Curio followed him down to plant his dagger into the brigand's liver. He cried out, sharp but short, then slackened beneath Curio as dark blood flowed into the dirt and sparkled with the campfire.

Only Varro and Siculus remained standing, while both Curio and Falco crouched to hide themselves.

"I am surprised to see you, sir." Siculus glanced at the man twitching in his last moments of life at his feet. He kicked him in the face, snapping his head back. "Thank you for relieving me of such vile company."

"Falco says you were captured by the brigands and forced to serve them. Is that true?"

"Of course, sir. But now that you and Master Falco are here, I know the gods smile upon me again. So, what must I do for my freedom?"

A bright smile appeared in Siculus's impossibly thick and black beard. He and Varro clasped arms as old friends rather than master and slave.

"Only face death alongside me. If we walk away from here tonight with my objective complete, then you will be a free man."

Siculus nodded appreciatively and slowly looked around. The fight at the other campsite was intensifying, drawing others from nearby camps.

"We should move away from here, sir. Those fools get drunk every night and fight until they pass out. But by morning, they are as good as brothers again."

Both Varro and Siculus walked calmly from the campfire while Falco and Curio dragged the enemy corpses out of the firelight. Soon, all four of them crouched in the grass down the slope from Falco's walled villa.

Siculus detailed how he had been captured the day after the attack on Falco's camp. He had been running for Rome, but in his panic had taken the wrong road. A pack of roaming brigands had captured him, and he played up being an escaped slave. "They claimed I would be free with them, though they only offered me a choice to join or die. You see how I chose. Your objective must be Marcus Longus, the monster who leads this scum."

"Is he here tonight?" Varro grabbed Siculus by his shoulder, shaking him.

"They don't let recruits like me near him, sir. All of us outside the gates are his guests. His faithful are inside with him. They are no better than rabble. I could not tell his chosen from his guests even if you put a knife to my throat."

Varro did not release his grip but stopped shaking his slave. "How many are here and how many do you believe Longus has under his command?"

Siculus tilted his head and ran his dirt-encrusted fingers through his beard.

"A hundred fifty to two hundred men are camped here. Spread over the countryside, I imagine two times more. Brigand groups from all over have been answering a call to join forces. We will retake the countryside for the people. Rich monsters, men like you and your friends, are all to be killed and their slaves freed. Those are Longus's words, sir, and not mine. Anyway, he has delivered one speech since I joined. I can at least see why men follow him. He could've been an orator in Rome."

Varro thought back to the few exchanges he had with Longus, recalling his refined accent.

"That might have been one path his life could have taken. Have you seen him recently? What is his plan?"

Siculus shrugged. "He arrived only a day ago, and at dawn, when I was asleep. He came with a wagon full of food and wine. He has rationed food and drink, but you can see from those drunks that many have their own supply. Still, these scum have been grumbling about hunger. Like me, sir. My two dead companions didn't bring much more than their dull swords. That wagon of food might be a more tempting target for Longus's brigands than a distant farmhouse."

He paused to look back at the villa, then scratched his beard again.

"He has not left his room since arriving. It is on the top floor of Master Falco's home. As for our plan, well, I am to sack the countryside with my companions once the word is given. When it will be, only Longus knows."

Varro at last released his grip on Siculus. "Good, because after tonight Longus will not be here to give the word. So, these are all different brigand groups with their leaders and their own goals. Longus is holding them together, and when we remove him, this alliance will collapse."

Falco chuckled. "They'll collapse when the Senate sends an urban cohort out here to put them down."

Varro stared up at the dark walls of Falco's villa. Beyond them, the top floor of the main house was dark. Singing carried over the walls, but Varro would soon turn their merriment to horror.

"All right, we've been chasing Longus around Rome for too long. He's hurt and hiding in that room, clinging to life just long enough to start his attack. He has much to answer for, and we're going to have it from him tonight."

Varro shared a smile with the three men huddled with him in the grass and darkness.

"Curio and Siculus, you two will create a distraction for me and Falco. You'll also help us escape. We've got a lot to do tonight. So let us beg another favor from the gods and get to work."

24

Varro and Falco huddled together in the darkness at the corner of his villa walls. They watched the front gate for Siculus and Curio to appear. Stars now glittered above, and Varro hoped the gods would look upon them with favor. They faced an impossible task, for Longus was protected among scores of loyal followers. According to Falco, Lars had used the same second-floor room as his base and had filled the bottom floor with his men. They could not expect to pass among that many brigands undetected, especially when they had to capture Longus alive.

"What's taking them so long?" Falco spoke in a whisper, and both looked up as if a face might appear over the wall. However, there were no parapets, and the only lookouts were stationed at both the front and rear gates.

"I don't know," Varro said, pressing against the cold stucco wall. A thin globe of orange light fluttered at the front gate, where both were expected. The lookout might have been asleep for his silence. Varro and Falco had both seen Siculus fetch one of the combative drunks from the neighboring campsite. They convinced the drunk that he had captured a Roman spy and that they would be rewarded for bringing him in. Since the other two drunks had passed out, the last standing drunk had no one to dissuade him and his greed got the better of his wine-fogged mind.

Curio had left between Siculus and the staggering drunk, his head hung in defeat but his pugio hidden beneath his tunic. Also, his gladius was conveniently strapped to Siculus's side alongside his own battered sword.

Varro clutched the lamp oil close to his chest as he waited. Falco carried their flint, and once inside, would light the clay lamps he carried. They had collected the oil from Siculus's supply, along with extra clay lamps they carried in their packs.

They could not reach Longus, but they could have Longus delivered to them.

The singing was louder up close and certainly came from within the main house. Varro hoped their celebrations would be a distraction. But with the late hour, the singing voices dwindled.

"You should get the horses ready, not me." Falco still spoke in a whisper, but it sounded loud enough that Varro winced.

"The horses will know you, at least the ones you owned. Besides, it'll take a strong hand to keep them under control when the fire and fighting starts. That's a task better suited to you. I just need to peel Longus away from his defenders and get him on a horse."

At last, Siculus appeared with Curio. Both paused to wait for the drunk to catch up with them. It had been Curio's idea to have another brigand to make his capture appear more legitimate to the gate guard. But now it seemed their choice was too drunk to be useful. He nearly crashed into Curio, who, unlike a prisoner, had to help his would-be captor stand upright.

Yet they reached the gate and Siculus called up with the password.

"New Republic," he shouted. "We've captured a spy. Open up! Longus will want to see this one right away. Enemies are near."

As Varro expected, the lookout seemed to have just awakened at Siculus's call. The drunk beside him laughed and staggered backward, nearly falling over before Curio drew him upright.

"A spy? He looks like a boy."

"Fuck you!" Curio shouted. "When I don't report tomorrow, my commander will know just where to come. You're all as good as dead."

The drunk apparently realized he had to embellish his role, especially if he wanted to collect his imagined reward. Despite his condition, his bellicose shouting was clear.

"We gave you the fucking password. Let us in! This boy can fight. I'd like to see you try to take him down."

"You're drunk again," the gate guard said. But Varro saw him start down the ladder.

He pulled back to the other side of the wall with Falco. "Time to do our part."

He gave Falco a lift to the top of the stucco wall. With a grunt, he reached the sloped tiles which sloughed off like fish scales to crash around Varro. He cursed the clay tiles, but fortunately, none broke on the soft earth. Once Falco scrabbled to the top, he lay flat and dropped his pack on the opposite side. He then accepted Varro's pack and did the same before extending a hand.

Taking a brief run, Varro leaped up and grabbed Falco's extended arm. He pulled him up, using momentum to land on the clay tiles. Again, more tiles slid to the ground as Varro struggled for purchase. But Falco had already dropped into the darkness on the opposite side.

After Varro thumped down beside him, they both looped their packs on their backs. They had abandoned their shields and helmets and now carried only their weapons and the gear they needed for escape. Falco leaned close as he whispered.

"Well, that was easy. Next time I build a villa, remind me to set iron spikes on the wall. That sloping roof didn't provide the defense the architects had promised."

The brigands' singing reverberated through the walls of the main house. He and Falco had dropped into the corner of the front yard. Fortunately, two wagons of boxes and barrels offered cover. These also obscured the view of the front gate.

Varro crawled to the side of a wagon and peered around it.

The gate opened, and the guard on duty waited for Curio and

Siculus to enter. The brigand yawned and stretched as Siculus and his drunken companion dragged Curio inside. Varro's stomach tightened as he anticipated the next stage of the plan.

Though the singing nearby covered much of the exchange at the front gate, he could still hear Siculus.

"You must wake Longus. Who knows when the Romans will attack?"

The drunk echoed Siculus's demand, though he was so slurred in speech the brigand guard looked at him in confusion.

Now Curio began his scripted struggle. He wrestled against Siculus, all a ruse to cover his reaching for the pugio hidden beneath his tunic. The guard's only reaction was to widen his stance and touch his sword hilt. The drunken brigand fell over, seemingly of his own accord.

In the next instant, Siculus and Curio overcame the gate guard. Varro was interested to see how well Siculus fought. But the exchange was so brief and efficient that he only saw the guard stagger forward and fly out the front gate. Then, Curio cut the throat of the drunk on the ground.

Varro pulled back and nodded to Falco. "Front gate is secured. Let's start a fire."

"The gods hate me," he said. "I'm burning down my own home. Does that make sense?"

Hiding behind the carts, Falco withdrew tinder and a striking iron from his pack. Varro stood lookout, listening to Falco strike until a spark caught. Each bright chime of the iron sounded like a bell tolling. But the singing from the main house covered it.

Yellow light spilled out of the half-opened front door, and the windows revealed flickering shadows as men moved about the lower floor. Scanning up, the top floor windows remained black.

"All right, I've got the lamp burning. Time for mayhem."

Falco protected the nascent flame of the clay lamp, and Varro used the burning tinder to light his own.

They squeezed full skins of lamp oil to wet the side of Falco's house opposite the garden. The singing was stronger through the wall here. In this narrow and dark section of the yard, their fluttering lamps seemed no more than fireflies.

Once they had dumped all the oil along the stucco walls, each touched their open lamp flame to it. The fire spread in thin sheets, lighting the darkness with shaky orange light. Varro felt the heat spread on his face and backed away out of instinct. Falco, who had once braved raging fires in Sparta, was more fearful. He dropped his lamp and retreated against the wall.

The singing continued inside the villa as flames crawled higher along the stucco. Varro threw his clay lamp to land on the villa roof, then both retreated toward the rear gate.

Varro nodded to the front yard. "Get those horses ready. Siculus and Curio will keep the gate open. I'll make sure the rear gate sentry doesn't raise the alarm before the fire is unstoppable. Fortuna be with you."

Falco remained staring at the fire streaking up the forgotten side of his house. He glanced back at Varro with a twisted smile.

"If I had been thinking, I would've exited the other way. Now I've got to pass through the garden."

"Just get the horses ready, then watch for Longus. He could come out either door."

Varro now swept along the shadow of the villa wall toward the rear gate. The sentry there stared into the night beyond the walls, perhaps dozing like his friend at the front gate. Falco clung to the side of his house before disappearing around the corner into the garden and bright light spilling from the inside.

Bounding up the ladder, Varro's hand clamped onto his pugio. The sentry at the top turned on his small observation stand and frowned down. "Hey, it's not time for a shift change yet."

Varro saw the yellow fire reflected in the guard's eyes, and his mouth opened to shout a warning. But Varro was faster.

"Your shift is done."

His pugio cut across the surprised guard's throat, and dark blood spilled down his chest to catch the growing firelight behind them.

Varro then shoved him off the stand and over the wall, sending him to crash with a bone-jarring crunch on the opposite side.

Shouts came from the garden, and Varro realized Falco had alerted the brigands. Fortunately, the singing continued, even if it had diminished. He scrabbled down the ladder and then hid in the shadows by the gate.

The singing had turned to angry shouting and then panicked cries of alarm.

He watched the second-floor window where Longus rested. The layout of this villa was identical to his own. In his mind's eye, he could see alarmed brigands racing up the stairs to warn Longus of the danger. In his injured condition, no doubt the reason he hid from his followers, they would carry him down the stairs, hear the confusion from the front, and then choose to leave by the rear gate.

Varro realized his error too late. All the horses would be at the front, and if Longus came his way, then he had no easy means to escape with him.

As he watched for signs of this happening, he heard shouting from beyond the villa walls. The brigands camped outside now saw the flames licking at their stronghold.

His stomach twisted, unsure how much time he should give Longus before going in after him. With the fire now spreading to the rooftop, and all the one hundred or more brigands alert to danger, he counted his opportunity in mere heartbeats.

Light now leaked from the shuttered second-floor window, and he saw shadows flickering along the edges of the closed shutters.

He heard Falco calling him across the yard.

It was a gamble. He knew Longus was coming this way to escape. But he knew Falco called him for a purpose. His options must be diminishing even as he hesitated.

The shouting beyond the walls grew closer now, a stark contrast to the drunken singing that had filled the night a moment ago. The brigands were heading to the fire and coming by the rear gate as well as the front.

Again, he heard Falco bellow his name, but it was weak amid the shouting and crackling fire that now engulfed one side of the villa.

Then Longus stepped around the corner, supported by two men in black tunics. He slouched between them, his face pasty and shining with sweat. His feet half dragged and half walked with the help of his followers. His head hung as if he lacked the strength to hold it up.

They glared at Varro, and he realized they did not recognize him as a threat.

"Out this way," he shouted, pointing toward the gate and turning around in case Longus should lift his head. "The traitors are burning down the villa. They want the supplies."

Varro made as if to lead them into the welcoming safety of the dark beyond the rear gate. Longus cursed, his voice weak and wheezing. "Those greedy fools! Nothing satisfies them!"

"We will deal with them later, master." One of his guards spoke as he dragged Longus toward the rear gate. "First, we must get you away from the fire."

"This way," Varro said. "There are no enemies on this side yet. They're attacking from the front."

In the brilliant light of the burning house, shadows danced in crazed patterns across the rear gate door. Varro threw the bar aside, then pushed it open. He dared to look back and found both Longus and his two guards staring at the burning villa.

"This smells of the Romans," Longus said. "The men wouldn't burn their supplies."

Varro slipped out the rear gate, hoping their panicked momentum would carry them along. They had been acting out of fear, but Longus inserted sense into the confusion.

"Hurry, they are coming!"

But Varro's plea did not draw an answer. The gate hung open, and the mass of shadows from Longus and his two guards stretched through it, dancing with the blaze behind them.

He repeated his plea, but the shadows retreated as one guard stepped through the gate.

"Who are you? Not one of us, I suspect."

The brigand was a burly man, his muscles sharply defined by the violent firelight. He had drawn a long and curving dagger, nearly the length of a gladius.

Varro stood just beyond the gate and to the side. He did not waste the moment but struck with the speed of a snake.

His pugio flashed in the light, but the brigand was aware of the threat now. He parried Varro's strike with his dagger, stepping aside and throwing a punch into his wounded shoulder.

Hot pain flashed from the blow. But Varro gritted his teeth and circled the brigand. He felt the heat of the burning house on his back. His opponent now was framed in the gate, and beyond him, more brigands surged forward to answer the threat of the fire.

He feinted to the left, but the brigand did not fall for the trick and met him again. Their two blades ground together, sending bright sparks between them.

Varro, however, wore caligae rather than sandals. He stomped hard on his opponent's foot, the hobnails crushing bone, then shoved forward. No matter the brigand's strength, he toppled with a howl of pain. Varro followed him down, driving his blade under the man's neck. His powerful hands latched on to Varro's, but in the next heartbeat, they fell aside as his lifeblood spilled from his throat into the dirt beneath the gate.

Leaping up again, Varro found himself pinned between the growing fire and a mob of at least thirty brigands.

Rather than attempt to flee, he instead raised his pugio overhead and pointed at the burning house.

"Longus and his cronies were having a fucking party with our wine. It's time to take what's ours! Fuck him! No one owns us!"

He had tapped into the anger and suspicion latent in every brigand excluded from the villa. Just as he had struck a spark to burn the house, so had he sparked their rage. The mob now shouted as one, raising their fists and weapons at the burning house.

"That traitor!"

"I never trusted the bastard!"

"We deserve more!"

Those were just some curses Varro heard as he led the angry mob into Falco's garden.

He directed them toward the front, where a group of brigands had encircled the wagons and horses. He spotted Siculus standing atop the wagon and holding a flaming brand overhead. Falco and Curio were ready in the driver's seat. It seemed as if they had almost escaped before being cut off.

Longus stood before them, shouting at Siculus who threatened to set fire to their rations in the wagon.

The wave of angry brigands flowed out of the garden. What they saw only confirmed the doubt Varro had sewn in their hearts. It seemed as if Siculus, being one of them, had captured the rations and wine while Longus and his cronies tried to wrestle it back.

"Our wine and food!" Varro pointed at the wagons. "Get it before everything burns down."

As if to emphasize Varro's words, part of the burning roof slid into the garden and crashed in a bloom of orange sparks. The brigands ran screaming from the spreading fire.

But Varro had set enough fires for one night.

He charged through the garden, the world fading to darkness around him even as fire engulfed the house. His eyes focused only on Longus, still propped up by one of his men. Siculus had drawn his complete attention, and Varro's charge went unnoticed.

Ramming aside brigands in the way, he reached Longus just as his guard noticed him.

The guard understood the danger even if everyone around them remained confused. He allowed Longus to slump against the cart, then stepped into Varro's path.

He crashed shoulder-first into the strong guard, forcing him back against the cart. But his drawn pugio did not find its mark.

The brigand shoved Varro back and drew his long dagger.

"Get Longus to safety," Varro shouted. He had been addressing Curio and Falco, but in the confusion, Longus's loyal men mistook the situation. Varro had only a moment to see men helping the feebly protesting Longus onto the cart.

A heavy punch connected to Varro's temple, sending him backward into the crowd. He expected to be dragged down and overcome. However, the brigands now fought amongst themselves. There was too much confusion, too much suspicion, and too much wine for any other outcome. A brawl now erupted in the front yard and led back to the garden. Amid all this, Falco's home now blazed into the night sky, painting low clouds with an orange glow.

The wagon pulled away, and the horses cried out against the sudden violence. Also, the growing fire panicked the remaining horses, and these now fought through the press of brawling men.

Another punch grazed his chin, driving him back. He faced the burly guard, who had not surrendered to the madness all around. He followed up with a strike from his dagger, and it took all of Varro's speed to dodge it.

The melee was thicker than a shield wall, but more deadly for the unarmored combatants. As Varro danced with his enemy, he stepped across the fallen bodies of both the dying and the dead. The fight was as out of control as a fire.

He glimpsed the wagon with Longus exiting by the front gate. Siculus had crawled to the rear and hung out to call Varro's name. But the cart charged away, and men intent on killing each other by the light of the burning house filled its wake.

25

Among the press of screaming and cursing brigands, Varro wrestled with his enemy. The burly guard who had tried to prevent him from capturing Longus now gritted his teeth as he latched both hands on to Varro's arm. He strained to keep the point of Varro's pugio from his neck.

They had clashed twice before Varro disarmed his opponent with a lucky cut to his wrist. Blood flowed down the brigand's arm, mingling with his sweat. His eyes blazed with hatred equal to the fire raging from the house behind him. Despite his injury, he remained strong enough to keep Varro's blade from the killing stroke.

Furthermore, he evaded Varro's stomping feet. It seemed as if the two danced amid the swirling chaos of battle. They staggered in a circle, arms and eyes locked, teeth gnashed against their grunting. Varro's attempts to crush his enemy's feet were exhausting him. But his enemy was likewise tiring. Others bumped into them as they shoved each other around the hard-packed dirt yard.

One of those bumps caused the brigand to slip.

Varro's pugio stabbed home, plunging into the pit of the brigand's neck. He gasped and cursed, blood flowing down to stain the front of his black tunic. Varro let him crash to the ground. He cast about as if seeking to hold on to life. But all he could do was put both hands over the hole in his neck, then life fled from his eyes.

The wagon carrying Longus and the brigands' supplies had only escaped a moment before. But to Varro, it felt as if a lifetime had passed. His unrelenting enemy had prevented him from reaching them in time. All around, brigands fought and killed each other. With no armor to protect them, blades easily sliced through their naked torsos. In moments, the battle would end with the complete destruction of the brigands as a fighting force. There could be no reunion after such a bloody battle.

As winded as he was from the fight, he could not linger to catch his breath. He had to catch up with the others at the rally point. They had agreed to meet at the campsite of the previous day. From there, they could relocate to a more secure place to interrogate Longus.

Falco's horses had all fled or been taken. Yet Varro still heard one's terrified screaming. He searched over the heads of the brawling men and through the orange glare of the burning house. The horse had become trapped against the wall and struggled against its tether. Somehow, in the madness, it had been forgotten.

Varro pushed through his enemies, reaching the kicking and screaming horse. The heat here threatened to scorch his flesh, and he understood the horse's terror. But he had spent a year among the Numidians and learned much about these noble animals. Under these circumstances, he knew he couldn't hope to calm a strange horse. However, he knew that if he freed the animal, it would find the shortest way to safety. From there, he might earn its trust and use it to catch up with the others.

He dodged flailing hooves and the mad bucking of the terrified horse but managed to get aside of it. In step with the horse's wild motions, he watched for his moment. For an instant, he saw an exposed side of the horse, so he grabbed its mane and pulled up on its back.

It felt as if it would buck him away, but it was ensnared in its tether and too horrified to worry about a rider. Holding on to the horse as tightly as he dared, he used his pugio to cut the tether free then grabbed the horse's mane.

The moment it realized its freedom, the horse plowed through everyone in its path to reach the open gate. Varro rejoiced at its unbridled power but was terrified of it in the same measure. He now fled into the night on the back of a panicked horse, bolting in whatever direction it thought safest.

Compared to the heat within Falco's former villa, the night air was cold on his exposed flesh. Being soaked with sweat only enhanced the chill. The wind pulled across his face and back as he wrapped both arms around the galloping horse's neck and pressed his heels into its flanks. It did not respond to his direction, at least not until the beast had exhausted itself and stopped.

Varro was uncertain of his location in the darkness but had the fiery glow of Falco's burning villa to serve as a beacon. The horse did not protest him as much as expected. It tried to express its opinions, snorting and bucking when it had the strength. But eventually Varro sweet-talked it into a sort of partnership. It wasn't until the sun pressed against the eastern horizon that he could lead the horse northeast toward the rally point.

He found the supply cart first. It had overturned and spilled its contents everywhere, barrels of wine now dripping the dregs into the grass. The supplies had scattered, and the crash had destroyed one of the wagon wheels. He determined they had hit a stone that flipped the cart. Such an accident could have been disastrous, but he did not see blood around the scene. So, he followed the trail as best as he could in the twilight.

Even knowing where they had camped, Varro still struggled to find his friends. It wasn't until dawn when he saw Curio's outline on the ridge searching for him. He had overshot the camp, and now had to backtrack. His horse had grown weary, and so now he led it by the remains of its tether. It seemed to perk up when it discovered another horse in the camp.

Despite the flipped wagon, the horse seemed in perfect condition.

It must have recognized Varro's horse, for its ears pricked up and it joined his animal in a silent celebration.

Curio stood with both hands on his hips like an angry father ready to chide a wayward son. Falco and Siculus both lay on their backs in the grass. Falco raised a hand in greeting, but Siculus scrabbled to his feet.

"You made it out, sir. They said you would have no problems. But your situation was desperate when I saw you last."

Varro released his horse to join the other, and both went to graze on the thin grass of the ridge.

"It's still desperate. Where is Longus?"

Falco now sat up but looked aside.

"We flipped the cart." Curio mimicked an overturning object with both hands.

Varro bit his lip but did not dare to voice his fear or otherwise it might become true.

All remained silent, Falco lowering his head and Siculus staring into the distance.

"He died? If he did, where is his corpse?"

Curio scratched the back of his head. "He must be dead, but I don't know where his body is."

Varro searched all three of them for an explanation. But he already understood what had happened. After the accident, Longus slipped away.

"His men had to carry him out of the villa. How the fuck could he have walked away from a wagon crash? And none of you could find him? This is what you want me to believe?"

Falco remained seated but let out a long sigh.

"We searched for him, searched around and under the wagon, even inside the broken barrels. But he's just gone."

"Impossible." Varro pressed his eyes closed and set both hands on his head.

"Maybe we'll find signs of him by better light," Curio said.

Unable to stand it any longer, Varro screamed in frustration. It echoed off the ridge, his rage rebounding at him.

"He is dying. He can't walk, much less run. He is back at the crash site. If he is not, it's because you three fools were not thorough enough in your search. We had him. We had him captured in the fucking wagon."

He cut off his diatribe with a curse and turned his back to all of them. His anger had frightened the horses, and now both ran out of easy reach. He would never catch them again, but in his current state he did not care.

Longus had escaped them again. The gods had drawn him into the earth and protected him from sight. Now, they would heal him, make him whole, and send him against Rome once more. The gods were unhappy with Rome. The earthquakes proved it. Now, they sponsored whoever promised them to bring Rome to its knees.

Falco cleared his throat. "Thanks for asking if any of us were hurt in the crash. We might've missed something, since we were a bit dazed after flying through the air and landing on our heads. But to set your mind at ease, we just have bruises and scratches. We came here because this is the rally point. Before you pop your eyeballs screaming, I understand Longus was the primary mission. But he had vanished. What were we supposed to do? We can't make him appear on command, or we would've done that long ago. So, we decided to link up with you. I know you think your escape was simple. But we didn't know if you were alive or dead."

"Of course he was alive," Curio said brightly. "We've all been in tighter situations than that. It just feels worse to you, Falco, because your house burned down."

"Why are you disagreeing with me? We went flying out the gate like rocks launched from an onager. We left him with a hundred or more enemies to fight. And you thought those were good odds?"

"You were the one driving. You didn't slow down to let Varro catch up."

"Driving? I was holding on for my life. The fucking horse was mad."

While Falco and Curio went back and forth, Varro laced his hands behind his head and tried to concentrate. If Longus was not at the crash site--and he did not see him there only hours before--then had he even got into the cart?

"I saw his men lift Longus onto the cart." Varro shouted over Falco and Curio's argument. He then turned to face them and Siculus, who stood in ashamed silence. "What happened once you got him?"

Everyone turned to Siculus, who looked surprised to be the focus.

"Sir, I pulled him onto the cart, and he fell between the barrels and crates. He remained there until the crash."

"Are you certain? You never took your eyes off him? Because you did at least once. You were calling out for me when you escaped by the gate. I saw that much at least."

Siculus's brow furrowed, and he ran his fingers through his impossibly thick beard.

"It was a headlong rush, as master Falco described. The cart shook, and we hit several bad bumps. I admit, I do not remember what I saw after that. We were speeding through the night, hoping to escape that burning madness. I am sorry, sir."

Varro held up his hands. "No, I'm sorry. I've lost my temper, and when that happens, reason goes with it. But I've got to calm down and think this through. Obviously, somewhere between escaping Falco's villa and the crash, Longus fell out of the cart. This is no great mystery. If you think it through, that is the only possibility. Therefore, we need to retrace the path you took last night, and we will find him."

With no hesitation, they gathered their belongings and set out to retrace their path. Varro resigned himself to abandoning the horses, who fled at his approach.

They took supplies from the crash, but otherwise found no trace of Longus. Now that Varro inspected the crash site in detail, he understood how fortunate everyone had been to come away uninjured. His cheeks heated with the shame of his earlier conduct.

The trail from here was easy to follow, as the horse and cart had dug ruts and divots into the earth. Black smoke streamed into the air in the distance where Falco's villa had stood. High on its ridge, flames still flickered there.

Yet all along the trail, they found nothing. Of course, Longus would have left minimal traces behind in the short grass. By midday, they drifted close to Falco's villa and risked encountering the brigands who had survived the mayhem of last night. Varro saw their dark shapes picking along the ruins of their camp on the ridge.

Curio shielded his eyes and squinted alongside him.

"Do you think he survived, and his followers took him back?"

"No, even if he survived falling out of the wagon--which it appears he did--he would not trust those men. How could he be sure whoever came for him was not out for his blood?"

He turned back to where Siculus and Falco were both stooped over the grass and searching for prints or blood trails. He accepted that in their exhausted condition they might have overlooked obvious clues. His own stamina for the search flagged, and he imagined it would be worse for the others. But he could not give up.

"Stop searching. We will not find anything in the grass. Instead, we've got to step through this in our imagination."

Varro folded both arms behind his back and spoke as if he were addressing men on parade. Everyone gathered around him. Falco's heavy brows filled his eyes with shadow. Siculus stood attentively, just as a soldier would. Curio gave him a beatific smile, as if listening to prophecy.

"Imagine what you would do in Longus's situation. You believe your enemies have captured you. You expect to be tortured for information. But you are also dying, and the mission you have dedicated your life to is burning down around you. What would you do if suddenly the gods granted you a boon and set you free?"

Falco chuckled. "I'd cry. Then I'd sacrifice to the gods."

"But what if you were a fanatic bent on accomplishing your mission? The gods have just saved you. Therefore, they believe in your mission. You believe you will live to fulfill it, no matter how impossible it seems at that moment. You would not give up, but seek to hide somewhere."

"Sir, are you saying that Longus believes the gods support him, and that it inspires him to press on?"

"Exactly, but to do so, he must begin again. The gods did not approve of his first plan. So they destroyed it, taught him a lesson, but then at the last moment set him free to try again. Longus believes in his mission to destroy Rome. The gods seem to share his goals. It's easy to think of what he does next. Falco, this is your land. Where is there a nearby water source? We will find Longus there, cleaning his wounds, slaking his thirst, and waiting for the gods to send aid."

Falco looked around, then pointed east toward the hills. "A stream runs down the hills and drains into a pond nearby. I would expect the brigands are aware of that place."

"Then that is where we go. Longus might hope to rally his men who go there seeking water they can no longer get from your cistern."

He led them at the fastest march possible. The three of them strung out behind, unable to keep up with his ardent pace. But Varro knew he had at last cornered Longus in a bolt hole that offered no escape. He might believe the gods saved him. Perhaps they did. But Varro had always been careful to venerate his beloved goddess, Fortuna.

They followed the slope, and along the way picked up hopeful signs of human passage. Curio celebrated a drop of blood found on a leaf dangling from a broken branch. Before long, they arrived at the confluence of creek and pond.

And found Longus.

Siculus discovered him curled up in the bole of a tree that grew beside the pond. Even in his condition, Longus had selected a well-screened hiding place. Reeds and bushes concealed him from most viewpoints. When Siculus shouted, waving his battered sword overhead, Varro's heart leaped into his throat.

All of them converged on their hated foe, but it was Varro who pushed to the fore.

Longus wore a blood- and mud-stained tunic that had once been clean brown. He had torn it aside to reveal dirty bandages that wrapped his festering wound. Black rings circled his eyes, and the broken tooth in his weak smile enhanced the pallor of death hanging over him. Indeed, he was steeped in the miasma of death, and Varro decided the gods might not love him as much as he thought.

"Varro, you found me." His voice was weak and raspy, but still packed with arrogance. "I thought you would give up by now. My men didn't finish. Surely, someone will do me the favor soon."

The defiance seemed to have sapped his strength. His gap-tooth smile faltered and his eyes fluttered. His lids drooped, black and shiny with oncoming death.

Varro knew he had no time for banter. He dropped to his knees and grabbed Longus by his tunic.

"You can die quietly in the mud, or I could make you scream out the last of your life. Now, who do you work for? Who is the masked man?"

A thin smile formed on Longus's bloodless lips.

"You are an inefficient killer. You cut me once, and it took all this time for it to drop me. I'm poisoned, like the Republic. Poisoned and dying. We would do for it what you would do for me. Hasten its death."

Varro's hands slid from his tunic and down to the infected wound. He only had to press the bandage to elicit howls of pain from Longus.

"The name! Who do you work for? Is Carthage sponsoring you?"

Longus's screams became laughter, even as he tried to squirm away from Varro's touch.

"What is pain? You do not know. You know nothing! I came to this mud for my rebirth." He struggled to lift his arm to indicate his surroundings, but both plopped back into the mud. "And so I shall be reborn. My father and brothers continue to serve the people. Not the Republic, which is rotted from the inside like me. And so, if you cannot save me, then you cannot save the Republic. Today I die, and tomorrow so does the leprous body of the Republic."

Suddenly, Longus shoved back into the bole, and his drooping eyelids flicked open. His eyes bulged and his mouth fell open as he gasped his last breath.

Jutting from his chest was the tip of a bronze blade that he had been lying atop. He had only pressed down to drive it through his lungs.

Between his gasping and squirming, he tried to laugh as he left the world but only wheezed and gurgled blood.

Varro flailed at him, begging him to live even as he slumped in death.

He sat back, appalled at the corpse before him.

Siculus knelt beside him, putting his finger beneath his nose for the terrible stench of Longus's gangrenous wound.

"Sir, I did not realize he had prepared an ultimate escape. I should have known."

Varro stared at the broken-toothed, mocking expression now frozen in death. He stood up, brushing mud from his knees.

"A true fanatic. Any other man would've driven that blade into my neck when he had the chance. But Longus was so dedicated to his cause that he saved it for himself, just to keep his secrets."

The four of them stood in a ring about the body, dark blood now pooling in the bole where Longus had come to die.

Varro scrubbed his face, then stared at the dirty corpse he had spent so long chasing across Rome.

"What a waste. We'll take his head back to Flamininus. It'll stink, but let there be no question of justice for Facilis's murder. The rest of him can rot here. May worms and wolves gnaw on his bones."

26

Three days had passed since the debacle at Falco's villa. They once again convened in Flamininus's garden, invited for breakfast with the senator's compliments. They sat around a now familiar stone table and waited for him to join. Varro scratched at the wound healing on his shoulder and stared across the western horizon.

He had used up every excuse. Now he had to find his mother and inform her of Arria's death. Slaves hovered at the sides of the garden, Siculus among them. Varro's eyes kept flitting to his solitary figure waiting in the shadow of the garden walls. He would grant him freedom but regretted the loss of a loyal slave. He doubted he would find another like him.

"I can do it for you," Falco said. "I witnessed Arria's death, and I know you don't want to see your mother. Maybe it's better if you let me talk to her."

Varro bit his lip and shook his head.

"No, it is time I make peace with my mother. I should have done so before. I've blamed her for everything, but I understand now that it has always been my choice. Everything that has happened to me has come from my decisions. I've been angry with her all these years, blaming her for my father and going against my great-grandfather's will to keep me out of Servus Capax. But what could she have done about my father? And in the end, I accepted Consul Galba's offer."

Falco looked at Curio and both shrugged.

"I wonder if my villa is still standing?" Curio craned his head as if he could see his home over the walls of Flamininus's garden. "We will have to go check it out eventually."

Curio then mused on the condition of his villa long enough to distract the conversation from Varro's mother. He smiled gratefully, and the three fell into a companionable silence while they waited for Senator Flamininus.

After they returned to Rome with Longus's bloodless head, they reported directly to Flamininus. He verified the identity and then had a slave burn the head. He then consoled them on their losses but encouraged them with praise.

"It may seem as if Longus revealed nothing. But you got him to reveal more than we knew previously. And in chasing him, you exposed the power behind him. As always, you have done well. Besides poor Facilis, you have saved many important men. I believe our foes are on their back feet now. We need to press this advantage and cut off the head of the snake."

They continued to live in the central apartment Flamininus had designated for their use. With their homes now destroyed and their finances dealt a severe blow, they needed another place to stay. The countryside was not safe for now.

They rested for three days, and all the while wondered what came next. They wagered on their next orders. Varro bet that they would be dispatched to ensure Consul Merula's safety. Falco was convinced that they would be sent to Carthage as spies. And Curio bet they would be sent to clean up the brigands. Upon being summoned this morning, they set out their coins on the table before leaving, each hoping to claim the pot upon returning.

At last, Senator Flamininus emerged from his house, dressed in his plain white tunic with the purple senatorial stripe. He had his secretary in attendance but dismissed him before seating himself with the rest. His soulful eyes were bright with excitement.

"Before I tell you the news, I should let you know Senator Flaccus is deeply impressed. He is now your ardent supporter." He raised an eyebrow at Varro. "That is an interesting development, don't you think?"

"I believe he wanted me flogged in a public square, sir."

"And he may still seek that for you," Flamininus said with a wry smile. "But for now, you have brought justice for Facilis and broken up the threat against him and his protégé, Proconsul Cato. Enjoy the moment. When it comes to Flaccus, all such graces are fleeting."

Varro inclined his head, then cleared his throat. "Sir, you had news?"

Flamininus sat back and folded his arms with a satisfied smile.

"Spies report activity from Carthage. There may indeed be a coup in the works."

Falco leaned forward and arched his heavy brows. "Is that so, sir? Then you will send us to Carthage?"

Flamininus rubbed his chin in thought. "Perhaps, but not immediately. I have more work to do before we decide on the next steps. My investigation into those abandoned properties has reached a dead end. That in itself tells me something. Our enemy has taken every precaution to obscure his identity. Still, I have means available to me. While I dig at that mystery, I think the three of you have earned a rest. As well as financial recompense for your wounds and property loss. I cannot make you whole, but I can work within my budget to ease your pain."

They thanked the senator, even though Varro had wished for something more definite than working with a budget. But he knew better than to press the senator, particularly after straining the limits of his independence.

The senator pointed to Curio's arm. "You'll need a tattoo to match the others. Use this time to get it. Eventually, I will ensure all other operatives do the same."

Varro straightened up at the mention of others. "Will we ever meet them, sir? We've been at this a long time, and I have hardly met anyone else in the same service."

Flamininus's expansive mood seemed to contract, and his smile weakened.

"That's as it should be. Besides, there are never more than twelve at any one time. Since you three operate as a unit, you know one-fourth of our organization as it is."

The three of them shared a chagrined look. Curio rubbed his upper arm where his tattoo would be.

"That's more than I knew this morning, sir. Sometimes, it feels like it's just the three of us against everyone else."

Flamininus gave a solemn nod. "Let us pray it never becomes so. Now, you've enjoyed my hospitality, and soon you'll enjoy your rewards. In the meantime, take a well-earned rest. But remain prepared. The moment I have the shred of a new lead, I will call you."

They returned to their apartment and Siculus accompanied them. Once the three of them reached the third floor, they stared at the stack of coins on the table.

"I came the closest," Falco said as he reached for the coins. "So I win."

But Curio grabbed his arm and forced it down.

"He didn't say we were going to Carthage. You need to clean out your ears."

"So, what are we going to do with all this? I need money, and it's better when it comes out of your purse."

Varro left Falco and Curio to exchange good-natured jabs. The three stacks of coins remained unclaimed on the table when he closed the door. At the bottom of the stairs, he found Siculus preparing the kitchen.

"Master, what shall we have for dinner? I will visit the market this afternoon."

Varro smiled and patted him on the shoulder. "Thank you. As promised, you will be a free man, though I will hate to see you leave. When I return today, we will make it legal."

Siculus bowed. "Then you shall be as a father to me thereafter."

"Speak to the others about dinner. Right now, I have no appetite."

He left by the front door and followed the streets through the crowded city until reaching his mother's neighborhood. She had married into wealth, which surprised Varro. Therefore, her house was not far from the Palatine Hill. It was a narrow and tall building with a small yard enclosed with a stone wall.

He stood before the door as if facing off against an enemy ranked up across a field. Just like he would in battle, he did not think about the outcome, but simply charged forward.

He rapped on the door until a stooped and gray-haired woman answered. For an instant, he thought she was his mother. But she was too old and had blotches on her high cheeks. She might have been pretty in her younger years, but time had worn her down with heavy lines around her eyes and on her forehead.

"My name is Marcus Varro. I am here to see my mother. Please take me to her."

That simple statement of intent had required almost nine years to form on his lips. Speaking it aloud was like striking the first blow in battle. Now, he had to break through the enemy formation.

The servant stared at him in disbelief.

"Marcus, is it you? You, you...I cannot believe it."

Varro's chest tightened, and he peered harder at the old woman. He had not recognized her, remembering a less care-worn face, but the voice and Carthaginian accent revived his memory.

"Yes, Yasha, it has been too long. This visit is overdue. Please, take me to my mother. I have grave news."

Yasha had been his father's slave, and his mother had claimed her as part of his inheritance. He had fond memories of the old woman and felt ashamed he did not recognize her. The last time he had seen her, she wore a simple cloth over her head and waved goodbye in front of the family home as he went to join the legion.

The old Carthaginian slave nodded and pulled the door open into the sweet-smelling interior. He stepped inside, and familiar aromas flooded his mind with memories. Although this was another man's house, his mother and her faithful slave still cooked the same meals and still placed the same flowers in vases all around the atrium. It smelled like home, and it was both comforting and jarring.

At the back of the house, he heard a small dog barking and a girl laughing. He could not see Lucia, but expected it was her. Yasha led him inside and pointed toward the garden.

"Your mother is outside with her granddaughter and her dog. Her husband is not home. It is a shame. I know he wants to meet you."

Varro inhaled to make an insulting retort about how he had no wish to meet a stepfather he did not know. But he bit back on the impulse. He was here to create the beginnings of peace.

"Another time, perhaps. I don't want Lucia to see me or overhear our conversation. Could we meet in the cubiculum?"

Yasha flinched at the suggestion and looked furtively at the open cubiculum door beyond the small reflecting pool in the atrium. She seemed to settle an internal struggle and nodded.

She went to fetch his mother, and he seated himself on the guest's chair. He tried to evaluate the man who would normally sit at the austere desk. The most he could deduce about his stepfather was his frugality and orderliness. There was not one item unnecessary to commerce present in the room. He took care to arrange his papyri and wax tablets neatly on shelves, and he also ordered every other accouterment of business. It smacked of military precision, and Varro admired that, even if begrudgingly.

His mother appeared in the cubiculum's doorway. Varro nearly leaped out of his chair in surprise, despite expecting her.

She was shorter than he remembered and hair that had once only been mixed with gray had now turned nearly white. She wore it up, the same as Arria had done. Her dark eyes were sunken behind high cheekbones, and age had pulled at her flesh. Even so, she was still graceful in her sea green stola, pinned with a coiling gold broach.

His mouth hung open, unsure of what to say. He found himself staring at her nose and resisted an urge to touch his own. He shook the thought away, then forced himself to smile.

"Hello, Mother."

Never had any utterance felt so insipid as this. He wanted to slither away like a frightened snake.

Yet his mother nearly collapsed, her eyes shining with tears.

"My son, my beautiful son!"

She threw her arms wide and stepped forward, then stopped as Varro recoiled.

His head felt as if it were aflame, and he immediately regretted retreating and bumping into the chair. He stumbled, leaning on the edge of the desk for balance. His mother quickly folded her hands on her lap and lowered her head.

"I'm sorry." He was uncertain if he was sorry for his reaction or the news he planned to deliver. But if he were to make peace, then he had to surrender now. So he regained his balance, then opened his arms to receive his mother's embrace.

She did not hesitate and threw herself against him and crushed her arms around him. She wept violently, sweeping her hands over his back and burying her face in his shoulder. He stood to parade ground attention and stared at the wall opposite of him. It lacked any decoration, as blank as his mind.

When his mother finally recovered, she held him at arm's length and studied his face. Her own cheeks were red and stained with tears, and her brows formed a pained arch as she traced the scar over his eye. Her touch was warm and familiar, and her scent was like lilac. Until this moment, he did not realize how much he missed his mother.

It took all his strength to keep the tears out of his own eyes.

"What have they done to my dear boy?" Her fingers lingered on his cheek as her eyes settled on his. Her heavy blinking forced out more tears. "You were always a serious child, Marcus. But look at you now. They turned you into someone else."

"The legion made me a man, Mother."

She gave a slow nod, and her fingers slipped away from his cheeks. She drew a deep breath and sniffled before speaking again.

"The legion took the joy out of your eyes."

Varro turned aside and retreated to his chair, dropping into it. He rubbed his face, then glanced around the cubiculum.

"Mother, I have sad news. I've come to tell you myself. Perhaps you should sit as well." He extended his palm to the chair behind the desk. Rather than sit there, she dragged the chair to sit next to Varro.

"I know what happened Arria. Senator Flamininus visited and told me the news."

Varro shot up from his chair. "He did what?"

His mother leaned back, placing both hands over her chest.

"He knows you did not want to do it yourself and felt I should also know as soon as possible. He meant nothing wrong by it."

"He's interfering with my personal life. What else has he come to tell you about me?"

His voice filled the cubiculum and his mother cowered like a recruit under the vine cane. Realizing his outburst, Varro touched both hands to his temples and drew a calming breath before sitting again.

"I'm sorry for that. It's not your fault. Has the senator visited you often?"

His mother stared at him in silence. Her terrified expression made Varro slump in his chair.

"Never mind. It doesn't matter what he has told you. I'm sorry that I failed to save my sister. She came to me seeking protection but found death. That is why there is no joy in my eyes, Mother. It's not the legion's fault. So, what will we do about Lucia?"

Dabbing with the back of her wrist at the tears still staining her cheeks, his mother straightened in her seat.

"Of course, I will raise her. She has nowhere else to go unless you want to adopt her."

He raised both palms forward and turned his head. "I'm not good with children, particularly girls. Besides, I have nowhere to live appropriate for a child. If you will raise her, then I will help as I can. If you need money for her support, then just say so."

At last, a genuine smile touched his mother's lips.

"It will not be a burden to look after her. We have a good life here."

Such a simple statement unleashed a torrent of doubts in Varro's heart. Was their life good because of his father's criminal past? So many similar questions welled up in his throat, but he shut his mouth against them. He reminded himself that the past was done, and all that mattered was today. Besides, his father's past would not become his future. Varro was certain he had picked a better path to travel.

His mother studied him as he wrestled with his doubts.

"He does business with the legion, my husband. He has a workshop producing boots and sandals. It's good money, though the profit varies with the cost of leather. That's how he knows Senator Flamininus. They seem to have formed a friendship, and that you are my son is coincidental. Please, don't blame him for delivering the news about Arria. I'm certain he had your feelings at heart."

Varro nodded. Flamininus was an inspiring leader, generous to his men, and fair. But he was not a man overly concerned with the feelings of others.

"I'm certain he had good intentions."

With the burden of bad news now lifted from his shoulders, Varro fell into an awkward silence. He knew he should say more to comfort his mother, but could not think of what it should be. She sat before him; her aged hands now folded over her lap. She examined him with the rigor of a centurion reviewing his soldiers. It was the same examination she used to give him whenever Falco bruised him up, and he felt the same urge to squirm away now.

Another more recent memory popped into his mind, allowing him to break free of the scrutiny.

"Arria said you were dying. Yet, besides the natural changes of age, you seem as healthy as ever."

She touched her throat and laughed.

"Arria said that? Maybe it was her way of urging you to visit me. I am not dying, at least as far as I know."

"Well, that's a relief."

They smiled at each other in silence, until his mother lowered her head as if to acknowledge he had reached his limits.

"Won't you stay long enough to meet my husband? He would love to meet you, and I'm certain the two of you would get along."

"I'm certain I don't want to meet your husband." Varro stood, perhaps too abruptly. "I'm still on a mission for the senator. As you must know, the dagger you had blessed at the temple of Mars has marked me for special service."

Varro pulled up his tunic and revealed the owl head tattoo with the star above it. His mother's expression flattened as she stared at it. He held it forward until her eyes shifted aside.

"I'm sorry, Marcus."

"Don't be. For all that I've suffered, Servus Capax has been good to me. Falco and I take care of each other, as hard as that is to believe. I've made good friends, and I enjoy that life. I can't think of another way to live now."

His mother stood, and more tears flowed despite her smile. She once more embraced him. At least he did not resist the time, though he failed to return the hug.

"Be safe, Marcus. Protect your heart and your flesh. I don't like what I see in your eyes, but I believe it can heal with time."

He gently set her aside and now held her at arm's length.

"Perhaps I will visit again. I have many questions, Mother. But I doubt the answers will be of any benefit to me."

"It is better to walk the road ahead than to look behind. I've learned that through bitter experience. I am here if you want to speak with me again."

His mother suddenly pulled him down and placed a soft kiss on his forehead.

It felt like a burning brand, such was his shame at having reviled her for so many years. But at least today he had taken his first steps toward rebuilding their relationship.

His mother and Yasha escorted him to the door. He heard Lucia and the dog still playing in the backyard and nodded appreciatively.

"I will visit her again, as well."

"She would be glad to know her uncle better."

He left his mother to watch him slip back into the streets of

Rome. A hard lump had formed in his throat and his eyes brimmed with tears that he struggled to contain.

He let the traffic guide him through the late afternoon haze. The street was packed with every class of people jostling each other while going about their business. Merchants called out to passersby, promising whatever they sold to be the best in all the world. Carts jammed the narrow streets, and their drivers cursed each other, neither side willing or able to back away in the traffic.

Varro's mind remained clouded with questions about his past. Worse still, he fretted over his handling of the reunion with his mother. He felt as if he had become a child again, not an unexpected feeling when in the presence of one's mother, he assumed. So much of what he had hoped to say remained unspoken.

Yet, he would find another time for questions and better prepare for it.

As he wandered, he paused to examine decorative brass lamps laid out on a frayed carpet. The old man selling them haggled with a customer. They settled on the price, and as Varro was about to move on, he realized someone followed him.

He had the suspicion several streets ago, but it had been only a sensation. Now, he saw someone turn away as he looked back, then vanish into the crowd. While it could have been a coincidence, Varro knew to trust his instincts.

He continued to wander, but now checked across his shoulder at random intervals, all while pretending to shop along the street of roadside vendors. Each time, a dark figure shifted away into the faceless crowd.

Now, he did not doubt someone trailed him.

As he examined rolled-up carpets laid out on the bed of a wagon, the proprietor describing how they were carefully woven by master artisans in distant Numidia, he watched for his pursuer.

Once more, the same indistinct figure had likewise paused to examine market trinkets, but Varro caught him glancing his way.

Then Varro shot away like a hunting dog let off its leash.

He bounded through the traffic, curses and shouts echoing in his wake. He looked behind and found the dark shape chasing him.

Varro did not want to escape, but to lure his pursuer into an alley or dead-end.

He sprinted down a narrow street free of traffic, then ducked into a dark alley. He pressed against the wall, the rough stone scraping his back. As he waited, he struggled to control his breath. His hand reached for his pugio, but he was unarmed.

He muttered a curse. Of course he would not have brought a weapon to his mother's home. Nor could he carry one openly in the city.

Now he heard the heavy footfalls of his pursuer.

As the dark shape ran past him, Varro leaped out of hiding and tackled the man from behind.

He slammed into the hard body of his pursuer, and both crashed on the paving stones. The man grunted in surprise and pain, but Varro pinned him in place.

"I don't like being followed. I know who sent you. You're coming with me, and we're getting answers out of you."

Varro eased back to flip the man over, expecting a struggle but encountering no resistance.

Light streamed into the narrow street, framing them in a box of light the color of fresh cream. Varro's shadow fell across the man's face as he pinned him by his shoulders. When he shifted to get a better grip on his captive, Varro's shadow slid off the man's face.

He looked down at Longus's tight-lipped sneer.

Cold terror swept through him, and he lurched back from the ghost of his enemy.

Longus wasted no time, springing to his feet in a practiced and fluid motion. He wagged his finger at Varro, then spoke in a throaty whisper.

"You'll pay, Varro. Not today, but soon enough. You'll see."

Then Longus turned and fled into the darkness ahead.

HISTORICAL NOTES

This novel touches on several topics of ancient Roman life that may be unfamiliar to modern readers or might be influenced by anachronistic viewpoints. These topics are the patron and client relationship, law enforcement, and slavery. A nuanced and detailed review of any one of these topics could fill hundreds of pages, and I can hardly do justice to them in a short page of notes. Still, it might help some readers better understand the Roman world and provide a starting point for more serious research.

The patron and client relationship is prominently featured in this book, as well as in several prior volumes. Patronage was not a formal structure of Roman society, but still permeated daily life. It was a means for people of varying social statuses to help each other.

Powerful men, usually patrician-class citizens, would accept social inferiors as clients. Sometimes a patron, if powerful enough, might even have clients of the same social status. A patron was bound to be the protector and benefactor of his clients. He would offer financial and legal aid, arrange marriages, support a client for public office, and so on.

In turn, the client was obligated to support the patron in other ways, most obviously by voting for them during elections. But clients often did more than this. They would meet their patron in the morning and serve as escorts, security, or do anything else their patron might request. One of the most important duties of a client was to ensure others knew who his patron was. The more clients a patron had, the more status he accrued.

Now, as we speak of patrons and clients, we see legal assistance and security as benefits of this system. Yet why did this system fulfill this need? It is important to understand that there were no police in ancient Rome, nor was there any sort of city watch or other codified system of street-level law enforcement unless organized by a local community. Citizens had to watch out for themselves. Hence, powerful senators not only wanted a large escort to the forum so that they appeared famous, but also wanted them for personal security.

While Roman courts existed, it was the responsibility of the wronged party to bring their suit and the accused to the court. There was no one to call upon to assist with this, and therefore having a powerful patron would be a tremendous benefit in this regard. He could supply the force to bring in fugitives and criminals for trial. Yet, even so, magistrates had limited abilities to enforce punishments. Given this uncertainty, people seldom went about their days alone.

But what about urban cohorts? These were forces raised by the Senate for military actions close to home. Yet they could be called upon--or raised on demand--to deal with large-scale public disturbances. But they did not patrol the streets or arrest suspects for trials.

A wealthy man might raise a private force to deal with his problems. He could arm them and even train them as a fighting force if he had the means. You can immediately see what a tinder box this absence of codified law enforcement was. Private armies led to clashes between patron factions, leading to violence and death in the streets. Indeed, life in ancient Rome was fraught with danger.

Lastly, we come to the sensitive topic of slavery. The Roman Republic and Empire were one of the largest slave-driven economies in history. Undoubtedly cruel and inexcusable, it differed from later concepts of slavery, particularly as found in America. Roman slavery was not determined by race. Slaves were comprised of every race, age, social status, and gender.

Lines between the free and enslaved were far less defined than in other ages of history. People could move between both statuses, being slaves and freemen, and perhaps more than once in a lifetime. If a citizen could not clear his debt, he could pay it off with enslavement. For certain crimes, courts could impose slavery as a punishment. Desperate people could sell members of their family or even themselves into slavery. Of course, many slaves were captured in battle and taken back to Rome.

Freedom was usually gained after the slave had saved enough money to pay his own cost. Of course, most slaves were not well paid, if at all, and earning enough to fund a *peculium* might take a lifetime. Rural slaves, in particular, were often treated little better than animals and rarely earned their freedom. For a rough average, some historians believe it took seven years for a slave to earn enough to buy freedom again.

However, a slave owner might grant a slave freedom at any time, even after the slave's death. This was important because slave children inherited the status of their parents. Freeing the parents would free the children as well. This was a process known as *manumission* and was often included as a stipulation in slave owners' wills or done when a man grew up and freed his childhood slave friends.

Many slaves were skilled professionals, notably doctors. Due to demands for their specialized skills, these slaves had a greater chance to fund a peculium. In many cases, these slaves would enjoy better living conditions than free citizens. Some slaves were also given positions of responsibility and paid accordingly.

None of this is meant to condone or excuse slavery in any way. It is a horrible crime against the basic rights of all people to be free to pursue their own lives. While some slaves may have eventually earned freedom, many more suffered all their lives and died in abject misery. Roman slavery was like all other slavery in that it turned human beings into objects, and made the world a darker place for its existence.

Now, returning to our heroes, while they have suffered setbacks, they are drawing ever closer to the heart of an underground conspiracy. Is there a coup planned in Carthage? Will the Republic fall? Of course, we have the benefit of history to answer these questions. But what else might be lying in wait for our forgotten heroes of Rome? They will soon find out!

NEWSLETTER

If you would like to know when my next book is released, please sign up for my new release newsletter. You can do this at my website:
http://jerryautieri.wordpress.com/

If you have enjoyed this book and would like to show your support for my writing, consider leaving a review where you purchased this book or on Goodreads, LibraryThing, and other reader sites. I need help from readers like you to get the word out about my books. If you have a moment, please share your thoughts with other readers. I appreciate it!

ALSO BY JERRY AUTIERI

Ulfrik Ormsson's Saga

Historical adventure stories set in 9th Century Europe and brimming with heroic combat. Witness the birth of a unified Norway, travel to the remote Faeroe Islands, then follow the Vikings on a siege of Paris and beyond. Walk in the footsteps of the Vikings and witness history through the eyes of Ulfrik Ormsson.

Fate's Needle

Islands in the Fog

Banners of the Northmen

Shield of Lies

The Storm God's Gift

Return of the Ravens

Sword Brothers

Descendants Saga

The grandchildren of Ulfrik Ormsson continue tales of Norse battle and glory. They may have come from greatness, but they must make their own way in the brutal world of the 10th Century.

Descendants of the Wolf

Odin's Ravens

Revenge of the Wolves

Blood Price

Viking Bones

Valor of the Norsemen

Norse Vengeance

Bear and Raven

Red Oath

Fate's End

<u>Grimwold and Lethos Trilogy</u>

A sword and sorcery fantasy trilogy with a decidedly Norse flavor.

Deadman's Tide

Children of Urdis

Age of Blood

Copyright © 2024 by Jerry Autieri

All rights reserved.

No part of this book may be reproduced in any form or by any electronic or mechanical means, including information storage and retrieval systems, without written permission from the author, except for the use of brief quotations in a book review.

Printed in Great Britain
by Amazon